Heir to the Sundered Crown

The Sundered Crown Saga Book One

M.S. Olney

Copyright © 2014 by M.S. Olney

All rights reserved.

No portion of this book may be reproduced in any form without written permission from the publisher or author, except as permitted by U.S. copyright law.

The Sundered Crown Saga-

Heir to the Sundered Crown

War for the Sundered Crown

Quest for the Sundered Crown

Voyage for the Sundered Crown

Heroes of the Sundered Crown

The Sundered Crown Boxset

The Nightblade

The Crimson Blade
Danon
The Empowered Ones-

The First Fear

The Temple of Arrival

The Empowered Ones Boxset

PROLOGUE

Lightning lit up the sky and thunder battered the senses of the watchmen. All night they had guarded the palace's great gate, while the storm raged all around them. For hours, the elements had illuminated the sky in a cacophony of light. For most of their shift, the guardsmen had huddled in the limited shelter of a small guardhouse.

"Here, Jonas, who would be out here on a night like this?" the guard captain muttered to his fellow watchman. A stooped figure was shuffling along the road, the heavy rain obscuring the vision of the guards.

Jonas was a boy of no more than seventeen who had just joined the guards division and was in training to join the King's Legion proper. He leaned out of the side of the guard station to take a look at the figure.

"They must be ruddy mad to be out in weather like this. The poor bugger must be soaked right through." Jonas took a step out into the road and moved towards the shuffling person. As he approached, he could hear a strange sniffling sound. It sounded as if the figure was crying. It was a woman, Jonas realised.

"Here, Cody," he called to his colleague. "Come here. I think this woman's hurt."

"*Captain* Cody to you, son," the grizzled elder man growled irritably as he stepped in front of the hunched woman. He gestured impatiently for his inferior to halt the woman; she seemed determined to shuffle straight past them and through the gate.

"Here, love, are you okay? You'll catch your death if you stay out in this weather much longer," Jonas said, ignoring the pompous captain.

Jonas reached for the woman's arm. Instantly, the stooped figure stopped, before rising from her hunched position to a straight-backed one.

With an eerie silence, Captain Cody watched in terror as the woman grabbed Jonas's chainmail-covered arm and wrenched the terrified lad to the ground. Instantly, she was on him, a dagger in hand, slashing and hacking at the boy's head and neck.

Seconds later, the now blood-soaked woman stood and held the guard's severed head in her hand. Her robe had slid off, revealing a taut, naked body, the rain washing across her flesh, cleansing the young guard's blood into the road.

She turned her head and stared at Cody, a manic look in her eyes.

Cody stood and watched, paralysed with fear as she advanced on him. He staggered backwards, desperately trying to unsheathe his sword. With startling speed, the woman came at him; with one savage swipe of her dagger, Captain Cody joined his comrade in the underworld.

The woman turned to look out over the city. The city of Sunguard's lights looked like a vast sea of fireflies in the night, the effect only slightly dampened by the heavy rain. Occasionally, bright forks of lightning would flash on the distant horizon, making the night as bright as day.

The plateau was impregnable to any army willing to directly assault it. The long-winding road that led to the plateau's peak, and to the palace in the centre, was defended by a number of guard towers and defensive kill zones. The steep sides and formidable man-made defences ensured the king's palace would be able to fend off any enemies. Any enemies save one ...

She walked to the guardhouse, taking a flaming torch off of the wall and, with a smile, walked to the edge of the winding road and waved the torch three times.

It was the signal for the Crimson Blades ...

Elena cradled the gurgling baby in her arms. The little prince was restless; the storm had kept him awake all night so far. *Or was it something else?* Elena had felt uneasy this night. And yet she had no reason to be; it was a night like any other, aside from the vicious storm battering the palace. The gods were angry this night.

She shook her head and chided herself. "There's nothing to fear, my little prince," she said soothingly, in part to calm the baby, and partly to make herself feel better. "It's just the weather keeping you up, nothing more."

The nursery was a large, bright room, lit by candles and painted in soothing pastel colours. Pictures of dogs, cats and a friendly-looking black bear adorned the walls. It was a peaceful place.

Elena had been the nanny to the baby prince since he was born, six months ago, and was chosen from a number of prestigious candidates. She had felt great pleasure beating the rival girls to the job and was immensely proud of her position. Above all, she had learnt to love the baby as though he was her own. She would do anything for him, even give her life if needed. Little did she know that tonight she would have to put her commitment to the test. Elena eventually got the baby off to sleep, returning to her own bed which was next door to the nursery.

The wind was howling outside, and the rumble of thunder added to the sense of unease she felt.

She took her ivory brush and began dragging it through her hair, a habit from her childhood. It was something she did to ease her worries. But the nagging feeling remained, like an itch she could not scratch. She stood up after several minutes to pace her room.

"This is silly!" she muttered to herself.

The sound of running feet stopped her pacing. The footsteps were drawing closer to the nursery. *Who'd be running around the palace at this time of night*, she wondered.

She ran to her bed and felt under the pillow. The hilt of the silver dagger her father had given her gave her comfort as she picked it up. She drew the blade and moved quickly to the nursery.

The running footsteps were outside the door.

The nursery door was kicked in with a loud crash, waking the baby prince. In the doorway stood Commander Davik, the head of the king's guard. In his gold and black plate armour, he looked like a hero from the old stories.

"Elena, thank Niveren you're safe," he breathed in relief.

"What has happened, my lord, why are you dressed for battle?" she questioned, clutching the dagger tightly to her chest.

"There's not much time, Elena," he replied hastily, grabbing a travel bag off of the nursery wall. "We have to get you and the prince to safety. The palace is under attack!"

The king and queen were the first to die. After their guards had all been silently dispatched, the assassins entered the royal bedchamber. There, their victims lay soundly asleep.

Two quick cuts with the assassin's blades and the heads of the kingdom were dead.

In other rooms around the palace and in locations all over the kingdom, similar murders were taking place. The Diasect had failed to warn the king, and because of that failure, the royal family of Delfinnia was eliminated.

The princes, Drayson and Ryiar, were brutally murdered as they tried to flee their beds. And their sisters, the two young princesses, were strangled in their sleep.

"Pack what you need for a journey; the prince must leave the palace!" Davik shouted, urgency clear in his voice. "With the king removed, the kingdom will fall into chaos."

Elena wasted no time; she raced into her room and quickly dressed in loose blouse and trousers, before pulling on her travel boots. She grabbed the baby's essentials before finally reaching into the crib and picking up the squealing prince.

She looked to the doorway; Davik was blocking the entrance, sword in hand and a look of fierce determination on his face.

Down the long passageway, the palace's attackers were moving room to room, slaughtering the groggy residents. The assassins saw Davik and hastened towards him.

"You must flee, my lady," he commanded. "Stop for no-one and nothing. The prince must live! I will hold these bastards as long as I can. Now go!"

Davik stepped out of the doorway to advance down the passageway, roaring a challenge as he went.

Elena ran with the baby in her arms as fast as she could, tears streaming down her face, as all she had ever known was destroyed.

CHAPTER 1.

Three Years later…
Word had spread like wildfire through Caldaria, the last majestic city of the mages. Excited crowds ran through the streets cheering, peddlers made sure to put out their most precious stock, and the city's crystalline buildings were decorated in a plethora of dazzlingly colourful banners. Street magicians competed to the joy of the watching audiences; puffs of purple smoke and flashes of flame and lightning amazed and stupefied the excited crowds.

The news of the Baron of Balnor's rout at the Golden Hills had been warmly welcomed by the citizens of the West – a people whose loyalties remained strong to the Privy Council of nobles who'd assumed power upon the murder of the royal family. The War of the Six Claimants was deep into its third bloody year, and any victory was celebrated.

Trying to make his way through the bustling throng was a young lad named Luxon. He pushed and squeezed, dodged and dived until he could get clear and take a few hurried steps further towards his destination.

Glancing up at the huge clock tower dominating the city's plaza he cursed as he realised that time had once again betrayed him. It was a few minutes shy of ten bells; no way would he make it this time. He flicked his sandy brown hair from his eyes, frantically looking for a passageway through the sea of people.

He narrowed his eyes, holding an arm up to shield them from the bright, warm sun. Across the plaza, he could see his rival, Accadus, smiling cruelly and shaking his head tauntingly. Luxon swore loudly, thumping his hand against the stone ledge he was standing against. The sot was going to beat him again, and no doubt would land him in more hot water with Master Ri'ges.

No, he wouldn't get another thrashing from the old mage, not today.

He thought desperately.

Wagons, horses, cattle and, of course, the mass of humanity all barred his way through the plaza and to his destination at the school. He racked his mind for anything useful and laughed out loud at his foolishness.

"Of course!" he exclaimed loudly, causing some in the great crowd to turn inquisitively in his direction. Deftly, Luxon climbed onto the stone ledge just above him and hauled himself upwards, a move that caused more people in the thronging crowd to pay him some attention. Sitting down he removed his velvet shoes and cotton socks, the warm air feeling good against his bare toes.

The fourteen-year-old clapped his sweating palms together, licked his lips and waggled his toes. "Okay, here goes," he mumbled to no one in particular. Taking a deep breath he remembered what he had read in the fifth volume of *The Wizard's Craft*, a text that he'd managed to smuggle out of the Great Library only two days previously. Closing his eyes, he focused his mind. A tickling sensation passed through his body, sliding rapidly to his feet. He picked up his discarded shoes and tucked them into one of the pockets of his blue mage's cloak. A swirling of air formed underneath his bare soles, and then tentatively he stepped off the ledge.

The surprised gasps of the surrounding onlookers, and the fact that he had not fallen caused him to open his eyes. He almost laughed with delight. He'd done it! He'd actually managed to successfully cast a levitation spell. When he felt himself on the verge of falling, he flapped his arms like a newly-fledged bird. He narrowed his eyes and deepened his concentration. Through half-lidded eyes, he sought out the opposite end of the plaza and slowly but surely made his way towards it. The crowd by now had stopped what they were doing to gawp at the lanky boy floating above their heads. Men and women stood slack-jawed at the sight, whilst children laughed and pointed. A merchant almost crashed his mule and cart as he failed to notice a wall.

After a few moments, Luxon felt sweat trickle down his brow, and his limbs begin to feel rubbery. He picked up the pace, making it across the crowd to the archway leading to the school. Tiredness crept into every inch of his body, threatening to overwhelm him. Finally, it became too much, and the swirling wind under his feet began to peter out of existence.

Not good! Luxon thought, desperately looking around for another ledge to cling to or a soft place to fall. He grit his teeth, focusing even harder than before, putting every ounce of power he could muster into the levitation spell. He made three more steps before a wave of blackness blurred his vision. The archway to the school was right below him. He fell as his vision faded. Someone in the crowd screamed.

Luxon groggily opened his eyes to find himself in a large four-poster bed. Four thick, feather-filled pillows supported his head, and the quilt tucked about him was made of thick sheep's wool. A single candle lit the room, casting shadows upon several paintings adorning the walls. He recognised one as a portrait of Zahnia the Great, the wizard's long white hair and thick beard billowing in a mighty wind. In his left hand was his staff *Erdasol*, and in his right was the legendary sword *Asphodel*. The long blade was emblazoned with light, and the staff lived up to its name, *Earth's Fire*. Luxon slowly sat up, instantly regretting his decision to do so as a wave of nausea threatened to make him vomit.

"You're not Zahnia just yet," a chuckling voice spoke from the darkness. "Although, saying that, a lad just shy of fifteen summers being able to control a spell of the upper ring is certainly impressive."

Luxon slumped back miserably onto the pillows, another wave of dizziness causing the room to spin.

"M-Master Ri'ges?" he asked, already knowing the answer.

The elderly tutor rose from his high-backed chair and stepped into the candlelight. His wrinkled face was covered in liver spots, his grey hair was long and straggly, and only the small pair of spectacles perched upon a hooked nose hinted that he was an intellectual and not some scruffy beggar from off the street. He had taught Luxon and the other boys and girls for over two years in the School of the Lower Ring, and rightly had a reputation for his tough style of educating. On more than one occasion, Luxon had received whacks with the rod, either because of his wild curiosity, or because Accadus had baited him.

Ri'ges sat at the end of the bed smiling, an expression that took Luxon by surprise. He'd been expecting his teacher to raise fury at his latest stunt, not sit at his bedside with a smile.

"What happened?" he asked as he once more tried to sit up. The dizziness came again, but it was not as bad as before.

Ri'ges removed his spectacles and wiped them on his long grey robe.

"You fell," he replied simply. "Luckily, I saw the whole thing and was able to catch you with a telekinetic spell before you cracked your head open like an egg. The reason you feel so nauseous is no doubt due to you over-exerting your mind to keep the levitation spell intact – a spell, mind you, that one as young as you should never have attempted." The old master stood and stretched his back. "One as young as you, in theory, should not even have been able to have gotten the spell to work at all."

"I'm sorry, master," Luxon said miserably. "I just didn't want to be late for classes again. Accadus hid my shoes again and- "

Ri'ges held a hand up in annoyance. "I do not care for the follies of young men. Making a foe of Accadus was not a wise move on your part. Listen to me, Luxon. You are one of the most promising students I have ever seen pass through the Crystal Gates, and I will not have you ruin your chances of making apprentice because of some foolish feud."

Luxon looked at his hands. He hadn't had any idea that the old man thought that way about his abilities. He knew he was good, but his thirst for knowledge often saw him getting into scrapes with his fellow students and the school's other teachers.

The old man's expression softened. "Accadus will always loathe you, Luxon. His father is the Baron of Redbit, as you well know, and after what your father did-" he trailed off as he saw tears beginning to form in his pupil's eyes.

"My father was loyal to the king," Luxon spoke miserably. "The baron had no right to make a claim. My father swore he spoke the truth that day and lost his head for it."

Luxon's father had been a noble in the court of the capital at Sunguard. With the royal line lost, the realm's leaders had gathered to discuss the succession.

Garrick, Luxon's father, had testified to the gathering that the king's youngest child had escaped the assassins, swearing blind that he had helped a young woman smuggle a baby boy out of the city. Accadus's father had condemned Garrick as a liar of the worst degree, arguing that the palace had been burnt to ashes by the assassins and that all of the bodies had been accounted for.

After the summit, Garrick had hurried back to his home and told his wife and son to pack for travel at once. Luxon had been as afraid as any boy of just eleven years of age would be. That same night, the baron's men came to their home and, without preamble, dragged the stricken Garrick into the streets. In the confusion, Luxon and his mother managed to escape the city. It had been a month later that they had heard of his father's grim fate. Anger surged through him, his hands knotting into fists at the memory.

"Accadus hates me because I know his father is a lying sack of—"

A knock on the small room's door interrupted him.

"Come in," Ri'ges said, placing a calming hand on Luxon's shoulder. The lad choked back tears as another wave of nausea struck.

The door opened, and into the room walked a man dressed in black leather armour. He was no older than thirty, but his long black hair had traces of silver along the sides. His face was hard and a scar ran from the top of his right eye down toward his bearded jaw. Luxon's eyes widened as he realised the man was a Nightblade, an order of highly skilled agents and monster hunters.

Since the beginning of the war, the Nightblades had abandoned their posts across the realm. They were sworn to the king and no other. Until a rightful successor won the throne, they had vowed to play no part in the fighting. Instead, they had returned to Caldaria, the only city in Delfinnia where they could practise their magic freely.

"Ah, Welsly, I forgot all about the meeting, forgive me," Master Ri'ges said. The old man shook the Nightblade's hand before turning to look at Luxon. "I am afraid Luxon here distracted me from our business," he added, gesturing to his student. Welsly nodded to Luxon in greeting.

"Ah yes, the boy who caused all of that commotion in the Quartz quarter. I hear you put on quite a show," Welsly chuckled. "If you would excuse your master, the council has need of us, and we cannot tarry further. Get well soon, Luxon. Shall we, Ri'ges?" He held the door open for the ageing mage and followed him out of the room.

Luxon stared at the now closed door, a feeling of excitement in his gut. He'd actually spoken to a Nightblade. He was sure all of the other students would be jealous of that. Tiredness came to him, and before he knew it, he was once again drifting off into a deep sleep.

The Dream was always the same. The lone tree standing on the hilltop, its withered branches stretching toward the heavens. The sky a tumultuous riot of colours. A name is always whispered on the breeze, growing louder and louder as he walks numbly towards it.

The voice is familiar, as though he has heard it once before, long ago. A sense of dread wounds its way into his stomach as he approaches the tree, its knotted roots jutting out from its grotesque body, trying to trip him as he walks ever onwards to the top of the hill. Each time he dreams, Luxon always wakes before he reaches the summit, but deep down in his gut he knows that something lies beyond the horizon, something terrifying, something that he does not want to see.

The whisper grows louder and louder until it turns into a scream, a woman's scream, a woman in agony and despair, and she would always scream his name.

Just as he reaches the tree and crests the hill, the sky turns black, and silence descends, and there he sees it – a spectre. A shadow in the shape of a tall slender man. It stands there in the shadows staring, his features hidden by the darkness.

The sense that he knows its name frustrates him. Like in a dream where you can never reach where you want to go, a name that tries to claw its way through to his waking mind, a name that he knows is full of woe. The spectre raises its hand, pointing at him and then a menacing laugh emanates from the darkness – laughter that promises pain, despair, and evil intent.

The laughter becomes deafening, threatening to burst his ear drums, until finally he awakens covered in sweat, breathing hard, his heart racing with fear.

CHAPTER 2.

"You still not sleeping well?" asked Yepert, the boy who was Luxon's only real friend in the whole of Caldaria. The lad hailed from the small village of Plock on the Eastern shore. His broad eastern accent gave him away as someone who didn't come from wealth or prestige, but no gentler soul could anyone hope to find.

"The same dream every night," Luxon replied miserably as he wearily wrapped his cloak around his shoulders.

It had been two days since the incident in the plaza, and word of his deed had spread rapidly throughout the city's schools. Luxon's ego and reputation were at a high, but his energy wasn't.

The two boys were in their dorm room in the boarding hall. For the past two years, the place had been home, but to Luxon, it felt more like a prison.

"I overheard Master Kvar say that dreams were important to folk like us," Yepert said as he bent to tie his shoes. Even such a simple task as that seemed difficult for him, his rotund shape not making it easy for him to bend.

Luxon snorted. "I heard that Master Kvar is nuttier than squirrel poo and that he tried to transmute his cat into a horse. I'll be fine; it's probably just stress or something, and this whole thing with Accadus is getting to me."

Yepert finished tying his shoes and wrapped himself in his massive cloak. On the chubby boy, it looked more like a tent than an item of clothing. Luxon couldn't help but smile; his friend may appear to be an eastern simpleton, but he knew better. Behind those nervous eyes was a profound intellect, an intellect that almost matched his own. Almost.

The two of them left their room and began making their way through the city. Peddlers and merchants were already out on the cobbled streets, eager to sell their wares. The small stone shops that nestled underneath the massive crystalline walls were beginning to open their doors, and scholars and officials made their way to their places of work.

It always surprised Luxon just how busy the city became at such an early hour; how normal things were despite the vicious war being waged outside its walls.

"Uh-oh," Yepert exclaimed coming to a halt. Luxon stopped too, looking at his friend in confusion.

"What?" he asked.

Yepert's face had gone a deep crimson red. He pointed. There, through a break in the crowd of bustling folk, stood Accadus and his three thugs. They regularly persecuted Luxon and Yepert. With Luxon, they often just snarled insults, but with Yepert they got violent. Anger swelled up inside Luxon as he remembered the last time his friend had staggered into the dorm room, bruised, and battered.

He itched to teach the bully a lesson, but any use of magic for such a thing would instantly see him cast out of the city; and with the strict laws regarding magic users, he would very likely never be able to practise his skills ever again.

"Let's take the long way around," Luxon said through gritted teeth. He didn't want any trouble. Following his stunt in the plaza, he could ill-afford to come to the master's attention again, at least not so soon.

Just as they were about to turn around and head in the opposite direction, they heard a shout. Luxon spun at the noise. Accadus had seen them, and he and his cronies were hurriedly pushing their way through the flow of pedestrians to reach them.

"Run, Yepert, go!" he shouted, grabbing his friend's arm, and hurrying him back the way they had come.

"Wh-What about you?"

"I'll be fine," Luxon replied with more confidence than he actually felt. "Go on; I'll meet you at class."

He sighed as he saw the look of determination cross his friend's face.

"N-no. I won't leave you. I'll stay at your side."

Luxon clapped his friend on the shoulder. "Your funeral," he said wryly. Both lads turned to face their tormentors.

Accadus stood a full inch taller than Luxon, his broad shoulders hinting at his physical strength. His dark eyes were full of malice; his large nose dominated his face. He too wore a blue students' cloak, except his, had the emblem of his father emblazoned upon the breast. The crossed axes and the red crow of Redbit stood out proudly, allowing all to see that he was under the protection of one of the most powerful lords in Delfinnia.

Standing to one side of him was Douglas, a tall, skinny lad with shifty eyes, and on the other was Rudak, a large brute of a boy with a look that said that the lights were on, but nobody was at home. Neither of them studied at the schools; instead, they were in service to Accadus.

"Well, well, well, if it isn't the son of the liar and his fat oaf of a lover," Accadus said snidely, eliciting chuckles from his goons.

"That's funny coming from the son of a liar *and* a traitor," Luxon replied calmly, his steely blue eyes boring deep into his foe's. Accadus's false smile immediately dropped, his face reddening with rage. Without warning, he lashed out, and his fist connected with Luxon's nose.

Bright white pain shot through Luxon, blinding his vision, and causing him to stagger backwards. Yepert cried out, but Accadus's thugs quickly silenced him. Rudak grabbed him, putting him in a headlock and muffling his cries with a large hand over his mouth. Accadus gestured to his friends, and he and Douglas gripped the dazed Luxon under his armpits and hauled him and Yepert down a nearby alleyway.

CHAPTER 2.

Panic started to swell in Luxon's mind. Out of sight of the public, he dreaded to think what Accadus had planned for them. Perhaps calling the bully's father a traitor was a step too far, he thought, as his wits slowly collected themselves. Accadus had a mean right cross.

"You snivelling piece of scum," Accadus snarled, pinning Luxon to the alleyway's wall, an arm pressed against his throat. "My father is the rightful king. He is the strongest baron in all of Delfinnia; the crown is his through strength of arms. You think that just because you are skilled in magic that it will save you? Magic is dead in this world; if you use it outside this city, the Knights of Niveren or the Witch Hunters will gut you like a fish or burn you on a stake!"

Luxon was scared. He had never seen Accadus so angry. Out of the corner of his eye, he could hear Yepert's muted cries as the two thugs beat him yet again.

"Your father may be the strongest," Luxon wheezed, "but he *is* a liar."

He winced as he awaited another blow. Perhaps Master Ri'ges was right when he said that he was too foolhardy.

The blow never came. Instead, Accadus was on the ground, his hands around his throat, his face turning blue. Luxon stared in confusion, noticing that Yepert had gone quiet as well. The thugs who had been beating him just moments before were also on the ground. His friend was on his feet, a look of stunned disbelief on his face. The two thugs were in a similar predicament to Accadus.

"What the? What's happening, Luxon?" Yepert asked worriedly.

By now, Accadus had gone an unnatural colour as he gasped for air. Luxon gasped as he realised that his hands were tingling with energy. With horror, he realised that somehow, *he* was responsible. He wracked his mind, desperately trying to think of a way to break the spell he had somehow cast. He faced his friend.

"Yepert hit me!" he shouted in panic as the three bullies began to thrash ever more desperately. His friend hesitated.

"Damn it, Yepert, if you don't hit me then they will die. I don't know how but I'm causing this, I can feel it. I need something to break the spell, and physical harm is one of the most effective ways."

Accadus had now turned a livid purple. Luxon shouted out in annoyance as his gentle friend stood there stunned like a frightened rabbit. Spinning, Luxon faced the wall, gritted his teeth, and ran headfirst into the stone wall against which, moments before, he had been pinned against his will.

His head connected solidly with the hard stone, and the world went black.

"It isn't possible. No one has that ability."

"No one living you mean."

Voices drifted into Luxon's consciousness.

"They have-" responded another, a higher, lighter-pitched voice compared to the first's gruffness.

"Nonsense. If you compare this boy, *this child,* to him, then I seriously question your sanity."

Luxon stirred. Slowly, he opened his eyes and immediately regretted doing so. Once more he was lying in the bedchambers of the school. The same painting of Zahnia the Great greeted him, except this time there was no friendly voice to set him at ease. His head throbbed, and he tentatively touched the spot where it had connected with the alleyway's wall. He winced as pain radiated from the wound. Glancing around the room, he could see his robe hanging from the back of the high-backed chair that Master Ri'ges had been sitting in during his last visit.

The voices were coming from the hallway outside of the room. Gingerly, Luxon sat up. Stars exploded before his vision, causing him to cry out. The voices stopped, and the door opened.

In walked a woman, who Luxon guessed must be the owner of the second voice that had drifted into his consciousness. Her long blond hair framed a delicate face; her deep blue eyes caused his breath to catch in his throat. She was beautiful.

"So, you're finally awake," the woman said, walking over to the bed. "My name is Hannah; I am an apprentice to Master Enil," she explained as she checked Luxon's bandages.

"The master healer?" Luxon asked, his mind racing to recognise the name.

Hannah gave him a wide smile; her perfect teeth shone like polished ivory, causing Luxon's heart to beat quickly. "That's right," she answered. From the youthfulness of her skin, Luxon mentally guessed that she must have been only a few years older than himself. He took a wild stab in the dark: she was around eighteen.

"You took a very nasty knock to the head. According to your friend, you deliberately knocked yourself unconscious." She raised an eyebrow questioningly. "He was much shaken up when he sought help."

Luxon simply shrugged his shoulders. "I had to do it. Something happened- something that I couldn't control," he added miserably. The memory of what occurred flashed into his mind, and a dreadful thought struck him.

"Accadus! The others!" he blurted out, sitting up in panic. "What happened to them? Are they okay?" His head swam again as the concussion threatened to drag him back into the realm of sleep once more.

Hannah gently eased her patient back down into the pillows beneath him. She turned to face the door to see that the man she had been talking with earlier had now stepped into the room. He wore a black cloak with the hood up; it was drawn tightly, casting his features in shadow. The silver seven pointed star on his cloak identified him as a Battle Mage, the mages tasked with upholding the law in Caldaria.

"Your friends live," the man answered with not a shred of kindness in his deep, gravelly voice. "However, you have broken the law and have been charged with attempted murder under the Act of the Sacred Flame."

Luxon gasped. He tried to speak, but this time the darkness took him, and he started to fall back into unconsciousness.

Hannah rounded on the cloaked man. "Why did you say that? Could it not have waited until he was feeling better? Whatever this lad has done it is decreed by the law that he remains in a healer's custody until he is fit and able to stand trial."

The man shrugged nonchalantly. "It matters not. Either way, he will be judged ..."

Three days passed before Luxon was able to stand without being struck by nausea, or without the world spinning before his eyes. On more than one occasion he had attempted to walk but had collapsed into a painful, messy heap. The healer's apprentice had looked after him throughout his time of incarceration.

At first, he hadn't realised that he had been arrested, but it dawned on him when Hannah had not allowed anyone to visit him. He had heard Yepert enquiring about his health before being gently turned away with a polite refusal. Even Master Ri'ges had not been allowed entry.

Luxon was afraid.

On the second day, Hannah told him what he had been charged for. Aside from the claims from Accadus for attempted murder, he had been brought up on the serious charge of uncontrolled use of magic – a crime that, since the days of the fall of the Golden Empire, meant death for anyone committing it.

Magic wielders were feared in all the corners of Delfinnia, except for Caldaria. For centuries, magic had been strictly controlled. It had been magic users that had caused the Empire's fall and brought the world to the brink of annihilation in the Magic Wars. Witch hunters and the Knights of Niveren scoured the realm in search of those who abused their power, and hunted the remnants of the wicked things conjured into the world during the wars. Fell Beasts, spirits and other abominations had been unleashed as mage battled mage, and wizard waged war upon wizard.

Before the war of succession had begun, mages and wizards had kept mostly to themselves, choosing lives of seclusion in Caldaria or using the skills learnt at the city's schools to help the peoples of the realm. Wizards and mages were often found as court advisors to the king and his barons, but now even they had been forced to return to Caldaria. Those that left Caldaria were not allowed to use any magic – to do so would mean certain death. Nightblades were the exception. Often employed as bodyguards or agents, the Nightblades used their skills to do the deeds that a normal person could not. Their main purpose, however, was to hunt the beasts of the void that stalked the realm's dark places.

Luxon sat in the room's high-backed chair, wracking his brain to figure out what had happened. He had asked Hannah to scour the great library for any tomes that could answer the mystery, but none had contained the information he sought. A book he had not yet read lay on the small table at his side. *The History of Magic, Volume 47* was emblazoned on the cover. He sighed in exasperation and settled into the chair to read the massive tome.

CHAPTER 3.

Dungeons of Retbit, Barony of Retbit.

Kaiden wasn't very comfortable, not one bit. His hair was long and unkempt, and his clothes stank with several days' worth of dirt and sweat. The smell of the dank, damp dungeon added to the foul aroma. The fact that he was chained to the small cell's wall meant that he had very little room to manoeuvre, a fact that had resulted in several unpleasant instances when it came to relieving himself. His once spotless mantle was covered in filth. The gold seven-pointed star on his chest was faded and muddy.

Kaiden was a knight, a member of the order of Niveren, sworn to defend the weak and to root out heresy. The order had been founded after the end of the Magic Wars, a war that had seen the ruin of an empire.

Kaiden had been proud when he had finally been ordained as a knight at the age of twenty-two. Now, four years later, he found himself in the flea-ridden dungeons of the Baron of Retbit, the ruthless warlord who laid claim to the throne. His mission had been relatively simple; the people of the county of Retbit had asked the Knights of Niveren to intervene in a dispute between the baron and his eldest son over the rights to conquered territory. Murmurs were growing that the baron's eldest son was planning to overthrow his father. Unfortunately for Kaiden, he had sided with the son, and in his temper, the baron had him locked away in the stinking hole that passed for a dungeon. That was three months ago, no release was looking likely. Outside, the war was still raging.

He scratched himself, finding another flea and crushing it between his fingers. Several times he had tried to send a message to his brother knights at the priory at Lake Sumil – but every time, the baron had found out and increased the jail sentence. Kaiden had eventually given up. At this rate, he'd never get out of there.

He longed to breathe fresh air and bathe; to trim his itchy, greasy beard and to make himself feel like the man he once was, respected and feared in equal measure. If his fellow knights could see him now, they would probably all collapse from laughter. He knew he was a good swordsman and was skilled in the ways of combat, but now it seemed obvious that he had to work on his powers of diplomacy.

The voices of the jailers broke into his thoughts as they came close to his cell. They stopped outside. Being roughly manhandled and leered over by the two wicked men was a young woman. She looked no more than nineteen years old. Her once golden hair was covered in filth, and she looked as though she had been through a very tough time. Kaiden could appreciate that.

"Here, sir knight, we've found you some company," the fat, bald jailor laughed. His thick beard hid the menacing smile underneath. "A pretty little whore for you to play with. The other cells are full thanks to the baron's crackdown on beggars."

The skinnier jailor took a set of keys from his belt, unlocked the door and unceremoniously pushed the girl into the cell, causing her to fall into the slop bucket in the centre of the tiny room. She clambered to her knees, coughing and gagging at the smell. Kaiden watched her with interest; the fire in her eyes was mesmerising. She rounded on the jailors and tried to force her way past them, but the bigger man simply pushed her back to the ground. With a click, the cell was locked, and the two jailors walked away cackling to one another.

"Bastards!" the girl screamed.

"Let me out of here!" Another twenty minutes passed with the girl screaming obscenities at the jailor's.

Finally, Kaiden had had enough. "They won't listen to you. And where in God's name did you come up with such foul words."

The girl jumped, only just noticing the chained knight on the far wall of the cell.

"You startled me. I didn't know you were there ..." she said nervously. She paused as she remembered what the jailors had said. A look of fear and doubt passed over her face. "I'm no whore, so don't you touch me," she said defiantly.

The girl was attractive, even though she was covered in mud and dirt. Her green eyes were mesmerising, and her determination gave her a look of strength. Her golden hair fell to her shoulders, matted, and knotted but nonetheless appealing. Her tunic was ripped, almost revealing her breasts. She covered herself as best as she could and held the torn material in place.

"What's your name?" Kaiden asked.

The girl looked at him, curiosity, and mistrust in her eyes.

"Alira."

"Well, Alira, my name is Kaiden; I am a knight in the Order of Niveren. I promise I won't hurt you."

Alira's eyes went wide as he told her who he was. A look of respect showed in her eyes, which was quickly replaced by suspicion.

"What is a Knight of Niveren doing in a hole like this?"

Kaiden sighed and told her his story. Afterwards, Alira laughed at the knight's predicament and his foolishness.

"I never thought a knight could judge something so badly," she said sarcastically. Kaiden scowled at her, embarrassed that this peasant girl thought him a fool.

"Well then, what's your story?" he asked brusquely.

She went to the cell door and checked to see that the jailers were nowhere in sight before she turned to him with a mischievous look in her eyes.

"I'm a mage," she whispered.

Kaiden stared at the girl in disbelief.

"That's impossible. A Mage hasn't been seen in these parts for decades. They all went into hiding or fled to the Mage realm of Caldaria to the far north. And another thing ... a mage would never let herself be caught by the baron of Retbit." He shuddered at the thought.

Alira looked at her feet.

"I'm not a very good one, okay," she admitted sadly. "My father died before he could teach me anything important, and I was sent to live with my grandmother when I was eleven. She hated magic, and she hated me and all of what my father stood for and practised."

Kaiden nodded his head in sympathy. He too had lost his father when he was young. Sir Fredrik of the Marble Shore had been killed in battle against one of the many warlords that threatened the peace of the kingdom. The Knights of Niveren and other orders were constantly fighting to remove them from the world.

"It's a pity. I was hoping you were some mighty warlock and could make these goddamn chains remove themselves from my wrist," Kaiden replied jokingly.

"You're a Knight of Niveren; your kind hunts us just as much as the others, and yet you joke," the girl said seriously.

An awkward silence followed, but for the next two days and nights the two talked and told each other tales.

On the dawn of Kaiden's fifth month of captivity, the Baron of Retbit himself came to the cell. He was a dour-looking man in his early fifties; his grey and balding head was covered in pox marks. He was a short man, no more than five feet tall, but nonetheless, he gave off an imposing aura. Now, as he stood before the cell of the knight who had dared favour his son, he smiled evilly.

"I thought you would like to know, sir knight, that I have taken the castle at Rook's Peak. The siege was long and costly, but finally, my son is in chains. Just like you, in fact," he tittered mirthlessly. "So now that my quarrel with you is over, I have decided to release you. Your imprisonment no longer amuses me, and your fellow knights have begun sniffing about asking questions, a distraction I can ill-afford whilst I press my advantage in the war."

Kaiden stared at the baron, a mixture of relief and hatred coursing through him.

"You made a big mistake imprisoning me, baron," Kaiden growled back. "My brothers will not look kindly on what you did. You can be sure the council will take the castle back from you. After all, a Knight of Niveren's decision is the law."

Alira was hiding behind Kaiden; the months of imprisonment had gone badly for her. The jailors had treated her badly, and the lack of food had made her gaunt and pale.

The baron snorted derisively. "We shall see, knight. We shall see. Be assured that you have an enemy here in this county. If I hear of you set foot here ever again, I will cut off your balls and feed them to you." He nodded to the jailors; warily, they unlocked the chain holding Kaiden to the wall.

The months of being chained to the wall by the wrist had left him weak, and his muscles had wasted away. He rubbed at his wrist, trying to get the blood flowing once more. Fortunately, it was his left wrist that had wasted and not his sword arm. Kaiden was about to leave when Alira sobbed, stopping him in his tracks.

"What about the girl?" he asked.

"So, the so-called pure knight has taken a fancy to the little whore has he? Well, you can have the little witch. Tell your fellow knights that I am merciful."

Kaiden scowled at the baron. *That was too easy,* he thought.

Alira clung to him, and instantly his doubts evaporated. Once more he addressed the baron; he hoped it would be for the last time.

"Fair enough," he said. "I will tell my brothers of your mercy and generosity."

The baron nodded silently and stepped aside as the knight and the whore limped past him. He stared at their backs as they were escorted out of the dungeon. When they were out of earshot, the baron gestured to his lieutenant.

"Make sure that whoreson doesn't leave this county alive," he snarled. "The Knights of Niveren must not find out about this. Kill him; but make sure the girl is unharmed."

After their release, Kaiden and Alira made their way through the shit-covered streets of the city of Retbit, the county's capital.

"Thank you for not leaving me to rot back there," Alira said, finally breaking the awkward silence that had descended over the two of them.

Kaiden looked at her and smiled. "Think nothing of it. Just doing my knightly duty," he said with a roguish smile. "First thing we have to do is get a horse and get the hell out of this cursed county. You can be sure that the Knights will not take the baron's actions lightly. I never believed that he would besiege that castle and cast his very own son in chains."

Kaiden spoke sadly. The entire situation was his fault. His poor attempt at trying to resolve the dispute had led the county to the brink of civil war.

It was dusk by the time the two reached the stable where Kaiden had paid for his horse to be looked after. He had given the stable owner a large sum of gold to keep the animal safe, and luckily for Kaiden they had kept their word, even after his long incarceration. The large warhorse whinnied as he spoke to it in calming tones. It was a black gelding – one of the finest breeds from the plains of Bison.

"She's beautiful!" Alira exclaimed excitedly.

Kaiden paid the stable boy with the gold he had recovered from his hiding spot at the side of the road leading out of town. It was always a precaution the knights took just in case of capture. After all, they made for a valuable ransom prize.

Herald was the name of his horse, and now it stood saddled and covered in the mantle of the Niveren. The mantle's colour was bright and clean in comparison to his own messy and filth covered one. Kaiden helped lift Alira into the saddle; afterwards, he rooted in the hay bale in Herald's pen.

"What are you doing?" Alira enquired.

"Aha! There you are my pretty!" Kaiden exclaimed as he picked up his sword from its burial place. It had been carefully wrapped in a thick cloth to prevent it rusting, and aside from some dirt, it was in near perfect condition. The long, broad blade was a thing of beauty, as was the small red diamond on the pommel.

"Hopefully, we won't need this, but I don't trust that bastard baron as far as I could throw him." With that, the two rode along the road out towards the Priory of Niveren.

The two horsemen had waited patiently for hours. Boredom was setting in as they watched the dirt road for any sign of their prey. The baron had been explicit with his instructions: the knight was to die, and the girl was to be sent back to him as his prize. A mage was worth a lot of ransom money, and the market for mage slaves had increased tenfold during the past year. No one seemed to know why, and the slavers weren't about to ask. Rumours had spread that things were happening in the lands beyond the borders of the kingdom.

Finally, a lone horse came into view; a man and small woman were on its back. They were laughing and joking, despite their haggard appearance.

The taller of the men pulled up his cloak's hood and drew his sword from its scabbard.

"We go now," he snarled, and with that, he and his companion spurred their horses and galloped into the centre of the road. The knight slowed his horse and grasped the hilt of his own sword.

"Stay here," Kaiden murmured to Alira, who looked at the horsemen in fear. He dismounted and raised his arm to hail the two mysterious riders.

"Gentlemen," he began, "you seem to be blocking the road. My companion and I must continue on this route. As a Knight of Niveren, I must insist you allow us to carry on our way."

The two riders laughed at his insolence. "Let's kill this arrogant bastard," the hooded man snarled. His colleague nodded in agreement. They were hired killers, born and bred in the rough and dilapidated slums of Retbit – thugs who did anything for coin. Killing a knight meant no more to them than roughing up a family or burning down someone's livelihood.

The riders spurred their horses and charged at Kaiden who had now drawn his sword. The hooded rider aimed his blade at the knight's head and with a battle cry, swung it with all of his might.

Kaiden ducked at the last second, and from his crouch rose to his feet and ripped his sword through the charging horse's exposed flank. The blade cut deep, and blood sprayed from the wounded beast; its rider was sent flying and crashed to the ground in a heap.

Kaiden spun about and saw the second rider charging at him. There was no way to avoid the arching swing of the man's axe. He chided himself on his weakness; if he was at his peak, he would've dispatched the two vagabonds with ease, but all of the months incarcerated had slowed his wits and weakened his body. He said a silent prayer and closed his eyes as the axe drew closer and closer, but just as the blade would surely take his head from his body, there was a blast of sound, and a strange sensation as all the hairs on his arms stood up.

He waited for a few seconds, disbelieving that he still lived, and then slowly opened his eyes. There in front of him, where his attacker had been, was a smouldering pile of ash. Both rider and horse had been disintegrated. Gaping at the sight, he jumped when he heard Alira gasping for air. The girl still sat on his horse, but her hair was standing up and frazzled. She was breathing rapidly, and steam emanated from her hands.

"By the gods, was that you?" Kaiden asked.

Alira simply nodded, tears streaming down her face.

"Taught nothing good, my arse," Kaiden joked lamely. He hurried to her and held her as she sobbed.

"I killed him. I didn't mean to kill him. I just wanted to scare him, is all." Kaiden hugged her. He had never witnessed the power of magic before, and all the doubts he had about the girl's story evaporated as he held her.

"It's alright, love; those buggers would have killed us given a chance. I owe you my life," he said gratefully.

Kaiden released her and jumped back down to the road. He kicked over the body of the hooded rider, whose spine had been broken by his horse throwing him awkwardly onto the hard surface of the road. Reaching into the cloak, he found a bag of silver coins and a small note with the seal of the Baron of Retbit. Unsurprised, Kaiden remounted his horse, and they began their journey again.

CHAPTER 4.

Sunguard

The palace remained a ruin. Even three years after the assassins had burnt it to the ground, it stayed an empty blackened husk. Masonry continued to crumble and, during a large storm in the previous year, the Hall of Kings had collapsed. An ancient structure that had survived for millennia was now just a heap of rubble.

It was a fitting place to announce a new king. A small crowd had gathered on the clifftop, ushered into place by soldiers of the legion.

General Rason smiled as the privy councillors were roughly thrown to the ground before him, their cries of protest quickly made silent by the pommels of soldiers' swords connecting with their skulls.

Rason struck a powerful figure. His golden plate armour gave him an aura of invincibility as he stalked up and down the line of councillors. His grey tonsured hair was offset with a sharp pointed nose, and his steel grey eyes belied a keen and savage intellect.

"For three years I have fought for you noblemen," the general said, sneering at the pathetic bunch cowering at his feet. "I led the remnants of the King's Legion through the blood and filth of the grasslands. I routed the Baron of Balnor at the Battle of the Golden Hills and what did I get for my troubles?"

The general faced the grim-faced legionaries standing to attention behind the councillors and the crowd of cowering civilians. Legionaries were men who respected power and authority, but most of all they respected strong leadership. With the death of the king, and with no heir, the legion had turned on itself. The capital had almost ripped itself apart as cohort turned on cohort. They called it the Night of Tears, a night when twenty thousand men, women and children perished. The scars of that night were still evident in the city. Two whole districts remained wrecked; blood stains could still be seen on the streets, the rains having little impact cleansing it away. The people would simply obey.

Rason turned back to the nobles. "I saved this city, I saved you," he said, his voice barely louder than a whisper. "Foolishly, I put my trust in you good men to restore order to safeguard the throne for one who was worthy. Instead, what did we get?"

"Lies! Weakness!" his legionaries shouted in response.

Rason smiled wickedly at the men kneeling before him.

"Yes, that is exactly what we got. Instead of taking charge, of asserting your authority over the realm, you allowed it to be torn apart by the barons and their petty squabbles. Now we have six claimants all tearing Delfinnia apart. This is something ..." His voice rose in volume as he shouted out, 'This is something that I cannot allow!"

He put a boot on the neck of one of the terrified councillors. "Do none of you contest my judgement? That you are all sniffling cowards, that I am the only one who can bring order back to this realm; that only I can save Delfinnia?"

Only sobs and pitiful cries answered him.

He laughed, mocking their weakness.

"No one has the courage to stop me?" he said disbelievingly. He was amazed at himself that he had been willing to follow their orders for so long. He was the last general willing to do what was necessary. If he did not force the realm to heel under his boot, then Delfinnia would surely be lost.

"You have no right to the crown," said a deep voice from the crowd of onlookers.

Rason spun to face the cowering peasants. His face grew purple with rage at the audacity that a peasant, no less, would speak out against him. He raised his fist and thrust it at the crowd. Immediately, the legionaries drew their swords. Women and children screamed, and the men shouted in protest as the soldiers waded into the crowd, violently shoving and punching whoever got in their way. The peasants scattered, fleeing back down the cliff path to safety. All of them save one.

A hooded, cloaked man stood his ground.

"And who are you to say such a thing?" Rason said menacingly as his men approached the man. His legionaries smirked to one another; the man was obviously mad to defy their general in so public a place.

The man threw back his hood to reveal the face of a ghost. Rason took an involuntary step backwards as he recognised the former commander of the king's bodyguard.

The great warrior Davik stood before him.

He looked the same as he had always done, save for a scar that ran from his left cheek and down into his neck. The grizzled old veteran glared at Rason and the legionaries as though daring them to attack.

"You're supposed to be dead, Davik. You died the same night as the king and his family," Rason sputtered in disbelieve. A thousand thoughts whirled through the general's mind. Davik had been a friend. So where had he been all this time?

"I got better," Davik replied simply.

The legionaries looked to each other in confusion, unsure how to react at this revelation.

"This war has raged on for long enough. I had hoped to wait and see who the realm's true enemies were, but now I see that before then, we will destroy ourselves by infighting."

Davik smiled. "An heir to the Sundered Crown yet lives, Rason."

The general took another step back at his former comrade's revelation. He had been planning this coup for two years; he could not stop now, not with the crown so close to his grasp. If he freed the Privy Council or welcomed this heir, he would no doubt lose his head. Too much blood had been spilt for him to stop now.

CHAPTER 4.

"I have put too much on the line to stop now my old friend. *I* will be king, and *I* will save our realm." Rason paused, offering a hand to Davik. "Join me, and together we can restore order to Delfinnia."

Davik glared at the man he had once called a friend. He glanced from legionary to legionary, catching each of the men's' eyes in turn. None could bear to hold his gaze for long.

"You pledged your loyalty to the King's Legion, and I say a true king yet lives," Davik said to them. "And enemies greater than the barons are waiting in the wings. Would you forsake it all for your general's lust for power?"

No one answered him.

"My men are loyal to me, Davik," Rason said. "Under my rule, all enemies, whether real or ones concocted in your age-addled mind, will be destroyed." A sad look crossed Rason's face. "I am sorry, my friend but I cannot allow you to leave this place alive. If word of this so-called heir got out, then ... well, my rule would not be accepted by the people now, would it?"

Davik frowned; he knew what would happen now. His right hand edged to the sword on his hip, unseen under the cloak.

"Kill him," Rason barked as he drew his own sword.

With a speed that startled the legionaries, Davik whipped his blade out of its scabbard and buried it deep into the nearest legionary's throat. Blood erupted from the dying man's throat as Davik ripped his sword away. He spun, countering a thrust and bringing his knee hard into the face of another attacker who fell to the ground, his nose shattered.

He might have been old, but Davik had been in more battles than he could count, and the young legionaries didn't have half his skill or experience. He pivoted on his left foot, spinning around to face the rest of his attackers. He glanced behind him to see a full platoon of troops hastily marching up the hill, their spears at the ready.

Davik swore under his breath. He had been far too reckless. Two legionaries charged towards him. He ducked the first's wild swing and stabbed his own blade savagely into the man's gut. The metal slid in underneath the legionary armour and deep into meat. The man squealed in agony and crumpled to the ground in a messy heap.

Davik stepped over the corpse, ducked the second attacker's thrust, and brought his sword down onto the legionary's wrist, slicing clean through the bone and sending him crashing to the ground in a whimper.

Rason felt a twinge of fear at seeing his men being bested by the famous warrior but breathed a sigh of relief as the cohort crested the hill. One man against fifty – the old fool wouldn't stand a chance.

Arrogantly, he turned his back on his new enemy and turned his attention back to the councillors who sat stunned at the sight of the legendary old commander battling his former comrades. The general gestured to the two legionaries guarding the councillors.

"Kill them too," he said with not a hint of emotion in his voice. If murder was what it took to become king, it didn't bother him. Rather he was king than some fool baron or some mysterious claimant; the lady's prophecy had to be fulfilled.

The soldiers drew their swords, setting upon the defenceless councillors with a brutal determination. Each of their screams was silenced as cold steel took their lives in a spray of blood.

"No!" Davik screamed at the sight. He was holding off the cohort who edged towards him warily, the sight of their dead colleagues checking any foolish charge. He stood stunned at the slight of the slaughter. Madness had descended upon Delfinnia, a madness that would play into the hands of the realm's true enemies.

With a roar of anger, Davik attacked the cohort. His arm was a flurry of swings and thrusts as he hacked and slashed his way through the soldiers. A single thought filled his mind: Rason would pay. Despair filled him. He had been counting on Rason to hear him out about his fears, about that night when the royal family died.

Foolishly, he had hoped that together they would restore the legion and exact vengeance upon those who had hired the assassins. Now, all that was left of the man he had once trusted was a lust for power; Rason had lost his soul through murder and savagery.

A spear stabbed painfully into Davik's side, knocking the wind out of his chest. He staggered, grabbing the spear shaft to steady himself and plunged his sword into the spearman's throat. Blood poured from Davik's wound; if he didn't find a way to escape, then he would surely die. He edged the fight toward the steep cliff edge. Below lay the sprawling city of Sunguard, its high towers glinting in the sunlight. On any other day he would be thanking the gods for such a splendid sight; now, however, he prayed for something else entirely.

He pressed his attack forcing the soldiers back until they reached the side of the steep path. Madly, he glanced downwards; the drop must have been over two hundred feet at least. He closed his eyes in acceptance. There was no other way.

With one last look at Rason, Davik whispered a silent prayer to Niveren before stepping back off the cliff's edge.

CHAPTER 5.

The journey took almost four whole days, and on the eve of the last, they finally saw the Priory of Niveren. The two high towers of its battlements made an imposing sight compared to the beauty of its surroundings. The priory was in some respects like a small town – it contained a variety of craftsman, and it owned the surrounding farmland. The large walls and castle stood on a hill that allowed it to tower above the other buildings that were needed to keep the Order of Niveren running. Surrounding it was Lake Sumil, its shimmering waters only adding to the scene's beauty.

Kaiden reigned in his horse and admired the view. He turned to Alira. "Only Gods could have made such a place," he said. "A fitting home for our order, is it not?" He was happy that he was close to his home, yet he saw Alira had a sad look on her face. The ordeal on the road had scared her deeply.

"What's the matter?" Kaiden asked concern showing on his face.

Alira slumped in the saddle.

"I won't be safe there," she said. "You're a Knight of Niveren, and I am a mage. Your people hunt down my kind. And I fear I would hurt someone else. The power I felt was like nothing I've ever felt before. It scares me." She wiped a tear from her eye. "No, it *terrifies* me," she said tearfully.

Kaiden was about to try and reassure her that she would be safe, that he would protect her when a rider in a sergeant's uniform hailed them.

"Wait here," Kaiden said. "We can discuss this later when we've had a good meal and some sleep. That's the least I can offer for the lady who saved my life."

He dismounted, and the sergeant trotted closer.

"Hail Sir Kaiden. One of our scouts saw you whilst travelling back from Retbit."

Kaiden nodded. They had seen a rider yesterday; he gave them some wine but didn't have time to share any news. "He seemed to be in quite a hurry."

"Yes, the grand master sent him to deliver a message to the Baron of Retbit demanding your release, but on his arrival, you had already been set free. The grand master has recalled all of the knights back to the priory." The sergeant was a young man of no more than eighteen. On seeing Alira, he seemed to forget Kaiden was even there.

"Yes, she is a pretty one," Kaiden said. "Now, Sergeant; please tell me, why is the grand master recalling the Order?"

The sergeant snapped his attention back to Kaiden.

"Sorry," he said, blushing before regaining his composure. "The grand master is recalling the Order because he is preparing to go to war!"

"War? By God, what has happened?" Kaiden asked, a sense of dread knotting in his stomach.

"New intelligence has come to the grand master's attention; apparently, he now knows who was responsible for hiring the assassins that murdered the royal family and started the war for the crown."

It was an ominous-looking day when Kaiden awoke. Large dark clouds filled the sky, bringing the promise of rain. It was nice to be back in a comfortable bed and to be fed well, but he was most happy about his chance to clean and trim his beard.

The bell for Morning Prayer rang out in the courtyard, a tradition that had existed since the Order's founding. Kaiden pulled on his tunic, breeches, and boots before walking to his closet and taking out a brand new mantle. The white and gold almost shone, it was so new. Finally, he picked up his sword and attached the scabbard to his belt.

He was still tired after having to stay up until midnight talking with the masters of the Order about his imprisonment and of Alira. None of them liked the idea of having a woman capable of magic in the priory, but they all agreed they would allow her to stay for a time in respect for her rescue of their brother knight. As for the Baron of Retbit, he could wait as other events were taking place.

The baronies were on the verge of escalating the war. With the Baron of Balnor's defeat in the Gold Hills, the route to the capital was now open for the Baron of Champia to make his move northwards, and Retbit would surely not waste his chance to try and take Sunguard. Hiding behind the capital's walls was the Privy Council, who was rapidly losing control of the realm. Even those in the King's Legion that remained loyal were said to be manoeuvring to launch a coup d'état.

Rumours were also spreading that the baronies of Bison and Robinta had fallen under attack from rampaging warlords. And in the far north, the mountain kingdom of Eclin had sent messages for aid to the rest of the realm, telling of fell beasts had been ravaging its towns and villages. The details were far too vague for the knights to understand, though, so only a few scouts had been dispatched to the region.

Kaiden walked down the chapter house's long passageway, passing several other knights and squires along the way. Eventually, he reached the small room where Alira had been billeted. He gently tapped on the door.

"Come in," came her voice.

CHAPTER 5.

Kaiden opened the large oak door and saw Alira sitting at a small dressing table brushing her long golden hair. She wore a long shift dress of royal blue and smiled as she saw him. His heart almost skipped a beat; she was beautiful. Composing himself by clearing his throat, he said, "Morning. I hope you slept well. Have my brother knights treated you well? I am sorry I haven't come to see you before now, but I've been very busy."

She smiled. "I understand. I've been treated very well, and for an order that isn't supposed to have women, I was surprised to see such a lovely collection of dresses."

Despite her happiness, Kaiden could see the rings under her eyes. She had been having nightmares ever since the incident on the road. It was something she would have to deal with and accept; that would come in time, he knew.

He still remembered the first time he had killed a man. He could see his victim's face every time he fell asleep, but over time he had come to accept what he had done. Killing to save others was something he could live with; after all, that was what Niveren commanded. Kaiden laughed and pushed those thoughts out of his mind.

"Well, the Order often receives visits from noble ladies in need of our aid. Although some of my brothers do bring their wives here on occasion. Anyhow, I was going to tell you that the grand master has called another council. More knights have arrived, and he believes the Order cannot wait any longer."

Alira was scared; she had never seen a war before. She had seen the refugees and the resulting chaos a few times in her short life. Being brought up in the borderlands, there was always some conflict or another being fought by the barons and dukes. But this was different, she could feel it. Something had changed in the world, something she couldn't quite place, but the mage in her knew it was terribly wrong.

"What's the matter?" Kaiden asked as he saw the haunted look on her face. Distractedly, she shook head as if coming out of a daze.

"I'm not sure; I just have a strange feeling, is all. My dreams are filled with places and people I've never seen before, but all have been tainted by magic, or at least that's what it feels like. I don't know; I'm probably just being foolish."

"You have the blood of a mage within you, Alira," Kaiden said. "That is not something to dismiss. I've heard old tales that some mages could see glimpses of places and events, in some cases the future. I'll tell you what; I'll discuss this with the grand master. He is the keeper of the Order's knowledge of magic and the mages. Perhaps he could find out something."

"Thank you, Kaiden. You are too kind."

"No problem. I had best be on my way to prayers. You're welcome to join me; perhaps Niveren can give you some answers."

Alira agreed, and the two of them walked together towards the chapel and to Morning Prayer.

Over three hundred knights were gathered in the priory's courtyard. Many had travelled from all around, and rumours were writhe. Kaiden and Alira stood at the back of the crowd awaiting Grand Master Thondril's arrival.

The crowd fell silent once the masters stepped onto the makeshift podium.

"Brother knights," the grand master boomed. "We have recalled you back here because the kingdom stands on the verge of destruction. An unknown enemy assails the land. Assassins killed the king and queen, sowing the roots of mistrust and war amongst the realms. Rumours of death and evil come from the northern mountains. Ancient rivalries threaten to divide us further. Word has reached us that the Privy Council has been overthrown and that, yet another usurper has claimed the throne."

The crowd of knights gave out a roar of protest and anger as they heard the news. Kaiden was shocked at how quickly the situation in the world was worsening.

"We can no longer stay neutral in this war. We will not fight for those claiming the crown; instead, we will do as Niveren commanded and will do what we can to protect the helpless. The fell beasts and dark magic-users long hidden from the world will no doubt use this time of chaos to strike, and so it falls to us to carry out our sacred duty –"

Suddenly, Alira gave out an ear-piercing cry and collapsed onto the ground. Kaiden immediately knelt down next to her and cradled her in his arms. The other knights nearby all turned their attention to the girl who was now writhing on the ground.

"Alira, Alira! What's wrong? What's happening?" Kaiden cried desperately.

Flashes of horrific images screamed through Alira's mind. War, death, terrible creatures rending men and women limb from limb, their screams of agony reverberating in her ears. The screams turned into a wailing which then merged and changed into the cry of a child. She saw a woman, scared and alone, clutching a small child to her chest as a dark shadow appeared over them. Then there was a blinding flash; a halo of white light surrounded the child, casting back the darkness. A roar of anger and then suddenly a robed figure appeared in the image. His face was white and decayed with eyes of pure black. Tendrils of darkness emanated from him, and his fury was aimed at the child. A figure stepped out from the light and raised a sword high into the air. Light and fire blossomed forth, driving back the robed figure's fury.

'Alderlade, Luxon' whispered a malevolent voice.

Alira gasped awake. She sat up suddenly, only to see the concerned faces of Kaiden and the other knights. Kaiden sighed in relief.

"Alira, thank God. Are you alright?"

The grand master had stopped speaking as the commotion spread through the crowd.

"Sir Kaiden, what is happening?" he demanded.

Kaiden called for a healer and told the Master of Alira's collapse. Quickly, three knights picked up the dazed girl and carried her to the priory's infirmary.

Alira explained all that she had seen in her vision to the gathered masters. She was seated in the grand master's chamber. Once she had finished, Kaiden asked, "Masters, is it possible the vision was magical in origin? Since we left Retbit, Alira has been experiencing more and more magical activity."

The grand master glanced at the others. The vision had shaken them all.

"Sir Kaiden, what I am about to tell you cannot leave this chamber." He cleared his throat before continuing. "The name Alderlade was the name of the king's youngest child, a boy who was no more than a few weeks old. It was thought that he had perished during the attack on the Royal Family and the destruction of the palace three years ago. Very few of the commoners or even nobility knew the child's name. The birth of a child fifth in line to the crown isn't normally seen as that important."

Alira sat stunned; the name she had heard was a real person.

"If the child is alive, then they are in grave danger!" she cried.

"If that is the case, and the child does indeed live, then he is the true and rightful heir to the kingdom," one of the masters said.

"If that is the case then we must inform the Diasect," said another. "They must verify if the prince still lives and bring him to safety."

The grand master nodded in agreement. "Yes. We will send word to the Diasect about this and we must discover more about Alira's vision. Sir Kaiden and Alira will travel to Caldaria and find out what the mages may know of these troubling visions."

He paused, thinking. "What of the other name? Luxon was it?"

Kaiden shook his head. "I have never heard of such a person, but whoever they are they must be important."

CHAPTER 6.

The high ceiling of the Crystal Tower of Judgement was spellbinding. Orbs of bright light flitted and flew among the rafters in a rainbow of colours. The balls of magic were said to have been cast by Zahnia himself a thousand years ago as a test of his power. The mage lights had lasted for millennia, attesting to the long-dead wizard's connection to his power. Others said that the lights were simply created early every morning by the masters as they warmed up for the day ahead. If it was them, then they kept it a closely guarded secret.

A month had passed before the trial had finally been confirmed by the council of masters. With the war raging in the outside world, the masters had been kept exceptionally busy tending to the city's needs. Remaining a neutral party was proving hard, as each of the claimants were pressing to enlist the power of the mages to their cause.

Luxon stood on a raised platform facing a long crystal table. Sitting behind it, grim-faced and serious, were five of the city's masters. Each was the leader of their specific school.

To the far right was Master Dufran, the head of the School of Illusion. His bald head was tattooed in a plethora of mystical-looking patterns; his piercing green eyes regarded Luxon with amused interest.

Sitting at his side was Master Fy'odo, the master of the School of Alteration. His big, bushy black beard and raggedy hair hid virtually all of his features. Only his small grey eyes could be seen poking through his hair.

On the far left sat Master Enil of the School of Healing. He gave Luxon a reassuring smile. For a master, Enil was remarkably young – perhaps no older than thirty at the most. His head of red hair mixed strangely with his yellowish eyes.

Luxon nodded to the master, thankful to have a potential ally on the judging panel. Hannah had told him that Enil had taken a keen interest in him. When he asked why, Hannah had shrugged her shoulders, but something in her eyes made Luxon curious.

Sitting next to Enil was Master Kvar of the School of Transmutation. The man had a reputation for being slightly mad, and Luxon understood why. Kvar was the skinniest man he had ever seen; the master's robes hung loosely about his body. Under a head of long unkempt white hair, Kvar's eyes were always darting around as though he was looking for something. It was said that transmutation often had a strong impact on the caster's mind; after all, turning things into something else required a huge mental strain.

The centre seat was empty and reserved for the grandmaster.

Luxon looked over his shoulder to see Hannah, Yepert and – to his surprise – Master Ri'ges sat in the small gathering of folk who had come to watch the proceedings. Yepert looked petrified, but Hannah gave him a reassuring smile.

Luxon twiddled his thumbs nervously. Aside from himself and the masters, the hall was filling up with other mages and even a couple of Nightblades. His nerves were threatening to get the better of him, and he itched to run away, but that thought was immediately quashed as he heard the heavy metal doors to the chamber close with a loud thud. He turned in his seat to see Grand Master Thanos stride towards the master's table.

Thanos looked remarkably young for the title that he held – no older than forty at most, but as with all things magic, not everything was as it seemed. The grand master was tall and strong, with a head of thinning black hair. His serious eyes were a bright blue as though magic flowed through them. Thanos stepped up onto the raised platform and raised his arms to signal that the hearing was about to start. Those in the small crowd stopped their whispering, their eyes all focusing on Luxon and the masters.

Thanos spoke in a clear, assertive voice; he pointed a finger at Luxon who shrank back under the grand master's gaze.

"We are gathered here in the Tower of Judgement to determine whether this student is guilty of committing the serious crime of attempted murder" – the crowd murmured at that – "and the crime of uncontrolled use of magic."

Thanos sat in the centre chair, his hands resting limply on the table's smooth surface.

"Luxon of Edioz, son of Garrick Edioz and Drusilla Edioz. You have heard the accusations against you. How do you plead?" Thanos's tone was grave and threatening.

Luxon swallowed, his mouth suddenly felt dry. It took all of his courage to stand and say in a clear voice, "Not guilty, my masters."

Another murmur came from the crowd.

"Very well," Thanos bellowed. "Bring in the first witness."

A side door creaked open and in walked Accadus, a smirk on his face. Luxon felt his stomach fall; his enemy had him right where he wanted him.

The trial went on for the better part of the day. Accadus greatly exaggerated the incident and basically branded Luxon and Yepert as the bullies and aggressors. The more he had exaggerated, the less scared Luxon became. He knew that all of the masters were aware of Accadus's reputation, so they would surely never believe him. The other boys who had been injured in the fray also gave their testimonies, but due to their stupidity, neither one of their stories matched up. In one, Luxon had used telekinesis to knock them all to the ground, in the other he had muttered a dark incantation.

CHAPTER 6.

Luxon was glad the boys had not been allowed to see one another until the trial. They hadn't had a single opportunity to come up with a lie. Ironically, if they had just told the truth, then things would have probably been worse.

Once the boys had given their testimony, it was the turn of the defence. Yepert told the truth of what had happened, and Master Ri'ges vouched for both of them. It hadn't taken the masters long to pronounce Luxon innocent of the charge of attempted murder.

Thanos stood and addressed the court. "Now, we come to the charge of uncontrolled magic use. We would ask that all non-essential mages and onlookers leave the court."

After a few minutes, the chamber was empty leaving Luxon all alone to face the masters. Then to his surprise, all of the masters except for Thanos left as well.

"We have heard some interesting things about you, Luxon," Thanos said. "Your teacher, Master Ri'ges, assures us that you are one of the most naturally gifted students he has ever met – that somehow magic comes as naturally to you as eating or drinking.

"Do you know of Zahnia the Great?" Thanos asked.

Luxon nodded his head in the affirmative. "Yes, master, I do. Everyone has ... haven't they?"

Thanos smiled. The grand master sat casually on the crystal table's surface, his legs just about touching the ground.

"Zahnia was just a boy, no older than you are now before he entered into legend. You see, he lived in a time long before Delfinnia even existed as a kingdom. In his day, darkness ruled the world. He was born with a gift so great that he was able to defy the darkness and eventually defeat it. With his power, he was proclaimed a king, and it was he that founded the Golden Empire. Magic can change the world, both for good and for ill."

Thanos paused. The grandmaster looked around the room as though he was listening to something. Luxon strained his ears but couldn't hear a thing. A few moments of uneasy silence passed before Thanos's attention once more focused on the boy before him.

"What you did to those boys is the reason why the ordinary folk fear our kind."

Thanos held up a hand to stop Luxon's reply. "You were lucky none of them were killed and that you were smart enough to do what was necessary to stop it."

Luxon looked at his hands, dumbfounded.

"B-but master, I couldn't control it – the magic just happened," he said miserably, tears threatening to fall from his eyes.

Thanos's expression softened. The tall wizard walked over to Luxon and placed a reassuring hand on the young man's shoulder.

"In time you will learn to control it, Luxon. What you have is a very rare gift, one that only a few possess. You are quite possibly the first true *thaumaturgist* to have appeared in this world in several generations. It is a gift that enables you to do magic without the need for spells or incantations."

Luxon raised his head and looked at his master in confusion.

"How ... how is that possible?" he asked.

Thanos smiled. "The magic within you is like a second skin, Luxon. It is a reflex to you, just like when you blink or your knee jerks when hit with a healer's hammer.

"To me, and everyone else, magic is something that we must spend decades in near constant practice to bring such power out in us. It is a gift, Luxon – one that is both wondrous and terrifying in equal measure."

Luxon frowned at that. "Terrifying? I don't like the sound of that," he muttered. A thought entered his mind. "If magic is like a reflex to me, then why has it only come to me like that now?"

Thanos began pacing up and down the chamber. "Your life was in danger; it is as simple as that. Is it not a reflex to fight or flee when threatened?

"Your gift is dangerous if not controlled. I emptied the chamber because I did not want your abilities to become common knowledge. Unsavoury folk of all kinds would no doubt attempt to take advantage of your gifts.

"In that respect, I will be taking you on as my apprentice in order to teach you how to control your power. As for Accadus and his oafs, they will be expelled from this city and returned to Retbit. Too many times have I had to deal with the consequences of that boy's misdemeanours."

Luxon was stunned. He was being left off, and he was going to obtain the rank of apprentice, an apprentice to Grand Master Thanos no less! He didn't know what to say, so instead, he smiled.

CHAPTER 7.

Mountains of Eclin

In the scarce scrub of the mountain pass, two rangers watched and waited. Howling winds battered the senses, and the blizzard caused a near whiteout. Dressed in their grey robes and cowls, they were almost indistinguishable amongst the landscape.

Carlock shifted uncomfortably, his hands tensing and relaxing on the shaft of his longbow. His silent companion was as still as a statue, his grey and hard eyes never leaving the scene unfolding on the plain far below.

"How much longer must we wait, Woven?" Carlock mumbled to the stern looking older man. "It's been hours now."

Woven glanced at his comrade with an annoyed look on his face. "We wait until they've all passed. Down there is an army the likes of which we have never seen before."

The two rangers had been dispatched to the mountain regions after reports flooded in of massacres and a terrifying enemy. For days, the region of Eclin had been besieged. Towns and cities north of the mountains had fallen silent as thousands of refugees fled the horror that was quickly consuming the land.

Baron Lido had ordered his forces to defend and barricade the mountain passes that led to the south, to Delfinnia's capital and heartlands.

The reports of spectres and monsters had at first been scorned as mere panic-induced rumour, but after survivors from the garrisons of the mountain forts collaborated with the testimony of the refugees, fear had truly set in.

Down in the valley, a seemingly never-ending column of black armoured figures marched. Their destination, the barricade at Fuio pass.

"They look like men to me," Carlock said as he shifted slightly.

"Yes ... Wait look there," Woven whispered. "By Niveren, it can't be."

There, unbelievably, was a shambling horde of people. At first glance, they looked like prisoners of war – men and women. But Woven's keen eyes could see what they truly were. The faint stains of red on the snow around them were the first clue. It was blood. Many were headless, stumbling and staggering as they followed the armoured troops.

Then came the sound. It was the moans and cries of souls in torment, and it emanated from those walking corpses still with heads and throats able to unleash the bone-chilling sound. They numbered in their thousands.

"All of those people were killed in the towns and villages. Then they were brought back," Woven said. Carlock stared in terror; he remembered the horror stories his grandfather used to tell him and his brothers when they were small, sat around the fire on those long cold winter nights; tales of the dark mages' magic and the Great War.

"Magic. It has to be. The darkest of all."

A roar caught the Rangers' attention. Below their hiding spot, two rapidly-approaching horrors came: snarling beasts with thick fur, razor-sharp claws and talons of steel.

"Werewolves!" Carlock warned.

The creatures were rare, but not unknown in the mountain regions. They were the remnants of the Magic Wars, men cursed by the dark mages in battle. For centuries the beasts had roamed the peaks picking off the unwary traveller.

"They have our scent," Woven swore and drew his bow. "Let's move. They could be scouts for that army." The two rangers quickly clambered down from the overhang and ran through the dense brush. Naked trees with their sharp twigs and limbs tore at their clothes as the two men bounded down the mountainside.

"Hurry!" Woven shouted as his companion stumbled in the snow. The beasts were fast approaching – their panting breaths and snarls sounded close.

Carlock picked himself up and scrambled back to his feet, almost falling again as the thick snow shifted under his weight. Panicking now, he glanced over his shoulder to see the two wolves closing fast. The beasts' fearsome muzzles were full of razor-sharp fangs, and saliva poured from their snarling jaws.

"Down!" Woven shouted, just as one of the creatures leapt at Carlock's back, talons extended for the kill.

The creature covered the large distance in a single bound, almost taking the elder ranger by surprise. But Woven was a man of the mountains; his entire life had been spent hunting and fighting amongst the frigid peaks.

Instinct was his greatest ally in what was often a blizzard-filled landscape, a place where the senses often failed or deceived. He notched an arrow, drew back the longbow's cord and loosed. He shot with hardly taking aim; he never had to. After years of practice and use, he shot the bow from reflex alone.

Carlock turned as the werewolf flew at him. Just as he thought he would surely die, Woven's arrow struck the beast.

With a howl of pain, the creature lost its momentum and crashed to the ground at Carlock's feet. The arrow had pierced the creature's thick hide and its heart.

Carlock spun around as he heard the second wolf snarling. His adrenaline now pumping and buoyed up by his friend's kill of the first; he drew his own bow.

The remaining werewolf was more patient and cautious than its deceased companion had been. Slowly, it circled the young ranger, its feral eyes never leaving those of the man before it. Despite the cold, sweat poured down Carlock's face, almost blinding him. The monster before him continued circling, just waiting to strike.

Its fangs looked like knives capable of rending flesh with ease; its coarse, thick fur was aglow with ethereal cursed energy. Carlock slowly notched an arrow to his bowstring. He didn't want to startle the creature into attacking; he could see Woven moving slowly behind the beast, a new arrow strung on his great longbow. Delicately, Carlock took aim and drew back the cord. His breathing was deafening, and his heart pounded like a drum.

The werewolf snarled, and its eyes narrowed; it sensed the ranger was about to attack. With a blur of speed, the beast crossed the distance to its prey in a split second. It pounced, and Carlock hardly had the chance to scream – with lightning speed, the monster was upon him.

Woven shot his arrow, but this time the point only grazed the wolf's flank, bouncing harmlessly off of the beast's thick hide. Swearing, Woven drew his silver sword and raced towards the downed figure of his comrade who was desperately struggling to hold the monster's fangs away from his face. He winced as he heard Carlock's arm snap as the wolf's jaws clamped around it. He felt pride, however, that the younger man did not scream out the pain he must surely be feeling. To do so would alert the army still marching through the valley below.

Blood sprayed as a talon raked the Carlock's chest. Woven reached the struggling pair, and without hesitation raised his sword high into the air. With a two-handed downward thrust, he stabbed the werewolf between its shoulders. The tip of the blade ripped through flesh and bone until it burst the monster's heart, ripped through its chest and stopped just inches from Carlock's face. Before the wolf could roar out its pain and give away their position, Woven drew a dagger from his cloak and deftly sliced the snarling monster's throat, cutting off the gurgling scream of pain.

With a kick he rolled the heavy corpse off of his companion, only to find Carlock covered in blood and gasping for air. His chest was a mass of cuts where the talons had scratched at it, and his arm was at an impossible angle.

It was then he saw the bite mark on the younger man's neck, and despair filled him. Woven slumped to his knees; the bite of a werewolf meant one thing to anyone who was not eaten or killed outright. The werewolf's saliva spread into open wounds, passing the cursed magic onto the victim. Carlock would turn into the very thing the rangers hunted: a monster of evil.

Carlock grabbed Woven's shoulder and drew him close. His breathing was rapid with fear.

"Woven," he tried to say. He coughed, causing blood to foam at his mouth. "Already I can feel it," he managed to utter. His eyes turned glassy, and then their colour began to change – first to black, and then slowly to yellow.

Woven picked up his sword and put the blade to Carlock's neck. "I am sorry, my friend. It is better to die a man and under the grace of Niveren, than a monster of the darkness," he said reverently, reciting the Rangers' code. With a thrust of his blade, Carlock was silenced, never to rise again. Woven fell to his knees and sobbed, and all the while the army below continued its march; it seemed as though the horde would never end.

He respectfully said a silent prayer to Niveren for his friend's soul and knelt to retrieve the pendant around his neck. The young man's fiancée would despair at the news. With a final glance at the scene below him, Woven turned away and began to move down the mountainside. He had to warn the soldiers at Fuio pass.

CHAPTER 8.

The barricade had taken three days of constant building to finally be constructed. It was an engineering feat worthy of the ancient Golden Empire. The manpower needed to erect the massive mounds of earth, in order to block a pass over a mile wide, was immense.

Twenty thousand soldiers of the barony of Eclin had been put to the task, and none had protested. They had each heard the rumours of the nightmare that was threatening to overwhelm their homeland, and they were itching for the chance to deal out death to their foes.

Baron Lido watched as the final wooden stake was hammered into place, finishing the last line of defences.

A hundred paces in front of the stakes were the hastily built watchtowers and palisades. Archers would take up position in the towers, whilst the infantry would hold the walls. In front of that was the great mound of earth that was so steep it took a man several attempts to reach the top. There, the skirmishers would be placed; among them, the rangers and hunters, experts at hit and fade tactics. The baron hoped they would deliver such a hail of arrows that any enemy would turn tail and flee, even one that was said to have magic as its ally.

Finally, there was the field of stakes that would slow down any attackers and would buy his forces time to regroup and counterattack if the battle began to go ill.

Interspersed between the stakes were pits filled with sharpened sticks and nails. At a signal, the pit could be collapsed by one of the many squires that would be waiting behind the battle line. The baron had made it clear to the young boys that they would have an important role to perform. They would be the ones who would resupply the arrows and weapons of the troops, as well as bring food and water.

Lido was a confident commander; he had ruled the mountain lands for thirty years. He had seen his fair share of battles, both against mortal enemies and the remnants of the dark mages that sometimes attacked. Zombies and ghouls were of no concern to him; he had seen and fought them before and had emerged victorious. This time, however, something made him doubt. A nagging feeling that this time he would face something far more terrible than the centuries-old leftovers of the Magic Wars.

The war raging for the crown in the southern lands was of little concern to Lido. His name was listed as one of the so-called six claimants, but in reality, he and his men had not even marched against the other claimants. His war was here like it always had been. His task was to defend Delfinnia from what lay within and beyond the vast Eclin mountain range.

A zombie was a feeble thing, slow and weak. The ghouls, however, never lost their power and were formidable foes. He adjusted his sword belt and gripped the hilt of his sword tighter. It was named the Mountain's Hammer, and it had once belonged to his ancestor who had fought in that terrible final battle of the Magic Wars. The hilt was ornately decorated with golden serpents, and at the centre was laid a blue channelling crystal, which enabled the magic inside to enchant the blade.

"The mages toppled mountains in their battles; rivers turned to blood and men died by the thousands. Only Niveren had saved them that day," his grandfather had said. "But it was never a victory."

Those words now came to haunt Lido. What had the old man meant by that? All of the historians claimed it had been a total victory; the Knights of Niveren had slain the Necromancer and the Diasect had successfully defeated Danon, the master of black magic. A champion had slain the evil mage, and white mages had sent his soul into the void of damnation.

Lido began to doubt the old tales. With an enemy that was sounding more and more like the great enemy of old, he began to think the old man was onto something.

***

It was at dawn the next day that the ground began to shake and tremble. Men groggily stirred from their tents, wrapped in thick furs against the frigid cold, to see what was happening.

The alarm bells began to toll out over the vast camp. The enemy had arrived.

Running at the point of exhaustion, Woven reached the barricade just ahead of the coming horde.

"Halt. Who goes there?" challenged the knight defending the mound.

"My name is Woven," he replied tiredly. "I must speak to the baron at once." He showed the knight his blue crystal pendant, the identifying mark of the rangers, and was promptly allowed entry.

He made his way through a camp in chaos as thousands of soldiers armed themselves and moved to their positions. The squires ran about stamping out the cooking fires before heading to their posts. Horses were saddled as the Knights pulled on their armour and fastened their sword belts.

A horn's low warning tone echoed over the camp, causing the activity to pause for a moment. Woven stopped and listened just like all of the others around him. Carried

CHAPTER 8.

faintly on the wind came the sound of inhuman moans, the snarling of beasts and the steady stomping of thousands of armoured troops.

The forces of Eclin were afraid. Woven could see it in the eyes of his countrymen, and he said a silent prayer. He prayed his people would win the day.

"Why are you bastards just standing around?" roared a squat man in plate armour. "Pull your fingers out of your arses and get ready to kill!" He was short, but his chest was massive. It exuded physical strength. The troops all turned to the man; questioning looks on their faces.

"You're all afraid? You are the sons of Eclin, the wolves of the mountains! Let our foes hear us roar. Let them come and die. Roar with me!"

With that, the man bellowed his anger and defiance. Men around him joined him, and before long, twenty thousand soldiers were roaring along with him. The sound was like thunder blasting through the canyon and the mountain peaks.

Woven glanced around him; it seemed his prayer had been answered for now. With that one act, the men of Eclin now looked determined and fearless. He just hoped their newfound courage would last. Once more, the camp burst into activity as troops assembled and archers mounted the towers and palisades.

Woven turned as the sound of galloping hooves caught his attention.

None other than Baron Lido was approaching, riding a black stallion. The baron's shoulder-length grey hair and piercing green eyes were covered by a coif of chainmail. As the horse passed through the camp, the men bowed their heads or knelt in respect and fealty. The Baron stopped in front of the squat man.

"Hail, Sir Grandir. I see your way with words has not lessened since we last met," Lido greeted dryly.

Grandir bowed his head.

"Niveren will always be there to give courage to those who are lacking, my lord," Grandir replied icily. "Eclin has always been a stalwart and worthy member of the realm. It is an honour for me and my company to fight beside you, my lord."

The baron huffed and rode on to Woven. His face betrayed his annoyance at having the Knights of Niveren at his side. Lido, among many nobles and regents, felt that the knights had outstayed their welcome and had become too powerful. Eclin especially resented the Order due to the Knights' persecution of those who followed the old ways.

Long before the Magic War and the founding of Delfinnia, the Golden Empire had ruled the land. They had worshipped forgotten gods and practised insane magical arts.

Eclin was said to be the land where Danon and his bride, the first witch Cliria, discovered their power, and it was for this reason that the knights regularly sent crusades into the barony to root out any users of the old ways. The barbaric mountain tribes had always raided Eclin, so the kings of Delfinnia had allowed the knights to wage their wars.

Lido resented having to allow them access to his men and resources, but he disliked Sir Grandir especially. He was the head of the Eclin chapter of the Order and was constantly undermining the baron's commands, often overruling him with the law of Niveren. Lido knew the knights were fearsome warriors and knew any baron would want them to fight at his side, but the knight was infuriating to deal with.

"The guards informed me of your return, ranger," Lido said to Woven. "What news do you bring me? And where is your comrade?"

Woven took a deep breath and recounted all that he had seen: the death of Carlock and the horde of undead.

The Baron stared at the ranger; his eyes hard.

"Werewolves, Zombies? These are the aspects of the old enemy, are they not? How is this possible?"

Fear gripped the baron's heart; he had hoped and prayed that the stories were just fantasy. The stories his father had told him flooded his mind. How could he face such a foe by himself? Eclin could not hope to stand against such evil alone.

"Danon is dead," Grandir said certainly. He approached the baron and Woven after overhearing the conversation.

"The bastard's body was thrown into the void. No, this new threat must be the result of meddlers in the dark arts. For too long, I've tried to get my master to launch a full crusade against these mountains, but he felt the threat from magic had left us. Danon has not returned – it's impossible," he declared, albeit with some doubt in his words.

The baron scowled at the knight but seemed to relax at the words spoken.

"You are correct of course, Sir Grandir. Danon is gone forever. When this is over, I will allow full access to my lands for you to launch your crusade. Never again must these relics from the Magic War threaten the realm. We must root them out and burn them."

Just as Grandir was about to reply, the horn sounded again. This time the enemy was in the range of the first line of defences. The Battle of Fuio Pass was about to begin.

The pass was a mile across, with steep mountains on either side. It was a perfect spot to mount a defence, and the forces of Eclin were confident of victory. The horde of the enemy stood five hundred paces from the vast pile of earth that formed the first line of defences. Thousands of black-armoured figures stood in eerie silence, their faces concealed by their helmets. Behind them staggered the zombies, moans filling the cold air, chilling the defenders' blood with fear. At the flanks came the werewolves in numbers not seen for aeons. They roared and snarled at the rangers who took position at the top of the earth mound.

Woven was among them. Being one of the most skilled archers in the kingdom, he insisted on joining his fellow rangers. He was still weary from his journey to the camp, but fear and adrenaline kept his mind sharp and gave his arms the strength needed to draw his massive longbow.

Six thousand rangers stood with their bows drawn, arrows of death notched and ready to fly at the enemy. Tension filled the air, men sweated and prayed.

And then came the roar.

The black-armoured troops surged forward, swords and spears at the ready, charging headlong at the Eclin defenders. Within moments, they came into range of the rangers who, as one, loosed the first volley of arrows.

The sky turned dark as thousands of arrows momentarily blocked out the sun and slammed into the attacking forces with a deafening crash.

Woven stood stunned as he watched the arrows strike. Hundreds of the armoured figures had been struck, and yet none fell or even screamed out in either terror or jubilation at having survived. It was then, as the horde continued to come at him that he realised with horror that he had been mistaken. The armoured figures were not men or even mortal. They were ghouls!

Another volley of arrows was loosed, and another, and still not a single figure fell. The Rangers began to desperately shoot shaft after shaft, but still, none fell. Panic swept through their ranks as they realised that they could not harm the enemy.

It was then just as the first defenders were about to break that Woven saw the werewolves charging along the flanks. Those, he knew they could kill.

"Target the flanks! Kill the wolves!" he bellowed. Putting his words into actions, he swung his bow to the right and loosed.

The arrow pierced his target in the eye. With a satisfying roar of pain, the beast collapsed to the ground. Now all the other archers shot their arrows at the werewolves, killing dozens at a time, but still the armoured figures inexorably approached the rangers. Soon they would reach the foot of the earthworks, and the sword work would begin.

The armoured figures reached the mound and halted. The werewolves fell back, having learnt not to approach the stinging arrows.

Once again, an eerie silence filled the pass. Woven stopped shooting and shifted nervously. He could see that the Rangers had slain at least fifty wolves. But they hadn't even inflicted a scratch on the armoured enemy that now stood in ominous silence.

"Draw swords," Woven growled. With the wolves out of range, their arrows were harmless against the armoured ghouls. He wasn't even sure if the sword would harm them. He just knew they had to try.

The ghouls stamped their feet, causing the ground to shake. Incessantly, they carried on stamping, unnerving the defenders.

Then came the zombies.

Thousands of them swarmed through the ranks of ghouls and scrabbled up the earthworks. Some were headless, others had limbs missing, but all had once been villagers. A father, a husband a wife or a sister – all had once been mortal human beings.

Many fell backwards down the steep mound, but as soon as they fell, they would right themselves and try again. Hundreds managed the climb, and immediately attacked the rangers, who now stabbed and fought desperately.

Woven saw that the horde was swarming all along the earthwork. When one zombie was finally slain, two more would take its place. The foot of the earthworks was soon filled with their corpses, over which more zombies climbed to get up the steep bank.

Woven decapitated a zombie and impaled another on his blade. They were easy to destroy, but the sheer number was starting to cause the defence line to collapse. Hundreds of rangers were now falling under the swarm of undead, their screams muffled by moans and the sound of battle. Blood sprayed Woven's face as a zombie sunk its teeth into the neck of a nearby ranger.

"Fall back!" roared the now-familiar voice of Sir Grandir.

Charging fast from the direction of the second defence line came the Knights of Niveren. There were only forty of them, but their warhorses smashed into the zombies that had successfully scaled the earthworks. Now Woven and the surviving rangers turned and jumped, scrambling down the steep bank towards the second line. Once more, the roar of the werewolves filled his ears.

Now that the archers had been driven off, the beasts attacked en masse. Hundreds of fleeing rangers were chased down and torn apart by the monsters.

Woven didn't look back as he ran past the charging knights. The mounted warriors hacked their way through the zombies, rescuing wounded rangers. A werewolf leapt, sending a knight sprawling to the ground; his horse whinnied in fear and was abruptly silenced as the wolf sunk its teeth into the poor creature's neck. Zombies overwhelmed one knight, throwing him to the ground before ripping away his armour and ripping into his flesh. Woven wished he could block out the screams; never before had he witnessed such horror in battle. Yet more horror was to come …

Stood behind the ranks of the undead was a tall figure. Its flesh was rotted, and its bones were visible. At first glance, it looked like a walking skeleton. In fact, it was a Lich.

A tattered and torn cloak billowed in the cold breeze sweeping through the pass. In the lich's hands was a long black staff, which it now held high in the air.

With an unearthly scream, the ghouls advanced upon the Eclin defenders. Victory for the undead quickly followed.

CHAPTER 9.

Caldaria was a riot of colour. Fire jugglers and circus acrobats cartwheeled and danced their way through the streets. Even the mages got in on the celebrations – fireworks lit up the sky, and magic dazzled and amazed the stunned onlookers. All thoughts of war and evil were cast out of folk's minds as they celebrated the *Feast of the Brave Knight*.

Luxon pulled his cloak tighter about his shoulders. Despite it being the height of summer, an unnatural chill was in the wind. He stood on the balcony outside the dorms, leaning against the rough stonework; despite the festivities, he couldn't shake the feeling of unease that had been tormenting him for the past few moons.

Word had come from Sunguard of the overthrow of the Privy Council. According to all accounts, the Midlands were now under the command of what folk named in whispers *the Legion of the Usurper*. Rason hadn't wasted any time in establishing his authority over his new "kingdom." The sot had even tried to have himself crowned in the ruins of the old king's hall on the summit of the peak which rose over the capital. Resistance had been virtually non-existent. The legionaries that had supported the council quickly bowed the knee to their general.

In the days that followed, Luxon had spent long hours under the tutelage of Thanos. He had learned so much already.

A firework exploded high in the sky in a breath-taking riot of colours, causing Luxon's companion to shout out in joy. Despite all that was happening in the world, and to him, he couldn't help but smile at the sight of Yepert clapping his hands in glee.

"Oh, that was incredible!" the chubby boy laughed. More fireworks shot into the sky, one exploding into the image of a knight whilst another took the form of the monster Necron. Upon seeing the beast, Luxon heard the booing of the crowd.

"Why are they booing, Lux?" Yepert asked, confusion evident in his voice.

Luxon rolled his eyes.

"Come on, Yepert, you must have heard the story of Necron and Estran; we celebrate it every year!"

Yepert had a look of confusion on his face, as though he was deep in concentration. After a while, his eyes went wide.

"Oh yeah ... but you tell the tale so well, Lux; go on, tell it again."

Luxon sighed. He knew he was a good storyteller; the two boys had spent many a night telling each other tales from their respective homelands. The tales from Plock where Yepert was from made for some pretty interesting, if far-fetched, stories. His favourite involved a witch, a mage and a rather amorous chicken.

"Alright, so here goes," Luxon said, walking back inside the dorm room. He took a cushion from his bed and threw it on the ground, before sitting carefully upon it. Yepert also settled himself onto the floor in eager anticipation of the tale. Whenever Luxon told a tale, he liked to be as dramatic as possible, so he pulled his hood over his head, hiding his face in shadow.

"Long ago, before the days of the kings of Delfinnia, and even before the Golden Empire, the descendants of the first man, Niveren, prospered for thousands of years. But always lurking in the shadows was the spirit of Niveren's evil brother, Danon.

"The offspring of the dark one and his wicked wife had not been idle after his first defeat in the days of the gods, and whilst the world above them witnessed the rise and fall of kings and empires, they focused on furthering their power in the dark arts of witchcraft and the blackest of magic. In the age of three empires, a powerful wizard known as Necron, who was also secretly a disciple of Danon, bound his soul with magic so foul that the site of his wicked experiments remains tainted to this day, and the first Lich was created."

Yepert shivered at the thought of such a terrifying monster. He had seen pictures and read about them in the ancient texts found in the great library.

"Necron rose to dominate all other followers of the N'gist cult, and his foul influence spread to the world of men. With promises of power and riches, he seduced the rulers of the Sarpi Empire. Within less than a century, that noble and rich empire had fallen into decadence and corruption, its once good and fair people fallen into wickedness.

Soon the lich's influence had spread to the Yolla and Tulin Empires until only the fractured and broken Nivion Empire remained. Once more, conflict erupted on Esperia. Millions perished in the bloodletting as the Nivion Empire desperately tried to halt Necron's power."

Yepert's eyes had gone wide.

"What happened? Not everyone had gone bad, surely!" he cried.

Luxon smiled. "Not everyone went evil, of course. As is the way in most of the old tales, there is always a counter to the bad. After all, isn't it always preached by the church that the light always balances out the dark?"

Luxon cleared his throat and once more pulled his cloak tighter around his shoulders. There was definitely something on the air. The summers in Caldaria were rarely so cold. He continued telling the tale:

"At the Battle of the Greenmoor, the armies of the three empires clashed and their fleets fought at sea. The already weakened Nivions fought bravely, but the power of Necron could not be broken. When all hope seemed lost, a knight of the Nivion Empire called Estran rode forth on his white stallion and bellowed a challenge to the Lich, vowing to never surrender.

'By the way," Luxon said, pausing the story to Yepert's obvious dismay. "I once visited the place where the battle took place."

Yepert scoffed. "You've been to the Blackmoor? As if. You'd have to be mad to go there; they say that banshees and the ghosts of the dead roam those evil moors."

Luxon chuckled. "I went there with my mother when I was younger. If it was as evil as everyone says, then why is the city of Blackmoor there?"

A look of concentration crossed Yepert's features as he tried to argue. With an exasperated sigh, he admitted defeat. "There are banshees ..." he grumbled.

"Anyway," Luxon interrupted, "back to the story."

A large firework lit up the boys' room, followed a few seconds later by the loud explosion of the black powder. The cheers of the crowd followed on the breeze.

"The scars of that mighty battle are evident in Delfinnia today, as the once prosperous region of Greenmoor was turned into a wasteland. Today it is known ..." he paused for effect, "as the Blackmoor. Anyway, Estran rode forth from the lines of his battered army and drew his sword, Asphodel."

Yepert cooed at the name. "The sword of light!" he cried excitedly. Everyone in Delfinnia had heard of the legendary blade, the sword that had been wielded by heroes throughout the ages. Most of the tales of the mythical weapon were probably just fairy tales; after all, any story that had the sacred blade in it always went down well with the common folk.

Luxon smirked at his friend's expression. "With the sword thought to be that mighty blade Asphodel, the two battled for hours until finally Estran mortally wounded Necron in single combat. Sadly for our hero, he too was killed by the lich's forces, and to this day the peoples of Delfinnia celebrate Estran with the Feast of the Brave Knight on midsummer's eve.

"The end," Luxon said, spreading his arms wide.

Yepert sat in silence, confusion evident on his face. He blinked.

"Wait ... that's it?"

"Yep," Luxon replied simply.

"But ... But Estran died! What happened next?"

Luxon sighed and stood up from the floor. Even sitting on the cushion, his bum was growing numb from the hard stone surface. He pulled his hood down and ran a hand through his hair before answering his confused friend.

"Estran died, and the forces of Necron obliterated the warriors of Nivion, hailing in the thousand-year-long age of darkness.

"Not a very happy ending I know, but that's why most storytellers stop at the point when Estran cut down Necron."

Yepert sat on the floor looking from one hand to the other. He was a bright lad, just not when it came to history or the meaning of things.

"If Estran died and the goodies lost, then why on earth do we celebrate the Feast of the Brave Knight?"

Just as Luxon was about to answer, a deep voice interrupted him, causing Yepert to jump in fright.

"Because the tale of Estran shows that it is noble to stand against evil at all costs, and to never fear death. If people follow his example of courage and bravery, then evil can always be defeated."

Standing in the doorway to boys' room was the man Luxon had met when he came to after his failed levitation experiment.

The Nightblade Welsly gave a bow.

Yepert jumped to his feet, his mouth hanging open in surprise and awe; he'd never met a Nightblade before.

"Forgive me for my intrusion, Luxon, but Master Thanos wishes for you to come to his chambers in the Arch Tower. He sent me to escort you there. Some riders from the south arrived earlier this evening, and your name cropped up," the Nightblade explained.

Luxon quickly pulled on his shoes and followed Welsly out of the room, throwing a bemused look to his friend as he went. Curiosity filled him as he wondered at the identity of the riders who had named him. As far as he knew, no one outside of Caldaria knew him except for his mother.

Together he and Welsly walked out of the dorm and into the bustling streets. The bangs and pops of the fireworks and the host of entertainers couldn't shake the feeling of unease that reached into Luxon's chest.

CHAPTER 10.

Kaiden paced the opulent room, a frown adorning his features. His blue eyes were shut tightly in prayer as he walked, and the mutterings of his appeals to his god broke the silence.

Alira sat in one of the high-backed leather chairs, her feet resting on the edge of a large crystal desk that dominated the room. She struggled to keep her eyes open; all knowledge of time was lost to her as she battled against her weariness.

The two had travelled for three days up the Kings Highway, and the stress of the trip had finally caught up with her. The journey would normally have taken a day at most, but with marauding bandits and battered armies using the same road it had taken a lot longer.

At one point, they had been forced to abandon the road entirely as they encountered a battalion of the Baron of Balnor's men being butchered by a mob of bandits. She shuddered at the memory; there had been so much blood.

"You're going to wear the nice mage's carpet out if you don't stop your pacing, Kaiden," she sighed wearily.

The knight stopped dead. His formerly pristine mantle was covered with mud, as were his boots; and the rest of him looked no better. Alira, too, was covered in dirt and grime. Her travelling cloak was torn, and her trousers had tears in the knees. Their night hiding in the wild woods from a hunting band of sinister-looking shades had taken its toll. More than once, they had encountered things that should not have been there. The wails of banshees and other fell beasts had haunted the nights, highlighting just how low and dangerous the once peaceful kingdom had become.

"I'm sorry," Kaiden replied, tiredness evident in his voice. "I don't feel comfortable being in this city. It's the home of folk that my brother knights and I are often tasked with hunting down ... I don't trust them."

Alira stood and placed a hand gently on his arm.

"I understand,' she said kindly. "You feel what I felt like when I was at the priory," she said comfortingly.

If she was honest with herself, she would have admitted that even being in a city of her kind made her just as nervous as being with the knights. She had never met another mage before, let alone a grandmaster.

Kaiden sighed, turning to face his young charge. The days on the road had given him a new-found respect for the young woman before him. Gone was the scared, frightened girl he had met months previously in that cold damp dungeon in Retbit. The time they had spent together in the priory was some of the best times he could ever remember. She had practised with a sword every day until the knight masters had deemed her capable enough to risk the roads.

"I am sorry, Alira. I forget that this place is just as strange to you as it is to me. No doubt you will wish to learn all you can about your heritage." He placed his hand upon hers. Her skin was soft and warm.

They looked into each other's eyes, a silence passing between them.

A knock on the oak door broke the tension, causing them both to blush. Into the room stepped a tall man in the robes of a master mage. A pleasant smile was on his face as he offered his hand to Kaiden. The knight hesitated before he shook it.

"Greetings, I am Thanos, Grand Master of the Upper Ring and Magister of the Mage Realm of Caldaria. I welcome you, sir knight, and offer you and your companion shelter in these troubled times. What is ours is yours."

Alira almost gasped when the mage gripped her hand softly. She felt a jolt like that of being stung by a wasp shoot up her arm as his skin made contact with hers. For a brief moment, his piercing bright blue eyes widened in surprise. He composed himself quickly. Alira stood stunned, the tingling sensation spreading up her arm.

"Forgive me for the delay in my meeting with you. As you can hear, the celebrations are rather exuberant," Thanos explained with a smile. The distant sound of fireworks and drunken songs could be heard outside of the chamber's solitary window.

"You told my steward that you were here to look for someone called Luxon?" the grand master queried as he sat in the chair on the opposite side of the crystal desk. "I have taken the liberty to send someone to fetch the only person in the city going by that name." When seated, he poured himself a cup of wine from a clay jug. Alira blinked – she didn't recall seeing a jug on the desk's surface when they had arrived.

Kaiden sat in one of the chairs and accepted the cup offered to him.

"Yes," he said. "This may sound strange, but we were sent here by the order to try and find this Luxon person. We believe he can help us find someone." Kaiden shifted uncomfortably under the mage's gaze.

"And *how* did you learn about this person?" Thanos asked, his eyes flicking to Alira.

Kaiden stammered, unsure of what to say. Alira stepped forward.

"I heard the name in a vision," she said, her tone hinting at a challenge. She knew she wasn't crazy. She knew that the mysterious man before her would understand. Surely the grand master of the magic-wielders in Delfinnia had similar visions of his own.

Thanos sat back in his chair, his eyebrows arching in surprise before sitting forward and knotting his fingers together.

"A vision, you say?"

CHAPTER 10.

"Yes. A vision. One that has been haunting me more and more over recent days" Alira explained.

"Truth be told, they are the main reason we are here, to try and discover their meaning," Kaiden added.

Thanos looked at the girl with renewed interest. The spark he had felt when he had touched her hand, the strange way in which the magic appeared to be distorted around her aura, and now the revelation that she had visions. An amused smile briefly touched his lips as he wondered whether the noble knight knew what exactly it was he had been travelling with all this time.

The door to the chamber opened. Standing in the doorway was Luxon. At his back was the tall Nightblade, Welsly. The young lad looked sheepish and nervous; his bright eyes darted around the chamber until they focused on the knight and the strange girl.

Thanos leaned forward in his seat, slightly curious as to whether his young apprentice would notice something out of place. To his surprise, Luxon's eyes stayed fixed on the girl a tad too long. The boy blushed slightly. Thanos had to restrain a chuckle. He had noticed something alright – he had noticed her good looks. Boys will be boys.

"Ah, Welsly, Luxon, welcome. Come in and take a seat," Thanos greeted warmly.

"What's this about, Master?" Luxon asked, recognising the mantle worn by the knight. A knot of fear twisted in his gut. All of the apprentices and students knew the stories of the merciless knights who hunted down their kind.

Welsly remained standing. He too had noticed the knight. His hand drifted lazily to the hilt of his sword.

Feeling the tension rise in the room, Thanos stood and smacked a palm on the crystal table's surface.

"Listen here," he said. "These two are our guests. Sir Kaiden serves the Order of Niveren, but he is not here to harm anyone. His companion is Alira, a girl who has been having visions of late. Visions in which you have been mentioned, Luxon."

The boy took a step back in surprise.

After a few minutes of awkward introductions and explanations, Luxon found himself alone with Alira in the grand master's chambers. The two sat in silence, he twiddling his fingers, she checking her fingernails for dirt. As to where Thanos, the knight and the Nightblade had gone, he didn't know, but he got the sense that his master had intended for him to be alone with the girl.

She was pretty, he couldn't deny that, but she wasn't a patch on Hannah.

"You're younger than I thought," Alira said, causing him to jump in surprise. "I thought that you would be some mighty powerful mage, with white hair and a long beard—"

"—and the ability to shoot fireballs from my arse, no doubt," Luxon interjected.

Alira glared at him. Luxon sighed in annoyance.

"Listen," he said. "I don't know what you and sir what's-his-face want with me, but I reckon I'm not the guy you're looking for. I'm just a lowly apprentice mage who's never even travelled south of the Ridder River."

"I have dreams too. That's all your visions are," he explained, trying to sound authoritative. "Just dreams."

Alira stared daggers at the boy. "You just said you're nothing but a lowly apprentice ... so what do you know about things?" Her voice rose in pitch as frustration and fear edged into her words. "I haven't been able to sleep in months. I keep hearing names, seeing things I never want to see and, always I see the face with the black eyes."

Luxon stared at her in disbelief.

"You hear names?" he asked quietly.

Alira nodded. Her golden hair falling into her eyes in the process. She swept it back over her ear.

"Every night I am told two names." She stared at one of the tapestries on the walls of the room. A blue and golden pentacle was emblazoned on a blood red background. It was the sigil of the first ring of magic. "Names that I do not know. Alderlade is one and the other ..." She paused and stared at him, her eyes filled with something akin to yearning, a yearning for answers. "The other name is Luxon ... always Luxon."

Luxon looked away from her gaze. He didn't know what was happening. First, had come his own dreams. He had always dreamt, but now the dreams were growing more vivid, stranger and more terrifying. Then he had been told of his unique gift of being a thaumaturgist, a magic-wielder able to cast spells just through thought and feelings. And now he was being told that he was appearing in the dreams of this strange girl from half a world away.

The fireworks and the festivities were the perfect cover. Moving quickly through the unsuspecting crowds of drunken revellers, the group of men went unchallenged. Their crimson cloaks didn't stand out on this most festive of evenings. Getting over the city's crystal walls, however, had proven problematic, but to the Crimson Blades, nothing was impossible.

After walking through alleys and down backstreets, the assassins reached their destination. The Arch Tower stood strong and tall above the city like a giant. It was the tallest structure in Delfinnia now that the Sun Spire in Sunguard was now just a ruin – a once magnificent structure toppled during the Night of Tears, along with countless other irreplaceable buildings and monuments.

Inside the Arch Tower was the assassins' target.

CHAPTER II.

The sound of leather-soled boots stealthily creeping along the stone-flagged floor was almost indistinguishable over the background noise of the celebrations, which seemed like they would never end. Only a man who was trained to notice such detail would be able to pick it out and Kaiden was such a man.

He thought they would be safe in the city, but it seemed that danger had once again caught up with him.

He deftly slid from his bed onto the balls of his feet, moving as quickly and as silently as he could to the corner of the small room where he had billeted for the night. After their long journey, Kaiden had jumped at the arch mage's offer of a room and clean sheets for the night. He had talked at length with the man, but it felt as though their conversation was but a sideshow after he had left Alira with the boy, Luxon. They had spoken of events in the world, of the war and of dark murmurs emanating from the outer reaches of the realm.

The creeping noise was drawing closer to the room, he was certain.

He drew his long sword from its sheath, the familiar weight giving him some comfort as he prepared to defend himself. He'd kick himself if it proved to be nothing, but being in the city of the mages, he wasn't prepared to take any chances.

The room in which he found himself was comprised of a small chest, bed, a worn out leather-backed chair and a tiny window high on the wall. There was no visible way of escape, aside from the door to which the footsteps now approached. There was no access to the outside. Kaiden set his jaw; he would have to make a stand or at least hold them off until he could think of some way out of this.

He was one of the best swordsmen in the Order, but he had no idea if the people sneaking up to his door knew who and what he was. But he wasn't about to let them find out. His thoughts flashed to Alira, still in the arch mage's room with the boy. He almost swore to himself. Were the mages betraying him because he was a Knight of Niveren? It was certainly possible; after centuries of his order hunting rouge mages and magic wielders, why would they not want to seek vengeance? With no king and no king's law, there was nothing stopping them from murdering him. The land was in chaos, and the other knights would never learn of his fate.

As his mind ran wild the sound of the stealthy footsteps had now stopped directly outside of his door; he knew now for certain that his suspicions had been right, if they were mages he wouldn't make it easy for them. He positioned himself to one side of the doorframe and waited for his adversary.

The door handle turned slowly, and with a quiet click, the door silently began to open. Kaiden tensed, ready to make his move.

Two throwing knives flew through the open door, digging themselves deep into the bed right where his head would have been.

The assassin noticed that his quarry was not where he was supposed to be and moved into the room, a sharp and lethal curved blade in his hand.

Kaiden wasted no time and immediately hacked his sword in a downward stroke, slicing his attacker's arm clean off at the elbow.

The knight bellowed a challenge and struck again, this time burying his blade up to the hilt into the assassin's chest. The lifeless corpse slid off the blood-soaked blade and slumped to the floor.

Kaiden ducked just as another thrown knife struck in the wall where he had just been standing. He immediately threw himself to the floor and rolled to his feet as two more of the robed figures charged him with familiar curved daggers in their hands.

He was now in the main upstairs corridor of the tower's dorm area. It was narrow, with various doors leading to other guest rooms on either side. His attackers blocked the staircase that would lead him to the main hall and perhaps to safety. He could see only one other possible escape route: the large window at the far end of the passage.

He parried a quick strike from the lead attacker, bringing his elbow up and striking the assassin square in the throat. The robed figure immediately fell to the floor clutching his throat, gasping for air now that his windpipe had been crushed.

The second assassin was more patient, holding back and watching Kaiden for any sign of weakness. The knight didn't give him a chance and instead charged. As he made a lunge for the assassin's head, the robed figure moved with astounding speed, slashing him in the face. The pain was extraordinary, and a burning sensation began to emanate from the wound.

Kaiden had no time to think, as again the assassin was on him, curved dagger swinging and stabbing savagely. It took all of his concentration to parry the blows that were raining down on him. The pain in his face had begun to subside, but now numbness was spreading out from it – one side of his face had now lost most of its feeling.

It was a poisoned blade, he realised with horror. Just what poison it could be, he didn't know, but it would surely kill him if he couldn't escape and find a healer soon.

He now knew the assassins intent: they would keep him occupied long enough for the poison to take effect, and then they would watch him die a slow death, or perhaps capture him alive. The realisation struck him like a fist: the poison wasn't intended to kill him, but to paralyse him. He could feel the numbness spreading through his body now; he had to escape, and soon. Questions flashed through his mind – were they trying to capture him and Alira? Had they been followed on the king's road? Or were they here for some other nefarious purpose?

Kaiden feinted high with his sword and rotated his wrists so that now his blade was ready for an upward slash to the assassin's face. The assassin, however, moved to parry the cut, and as he did so, Kaiden twisted again, causing his sword to catch the assassin in the throat.

Scarlet blood hit the corridor wall as the sword sliced clean through the attacker's throat. The robed figure crumpling to the floor in a heap as blood continued to spurt from the wound.

Kaiden leaned against the passageway wall, his breath now wheezing out of him. His whole face felt numb, and the sensation was spreading through his arms. He made to head for the staircase, but the familiar figure of yet another assassin was cresting the top step. His dagger was drawn, looking for vengeance for his comrades' deaths.

Where was the tower's security? Where were the mages?

The large window was his only possible escape route; he was in no condition to take on another of these vicious killers. Steeling himself, he ran as fast as he could at the window.

With an ear-piercing smash, he went flying through the air, hoping that there would be something soft to cushion his fall.

The fall felt like forever, and with a bone-jarring thud, Kaiden hit the ground, fortunately landing on a hay basket that took most of the impact. His shoulder was dislocated, but apart from that, he was alright. Dragging himself to his feet, he staggered away from the tower. He made it only a few paces before falling into unconsciousness.

The last thing he heard was the city's alarm bells beginning to toll out in the night air. He had escaped.

CHAPTER 12.

The door to Thanos's study burst open with an ear-splitting cracking of wooden timbers. The alarm bells were tolling loudly outside the Arch Tower, and the sounds of frightened screams from the partygoers on the streets clawed at Luxon's nerves. Whatever was happening outside the tower sounded like the entire Void had been set free.

Luxon and Alira were hiding behind Thanos's desk. The sturdy crystalline surface was far stronger than it appeared, and its opaque service offered them some semblance of cover. The girl was breathing hard; if she was reacting like Luxon was then her heart was pounding a mile a minute.

Cautiously, Luxon poked his head above the lip of the desk. His eyes widened as he saw a robed figure standing in the doorway. The material of the robe was the colour of fresh blood. The hood hid the person's features, but it was clear as to their intentions. In their hand was a vicious dagger, and slung across their back was a lethal looking crossbow.

Luxon ducked back down holding a finger to his lips to tell Alira to keep quiet. He could have kicked himself. He hadn't been trained in combat magic; all he knew was basic tricks and ... the levitation spell! The mages of the lowest ring, like he was, were only taught the most basic of spells. Things like illumination and basic healing; he'd give anything to be a higher mage with knowledge of the elemental combat magic such as lightning or flame.

The robed figure stalked into the room; the creak of leather boots the only sound coming from the assassin. Alira's eyes widened in fear as she heard the killer creep closer to the desk. Luxon gestured for her to stay still.

He closed his eyes and focused. He could feel a tingling sensation spread up his arm as power flowed through his body. He had to refrain from laughing as he felt the magic build within; the tingling became more intense as he focused on the heavy desk. He raised a hand slowly. Alira stifled a gasp as the desk began to rock, the noise instantly drawing the attention of the assassin.

The footsteps grew closer. Luxon had his eyes shut tightly as he concentrated.

Alira screamed as the assassin leapt on top of the desk his dagger pointing menacingly at her. She scrambled back away from the killer.

"Luxon! Help me" she cried.

Luxon smiled.

"Of course."

He flung his arms upwards. Alira screamed again as the desk shot into the air, the surprised assassin on top. With a smash, the desk, complete with the stunned assassin, slammed into the crystalline ceiling, a sickening squelch the only clue as to the assassin's fate.

Luxon leapt backwards as the debris of the desk and the gory remains of the assassin crashed back to the ground. A red smear was clearly visible on the ceiling.

A wave of tiredness threatened to overwhelm him, but Alira caught him before he collapsed in exhaustion. He placed a hand on her shoulder to steady himself and shook his head to clear the dizziness that threatened to overtake him.

"Thanks, I forgot how tiring that spell was," he muttered.

A loud crash came from the hallway outside the chamber. The sound of alarm bells from the city had now been replaced by screams and the sounds of clashing steel. The city was under assault!

A ball of fire zipped passed the doorway, accompanied by an agonised scream. A crimson-robed assassin appeared in the doorframe, his robes aflame as he writhed on the stone floor. Alira recoiled at the sight and the smell of a man being burnt alive by magic fire.

The Nightblade Welsly stepped over the charred corpse, relief evident on his face as he saw Luxon and the girl.

"Praise be that you two are safe," he said.

"Welsly, what's happening?" Luxon asked. The sounds of battle were growing fiercer and louder.

"Caldaria is under attack. Assassins somehow managed to infiltrate the city and open the gates for an army that was hiding in the woods to the southeast," Welsly explained, fatigue evident in his voice. "What Nightblades there are in the city will be attempting to retake the gatehouse, but as for Master Thanos and the other mages, I have no clue."

Welsly's black leather armour had been ripped by a knife blade. "Are you hurt?" Alira asked as she noticed the damage. A rivulet of blood was oozing from the tear.

Welsly shook his head in the negative. "No, I'll be fine; the bastard only dinged me. He took me by surprise, is all." Tentatively, he touched the wound, only for his black gloves to come away sticky with blood.

Cautiously, he leaned out into the hallway before gesturing for Luxon and Alira to follow.

"Stick with me and stay close. These Crimson Blades may look like ordinary men, but they move like something unnatural. We need to reach the top of the Arch Tower. That's where Thanos and the other masters are likely to be."

They passed a number of chambers. In several, the unlucky occupants lay dead. In one, a mage had taken out several assassins, their charred remains releasing a foul smoke out into the hall. In another, a female mage was knelt over a wounded guardsman, the light emanating from her palms was her attempt at healing the knife wound in the man's chest.

The three continued slowly through the tower's lower floor. Despite the carnage all around them, they had not encountered any more assassins. Finally, they reached the great staircase which led to the levitation platforms that would take them to the tower's higher levels.

Welsly crept forward, taking cover behind one of the crystal pillars that dominated the base of the stairs. Each step was made of brightly coloured glass which gave the stairs their nickname, the *rainbow staircase*. Luxon and Alira both took cover behind another pillar.

Standing at the top of the stairs was a young man clad in steel plate armour, a red bird emblazoned on his mantle.

"Accadus …" Luxon whispered savagely as he recognised him. The youngest son of the Baron of Retbit was barking angry orders to a half dozen of his soldiers.

"Might explain how they knew how to get inside the walls," Welsly muttered.

The Nightblade drew the hilt of his tourmaline blade. These special swords were only used by Nightblades as they were the only ones skilled enough to wield them. Comprised of magical energy, the blade was pure magic, harnessed through the Nightblade's own reserves.

"He's just an arrogant, stupid boy," Welsly said angrily. "Who knows how much blood has been spilt on his account this night?"

Luxon knew what the Nightblade intended as he saw the man's shoulders tense. He desperately wanted to stop him, but Welsly shrugged off his hand as he tried to hold him back. Luxon grabbed Alira's hand and pulled her further behind the pillar they were hidden behind. The girl resisted at first but relented as she saw the look in his eyes.

"Accadus!" Welsly shouted as he stepped out into the open. He pointed his sword threateningly towards the boy.

"Well, well, well. If it isn't the high and mighty Welsly," Accadus sneered. The group of soldiers gathered behind their leader, swords and spears at the ready. Each wore a tunic with the red bird of Retbit upon the jupon and a suit of chainmail underneath.

"I can take your goons Accadus," Welsly said confidently as he stepped closer to the base of the stairs. "Why are you here? What do you want?"

Accadus laughed.

"I want payback for the shame bestowed upon me," he shouted, a tinge of madness evident in his rage ravaged voice. "I want Luxon and his fat friend hanging from hooks! And, oh yes, I want the power of the mages to give to my father so he can end the war and claim the Sundered Crown and become king!"

Accadus pointed at Welsly. "Kill him!" he screamed.

The Retbit soldiers charged down the staircase. It was six against one, but Welsly did not turn to flee. Instead, he readied his blade and waited. As the first soldier got within striking distance, the Nightblade raised his left hand and unleashed a bolt of lightning from his fingertips. The blast sputtered out of existence. Welsly's eyes went wide in surprise.

The soldier smiled wickedly.

"Okay, so no magic," the Nightblade muttered. With a flick of his wrist, his sword struck like a flash to strike the chuckling guard in the throat.

With a gurgled cry, the soldier collapsed to the ground, his hands feebly trying to close the wound which pumped crimson blood onto the shiny floor.

The other troops hesitated – a fatal mistake. Like a blur, Welsly fell upon them. His bright yellow tourmaline blade flicked and slashed in all directions as he carved his way through limbs and armour. He parried a spear thrust and lashed out with a blast of flame which blinded his attacker, allowing him to bury his sword deep into his chest.

Within moments, all six of the Retbit soldiers lay dead at the Nightblade's feet. Not a single sword or spear had even come close to wounding him.

"Well done," Accadus laughed sarcastically, his slow claps echoing up the staircase. "How about you take on someone a bit more akin to your own skills?"

Welsly raised his arms as if to challenge the arrogant boy.

"Comparing yourself to a Nightblade just shows how stupid you are little man. Come and pay for what you've done here," Welsly challenged.

Accadus simply smirked. He clicked his fingers.

Luxon held his breath in anticipation. The sight of the Nightblade in combat had been incredible; Welsly confirmed all of the tales about their legendary feats. He narrowed his eyes at Accadus. The boy had always been a bully, but never had he seen him so cocky, so sure of himself; not even the sight of his men being slain had fazed him. Something was terribly wrong, he could feel it. Just as he was about to shout a warning to Welsly, a crimson-robed assassin leapt from the shadows.

The Nightblade swung about to face his attacker but was too slow to counter the impossibly fast dagger thrust. The vicious blade sunk deeply into his abdomen, causing him to cry out in surprise and pain. The assassin pirouetted upon his left heel, delivering a vicious roundhouse kick and sending the Nightblade crashing into a heap at the base of the stairs.

Visibly stunned, Welsly staggered back onto his feet. But before he was able to raise his weapon or use magic the assassin was on him and raining savage blows. He was being beaten to death, and all the while Accadus cackled.

"I must be leaving now, Welsly. Send my regards to the other dead mages you'll soon meet in the afterlife."

Luxon darted out from his hiding place, Alira hot on his heels.

The assassin was focused on the Nightblade, who was desperately trying to defend himself. Blood poured from the knife wound, but still, he fought. Accadus meanwhile had stepped onto one of the levitation pads and was now flying upwards to the tower's upper floors.

Luxon watched helplessly as the assassin parried a sword thrust and grabbed Welsly's arms. The Nightblade tried to break free but to no avail. The assassin twisted. A sickening popping noise reverberated around the hall, quickly followed by the Nightblade's agonised screams. Welsly collapsed to the floor unconscious from the pain, his arms flopping uselessly to his sides.

CHAPTER 12.

Anger surged through Luxon. He raised his hands at the assassin who now spun to focus on the boy and the girl.

With a roar, Luxon unleashed his fury. Heat flowed through him until fire erupted from his palms, engulfing the assassin and setting fire to the tapestries hanging above the stairway. Within moments, the killer's robes were aflame, his skin blistering and vaporising, his blood boiling. It happened so fast that he didn't even have time to scream.

The stench of cooked meat almost made Alira vomit, but her attention turned to the unconscious Nightblade.

"Do what you can for him," Luxon panted, his breaths shuddering out of him. His hair and clothes were steaming; Alira winced as she remembered that time on the road when she had used such magic.

"There's a medica back down the hallway and through the library," Luxon told her. "Ask for Hannah – she will know what to do."

Before Alira could ask him what he was going to do, Luxon bolted up the stairs and towards the levitation platforms.

Accadus would pay for this.

Luxon stepped onto the levitation pad and braced himself. Within seconds, a white light emanated from the floor and propelled him skyward. The feeling of weightlessness was disorienting, but he shrugged it off. Instead, he focused on what he might find at the top of the tower. Accadus was too cocky; Luxon didn't understand how his old foe from Redbit had managed to infiltrate the city of the mages – it should have been impossible.

He glanced upwards. A sense of panic coursed through him as the ceiling rapidly approached. He always hated the levitation pads. At the back of his mind was always the possibility that they could malfunction and leave him as just a red stain on the crystal ceiling's surface.

To his relief, his ascent slowed until he stopped completely and was left floating in mid-air. He stepped forward onto a solid platform which led into the Arch Chamber, the council room of the mages of Delfinnia.

Being just a lowly apprentice, he had never been allowed this high in the tower. Ahead of him was an imposing bluish crystalline door. Angry voices were coming from the other side.

Luxon dashed towards it, slowing as he got within earshot of those in the chamber.

"The other claimants will not stand for this, you do realise. Assaulting the mages cannot be ignored; they will not accept you coercing us into using our power for your gain." The calm tones of Thanos drifted through the crack in the doorway. Luxon edged closer until he could peek inside the chamber.

Standing in a semi-circle were Accadus, a number of Retbit knights and a short, dumpy man with an angry face. The short man wore ornately decorated armour painted with the red birds of Retbit. In his right hand was a long sword which he pointed menacingly at the other occupants of the room.

Opposing them stood the masters of Caldaria: Thanos, tall and statesmanlike stood in the middle. At his right-hand side was Master Ri'ges, and on the other, Master Dufran. The other masters stood behind those three, their expressions a mixture of anger and confusion.

Why don't they just strike Accadus and his men down? Luxon thought. By all rights, the mages should have had no trouble driving off the attackers who had no magic of their own to speak of. Aside from Accadus and the supernatural assassins, the soldiers seemed to possess no arcane ability.

"Your powers aren't that impressive," the small man tittered. "I have rendered you powerless just by using these."

Luxon squinted to see what the man held. In a gauntleted fist dangled what looked like a necklace.

Upon seeing it, Thanos took an involuntary step backwards. Shock was evident in the other master's faces as well.

"A talisman of N'gist," the grand master whispered in surprise. "Baron, where did you obtain these?"

The Baron of Retbit laughed, and his goons followed suit. Accadus simply smirked.

"A witch told me the secret. I believe they make your spells ineffective ... or was it that they drain your kind's powers? I forget the details," the baron mocked. "Anyway," he continued, "I am here to exact vengeance for you dishonouring my son's good name, and of course to enlist your aid in the war. With you mages as my servants, I will be able to destroy my enemies and finally take the crown that is rightfully mine."

"You're mad," Thanos replied defiantly. "We will never serve you, nor will we serve any other claimant. We are neutral in this war; the struggle for power is not our concern. The days when mages intervened in the wars of men ended centuries ago. King or no king, we will not break our oaths."

The baron clucked his tongue against his teeth for a few moments. An awkward silence descending upon the room.

"I have three thousand men inside this city all wearing these amulets and another six thousand that are not. If I give the order, then every mage and civilian in this city will be slain, and you will be powerless to stop it- unless of course, you join me."

Luxon frowned. The man was lying – he had seen a number of his men being bested by magic; Welsly had slain several with it himself. Unless of course, his being close to those soldiers and their amulets was what had weakened him enough to allow the assassin to strike.

A knot of fear wormed into Luxon's gut. The baron had them right where he wanted them. Caldaria would fall, and there was nothing the mages could do to stop it.

A memory popped into his head – something that Grand Master Thanos had said: "To me, and everyone else, magic is something that we must spend decades in near constant practice to bring out such power in us. The magic within you is like a second skin, Luxon. It is a reflex to you, just like when you blink."

CHAPTER 12.

The amulets didn't work on him! That was why he was able to cast fire on the assassin that had wounded Welsly. His magic was unaffected.

Taking a deep breath, he pushed open the doors to the chamber. The crystal door swung slowly, its heavyweight causing its hinges to creak, alerting the baron's men inside. Luxon strode into the chamber with as much confidence as he could muster. He was nervous; if he was wrong, then he had doomed himself.

The baron turned to face the young man who brazenly walked into the chamber.

"Who in blazes is this?" he demanded.

Luxon's stomach fluttered with nerves. The masters were all watching him in disbelief, but Thanos stood still, a faint smile on his lips. Taking a deep breath, Luxon pushed his shoulders back and held his head high in an attempt to look as tall and as menacing as possible.

"I am Luxon Edioz, master of the arcane, weaver of spells, destroyer of worlds!" he boomed in what he hoped was a terrifying voice. He felt his heart sink as the baron, and his cronies simply broke down in laughter. Thanos, though, was still smiling and nodded his head in encouragement.

Accadus stepped forward. No amused smirk was on his face. Instead, his green eyes were narrowed in hatred. In his armour, the bully looked even taller and more imposing than when they had last met.

"Luxon the coward, more like," Accadus spat angrily. "Luxon the liar, Luxon the little shit ..." The shame of being banished from Caldaria had been almost too much to bear; the insult to his family name deserved retribution.

The baron placed a hand on his son's chest, halting his tirade of insults. His pig-like features gazed at Luxon in amusement.

"So, this is the boy who bested you in a fight and got you exiled from your studies. The son of Garrick, the liar, seems to have more balls than his father at least," the baron tittered humourlessly. "It was your father that started this war, you know, boy. If he had just kept his mouth shut, then I would now be king unchallenged. His foolish talk of a surviving heir has caused more bloodshed these past three years than even the Yundol invasions did!"

Luxon stepped back. Anger swelled within him as the fat baron insulted his father's memory. His right hand clenched into a fist, and once more he felt the magic fill him. The sense of power was addictive. Heat flooded up his arm.

"Take care of this little fool. Whatever power he thinks he has, the amulets will dispel," the baron said dismissively, turning his back to face the masters. "Now, where were we?"

Accadus and the baron's men advanced upon Luxon. Seeing the boy was unarmed, they kept their swords sheathed.

"You deserve nothing less than to be beaten to death," Accadus chuckled evilly. "I'm going to finish what I started in that street, and I'm going to enjoy it."

With a roar, he charged at Luxon.

Magic like he had never felt before surged through Luxon's body, power like nothing he'd even read about coursed through his veins. He felt stronger, faster, and to his amazement, his attackers appeared to move as slow as a drunken slug. The world around him faded from his consciousness; only the charging Retbit soldiers remained in his vision. All sound was muted.

He easily sidestepped the first punch swung by Accadus and ducked the next. To him, they were in slow motion, but to anyone watching the vicious punches were coming in fast and strong. The other soldiers joined the attack, but Luxon dodged and weaved through the men's flailing limbs. Not one hand even got close to him.

"What the–" the Baron shouted as he watched. The boy was literally dancing through the hail of blows. He should have been a bloody heap on the floor; instead, the baron's men were growing tired, and more than a little afraid.

The soldiers stepped back from the boy, their breaths coming in ragged gasps. Their heavy armour had weighed upon them, draining their strength. Only Accadus remained, his fury quickly being replaced with desperation. Again, and again, he tried to hit Luxon, but couldn't.

The baron spun to face Thanos, pointing at his son's failing attempts to strike the young mage.

"What devilry is this? How can this be?" he shouted, his voice rising in pitch to make him sound like a petulant child. Thanos simply shrugged his shoulders, not saying a word.

Finally, Accadus slumped to his knees in exhaustion.

"What are you?" he gasped at Luxon.

"Someone you do not want to trifle with again," Luxon replied coldly.

It would have been so easy to strike down his foe, but something stayed his hand. A whisper at the back of his mind gave a warning against such action. The dream of the gnarled tree flashed into his mind. The mysterious spectre was there.

He has a part yet to play, it whispered.

"Kill the little wretch! Kill him!" screamed the baron. His face was red, flushed in anger. He would not allow a boy to unravel his plans.

The tired soldiers wearily drew their swords, once more advancing on the strange boy.

Luxon faced them. The power was still surging through him. He knew that at this moment, anything was possible. He had fully channelled the magic of the upper ring, something that even the most powerful of masters had difficulty doing. *What am I?*

He raised his hand. With a flick of his wrist, he unleashed a telekinetic blast that flung the soldiers back into a startled pile; their swords flew from their hands to hover around Luxon. Each of the blades then turned their aim at the panicked baron.

The soldiers staggered to their feet, looked at their lord and then at the boy, whose sandy hair was standing up and whose eyes had turned an unearthly bright blue. With shouts of terror, they fled the chamber. Luxon let them. Accadus stared at his foe, both terror and awe etched on his expression.

"Leave!" Luxon boomed at Accadus. His voice, too, resonated with power. Its volume shook the chamber causing dust to fall from the high ceiling.

He didn't have to ask twice. Accadus scrambled to his feet, and he fled, leaving the baron alone with the masters and the boy with the powers that rivalled the tales of Zahnia. The baron was quaking visibly, his lip trembling as though he were about to cry.

Luxon glared at the baron, his magic-infused eyes boring into him.

"You will leave this city never to return," Luxon demanded. "You will flee back to your castle and never threaten the mages ever again."

Feebly, the Baron took the amulet from his neck and thrust it at Luxon.

"Your magic will not work on me! I have this," he said, trying to sound defiant.

Luxon glared at the talisman of N'gist. He could sense the dark magic flowing from it. Angrily, he batted it out of the baron's hand, sending it skidding across the crystal floor. Master Ri'ges quickly gathered it up into his robes. The baron shrank under Luxon's gaze. Thanos and the others crowded around him.

"Heed the words of Luxon, baron, or be destroyed," Thanos whispered threateningly into the man's ear. "Magic is not to be used by the likes of you for selfish gain. Order your troops to leave this city, and we will spare your foul life."

The baron nodded.

"We will leave ... forgive me; please don't kill me," the mighty and powerful baron of Retbit cried pitifully. The smell of urine wafted as the warlord wet himself.

"Be gone and never return," Thanos shouted. The baron fled from the chamber.

The grandmaster turned to Luxon. The unnatural blue from the boy's eyes had faded, and his skin had turned pale. Thanos smiled, catching the boy as he collapsed from exhaustion.

"Thank you," he whispered

CHAPTER 13.

The sound of knocking drifted into Luxon's consciousness. The big bed was just as comfortable as before, albeit there were more blankets covering him than last time. Slowly, he opened his eyes. Once again, the portrait of Zahnia greeted him as he awoke.

"Really need to stop meeting like this," he muttered to the picture. His limbs felt heavy, and he felt drained. The room hadn't changed aside from there now being a huge basket of fruit laid on the bedside table, and several dozen bunches of flowers laid haphazardly on the floor. A few were in vases.

"Really must find more vases for all of these flowers; it's sad to see them all die," Hannah grumbled as she strode into the room, another bunch in her arms. She stopped as she noticed that Luxon was awake. Her large blue eyes widened, and she gave a joyous smile.

"Finally, you're awake," she said sitting on the bed and taking his hand in hers. She frowned slightly at his touch.

"You're still so very cold ..." she muttered.

Luxon arched an eyebrow.

"How long was I out this time?" he asked. His stomach rumbled. He was famished. "And can I have something to eat; I feel like I could eat a whole herd of cattle!"

Hannah smiled again. She placed the back of her palm to his forehead.

"Yes, you can eat. I'll send your friend to go and get you something. As for how long you were unconscious ... well, let's just say it was a few days." She smiled sweetly. Her eyes, however, looked away. She wasn't telling him something.

"How long was I out?" he asked again, a hint of worry in his voice.

Hannah sighed and stood.

"You we're out cold for three weeks, Luxon," she explained, concern evident in her tone. "We were ... *I was* terrified that you'd never wake up."

Luxon slumped back into the thick pillows.

"Three weeks!" he whispered in disbelief. His mind whirled at the revelation. What had happened to him? He remembered feeling powerful, *god-like powerful*, standing up to Accadus and the baron, and then ... nothing.

"Don't worry," Hannah said. "The city is safe. The Nightblades and the masters chased off the baron's men. As for the assassins, they simply disappeared once the baron retreated. We lost good people, but most are safe and well."

"What about Welsly? Alira? Yepert? What happened to them?"

"Welsly is fine. In fact, he's in a room just down the corridor from here. Your friend Yepert has been at your bedside every day and has been tending to your needs." She paused, a scowl denting her beautiful features. "As for Alira, she's still hanging about ..."

Luxon smiled at her tone.

"Jealous, are we?"

Hannah glared at him.

"No. Just because she is pretty, does not mean I am jealous. There's just something about her I don't like. I mean, she's been a real help dealing with the injured and getting supplies from the markets but ..." She paused and laughed. "I do sound jealous, don't I?"

Luxon chuckled. "Yep, you sure do."

A gentle knocking on the door interrupted their conversation.

"Grand Master," Hannah said, bowing to Thanos.

The tall man wore a simple tunic of blue and a pair of dirty black trousers. His boots, too, were covered in dust. His face was smeared with black soot, and tired rings were under his blue eyes. He returned Hannah's bow and smiled pleasantly as she scurried out of the room. Luxon was sad to see her go; it was the first time he'd been able to be alone with her in weeks.

"I see you're finally awake, oh saviour of Caldaria," Thanos said chuckling as he gave an exaggerated bow.

"The what?"

"That is what everyone is hailing you as, my boy. The people of this city know that it was you who saved them from the baron. Just look at all the gifts you've received ..." Thanos looked around at the flowers and other gifts that were scattered about the room.

"Master ... why are you covered in dirt?" Luxon asked. Normally the grand master wore his robes of office or the garb one would expect of the Arch-Mage. The tall man waved a hand dismissively.

"I've been helping with the clean-up. The baron's men left us quite a mess in the alchemist district," Thanos explained as he read a card from one of Luxon's many well-wishers. "I swear the fumes released by some of the alchemists' potions contained contraband goods. The fires set by the soldiers sent a great big plume of smoke over the city, and now half the populace are high as kites."

Luxon couldn't help but smile. From his glassy gaze, the grand master, too, must have inhaled his fair share of fumes.

"Now," Thanos said turning to face his apprentice. "I wish to discuss your health, my lad. How do you feel?"

"I feel exhausted, truth be told, and cold," Luxon replied, shivering.

The grand master stood over the bed and pressed a hand onto the boy's head. He muttered something under his breath, and as he did so, Luxon felt a surge of warmth pour into his body.

"Ah that's better; let's get some colour back into those cheeks, eh?" Thanos smiled kindly. "The reason you blacked out is that you tapped into the highest ring of magic. I didn't realise that your special talent would allow you to do so, especially since you have had very little training."

He paused tapping his chin with his fingers.

"Some might say you could be a wiz— ... no, no, that's silly. There hasn't been one in Delfinnia for a good two hundred years ..."

Luxon shifted in his bed uncomfortably. Whatever Thanos had done had made him too hot.

"What hasn't been around for two hundred years?" he asked, throwing back the heavy blankets to allow some air to reach his body. He was wearing his nightshirt which he assumed Yepert had brought to him from their dorm room. Sweat was starting to pour from his forehead.

"A wizard of course. The most powerful of magic-wielders. I am strong in the ways of magic, but even a wizard would best me." Thanos stared at his young apprentice, his eyes boring into him. Luxon shifted again; something was definitely not right.

"M-master, I'm boiling up," Luxon said, a hint of panic in his voice.

Hannah re-entered the room; concern etched on her face. Her eyes went wide as she saw her patient's condition. Sweat was literally running off the boy.

"Oh my, what's happened here?" she said as she rushed over to him. She glanced at Thanos and scowled.

"Did you do something, Master Thanos? You shouldn't be doing any magic in your state," she scolded. "You breathed in far too much of those fumes from the alchemist's district."

Thanos simply shrugged his shoulders, his eyes glazed. He was high.

"He said he was cold," Thanos slurred. The grand master staggered slightly as Hannah gently pushed him out of the way. She leant over Luxon and pulled a bottle of brown liquid from the pouch tied to her belt.

"Here drink this. Nurse!" she called out into the hall. A squat woman with greying hair hurried into the room.

"Take the grand master back to his bed and make sure he doesn't leave. I swear intoxicated mages are the worst."

The nurse took hold of Thanos's hand and guided him out of the room like a drunkard. He staggered more than once. Luxon would have laughed at the sight, but the heat was becoming unbearable.

Hannah opened the bottle, tilted his head back and poured the sticky fluid down his throat. It tasted foul, but almost immediately the heat began to fade.

"Gah, what was that?" Luxon sputtered.

"A dispelling potion. The grandmaster must have cast a spell – one that he couldn't control in his; condition."

Luxon sighed in relief as the heat dissipated.

"How long will I have to stay in bed?" he asked, sitting up and stretching his tired limbs. The tiredness was weighing him down like an anchor, but he had to get out into the world. He'd seen enough of the medica to last a lifetime, and he was starving.

"I'll probably let you leave this afternoon if you feel well enough. I'll get Yepert to get you some food and take you back to the dorms. I have a feeling that once the master recovers from his condition, you'll be a busy man."

Luxon's cheeks flushed red; she had called him a man! Without realising it, he puffed his chest out.

CHAPTER 14.

Luxon was happy. He'd eaten his weight in food, slept for an entire day and was now sitting out in the sunshine. He'd also been able to spend some quality time with Hannah. Their walks through the woods and city had only made him fonder of her. The small balcony looked out over the main thoroughfare of the quartz district and was an excellent sun trap. The warmth was relaxing and allowed his mind to drift.

Yepert sat in a chair next to him, his feet resting on the balcony's stone rail and his eyes covered by the book he was reading. Life was pretty good.

The bustle on the streets far below continued as usual as traders and craftsmen rushed to and fro. Parts of the city had been damaged by the baron's raid, the rainbow quarter receiving most of the damage. The fire had ravaged a large portion of the alchemist's district, and the smoke was still seen drifting lazily in the midsummer sunshine.

"This is the life," Yepert exclaimed happily. Gravy from their earlier meal of mutton and potatoes was covering his face. "You know what, Lux, I reckon things are going to be fine. That knight I found in the alley outside the Arch Tower is doing well, I hear. That makes me happy."

Luxon smiled at his friend's optimism. The wider world was in chaos, but on the balcony, peace reigned supreme.

"I hope you're right, but from what I overheard in the dining hall the war is escalating in the south," Luxon replied after taking a sip from his cup of tea. "One of those refugees from Kingsford said that the Baron of Balnor had regrouped and was launching an offensive against the Baron of Champia, who in turn is fighting the Baron of Blackmoor. It's a right mess, and the news from the mountains of Eclin is just; well, weird."

Yepert waved a hand dismissively. "These things always used to happen in the olden days. They always get fixed in the end. I am quite happy to stay here, learn my lessons and eat like a king."

Luxon chuckled.

"What did you mean the news from Eclin is weird?" Yepert asked, a hint of uncertainty in his voice. "Plock isn't far south of its borders."

"I overheard a trader who had come from that region that a great battle had taken place in the mountains at Fuio Pass and that the Baron of Eclin was in retreat. He wasn't sure whether the battle had been against some of the mountain folk or something worse ..." As Luxon spoke, the sense of unease returned, and again he felt the cold breeze coming from the north.

"I don't like the sound of that ..." Yepert fretted. "Surely my ma and pa would have sent word if they were in danger."

Luxon shuddered slightly. The voice of the spectre drifted into his consciousness: *More in Eclin than you know.*

"What time is it?" Yepert asked, suddenly sitting up with a wide yawn and snapping Luxon's attention back to reality.

He shook his head as the spectre's rasping tones faded.

"Er ... I think it's close to three. Why?"

Yepert leapt to his feet, panic on his chubby face. "Oh heck. I was supposed to take you to the council chambers then. Master Thanos has called for a moot of all the mages in the city." He ran inside to gather their mage's robes and shoes.

"C'mon, no lying about. I promised I'd get you there on time. I reckon you're going to get a big reward for what you did!" he added excitedly.

The chamber was enormous. Its ceiling arched impossibly high until Luxon could no longer see the ceiling. Huge, stained glass windows were hollowed into the blue crystal that made up the biggest structure in Caldaria, the Palace of Zahnia. The structure was only used for formal ceremonies and mass gatherings of the mages. The rest of the time, it was used by the city's crafters as a trading centre.

There were no stalls or merchants in there when Luxon and Yepert filed through the big stone doors; instead, the chamber was full of robed mages. Every magic user in the city was there, from lowly students to the grand master who stood on the dais at the heart of the room.

The two boys pushed their way to the front. Upon recognising him, the crowd parted and began to clap. Luxon flushed red in embarrassment; Yepert clapped him on the back and smiled proudly. Calls of "Well done," and "Thanks," came from the mages. Both young and old smiled and applauded.

Upon seeing Luxon in the crowd, Thanos held up his arms for quiet.

"My fellow mages, your applause for Luxon Edioz is indeed warranted ..." his voice echoed throughout the chamber, "but I must insist that we save our celebrations for another time."

Yepert's smile dropped. Luxon stopped. Something in the grand master's voice halted the claps; the mages sensed that something was wrong. The crowd turned their attention to Thanos, the boy forgotten. Murmurs and rumour spread through the crowd.

Thanos held his right hand in the air. Dangling from it was the N'gist amulet the baron had worn "I have here in my hand ... a relic from the age of darkness."

Agitated murmurs spread through the crowd.

"It is now clear that the events that have ravaged Delfinnia have been orchestrated by an enemy we had long thought defeated – an enemy whose sole purpose is to restore darkness to the world. This is an amulet of the cult of the N'gist, necromancers and the disciples of the dread lord Danon."

Shouts of protest came from the crowd.

"Impossible," yelled an elderly mage whose green robes were frayed from decades of use, and whose grey hair was long and wild. "They were all destroyed in the Magic Wars. None survive!"

Other mages took up the old man's call. Thanos held a hand up to quell the crowd. The feelings of anger and fear were palpable.

"It was with these that the Baron of Retbit and his forces infiltrated our city and bested our Nightblades. They were immune to our powers. Tell me, Yinger," the grandmaster said glaring at the old mage, "how else do you account for what happened? The question now is, what are we going to do about it?"

Silence once more settled over the crowd. Yinger, the old mage, looked at his feet uncomfortably as the truth sunk in.

"What can we do?" Master Duvak called from the front rank of the crowd. "By the laws of the realm, we mages are confined to using our power only in Caldaria. Even as the war rages, we are bound by the law not to interfere. Only a king could give us the authority needed to do so and with no king, our hands are tied. If we do intervene without a mandate, then the realm will unite against us and destroy us. They do not trust us! Whilst the barons slaughter each other for power, and we are bound here by law, then the true enemy is on the march. Delfinnia is a land divided; it is the perfect time for them to strike!"

"Damn the law!" came a deep voice.

The crowd fell silent. Thanos's eyes widened as he recognised who had spoken. The crowd parted as a tall man with shoulder-length black hair strode toward the dais. He wore the black garb of a Nightblade. A silver chain hung from his neck, and a bow and quiver hung across his back. His face was fierce; there was a scar on his cheek as though a claw from some beast had raked it.

The man leapt up onto the dais to stand next to Thanos.

"You know me. I am Ferran of the Blackmoor," the Nightblade said. Another bout of whispering and murmurs spread through the crowd.

Luxon wracked his brain. He had no idea who the man was. Yepert leaned closer, sensing his friend's confusion.

"That's the Rouge Blade, the Nightblade that refused to return to Caldaria when the war started," Yepert whispered conspiratorially. "He refused the summons and continued his work hunting the beasts of the Void. Some say he's a hero, others that he's a traitor."

"I have continued my mission to defend the realm from the fell beasts of the Void whilst my brother Nightblades scurried back here to hide," Ferran said. A roar of protest came from the crowd. Luxon noticed that the Nightblades amongst them lowered their heads as though they were ashamed.

"I have seen the true face of the war that you choose to hide from. Innocents perish at the hands of monsters and men, whilst you who have the power to defend them hide away because of your fear of some law made centuries ago. The king is dead, and not one of those Barons deserves to replace him," Ferran enthused, drowning out the calls of protest.

The Nightblade paced the dais, his anger visible in his energetic strides.

"We could appeal to the Diasect for a repeal of the law," a voice in the crowd said. Some of the mages nodded in agreement; most tried to shout down the suggestion.

Ferran scoffed. "The Diasect! Where have they been these past few years? No one has heard from them in a decade, the self-proclaimed guardians of the realm have been silent. No help will come from them."

Thanos placed a hand on the Nightblade's shoulder.

"I understand your frustration, Ferran. Come let us discuss this matter privately," the archmage said, softly but sternly. He faced the crowd. "This meeting is dismissed. A decision will be decided upon. Just know that you must be ever vigilant. If the N'gist cult has survived, then we must all be on our guard."

The crowd began to disperse, and the noise rose as the mages chatted amongst themselves. Arguments broke out over who was right. Should the mages break the old laws and intervene in the war? Most were opposed. The last time mages had interfered in political affairs or matters of war they had abused their power to take control and had caused the worst conflict in the land's history.

Luxon and Yepert were just about to leave when Thanos called out: "Luxon! Come with me."

Yepert raised his eyebrows in surprise. Luxon's stomach fluttered with nerves.

"Now what?" he grumbled. Yepert simply shrugged his shoulders and clapped him on the back before joining the other mages filtering out of the great chamber. Luxon took a deep breath and walked towards the dais. As he approached, he noticed that a few other people had remained behind.

The girl Alira stood nervously next to the Knight of Niveren. Kaiden wore the mantle of his order, his hair and beard impeccably trimmed. Only the cane he was holding gave any clue to the injuries he had suffered on the night of the baron's attack. Next to them was Ferran who was having an animated discussion with Welsly. The Nightblade was bent over slightly due to the bandages wrapped around his knife wound.

As Luxon drew near, the others stopped their conversations.

"Really, Thanos, you honestly think the boy is ready?" Ferran said, doubt and scorn evident in his tone as he appraised the boy.

Thanos smiled kindly, offering a hand to his apprentice and pulled him up onto the raised dais. "I do. He has proven himself capable, and I know that he has a part to play in coming events."

Luxon hesitated.

"Ready for what, master?" he asked nervously.

The Nightblade Ferran strode over to the boy grabbing him by the scruff of the neck. He pulled him closer so that they were eye to eye. Luxon cried out in protest. Kaiden reached for his sword but stopped as Thanos waved a hand in warning.

"To go out into the big wide world," the Grandmaster said. "To go to see the Diasect first hand, and to face danger from both mortal and undead foes alike."

Luxon stared into Ferran's brown eyes. The man had seen so much; it was evident in the dark rings and the haunted look. Here was a man who had seen death, someone who knew loss and definitely a man who knew hate. Luxon wanted to look away but didn't; instead, he held the Nightblade's gaze. Ferran smiled wickedly and released his grip.

"You have guts, kid. Perhaps you *are* ready; not many men can hold my gaze for long, let alone a boy." Ferran chuckled, offering his hand to the boy. Luxon sighed in relief before shaking it. The Nightblade had a powerful grip; respect had replaced the mocking look in his eyes.

Thanos coughed impatiently. The group gathered about him.

"I have a plan," he said conspiratorially. "As you all saw, the mages are against breaking the old law. They fear that the temptation to use their power for personal gain will be too strong, that once more our kind will bring the world to ruin. I understand that fear. What I cannot do, however, is stand idly by as our enemies gather strength.

"You five will leave this city and seek out the Diasect. From what Sir Kaiden tells me, his order has a similar goal in mind, albeit for a different purpose than what we seek."

The knight stepped forward placing a cloth map onto the dais floor. The realm of Delfinnia was laid out before them.

"The Order dispatched Alira and me here to find out about Luxon," he explained. "The rest of the Order, meanwhile, mobilised: a squadron of knights was dispatched to the Diasect's stronghold at Tentiv." He traced a route from the Niveren priory east to Tentiv. The stronghold was located deep in the heart of a forest known as the Fallen Wood.

"The masters of my order – like you, Master Thanos – want to know why there has been no word from them. As guardians of the kingdom, they should have intervened a long time ago. Instead, only silence has emerged from Tentiv."

Luxon thought for a moment. He had read about the Diasect in a number of history books from the library. It was a council charged with overseeing the affairs of the realm. Several times in the past, they had resolved disputes and offered guidance to the kings. Mystery revolved around them though, and the common folk had little trust for them.

Some books said that the Diasect was made up of the souls of dead kings, others that they were a council of solitude-loving wizards or even creatures of the Void. So rarely were they seen that many believed them just to be a myth.

"I thought that it was forbidden for anyone to seek them out, that Tentiv is forbidden for all but those chosen by the Diasect to be their servants ..." Alira said softly.

Luxon frowned at the girl. Her face wore an expression of worry, but there was something else there behind the nervous exterior.

"It is forbidden, my lady, but we must find out why they have not intervened, and we must also find out more about your visions," Thanos said kindly.

Ferran clapped his hands together loudly.

"Right then, I want us to be on the road by the end of the week. The healers say that your leg should be better by then, knight. As for you, Welsly, are you even able to come? We can't have someone with us who can't even move."

Welsly tried to stand straighter but winced as his wound pinched.

"I am afraid Ferran is right, grand master," Welsly said miserably. "I am in no position to travel, let alone fight if needs be."

"Very well," the grandmaster said distantly, his eyes unfocused as though he saw some far off place. "Yepert, Luxon's friend, will accompany you," Thanos said, raising a hand to cut off Ferran's protests. A twinkle was in the grand master's eyes. Luxon scowled slightly. What was Thanos up to? Both he and Yepert had no training in the martial arts, and neither of them could cast the magic needed to fight, at least not consciously.

Ferran fumed but kept his mouth shut. Too many times in the past he'd gone against the desires of mages, and every time he had paid the price.

"Fine. The boy can come, but I cannot promise his safety. If we are to reach Tentiv alive, then we are going to need more than just two men able to fight and three children with no training." He held up a hand to quell Alira and Luxon's protests. "There is another in this city that I want with us ... I just hope she'll forgive me enough to listen to what I have to say."

CHAPTER 15.

It had been a good six years since Ferran had willingly chosen to walk the streets of the stone quarter. This part of the city was renowned for being the home of Caldaria's less than respectable citizens. It was a well-known fact that the guild of thieves known as the Fleetfoots had a presence in the warren of ramshackle stone houses.

The sound of a barroom brawl came from an alleyway to his left. He pulled his black hood tighter around his face and took a deep breath. He hated this part of the city. It was here that he had spent much of his misspent youth. He smiled at the memories of being a snot-nosed cocky kid who wasn't afraid of anything or anyone. The smile abruptly faded as other, darker memories resurfaced.

He picked up the pace and made his way across the rickety wooden bridge that led across the pungent stream running through the quarter. Being just down from the alchemist's district meant that the fast-flowing water was often contaminated with all sorts of dangerous poisons and had strange magical properties. Many were the number of children that had played in the fetid waters only to fall ill, or worse, die. The mages from the medica did their best to help, but resentment towards the spell-casters who lived in their crystal towers was high.

It was ironic that even in the one city where the mages were allowed to practise their spells and magic, they were disliked. Ferran shrugged his shoulders; Master Durak had been right – if the mages defied the old law then most of the common folk would turn on them out of fear and old resentments.

Even he, a Nightblade, had to be careful outside Caldaria's walls. In the small villages and towns in the countryside, he was often met with distrust. Even when saving them from the beasts of the Void, they would be reluctant to offer him any thanks.

He knew the stone quarter like the back of his hand. It only took him a few minutes to find his destination. Nestled into a stone wall was a worn wooden door. Above it hung a wreath adorned with mystical objects and runes. Etched into the stone on the right-hand side was a sigil warding against evil.

He took a deep breath, his stomach fluttering with nerves. Would she forgive him? Would she even hear what he had to say? Cautiously, he approached the door and knocked on the wooden surface.

The door creaked open a notch to reveal a small lad. The boy was no older than eight, and his dirty face and long shaggy black hair gave him away to be one of the street urchins that lived in the quarter. The Fleetfoot thieves often used the many orphans and homeless children as lookouts, or in some cases as distractions.

"Is she in?" Ferran asked.

The boy's green eyes went wide.

"I don't know who you're talking 'bout, mister," the lad answered nervously. The boy was to about to slam the door shut when Ferran jammed it open with his foot and forced it open. The boy fell onto his backside and scrambled to his feet. Ferran moved quickly and grabbed the urchin by the arm. He spun the boy around and glared hard into his face.

"Is she in?" Ferran asked again. This time the boy nodded in the affirmative. Ferran released the lad and with his boot kicked him out into the street before shutting the door. He found himself inside a place that brought with it bad memories. A small candle was the only source of illumination in the living area, a broken chair stuffed with straw sat in one corner, and a simple bookshelf lined the wall. To the side was a tiny kitchen area complete with several baskets of dried fruit and bread. Directly in front of him was a narrow stone staircase which led up to the tiny home's bedrooms.

Absent-mindedly, he ran a gloved finger over the back of the chair.

It was here that I did it, he thought as memories came flooding back. He was jolted back to reality by the feel of a sharp blade pressed into the back of his neck.

"You have a lot of nerve coming here," snarled a familiar female voice. Ferran raised his hands to show he was unarmed.

"I had hoped you would have forgiven me by now, Sophia. I did what was necessary," Ferran said sadly. Slowly, he turned to see the woman who wielded the knife. She was standing on the stairs with a dagger aimed at his head.

He almost caught his breath. She looked the same as she had the last time he had seen her all those years ago. They had been lovers once, but any look of kindness for him was absent from her eyes. Instead, all he saw was hate. Her long black hair was tied into a top knot, and her large brown eyes were as fierce as he remembered. Sophia Cunning, the witch hunter who had won his heart, was as beautiful as ever.

"Forgive you? You murdered my father, you bastard, and then left me at the roadside to hold him in my arms as he died. I should kill you!" Sophia yelled.

For a moment, Ferran thought that she would follow through with her threat and plunge the blade deep into his heart. Keeping his hands up, he walked forward so that the tip of the blade pressed into his chest. At this range, his leather armour would do little to slow the weapon.

"Then do it if it will make you feel better. I did what was necessary; if you search your heart you will know it to be true," he said.

For a heartbeat, she hesitated. Then she lowered the blade. Some of the fire left her eyes to be replaced with sadness. He had wanted to see her so many times since that night but knew that it would only have brought them both pain.

Damn her father. Damn the witch hunter general and his foul deeds. What is done is done. I did what I did to save the realm and to save her. One day she must realise that. Ferran thought angrily.

"What do you want from me, Ferran?" Sophia said dully. She sheathed the dagger into her belt and sat heavily onto the broken and worn chair.

"I need your help. Grand Master Thanos has tasked a small group and me to seek out the Diasect, to find out why they have not intervened in the war and to find answers about this ..." He paused, pulling the N'gist amulet from his tunic pocket. He immediately sensed its power trying to feed off of his own.

Sophia's eyes went wide. She leapt out of the chair, knocking over some books from the shelf. She staggered backwards and leaned against the wall.

"Where did you get that? It's impossible! Get it out of here!" she yelled. Fear was evident in her face.

Ferran quickly wrapped the amulet back in the enchanted piece of cloth in which he used to transport it and tucked it back into his tunic pocket. The cloth had masked the amulet's power, preventing it from feeding on the magic-users around it.

"The Baron of Retbit used a number of these to infiltrate the city during his raid. We intend to find out who provided him with them and what the Diasect knows about them. Please, Sophia, you know about the N'gist cult better than anyone," Ferran begged.

He had known it was a long shot just to ask her. Showing her the amulet was bound to get her interested. She and the Order of Witch Hunters had spent decades rooting out those who followed the dark ways, and nothing was darker than the N'gist. Sophia glared at him, a mixture of emotions flooding through her. Finally, her expression firmed.

"What do you have in mind?" she sighed.

CHAPTER 16.

Luxon had triple-checked his pack and had spent the previous days constantly practising with Master Ri'ges. Kaiden had also taught him the basics of swordplay, something that he seriously doubted he'd ever get good at. Yepert, too, had been put through his paces by the old mage. Each of them had been taught most of the spells of the lower ring in a crash course of lessons that had pushed them both to their limits, both mentally and physically. Alira had joined them for one of the days. Her power was strong, as was evident when she set the training rooms curtains ablaze instead of the candle which she had been aiming for.

Ferran, meanwhile, had been busy gathering supplies and horses for the journey. With the gold Delfins given to him by Thanos, he had acquired two destrier horses for himself and the witch hunter Sophia. Kaiden would ride his own horse, Herald. For the two mages and Alira, he had bought three shire ponies. These sturdy animals came from the Caldarian countryside and were used to the rough ground after living and working in the region's rocky foothills.

The group met at the city's main gate at dawn. The horses were already loaded with supplies of food and weapons. To Luxon's surprise, Sophia's horse was covered in a sturdy harness which was filled with items.

"We witch hunters always go everywhere well-prepared," she said with a wink. She wore a purple cloak over a suit of tight-fitting black leather armour. The material pronounced every curve of her supple body. For a teenage boy like Luxon, it was a pleasant sight. Slung across her back was a longbow and on her hip a quiver of deadly-looking barbed arrows.

Yepert was already mounted on his pony. They all wore cloaks, but the mages wore no weapons save for small daggers which Thanos had given to them the previous night. The younger boy smiled with excitement.

"I can't wait to get going, Lux. This is so exciting!" he giggled. Luxon couldn't help but smile at his friend's enthusiasm. It was something that he did not share. The sense of dread had only grown stronger.

Alira wore a blue cloak over her travel tunic and trousers. On her feet, she wore leather boots that rose high on her long slender legs. Her blond hair was tied up in a top knot; she flashed Luxon a nervous smile before climbing into the saddle.

The knight Kaiden also wore a cloak over his mantle and chainmail armour. At his hip, in its sheath, was his trusty long sword. He was whispering soothing words into Herald's ears, which pricked higher at his master's words.

"Luxon!" came a shout. He turned to see Hannah running up the wide avenue. She skirted her way past a group of traders, ducking under a rug which two men were hauling across the street. She stopped in front of Luxon.

"I didn't want you to go without us saying goodbye," she said breathlessly. She gave him a big hug. He savoured the smell of her perfumed hair and squeezed her back tightly in response. He didn't want to leave her. Now that he was leaving, he realised just how much he didn't want to leave her behind.

"You come back safe," she whispered into his ear.

He stepped back, keeping her at arm's length and smiled. "I promise you; it would take the ending of the world to stop me coming back here … and to you," he added nervously. He could feel himself turning red. *I have all this power, and yet I get shy around girls*, he chided himself.

She returned his smile and kissed him on the cheek.

"I'll hold you to that." She glanced at a nearby clock tower. "I have to go, or else I'll be late for my shift at the medica. I'll miss you; write to me if you can!" She broke free from the embrace and ran off down the street towards the quartz quarter and the medica.

Luxon watched her go, his chest feeling heavy as she went. Yepert clapped his friend on the shoulder.

"You'll see her again, Lux, I promise," the chubby boy said reassuringly. "We have a Knight of Niveren, a witch hunter, a Nightblade and two of the best mages in Caldaria. What could go wrong?"

Ferran hauled himself into his saddle. "Mount up. We have a lot of ground to cover."

He waved to one of the gate guards, who pulled the heavy lever that opened the city gates. With a loud sound of grinding metal, the heavy doors swung open to reveal the wider world beyond. The sun was high and bright in the sky, and the sound of songbirds filled the air.

"Least it doesn't look like rain …" Luxon muttered as he mounted his pony and spurred it into a trot. The small band was finally on their way, the long king's road and its perils awaiting them.

CHAPTER 17.

Eclin Mountains

Woven ran as fast as he could through the deep snow of the mountain pass. His boots slipped, and in places, he sank knee deep, but still, he wouldn't stop, he couldn't. Behind him came the snarls of werewolves, the moans of thousands of undead echoing down the valley and the ominous thunderous noise of thousands of armoured boots.

He had barely escaped Fuio. Now, several months on from that disaster, he once again found himself fleeing the horrors that relentlessly advanced through the mountains. Numerous times, the forces of Eclin had tried to halt the horde's advance, and each time it had proven to be an unmitigated disaster. The Rangers' numbers had been decimated at the last battle. For three weeks, the fort at Dendros had held; the thick walls and heavy defences had slowed the monsters for a time, but once again magic had been their undoing.

"How much further?" gasped the young ranger at his side. The man was no more than twenty summers' old, and his brown eyes were wide with fear.

"A few more miles," Woven replied. Both men were close to exhaustion, but they couldn't risk halting. To make matters worse, the sun was setting in the west. Soon, the temperature would plummet. It may have been summer, but in the high mountains of Eclin, it was always cold.

The two rangers were heading towards the city of Eclin, the last barrier to the plains that led into the heart of Delfinnia itself.

"We're all doomed, aren't we?" the lad said despairingly. Woven stayed silent; instead, he grabbed the man's shoulder and pushed him to go faster. The wolves were drawing closer. He understood the man's fear. After the barricades had broken at Fuio, the baron had turned tail and fled south towards his capital. Only the Knights of Niveren had prevented a total slaughter.

On their white stallions, they had charged the enemy lines, again and again, buying valuable time for the rangers and Eclin soldiers to flee. It had been they who had led the defence of the mountain passes; it was they who had bought the kingdom some time.

"I can't go on, sir," the ranger cried as he collapsed into the snow. His breathing was ragged, and he was shivering violently. Woven knelt down and hauled the man up, wrapping an arm around his shoulders.

"Leave me," the man protested. "I'll slow you down, and we will both die."

"Shut up, Briden. I've lost too many brothers to this war already. I'm not losing another," Woven growled. Briden was right, though – they both would die unless they found somewhere to hide and rest. He looked around. The white snow capped mountains went on for miles in either direction. A small forest was at the base of the mountain they found themselves on. He shut his eyes, trying to remember the layout of the land.

"The Sigil Caves ..." he muttered as he remembered something. He glanced to the west. A ridge dipped downwards into a narrow valley, at the end of which was a network of caves. He had never considered entering them in the past.

"No ... those caves are cursed ..." Briden stammered.

"It's either we take our chances with an old wives' tale, or we get torn apart by werewolves. I for one would rather face the caves!" Woven snarled. He took a firmer grip on the ranger and made his way towards the valley.

As they reached a bluff, he lowered Briden to the ground and shoved. The ranger slid down the icy slope with a startled cry. Woven followed suit. Snow and ice were kicked upwards as he went. To someone watching from the opposite side of the valley, the two rangers appeared to be two boulders falling down the mountainside. Finally, he skidded to halt next to the other ranger.

In the distance, he could make out the three steeples known as the three kings. Standing tall and proud atop the peaks were statues of three of Delfinnia's greatest kings. Woven paused for a moment in thought. The three statues were used as landmarks by the rangers. From the peaks, the city of Eclin was ten miles to the south. The villages of Rintir and Unos lay three miles to the north.

He swore under his breath.

They couldn't head north – that way led the enemy – and the city was much too far to reach before nightfall. Once again, he hauled Briden up from the snow and carried him. Carefully, he made his way down the slippery mountainside until they finally reached the head of the narrow valley that led to the caves. The sun was beginning to set, and the cold was creeping in. The sounds of the enemy grew louder. Woven picked up the pace. His stamina was waning as the younger ranger's weight sapped at his strength.

"Over there," Briden pointed to a dark hollow in the valley wall. The dark grey stones and rocks weren't covered in as much snow as those found higher in the mountains. Woven staggered towards the mouth of the cave, collapsing in relief as they got inside.

Woven sat with his back against the cave's wall. The warmth of the fire he had made restored some vitality into his tired limbs. Upon entering the cave, the Rangers had headed as deep inside as they dared.

CHAPTER 17.

Briden had collapsed into a deep sleep as his exhaustion overwhelmed him. Woven, however, couldn't rest. He camouflaged the cave's entrance with stones and branches from a nearby dead tree. Then he took some sticks and used them to start the fire.

The fire cast shadows on the cave's wall and the flickering flames illuminated dozens of the mysterious sigils that gave the cave its name. He reached into his cloak and pulled out some of the bread from the knapsack on his belt. The dry, coarse food tasted foul as always, but he savoured it nonetheless. Briden was snoring loudly; his cloak wrapped tightly around himself to ward off the cold. Outside, the temperature was plummeting.

Woven paused in his eating.

A faint greenish light was flickering deeper in the cave. Slowly, he stood and drew his sword. Trepidation filled him. Had the enemy found them? Carefully, he crept towards the light until he reached the cave's rocky wall. The light was coming through a crack. He felt the wall for some sign of weakness. He knocked the wall with the hilt of his sword, leaping back as a hollow tone echoed around the cave. Briden shifted in his sleep with a snort.

The green light grew brighter.

"Magic ..." Woven whispered as he realised what he was seeing. Whatever was on the other side of the wall was magical in origin. He placed his sword on the ground before looking around. He grunted in satisfaction as he found a large heavy rock. With all his might, he smashed the rock against the hollow wall which shifted with a crack.

Briden leapt awake at the noise.

"What the? Woven ... Sir?" The young ranger awoke with a start; clumsily he scrambled for his sword.

"Easy, I've found something," Woven explained. He pointed to another rock. "Use that and help me get this wall down."

Briden got to his feet, picked up the rock and joined his superior at smashing down the hollow wall. A half-hour later, the two men had made an opening wide enough for a man to fit through. Both men were covered with sweat thanks to their exertions. Briden was gasping and collapsed back down onto the floor.

"Stay here and get some rest. I'm going to check it out," Woven ordered.

He pulled a number of arrows from his quiver and bound them together with spare cord for his bow. With the knife from his belt, he carefully removed the valuable bodkin arrowheads and removed the goose feathers. He took his hastily made torch, putting it into the fire until it ignited.

Carefully, he squeezed through the hole they had created, the eerie green light growing brighter. He gasped in awe at the source of the light.

Adorning the walls of the hidden chamber were sigils far larger and ornate than those found in the main cave. One was glowing brightly; to Woven it looked to be in the shape of a sword. An ancient language was scrawled on a stone tablet at its base.

He knelt down and looked at it; the symbols looked familiar but were so faded that they were near impossible to read.

"Looks like ancient Nivionian ..." he muttered. In his years as a ranger, he had spent a number of nights inside the ancient ruins of the Nivion Empire that dotted the wild lands of Delfinnia. Most folks avoided them, fearing that they were haunted by the souls of the dead. Woven knew better. Many were occupied by nefarious thieves on the lam, Pucks, or other fell beasts of the Void.

As he picked up the tablet, the light from the sigil faded, plunging the chamber into darkness. Only the light from his torch giving him light enough to see.

He tucked the tablet inside his cloak and exited the chamber. Whatever he had found was important. He could feel it in his bones.

CHAPTER 18.

The King's Road

They hadn't been on the road for long before they encountered their first taste of the war.

The group had only been on the king's road for an hour and had covered barely ten miles when they came across the bodies. Kaiden and Ferran rode ahead whilst Sophia stayed to defend the others.

"What is it?" Yepert asked as he happily munched on an apple he'd plucked from one of the many trees that lined the road. After leaving Caldaria, they had made their way through the farmlands and small villages that provided the mage city with food and other goods. Upon seeing the riders, the farmers had run into their homes. Anyone on a horse was a potential threat in these dark times.

"It seems the war is not as far away from Caldaria as we thought," Sophia replied grimly. Her horse whinnied and stamped at the cracked surface of the road. Luxon trotted his pony alongside the witch hunter.

"Could it be the baron?" he asked worriedly. He wouldn't put it past the spiteful ruler of Retbit to lay in an ambush after what had transpired previously.

"No. That pig is probably already in his castle with his tail tucked firmly between his legs," Alira spat as she joined the conversation. "He's a coward and a wretch." Alira's blue eyes were fierce and filled with hate at her former jailor. Her white pony was busy munching on the grass that grew through the road's cracked surface.

Luxon thought back to the last time he been on the road with his mother. It had been the day after his father had been dragged off and executed by the bickering barons in Sunguard. His mother had smuggled them out of the capital the same day. They had travelled for over a week up the king's road to Caldaria and safety.

He shut his eyes as he remembered the pain he had felt as his mother had left him at the city gates with nothing but the clothes on his back before kissing him on the cheek and saying her goodbyes. To this day, he did not understand why she had left him or where she had gone. One thing he did know was that back before the war had begun, not a single weed nor blade of grass had grown on the kingdom's highways. The King's Legion had taken meticulous care of that.

Kaiden galloped back to the group.

"It appears as though the baron's men may have done us a favour when they fled back south. There's an entire bandit camp burnt to ashes further ahead." The knight glanced at Alira and the boys. "It's not a pretty sight, however. Lots of blood, lots of bodies," he warned.

Yepert stopped eating, his face going pale. Luxon trotted over to his friend and patted him on the back.

"Just shut your eyes. Here," he said taking a cord of rope from the pack attached to his saddle and giving it to Yepert. "Hold this, and I'll lead you through, okay?"

Yepert nodded.

Together they spurred their mounts forward until they crested a small ridge and came across a scene of utter devastation. Hanging from some of the trees lining the road were bodies. Flies buzzed angrily over the corpses of bandits which lay naked in the summer sun. Several had spear wounds: others showed signs of sword or mace blows. Standing grim-faced in the centre of the carnage was Ferran. The Nightblade paced the clearing and knelt over one of the bodies. The corpse of the man he was checking neither wore the armour of a soldier nor bore the marks of a bandit. His eyes were missing, and a brutal tear had almost split him from neck to thigh bone.

"No man did this," Ferran muttered. "These bandits were slain, and this poor wretch must have come along later to scavenge their weapons and armour. He met with something he did not expect."

"What's the matter?" Kaiden asked, his hand dropping instinctively to his sword.

Sophia unslung her bow and gazed at the tree line.

"The Great Wood goes on for hundreds of miles. There could be anything lurking within its dark interior," she said as she dismounted gracefully. "With no Nightblades or legion patrols, beasts of the Void are certain to get loose and prey on the unwary." She walked over to the body Ferran was studying and pointed to the ground. "Here. There are tracks in the dirt. Something crawled out of the forest, all right. Something big."

Luxon looked around, trying his best not to heave at the sight of death. Worse than the blood was the smell. He told Yepert to hold his nose and keep his eyes closed.

"I suggest we keep moving," Ferran said, standing and mounting his horse. "This part of the road is not safe. There is a rune stone a few more miles ahead. We will camp there."

"Runestone?" Luxon asked. He remembered seeing them on his last journey. The big oval rocks dotted the realm. Most were located at crossroads and at the side of the major roads.

"Aye. Runestones are imbued with ancient magic which wards off fell beasts," Sophia explained her eyes not leaving the trees. "The ancient mages created them during the Age of Aljeron, the first wizard – the age when the Nightblades were formed to hunt the monsters unleashed from the Void by the stupidity of mages."

Night came quickly on the road. As the last rays of sunlight were fading, the group rounded a bend to see a black monolith standing high and proud. In the dim light, it was hard to make out the archaic writings etched into its surface.

The flicker of a campfire caused Ferran to call them to a halt. Someone was already camping at the base of the runestone.

"Hail there," the Nightblade called.

A shout of surprise and the sound of people scrabbling about came from the stone's direction. A cacophony of swear words and a crash as someone fell over caused Luxon to smile. Whoever was camped there was no skilled assassin or warrior, if anything they sounded like the clumsiest person in the world.

"H-Hail ... who goes there?" replied a voice. An old man wearing a long traveller's coat stepped out onto the road, his hands held high. Behind him was a younger man dressed in similar garb. The old man's hair was white and erratic, and his bushy unruly beard suggested that he hadn't had a chance to shave in weeks. In contrast, the younger man's black hair was slicked back with oil, and his beard was smart and trimmed. In his hands was a staff which he gripped tightly.

"We are just a group of travellers heading south to the sundial crossroads," Ferran explained politely. "Would it be alright if we shared the safety of the runestone with you?"

The two men conversed animatedly; Luxon could barely hear their whispers.

After a few minutes of comedic squabbling, the older man walked towards them his hands still high in the air.

"Seein' as you have young'uns with you, we figure that your band is safe. So yes, you can share our fire and the stone's safety." The old man moved his head from side to side as though he was looking for any signs of treachery. "You don't want to be on the open road at night. Especially not lately ..." he added.

The group trotted their mounts into the men's camp. Luxon and Yepert tethered their ponies to a nearby tree whilst the others did similarly to their own horses. Alira's pony was tethered to the runestone itself.

"Come, come sit next to the fire and make yourselves comfy," the older man enthused. "My name is Gric, and my young companion here is Huin. We are travelling peddlers from Ridder, wandering the king's road to find our fortune."

Huin snorted in derision. "Yes, old man, we're doing really well on that front ..." he muttered sarcastically.

Sophia had taken one of the packs off her horse and pulled out five sleeping blankets. She passed one to Luxon and the others and settled down to sleep a little ways from the crackling campfire. Kaiden pulled some food from one of the travel sacks on his saddle and passed some bread among them. He offered the peddlers some.

"Nay, lad, we have our own food. Can't be doing with taking from strangers," said Gric as he settled himself onto a pile of cushions next to the fire. A thin sheet of cloth had been stretched between the stone and a nearby tree to offer them some cover from the elements.

"We passed a bandit camp earlier in the day," Ferran said through a mouthful of bread. "No survivors. Do you know what happened there?"

"Aye we do," Gric answered, his tone going serious. "About three days ago there was three of us until we went to check out the smoke arising from that camp. We intended to strip the bandits' armour and sell it once we'd reached Caldaria, but poor old Euin bought it when he lingered there too long."

"That old fool got greedy and paid the price," Huin added. "I told him to get back here before the night fell."

"Aye, you did. We left him to it; we weren't willing to risk it, and especially after the noises we've heard at night during our travels. We got back here just after sundown, and then not long after we heard Euin's screams in the distance. Something got him; something fell."

Luxon shivered. Yepert glanced about nervously, and Alira huddled closer to Kaiden. The knight put an arm around her reassuringly.

"Fear not, we have a Nightblade, a knight and a witch hunter to protect us," Yepert said, more confidently than he looked. Ferran scowled at the boy. He didn't want everyone to know who they were.

"Get some sleep. We have a long day's journey ahead of us," Ferran said as he sat down under a tree and wrapped his blanket around himself.

Luxon couldn't sleep. The night was cold, but there was something else in the chill, something he had felt for several days. He wondered if anyone else had noticed it: a chill which made him shiver despite it being summer.

He also couldn't sleep. Usually, there were calls from owls or the constant shrill of grasshoppers, but there was nothing but silence, an oppressive silence that burrowed deep into his soul. He wrapped his blanket tighter around himself and edged closer to the fire, hoping that its warmth would put him at ease.

It's out there; Luxon almost cried out. He sighed in relief as he recognised Ferran sitting next to the fire, idly prodding it with a stick.

"What's out there?" Luxon whispered, not wanting to wake the others. Alira was curled up in a ball at Kaiden's feet, the knight's hand resting protectively on the hilt of his sword. Yepert was snoring loudly, and Sophia was happily catching flies.

The Nightblade looked at Luxon with a frown.

"What do they teach you in those schools about the Fell beasts and the Void? Surely a mage as powerful as you should already know the answer." Despite all his strength, Ferran couldn't hide his resentment for the lad.

Luxon glanced away, unable to meet the Nightblade's disapproving gaze.

"They didn't teach us much. I'm only an apprentice, and even then, a newly appointed one. I have a power that I don't understand," he answered miserably. He didn't want to be on the road; he didn't want to be in danger.

Ferran grunted and tossed a twig onto the fire, which flared brightly.

"I am sorry I spoke that way," he grumbled. "I shouldn't take my resentment of the mages out on one so young as you, and before you ask, I have my reasons which I do not wish to share this night." Quickly, he changed the subject.

"The thing that killed their friend," he said, gesturing to the two sleeping pedlars. "What do you think it was?"

Luxon shifted slightly as his leg started to go dead under his weight. He thought for a moment. The Nightblade was right; he didn't have a clue about the fell beasts or know anything much about the Void. He shook his head and shrugged his shoulders.

"I have no idea," he answered after a few moments.

A scream pierced the silence of the night, an unearthly, terrible scream. The others sprung awake in a panic and fright. All except Yepert, who remained snoring loudly.

Ferran stayed seated. "We are safe thanks to the runestone. Go back to sleep; it can't harm us here," he said reassuringly. Kaiden looked less than impressed, once again his blade was in hand.

"Listen ..." Alira whispered in fright.

Sure enough, the sound of rustling leaves grew closer and closer. Luxon scrambled to his feet, and Sophia knelt, her bow drawn. Still, Ferran sat, watching the trees impassively. The two pedlars cowered behind the runestone. Huin held his staff in a white-knuckled grip.

The tension rose as the thing drew closer. Luxon steadied his nerves, his hands going unconsciously to the dagger in his belt. He knew it wouldn't be much use, but he needed to hold something for reassurance.

The bushes across the roadside erupted, only to reveal a startled boar and its three piglets. The group all sighed in relief, the tension easing to be replaced with nervous chuckles.

"Ruddy pig; scared the snot out of me!" chuckled Gric. The old man picked up a stone and threw it at the boar, sending it running off back into the undergrowth. With a startled squeal, its tiny piglets following suit, and after another flurry of leaves and breaking twigs the boars vanished as quickly as they had arrived.

A few minutes later and the camp was quiet once more as everyone went back to sleep; everyone, that was, except for Luxon and Ferran.

"That scream was no pig, was it?" Luxon asked. The scream had shaken him deeply. He envied Yepert who seems to be able to sleep through virtually anything. He wished he could have been like the others and cast the night's horrors to the back of his mind.

"I'd guess it was a Banshee; a fell spirit which preys on the souls of the living. They're fairly common in this part of the realm. The Blackmoor to the west is full of them," Ferran reasoned. The Nightblade stared into the fire's flames and warmed his hands from the heat.

"Where do they come from?" Luxon asked. He couldn't help looking into the darkness. He felt as though a monster would burst into the clearing at any moment. If he could understand what the Fell beasts were then he wouldn't be as afraid. All he knew of them and their origins were just fairy tales told by parents to keep their children in line. Even the mage schools avoided the subject.

"It's a long story, and I wouldn't want to bore you," Ferran replied as he picked some dirt from under his fingernails.

"Dawn is a long way off, and I seriously doubt I'll be able to sleep, maybe a good story is what I need?" Luxon said, hoping that the Nightblade would change his mind.

With a reluctant sigh, Ferran relented.

"Very well, lad. Settle down and get comfortable, because this is the only time, I will tell you the tale of the Void and its origins. Only the Nightblades and the members of the Chantry and the Knights of Niveren remember the story. To everyone else, the Void is just a mystery or a legend. Although, people soon change their minds when one of its abominations terrorises their towns."

He took a sip from the water skin at his feet before beginning his tale.

CHAPTER 19.

"The tale of the Void goes all the way back to the very start of all things. At the beginning of the universe, there was nothing but darkness. Sitting alone in the empty cold was Aniron, the first of the Gods. She floated throughout the blackness, sad that she could not see. Boredom was her nemesis, and so to entertain herself she clapped her hands and created the stars. With light, she could see, but still, she was not impressed.

"So, she decided to create the worlds. For aeons she flitted from world to world, marvelling at their wonders, but still, she was not impressed.

"So, she decided to create life. If she could exist, then why couldn't others? She wanted to share what she had made. She took a part of her essence and gave birth to other gods to keep her company.

"For a while, the new gods played and were happy amongst the stars and worlds that Aniron had created; but one, her eldest son, grew sad.

"Vectrix grew jealous of Aniron's creations and wished for the power to create as she had done. One day when Aniron was walking on the world of Esperia, Vectrix came to her.

"'Why can only you create?' he asked of his mother. 'I too want to create. I want your power, for I have visions of such wonder and beauty that it would make you weep.'

"Aniron smiled at her son. She took his head in her hands and kissed him deeply. The two made love on the surface of Esperia, their lovemaking creating life in the process. After they were done, Aniron held Vectrix in her arms and whispered, 'Look what we have created – new life that is not god, but beautiful nonetheless.'

"Vectrix watched in awe at the life that had appeared. Beasts of all kinds roamed Esperia; the oceans were full of fish, the skies of birds and the land flourished with flowers and beauty. He wept.

"'This is beautiful indeed,' he said, 'but it is not mine. This is your favourite world.' His voice grew louder, creating the winds, and his tone grew angry, creating the mountains as it cracked the land. 'You tricked me into making life on your world,' he cried. 'The power is still yours!'

"Angry at Aniron's betrayal, he reached down and snapped off the top of the tallest mountain. With all his might, he hurled it at his mother, striking her down. In his rage, Vectrix stole his mother's power; the wounded Aniron powerless to stop him. He absorbed her until there was nothing left but her voice on the winds. Realising what he had done, Vectrix fled Esperia and cowered.

"When the other gods discovered what Vectrix had done, they wept. Their sorrow was quickly replaced with rage and greed. Aniron's power was up for grabs. If Vectrix could take it for himself, then what was stopping them from acquiring it from him?

"God slaughtered god, as each battled for the right to kill Vectrix and take their mother's power. The universe which Aniron had created was torn asunder as worlds were destroyed and stars extinguished. Finally, after aeons of fighting, only three gods remained.

"Vectrix, Rindar and Esperin were the final gods left standing. Vectrix had not been idle during the war – in his hidden sanctuary of the world of Vectra; the god had been busy using his mother's power. With it, he created the Void, his own universe that housed beasts of his creation. Instead of being beautiful, his creations were twisted and evil, his rage having corrupted his mother's power. He used his monsters to enslave the other worlds until only Esperia remained."

Luxon held up a hand to stop the story.

"So, the Void is the realm, of a god? How have I never heard of Vectrix?" he asked. He knew the names of many of the old gods, but Vectrix was new to him. Before the Golden Empire, there had been many religions devoted to the gods, but those were long gone. Only the followers of Niveren remained a man who was revered as a god.

Ferran shrugged. "He is a god who was lost. Folk forget things easily. Anyway," the Nightblade said with a hint of annoyance at the interruption, "I'll get back to finishing my tale."

"Rindar the god of Light and Esperin, the god of Darkness, defended their mother's world from their vile brother's hoards, but they were not strong enough to oppose him. The three gods battled in the skies of the world until Rindar was struck down. To stop Vectrix, the god of light came up with a plan.

"'We must become one to defeat evil,' he told his sister. Esperin, despite her powers, was no match for Vectrix, so she joined with Rindar. Light and Dark merged into one to become Chiaroscuro, the god of balance.

"The new god battled Vectrix, wiping out his monsters and casting them into the Void. However, despite their combined might, the new god could not destroy Vectrix. It was a stalemate.

"To break the deadlock in their struggle, the two gods met on Esperia. There they agreed to a challenge. Vectrix lent some of Aniron's essence to Chiaroscuro.

"'I will prove to you that my creations are worthy of life,' Vectrix said. 'Use the power I granted you to see if you are worthy of this gift you seek.'

"Seeing no other way to break the deadlock Chiaroscuro agreed.

"Vectrix created the Necrist. Millions of the hideous creatures burst from the dead things of the world.

"'I bring life from death,' Vectrix boasted.

"Chiaroscuro thought for a long time about what to make. Finally, the god created something that combined the essence of both light and dark: man.

"The first men were tall, strong and imbued with power. To give their new creations the power to defeat the Necrist, Chiaroscuro granted them some of its own power in the form of magic.

"Man, waged war with the Necrist. Using magic, the first men destroyed the Necrist, banishing the beasts to the Void. The war had taken a heavy toll on Chiaroscuro's creation. Out of the millions that had been created, only two men remained: Niveren and Danon. Niveren was the embodiment of light, while Danon was of the dark.

"'We have won the challenge, brother,' Chiaroscuro said. 'Too much death has resulted from this war. Instead of killing you, we will allow you to slink to your own creation and remain there until the end of time.'

"And so it was, that Vectrix was banished to the Void and Chiaroscuro became the one god of the universe.

"A long time later, a mage whose name was lost to history inadvertently opened up a portal to the Void. Unable to reseal it, the monsters of Vectrix burst forth from the Void and entered the world of men. At first, the beasts ran rampant across the world, but an alliance of the kingdoms of the first folk known as the Niver banded together, and over time they culled the beasts' numbers."

Ferran paused for effect.

"The best at hunting the monsters of the void was the specialist magic-wielding hunters known as the Nightblades, the order which still defends the realm from the Void's horrors today. That is when they aren't cowering in Caldaria," he added with resentment in his tone.

He looked over at his audience.

He chuckled when he spotted Luxon on his back and snoring loudly.

"Guess I'm not much of a storyteller ..." Ferran grumbled as he too settled down to grab some sleep.

Dawn came, bringing with it a shower of rain. The sky which had been blue and clear the previous day was now full of angry black clouds. Luxon awoke to find Gric and Alira sat next to the fire cooking some of the bacon and eggs that they had packed. The smell made his stomach growl loudly and his mouth water.

He sat up with a wide yawn and stretched. His muscles were tight, and he grunted with satisfaction as his back cracked. The sheet of cloth had done well to protect them all from the rain, all except for Sophia whose sleeping spot had been drenched. Now she was moaning about the weather. She had chosen to sleep away from the others, choosing to sleep under a tree rather than in the camp. Ferran was already up checking his horse and packs. Yepert, however, was gone.

"Where's Yepert?" Luxon asked, bleary-eyed. He wondered over to the fire and took a seat next to the old pedlar who was humming a happy tune to himself. He looked refreshed and spritely – not what you would expect from someone as old as the trader.

Alira looked up from prodding a piece of crackling bacon in a sizzling pan. She too looked as though she had slept well; her large blue eyes looked fresh and healthy. Her long blond hair was loose and flowed like a river down her back, and her fringe was in her eyes. Luxon had to stop himself from reaching over and pushing it back behind her ear. He was surprised to see her give him a warm smile; he thought she disliked him.

"He's down the hill over there," she said, pointing to the trees on the other side of the road. "There's a stream, so he's filling up our water flasks."

Ferran paused, checking his pack.

"He's gone where?" the Nightblade asked, his voice low and tinged with anger.

"The stream," Alira replied meekly.

Ferran pulled out the tourmaline sword which hung at his belt and snapped his fingers at Sophia, who jogged over to him.

"That foolish boy has wandered off of the road. I can't tell how far the rune stone's magic will reach and with a banshee about ..." He didn't have to finish his sentence. Sophia ran over to her horse, grabbed her bow and together they set off into the trees. Kaiden was about to join them when Ferran held up a hand to stop him.

"No, sir knight, stay with the others. Sophia and I have hunted banshees before. If we need backup, we will call for it."

With that, the witch hunter and Nightblade headed off after the missing boy.

Yepert was cheerfully humming a tune from Plock. It was a merry song that his grandfather always used to sing.

"The merry old fisherman left the shiny shore to sail the shiny sea ... hum de dum de dum ..." The fast-flowing stream was clear and cool after coming down from the mountains and foothills.

He was oblivious to the world around him as he dipped one water flask after the other into the water. Woodland and scrub bordered the river's course; the noise of insects flitting from flower to flower in frantic activity as they prepared for the coming change of seasons that filled the air.

He didn't notice the temperature fall.

He shivered, pulling his cloak tighter around himself. Still, he hummed merrily. He didn't notice when the sounds of nature ceased. Still, he hummed his grandfather's tune. His hands were growing numb from the chilled river water, but still, he was unaware of what was slowly moving up behind him. It was only when a shadow was cast over him, did he stop. The hairs on the back of his neck rose, and his breath came out as steam. Ice had formed in his hair. Slowly he turned and screamed.

CHAPTER 19.

———◆◯◆———

Ferran and Sophia ran through the undergrowth, snapping twigs and shoving branches from their faces as they went. The cry had spurred them into action. It was quickly followed by that unearthly of all screams – the banshee's call. Ferran leapt through a hedge, landed and rolled into the river. Sophia was right behind him, her bow raised with its cord drawn, a deadly silver-tipped arrow ready to fly.

Yepert was in the river. The boy was scrambling backwards on his hands, his feet desperately kicking as he tried to escape the monster that reached for him with its long pale arms.

The Banshee was a thing of nightmares. It drifted above the surface of the river, its body covered in a long, torn purple cloak. Its hands were claws, but worse of all was the smell of death it brought with it.

"Leave him alone, foul beast!" Ferran bellowed. He drew his tourmaline sword, conjuring the magic infused blade into life. The weapon hummed in his hand; its silver light aimed at the banshee which spun to face him.

Yepert was in the river on his back, his thrashings ceased as he blacked out. Now the lad drifted helplessly downstream and was being carried away by the river's rapid flow.

Sophia loosed her arrow, striking the banshee where a regular person's head would have been. It reeled backwards with a screech. Raising a hand, the fell beast blasted the witch hunter backwards with magic, sending her flying to land heavily on the riverbank. Ferran didn't hesitate. He unleashed his own magic. With one hand he launched a volley of fireballs at the banshee whilst he aimed his sword. The fireballs ignited the banshee's cowl, causing it to thrash about. With a shout, he leapt high into the air, slashing downwards with all of his might.

The tourmaline blade fell, piercing the creature and cutting it almost clean in two. The banshee screamed once more, trying to strike at the Nightblade who now rained blow after blow upon it. The Banshee was more a spirit than a monster, but still, the magical weapon inflicted it with pain. Ferran retreated a few paces, unbuckling a vial from his belt.

"In the name of the Nightblades, be gone from this world!" he yelled, hurling the vial at the reeling banshee. The vial lit up before shattering into a thousand fragments. The magic inside was released, sending the fell beast back to whence it came.

An explosion knocked Ferran off of his feet, sending him flying backwards to land next to the unconscious Sophia. The banshee was sucked into the created Void breach. With a final scream, the creature faded from existence to return to the gap between worlds.

"Kaiden!" Ferran shouted as loud as he could. The knight could look after Sophia. Yepert, on the other hand, needed help.

"The boy!" he shouted as he scrambled back onto his feet and dove into the river. He swam as hard as he could, the river's current increasing his speed. After a few moments, he caught sight of the boy's body floating face down against an outcropping of rocks.

Desperately, he swam towards him. He reached Yepert and hauled his head out of the water.

"C'mon boy, don't be dead."

He looked around for a way out of the river. He hooked an arm under the lad's and swam towards the bank where tree roots provided an ample grip to clamber out of the icy water.

Yepert wasn't breathing.

Ferran swore under his breath. He was no healer. He picked up the boy and carried him back up the river, desperate to reach the others.

"Help me!" Ferran shouted as he drew closer to the camp. He was soaked through. His sodden clothes were weighing him down. He crossed the river again and reached the tree in which Sophia had landed. He was relieved to see that the witch hunter was gone; Kaiden must have taken her back to the campsite.

A call came from the trees. It was the blond-haired girl, Alira. She was pointing and gesturing wildly. Soon Kaiden appeared. The knight burst through the hedgerows and jumped down to the bank to help Ferran carry Yepert up the slope.

"By Niveren, what has happened to the lad? His skin is as white as snow," the knight breathed as he hauled the heavy boy upwards. Luxon and Gric ran to their aid, each lending a hand. Upon seeing his friend pale and unmoving, Luxon's stomach fell. He fought to keep tears from his eyes.

"The boy is not breathing," Ferran panted breathlessly. The old pedlar pushed him aside to kneel over Yepert. His old face was full of concern, and also with profound concentration. There was wisdom in his eyes that Luxon recalled seeing on the face of many of the mages of Caldaria.

"Move aside. Let me look," Gric said irritably. He pulled some spectacles from his coat pocket and affixed them securely to his nose. Next, he pulled a small mirror from another pocket and held it above Yepert's face.

"Was it a banshee that did this?" Gric asked, in a business-like voice.

Ferran nodded in the affirmative. "It was. I sent it back to the Void. The boy's been struck by the banshee curse, hasn't he?" There was a hint of hopelessness in his tone. He was stunned when the old man slapped him hard around the face.

"Do not speak as though there is no hope. Be strong for your comrades if nothing else, oh fearless Nightblade."

The pedlar grunted in satisfaction as steam appeared on the mirror.

"The boy is not dead, just paralysed by the banshee's scream," Gric explained. "If it were the banshee curse then he would already be turning into a banshee himself." The fire in the old man's eyes faded somewhat as Ferran looked away, ashamed.

"Now, you," the old man said, pointing to Luxon and Alira. "You move your friend over there next to the fire."

He smiled kindly as he saw the worry on their faces. "Do not fear, young ones. Old Gric knows what to do. Your friend will be fine."

With Kaiden's help, they carried Yepert and settled him on a pile of the pedlar's cushions close to the fire, where Huin was preparing an iron pot full of water.

"How is your head, my dear?" Gric asked Sophia who was lying next to the runestone with a cold, wet cloth pressed against the back of her head.

"I'm fine. My head's a little sore, but I've suffered worse. Guess I must be a little rusty at the whole monster hunting thing." She winced as she tentatively rubbed her head. Ferran was about to walk over to her, but she flashed him a look that would terrify Danon himself. The Nightblade thought better of it.

"Girl pass me that satchel there," Gric asked Alira. "And get us some more water from the river. Perhaps the brave knight and Nightblade can assist you?" he cackled. The young girl picked up a large bag from the pedlar's makeshift bed and handed it over, its contents clinking noisily. Gric opened the satchel and rooted around its contents, all the while whistling a merry little tune.

Alira took the bucket handed to her by Huin and headed off for the river. Kaiden close behind, his sword already drawn. Ferran followed.

Something about the old man set Luxon at ease. Although he feared for his friend, he got the feeling that the pedlars had dealt with their share of wounds in the past. Something also told him that they weren't just any ordinary traders.

Gric emptied two vials of blue liquid into the pot and took a ladle from Huin who was piling more wood onto the flames. Luxon edged closer to the pedlars.

"Who are you?" Luxon asked the old man quietly after making sure the others were out of earshot. He got the impression that Gric and Huin didn't want anyone to know their true identities. Gric stopped stirring, his eyes going wide. Huin too stopped, his eyes darting about as though looking for an escape route.

"Don't worry. I won't say anything," Luxon said. He crossed his heart as he made the promise.

The surprise in the old man's eyes was replaced by a naughty twinkle as he smiled. Huin, however, remained twitchy. The younger man shook his head as though to plead with Gric to stay quiet.

"You are a smart one, young Luxon. Tell me, boy, what do *you* think we are?"

Luxon thought for a moment and then clicked his fingers.

"You're healers. Rogue ones. Ones who refused to remain in Caldaria. That's how you know how to heal my friend, and that's why you're so jumpy. If Kaiden found out, he'd have every right to ... well, kill you," he reasoned.

Gric laughed. Huin turned pale.

"By Niveren you are a clever lad," he chuckled, before suddenly turning all serious.

"You won't tell anyone about us, you hear me?" Gric whispered. "Promise me right now, or else I will refuse to help your friend, and he can remain frozen for all of eternity. These are dangerous times for folk like us, and for you. There are prices on all of our heads and not from the Knights ... Someone is hunting us all down like vermin

Luxon looked away, unable to meet the old man's intense gaze. Perhaps he was too clever for his own good.

"We are on our way to Caldaria to seek safety. The war grows worse, and magic-users are being killed as the common folk blame all the world's ills on us," Huin added darkly. 'We had a good business in Balnor until we were chased out of the city. It's a sign of madness that even healers are being persecuted. Once we were respected despite our magic ... Now we are murdered in the streets ..."

Gric held up a hand to stop his young companion.

"Fear does terrible things to people, but we shall rise above it. I fear that healers will be much in demand before the war is over," Gric muttered. He dipped the ladle into the now boiling water and scooped out the liquid that had turned a blue-green colour. Carefully, he took an empty bottle from out of the satchel and tipped the fluid into it.

Luxon held the bottle steady. A thought occurred to him.

"How do you know that I'm a mage? I've not used any magic since the city ..." he asked in confusion.

Gric cackled mischievously and put a cork in the bottle. A twinkle was in his eyes.

"Anyone who travels in the company of a Nightblade, witch hunter and knight must be a mage, for it is only a mage that would ever find themselves in such strange company. Also ... you do radiate magical power ... just like that girl you're with."

Luxon sat back in surprise. Alira? If she was as powerful as he, then why hadn't Thanos said anything? He'd assumed that the girl was even more of a novice than himself.

Gric clapped him on the shoulder, his expression turning serious once more.

"Be careful of the girl. There is something odd about her," the old man whispered.

"You're not the first to say such a thing," Luxon replied, feeling troubled.

"Let's see if we can rouse your friend. Huin, take hold of the boy's head," Gric said as he shuffled over to Yepert.

Luxon could see that his friend was as stiff as a board. His limbs were rigid, but his chest rose and fell slowly. Huin leaned over the boy and restrained his head while Gric opened Yepert's mouth and poured the contents of the vial down his gullet. The old man closed his eyes and muttered an incantation. A white light emanated from his palms as he chanted. The magic engulfed Yepert's body in a blinding flash.

With a start, Yepert's eyes fluttered open and his mouth opened in a silent scream.

"Yepert, easy," Luxon soothed as he knelt down next to his friend. Yepert's face went red as the blood flowed once more, and with a harsh gasp his breathing returned to normal, and his muscles began to twitch uncontrollably. Huin held him still whilst his body thrashed about.

"The banshee's spell is being broken. If Huin doesn't hold his head, then the boy could break his own neck as life returns to his body. I've seen it happen before," Gric explained.

A few moments passed until at last Yepert stopped moving. His eyes were wide and alert, and colour had returned to his skin. Luxon breathed a sigh of relief.

"Thank you," he said to the two healers.

Yepert sat up in confusion.

"Luxon. Wha— ... I'm hungry ..." he moaned as he held his stomach.

Luxon laughed.

CHAPTER 20.

Sunguard

The crowd's angry shouts were irritating Rason. The general was dressed in the regalia of a soon-to-be King. A purple robe was draped over his shoulders, and his white silk shirt and black trousers were ironed to perfection. His knee-high black boots were polished to magnificence and the jewels of Delfinnia shined opulently around his neck. The only thing missing from the outfit was the crown.

He posed in front of the full body length mirror affixed to his chamber's wall, marvelling at his regal appearance.

Soon after disposing of the Privy Council, he had taken possession of one of the former king's manors. The building's ornately decorated interior of gold and silver just oozed wealth and power. He felt at home there.

His thoughts were interrupted when a red-faced legionary burst into the room. The man was wearing plate armour, and his breaths came in ragged gasps.

"General, sir," the legionary rasped, giving a feeble excuse for a salute.

"A salute? Sir? Am I not the king? Bow, and address me by my proper title," Rason demanded, giving the tired soldier an angry, withering stare.

Annoyance briefly flashed across the legionary's face before he bowed low, his armour clinking as he did so.

"Now, what do you want?" Rason said airily. "I gave captain Odrin clear orders that I was to not be interrupted. I have a coronation to prepare for after all."

Again, the soldier scowled at his general's arrogant tone. "Sire," he said through gritted teeth, "the city's populace is growing restless. We've seen rioting in some parts of the city, and a large mob is heading this way. Captain Odrin requests that you order more troops to the manor. He fears that what men we have will not be able to get you to the crowning stone safely." As the solider explained, the sounds of the angry crowd grew in volume. A crash came from downstairs as a rock was sent through a window.

"Why are the people rioting?" Rason asked in genuine confusion.

"Begging your pardon ... sire, the people ... they say that you don't have the right to wear the crown ... that there is a true heir out there somewhere." The legionary cringed as he spoke.

Rason's face went red. Fury rose within him. His hands twitched uncontrollably. He hadn't betrayed everything he had loved, and worked so hard to achieve, for it to be laid low by rumours and lice-ridden peasants. He glared at the legionary, who looked away. Reaching into his boot, Rason pulled out a knife.

"I am the king!" Rason exploded in rage as he plunged the blade deep into the legionary's throat. Blood sprayed from the wound, splashing onto his fine cloak and face. The soldier's body slumped to the floor with a crash. The dying man gasped, his hands covering the wound in a desperate attempt to stem the flow of blood. His hands quickly grew slippery as he desperately fought for life. Eventually, he went still, eyes open wide in shock.

Rason stared at what he had done for a moment, before wiping the blade clean on the dead man's armour.

"I am the king," he muttered. The sound of the mob grew louder. "If they will not accept me as their king then I will make them."

He left his chamber and walked through the manor house. Portraits of kings and battles from long ago adorned the walls, and a vast golden chandelier hung from the painted ceiling. It was a cacophony of gold and red, designed to exude power and regal majesty to all who would gaze upon it. The staircase was made from crystal so pure that it glinted in the dimmest of light. Statues of marble and obsidian stood on every step. He bounded quickly down the steps to the ground floor.

Four legionaries were bracing the large oak doors, while two more were shooting crossbow bolts from the balcony above which overlooked the courtyard leading to the manor.

"Sire ... we can't hold them much longer. There are hundreds of them out there; they're threatening to torch the place!" One of the soldiers reported. Panic was in the man's eyes, but the long years of legionary training prevented him from fleeing.

Rason walked to a window and peeked outside. Sure enough, there were hundreds of peasants all baying for his blood. Shouts of, "Usurper," and, "Murderer," came from the crowd. After he had killed the council, the populace of the capital had been stunned into obedience. Now rumours had spread, and anger had followed.

He smirked as a peasant fell to a crossbow bolt fired from one the legionaries on the balcony. The bolt pierced the angry woman in the leg, knocking her to the ground. Immediately, other rioters pulled her to safety. He didn't envy the hundred or so soldiers that were preventing the crowd from getting any closer. Rocks were being thrown, as well as rotting veg and pig shit. He was pleased to see that Captain Odrin had formed his men up into a shield wall, an impenetrable barrier of steel.

"I have to reach the crowning stone by noon. Enough of this nonsense ..." Rason muttered. With a nod of his head, the legionaries opened the heavy doors and raised their kite shields high to protect their general and king. The roar of the crowd swept into the manor like a thunderclap, and for a brief moment, Rason hesitated. He shook the concerns away angrily, before stepping outside into the manor's courtyard. The line of legionaries held fast as the crowd tried to force their way through their ranks.

"Bastard!" shouted a man in the crowd.

"You have no right to the crown!" accused a woman.

"Prince Alderlade!" yelled another.

Rason stopped upon hearing the name. None of the common folk knew that name. A realisation struck him like a bolt of lightning.

"Davik!" Rason shouted angrily. They had never found the old warrior's body. Now it was clear that the old king's captain of the guard was spreading unrest amongst the populace. Rason raised his right arm into the air and thrust it at the crowd. They had tried his patience; now they would see that it was not wise to anger their king.

Captain Odrin saw his general's arm fall, and he swallowed hard. He knew what the command meant; it meant that things would only get worse in the capital now. He swore under his breath; he'd joined the legion to defend the people, not to massacre them.

At first, he had believed that Rason was the man to take the crown, but as rumours spread of a true heir, doubts had crept in. It didn't help that his general had become drunk on power. Before Rason's bid for power, Odrin had just been a private. Only the executions of his superiors had shot him up the ranks. Now his head was on the line; he had to obey or else he would die.

"Draw swords!" he barked to his men. Some of them glanced at him uncertainly.

"That crazy fool's going to kill us all," muttered another, a grizzled veteran of numerous campaigns against the wild tribes and Yundols. But despite their protests, they drew their weapons.

"Niveren forgive us," Odrin prayed quietly. The captain drew his sword, and the butchery began.

Rason was happy. The crowd was silent. It was also dead. The grim-faced legionaries had done their work with ruthless efficiency as always. Rason had ordered the manor's terrified servants to put blankets on the blood-soaked path. He didn't want to ruin his shiny boots.

Now he was on horseback in a procession of three hundred of his most loyal legionaries. The Sunguard Legion had been tasked with securing the rest of the city, and the smell of smoke and cries of terrified citizens carried on the air.

The marching steps of the legionaries resonated like thunder, and upon seeing the approaching soldiers, people fled back to their homes. Doors were bolted and windows locked as they marched. The people were afraid. Rason didn't see the looks of shame and anger that crossed many of his men's faces.

Word had spread quickly of the bloodbath at the manor, causing many of the rioters to flee, but others were emboldened by the slaughter. Anger was tangible, and as the procession wound its way through the cobbled streets volleys of rotten vegetation battered the soldier's shields. One soldier had been knocked unconscious by a thrown piece of masonry and torn apart by the baying crowds. The city's mood was ugly.

Some of the people had chanted the names of the barons, something once unthinkable before the demise of the Privy Council. The rebel barons had been loathed, but now some were seen as possible saviours from the usurper.

Finally, after a tense journey, they reached the heart of Sunguard.

The Plaza of Kings was a vast open space tiled with marble and other precious stones. Statues lined the plaza's edges and in the centre was a large domed cathedral, inside of which lay the King's Stone, the sacred stone where every king since the creation of the kingdom had been crowned.

The legionaries marched into the plaza, forming up into a pristine formation, their armour and spears glinting in the sunshine. More soldiers took positions around the plaza's edge to block the dozen roads that led into its heart. Mobs of rioters charged the lines on the north side but were repulsed with spear butts and shields.

Rason ignored the racket. All of his attention was now focused on the King's Stone. Standing outside of the large iron and wood doors of the cathedral were half a dozen members of the Chantry. The elders of the realm's sole surviving religion were adorned in their white robes of office, and their tall hats and staffs signalled that they were men of god. Each glanced at the plaza's edge nervously.

Rason trotted his horse to stand before the holy men.

"Archbishop Trentian," the man who would be king said, acknowledging the superior man of the cloth. Trentian was a man in his seventies whose skin was as brown as the sands of the Bison Plain, and his elderly features made him appear as though he was made of paper left under the heat for too long. Lines of age bore deep into the skin, and his yellow-tinged eyes were set deep in his head. A simple moustache of silver hair contrasted starkly with his bald head.

"General Rason," Trentian replied shortly. The other clergymen gasped in horror at their leader's lack of respect. The old man ignored them. He'd seen too many tyrants and fools to be quelled in fear by them.

Rason raised his eyebrows in amusement.

"I think you mean *sire* or *your grace*, Archbishop," he chuckled.

Trentian took a step forward, shaking off the warning hands of his fellow bishops.

"No. I mean *general*. For that is what you are. In no way have you proven that you are anything more to God or to the people of this realm," the old man shouted angrily. He wanted his voice to reach the ears of the soldiers at their general's side.

"Five other claimants to the Sundered Crown still stand and still tear this land apart through their lust for power. Some have legitimate claims. The Baron of Balnor was the dead king's right hand. The Baron of Retbit has support of the eastern lands, and Ricard of Champia is related to the dead queen through marriage to her sister."

The other bishops shrank back from their leader. The legionaries looked away, but unable to ignore the words. Rason simply glared at the archbishop.

Trentian gasped for breath but resumed his tirade. "And then there are the rumours of the prince in hiding. You, Rason, demand to be crowned because you butchered the Privy Council. You have done nothing to prove that you deserve the throne. If you become king, nothing will change. No one will accept you ... they will all still call you the usurper!"

Rason stared silently at the old man. He did not see a hint of fear in his weathered features. Instead, all he saw was belief and defiance. He chafed to draw his sword and take the man's head from his shoulders. Instead, he hesitated. Killing a few nobles and peasants was one thing, but to murder a man of the church was another thing entirely. He sighed angrily.

"Very well Trentian ... you win," he muttered darkly. He wheeled his horse about and galloped towards his legionaries who were standing at attention in the plaza. He trotted to stand before the front ranks. He raised his head and bellowed as loud as he could.

"Soldiers of the legion hear me. People of Sunguard hear me," his voice boomed.

The plaza was designed to carry sound, and his deep, powerful voice rang out to all corners of the square. What the defiant archbishop had said was true. Other claimants still lived. He would destroy them one by one.

"I came here to be crowned a king. Instead, I stand here before you all, and before God to make a vow. I will only return here to claim my throne when all enemies of the realm are defeated. When Retbit, when Balnor, when Bison, when Champia and all the others are carrion for the birds, that is when I will return to you."

He paused for effect.

Already he saw his words were going down well with the legionaries. All they wanted was to restore order; war was in their blood. His next words were aimed at the people.

"I will only return when I can bring peace and security to the people of Delfinnia. To atone for what many see as my crimes, I will vanquish the kingdom's true foes."

"What of Alderlade?" the crowd shouted in response.

Rason swore under his breath. What of the prince indeed? If the rumours were true, then they would never accept Rason as their king. No, if he found the child, he would have to end its life. Discreetly, of course.

He smiled.

"If the rumours are true and an heir yet lives, then I will stand aside and help put him on the throne myself. All I do, I do for you and the realm," he lied.

His smile widened as the crowd's jeers turned into cheers. The legionaries stamped their spears against their shields to show their appreciation for their general's words. Rason waved as the sound rose in volume until it roared like thunder.

He had a war to plan.

CHAPTER 21.

The Sundial crossroads was more than just a road which went off in all directions; it was basically a small bustling, prosperous town. Standing tall and proud was the legendary Sundial Arms, the biggest and rowdiest tavern in Delfinnia. Due to its strategic location, the Sundial had seen its fair share of skirmishes between the rival factions.

This day, the flag of the Baron of Balnor's sigil – an eagle clutching a bar of gold and a hammer in its talons – fluttered gently in the breeze. In a week's time, it would likely be replaced by the legion or Retbit's standard.

A tall, sturdy stone wall encircled the tavern, and a gateway was placed upon every road. Twelve different gates leading off in twelve different directions meant that, technically, Sundial was the heart of the land.

Luxon stared in wonder at the sight of hundreds of people milling about. He listened to the shouts and calls of the many traders, pedlars and other merchants that had set up shop outside and inside the walls. Most of the people appeared tired, their clothes were worn and their boots dusty. Standing tall was a runestone; Sundial was an ideal spot for one, and it was no doubt a major attraction for weary travellers.

Luxon licked his lips in anticipation of a hot meal and, hopefully, a nice comfy bed. The past few days had passed without incident, but the going had been slow as they encountered desperate folk fleeing the war. More than once they had to cross country to avoid bandits and bands of marauding soldiers.

Luckily, Ferran had known the countryside well, and at night he had led them to rune stones to stave off any of the fell beasts. "Refugees from the east and northeast, most like," Kaiden had said.

Now, as they approached Sundial, he held a hand up to shield his eyes from the sun's glare. "There should be an outpost of the Knights of Niveren here. I will ride ahead and see if I can make contact. It would be useful to learn the news of the land before we venture forth."

Ferran nodded in agreement. "Be my guest, sir knight. More knowledge couldn't do us any harm. We will meet you inside the Sundial Arms. I for one could do with a bath and a warm meal." It was the first time Luxon had seen the Nightblade smile. The hardness of his stern, slender face slipped away, and Luxon saw kindness in his dark eyes.

The others cheered the Nightblade's words before heading off after the knight and into the bustling Sundial.

The Sundial lived up to its reputation. Entering the huge tavern, the riotous sounds of drunks laughing, bards playing and people yelling was like a wall of noise. Ferran led the way through the crowds of people. Luxon had never been anywhere so loud or so busy; not even Caldaria's market got as chaotic as the Sundial tavern. They shouldered their way to a large oak reception desk, behind which sat a very thin and flustered-looking man. Alira stayed close to Luxon, her delicate hands holding tightly to his cloak.

"I swear! More guests, I presume!" the thin man cried despairingly, throwing his hands in the air theatrically. "I'll tell you lot what I told the last hundred or so poor sods: there is no more room at the Sundial tavern!"

Ferran glared at the man, causing him to shift uncomfortably. The Nightblade leaned on the desk and gestured for the tavern's owner to come closer.

"We have been on the road for over a week. We need food, a place to bathe and a place to sleep," he whispered into the man's ear.

"I am sorry, sir, but as you can see, we are overwhelmed. Refugees from Eclin and the mountain lands have swamped us, not to mention all the soldiers, and then—" The man was cut short as Ferran's hand snapped outward and grabbed him by his collar. The thin man squeaked.

"I am a Nightblade." The tavern owner's eyes widened as he spotted the tourmaline sword on Ferran's belt. "I am tired, as are my companions. I'm sure you don't want to anger me ... I may turn you into something unpleasant."

The tavern owner went visibly pale.

"P-p-please don't turn me anything unnatural!" he cried. "There is a room ... just become available ... it is on the tenth floor, the far chamber ... it has a bathroom and everything, sir! Here take the key!"

Ferran loosened his grip to allow the terrified tavern owner to pull a key from inside his tunic. Ferran smiled.

"That will do nicely. Thank you."

The room was huge. It was obviously the tavern keeper's own private room. A fine velvet couch was surrounding by other opulently decorated chairs, and the walls were a rich red complete with ornate gold trim. A rug made of a snow bear's hide lay in front of a large fireplace which was roaring away.

Yepert lay on one of the couches, stuffing his face with fruit from a bowl sat on a small wooden table. Alira sat in front of the fire brushing her long blond hair. Luxon, meanwhile, sat looking out of the large glass window which overlooked the tavern's large courtyard.

"I can't believe how good that bath was," Alira sighed happily.

Luxon chuckled as he heard the happy singing of Ferran who was at that moment scrubbing his back in the next room's large bathtub.

"Who'd have thought a Nightblade would enjoy baths so much?" Alira laughed.

"You knew him before all this, didn't you, Sophia?" Luxon asked, turning to face the witch hunter who was lazing on another couch. She had taken off her armour and now wore a simple white tunic and long brown cotton trousers; her hair was still damp from her own dip in the tub.

"Yes … I knew him. There isn't much to tell," Sophia replied quietly, pain evident in her voice. She sat up and walked closer to the fire. "Changing the subject, where did Kaiden get to? He's been gone a good hour, and the sun is setting."

"Oh yes … I forgot all about him," Alira said sheepishly. "I was enjoying the bath too much."

Kaiden was hiding. From behind a bale of hay, he could see the crimson cloaked figures stalking along the stables. The smell of horse dung and straw was almost overwhelming. The Sundial's stables were able to house over two hundred horses, and every stall was occupied. He had come to feed Herald after he had contacted one of his brother knights. The horse was standing nearby happily munching on some sugar cubes that Kaiden had bought from a scrawny old pedlar in the tavern's courtyard.

He hadn't been in the stables long when he heard the rickety wooden door slide open. Slowly and methodically, the Crimson Blade assassins had gone from stall to stall with their familiar curved daggers in their hands.

Kaiden edged further back into Herald's stall, hoping that the shadows would hide him.

"Good day sir … oh, my; nooo!"

The petrified cry came from a stall further down the row. A woman's voice was cut short as the assassins slit her throat. Kaiden wracked his brain. The woman had been one of the Sundial's stable staff. He whispered a prayer for her soul.

He went still as one of the robed killers stopped at Herald's pen. Slowly, the door swung open. Kaiden held his breath. What were they doing here? Were they looking for him and his companions? His worries were confirmed when he saw another assassin enter the pen.

"That is the knight's horse. It matches the description. They are here," said the killer. The voice was strange, otherworldly, like an echo that carried on for too long.

"All we need is the information the knight carries. Refrain from killing him and his companions; the mistress wants them alive," rasped the other assassin.

Kaiden itched to draw his sword and to get some payback for what they had done to him in Caldaria, but with six against one, he didn't favour those odds. He stayed still. So far, the bales of hay and the shadows kept him hidden. The letter tucked away in his mantle felt heavy.

"The other knight knew nothing," whispered the killer who had first entered the pen. His black gloved hands ran absently over Herald's flank, causing the horse to snort and stamp its feet. The animal's eyes were wide with fear as it smelt the blood oozing from the corpse in the nearby stall. The other horses were also beginning to panic. Whinnies and snorts grew louder; some of the animals banged against their pens' doors.

Kaiden sighed in relief. The racket that the panicked horses were making would surely draw attention.

"Hello. What's going on in here?" called someone from outside. Other voices joined the first as the horses' owners came to check on the disturbance. The assassins stopped their searching and silently slipped out of the pen. The stable's main door slid open. A dozen men armed with clubs and flaming torches entered.

"There's a body in here!" someone cried.

Kaiden let out a breath that he hadn't realised he was holding. The assassins had somehow vanished. He stood and placed a calming hand on Herald's nose. He had to warn the others that they were being followed.

CHAPTER 22.

Caldaria

Grand Master Thanos was in his study reading when a knock at his study door disturbed him. Irritably, he closed the tome and tiredly rubbed his eyes. Ever since Luxon and the others had departed the mage city, he had been troubled by nightmares.

Visions of great battles and of monsters plagued him, and all the while the sight of seeing Caldaria aflame burned into his mind. He couldn't help but feel as though he had missed something, and he was sure the N'gist was involved.

Despite his weariness, he had pored through the tomes in the great library, desperate to find any clue as to where the amulets that had almost brought the mages' low could have come from. He'd recruited over a dozen apprentices to assist him, but all had so far come up empty-handed.

He waved a hand at the door and muttered a simple spell. The door swung open. Standing in the doorway was Master Dufran. The man's normally bright green eyes were dull and ringed. He, like the other masters, had been suffering nightmares as well.

"What is it, Dufran?" Thanos asked tiredly. He stretched his limbs. He felt old.

Dufran rubbed his bald head.

"I have some disturbing news, Grand Master. It appears something has been stolen from the artefact vault in the Grand Tower."

Thanos stood up quickly.

"Impossible. Those vaults are magically sealed. Only I and the other masters can open it. What was stolen?" A worm of dread tightened in his gut. He knew something was not right. He had felt it since the Baron of Redbit's raid.

Dufran entered the chamber, a look of disbelief on his wise face.

"The staff of Aljeron is missing," Dufran answered.

Thanos took a step backwards and leaned heavily against his crystal desk. His mind whirled. Impossible!

"The staff of the Void ... Do you realise the damage someone could do with that staff?" Thanos cried. "If someone were to use it ... they could open a rift to the Void!"

"The staff of the first wizard had been sealed behind four magical barriers and encased in an enchanted chest," Dufran explained. "It would have taken someone with immense power to breach those defences. None of the masters would do such a thing; they realise the dangers."

"The attack by the baron ... it was all a diversion. A distraction to allow someone to steal the staff," Thanos whispered as the realisation came to him that they had all been played for fools.

"Even the Baron of Retbit would not be so foolish as to use something so dangerous," Dufran said dismissively.

"No. I don't think the baron knew of this. I could see it in his eyes that he genuinely believed that he was here to force us into helping him in the war. No, something else is behind all this. The nightmares I have been having ... they make sense now. The monsters I have seen in my mind are from the Void." He paused and looked at Dufran in horror. "Someone intends to unleash the Void upon the world ... perhaps even set Vectrix free."

"There are worse things than Vectrix in the Void ..." Dufran muttered.

CHAPTER 23.

The Sundial was behind them as they galloped as fast as they could away from the danger. They had let their guard down, and now they were the prey of the realm's most vicious killers. After Kaiden burst into the room to tell them of his run in with the assassins, Ferran had wasted no time in ordering them to move on.

Kaiden had found his contact at the knight's outpost dead with his throat cut, and the outpost itself had been ransacked. Now they were heading east at speed on the Balnor Road. Such was their haste that the Nightblade had ordered them to press on without the protection of the rune stones.

Luxon was exhausted. For three days and nights, they had ridden without much rest, too scared to stay still for long. Now, the darkness of the night had come again with only the faint reflected glow of Esperia's three moons lighting the way. Thick forest was on either side of the road, and only the sounds of night creatures broke the silence. The others were all feeling weary. Yepert was asleep in his saddle, and even Ferran looked bleary-eyed.

Alira, meanwhile, looked fresh-faced and alert.

"How far to Tentiv?" Luxon asked.

Sophia, who was riding next to him, put a finger to her lips.

"We must be quiet," she whispered. "These woods are not safe. The road to Tentiv is not far; we should come across it by the morning. The Fallen Wood is ..." She paused as Ferran stopped his horse. The Nightblade was at the front of the group, his hand in the air to signal the halt. Kaiden reached over and poked Yepert softly, stirring the boy from his slumber.

Luxon listened. The sounds of life had ceased. No owls hooted, and no crickets chirped. Even the trees themselves seemed to have resorted to holding their breath in anticipation of something.

A twig snapped in the undergrowth to his right, making him turn his head and stare into the foliage. He narrowed his eyes to try and see, cursing the faint moonlight.

He almost cried out as he saw shadows darting through the undergrowth. He hoped it was some boar like those they had seen earlier in their journey, and not some fell beast.

He looked at Ferran as the Nightblade slowly drew his tourmaline sword. Kaiden, too, unsheathed his blade, and Sophia carefully unslung her bow and notched an arrow.

"Get behind me," Kaiden said to Alira and Yepert, his sword held aloft in an en guard stance. The long steel blade was angled towards the ground, ready to deflect any sudden strikes from the trees. Luxon drew the knife from his cloak, his hands sweaty with expectation.

The scurrying figures had multiplied in number. Now he could even smell the creatures. Small white dots glared out of the dark forest, giving away their position. Luxon shivered as he realised the dots were eyes reflecting the dull moonlight. The whole forest seemed to be full of them.

A tense silence descended upon the group as they held their breaths. The scurrying noise continued, and with horror, Luxon realised that they were being surrounded. He turned around slowly to face the opposite tree line, fearful that any sudden movement would set off whatever was hiding amongst the trees. He stifled a cry as he saw hundreds of eyes glinting back at him.

Suddenly, without warning, the tree line exploded outwards in a foray of twigs, leaves and mud. The creatures charged out of the trees with a frightening high pitched roar.

With a whiny, Luxon's pony reared, throwing him to the ground.

Dazed, he could see that the others had tumbled from their mounts. All save Yepert, who was yelling with fear, and Kaiden, who leapt from the saddle. Ferran staggered to his feet just in time to parry an attack.

The first Puck ran straight at Luxon. Its short brown body was covered in long, sharp black hairs; its eyes were small white dots, and its mouth was opened wide to reveal a set of vicious looking teeth. In its clawed hand was a primitive spear, which it now pointed at Luxon's chest.

Without thinking, Luxon dove to the side, the spear point missing his heart by mere inches. He fell heavily onto the road, rolling onto his side as the Puck thrust its spear down where he had fallen. All around him the road had erupted into chaos.

Ferran was hacking and slashing wildly, the glow of his magic sword illuminating the night as it cleaved through the horde of Pucks. At his side was Kaiden, who was also swinging his blade with a skill and precision that only a lifetime of training could allow. Luxon took in the scene in a split second before he turned his attention back to the snarling Puck which paced towards him.

He lashed out with the knife, causing the goblin-like creature to snarl derisively. With its spear, it batted the knife out of his hand, sending it wheeling away into the dark. Panic threatened to overwhelm Luxon. All around, the Pucks swarmed. Only the swords of the Nightblade and knight kept Yepert and Alira safe. There was no one to help Luxon. The Puck leapt into the air, its spear held high and ready to kill.

Luxon shut his eyes in anticipation of the blow.

It never came.

The Puck crashed to the ground; an arrow lodged in its brain. Luxon spun to see Sophia standing behind him. The witch hunter grabbed his hand and hurried him between the terrified horses and ponies.

"Stay with the animals. We cannot allow these beasts to eat our only forms of transport!" she yelled over the screams and chaos. She put another arrow on the bowstring and loosed it into the ever-building crowd of monsters.

CHAPTER 23.

Yepert was shouting at the monsters. If a Puck drew too close, he lashed out with his own knife or lobbed a magical ball of fire at them. Three crispy corpses lay at the boy's feet. Luxon had never seen his friend so determined or so courageous in the face of danger.

"Get the horses out of here!" yelled Ferran. Even with his magic and tourmaline blade, the Nightblade was being overrun. He slashed his sword left and right, cleaving several Pucks asunder before using a telekinetic blast to send a dozen more flying backwards into the trees.

Kaiden parried a spear thrust before kicking his attacker in the face. His sword whirled as he rotated his wrists and thrust downwards with a mighty blow that cut the attacking Puck in half. A cut in his side had turned his white mantle red, but the knight ignored the pain. He calmed Herald and urged Yepert and the others to do the same, before spurring the warhorse with a kick of his heels.

Alira screamed as a dozen Pucks swarmed over her pony. Luxon watched as a Puck leapt at her. It snarled and snapped its jaws but did not strike.

Alira stared at the creature. Her lips moved and then the Puck turned away to join its friends in devouring her pony.

What the? Luxon thought.

The pony's piteous whinnies of terror were cut short as a Puck ripped the animal's throat out with its vicious teeth. Yepert grabbed the terrified girl's hand before climbing into the saddle of his own mount.

Luxon also ran to his pony and clambered into the saddle. Sophia continued to shoot arrow after arrow to hold the Pucks at bay. Yepert had mounted his pony and galloped after the knight. Alira sat behind him; her hands wrapped tightly around his waist. Luxon waited until he was sure that his friend had escaped before spurring his own mount into action.

The night whizzed past at speed as his pony galloped as fast as it could. The dark forest made it difficult to see. All around him he could hear the sounds of the Pucks. The trees whipped by and in the dark depths of the forest he could see thousands of white eyes watching him ride. He glanced behind him to see Sophia and Ferran on their horses riding hard to catch up with the others.

"Up high!" Ferran yelled.

Luxon looked to the sky. More of the Pucks were high in the treetops swinging from tree to tree at a terrifying pace.

"Keep riding! There must be a rune stone somewhere ahead!" the Nightblade shouted over the sounds of the horses' hooves and excited Pucks. The monsters had smelled and tasted blood. Now they wanted more.

Luxon concentrated and felt the familiar tingle of energy manifest itself. He watched as a Puck dove down from the trees at Yepert and Alira. He raised a hand and unleashed a bolt of lightning from his palm. The Puck was struck and sent whirling away to smash into a tree with a sickening squelch. More dropped from the trees, but Luxon blasted every one that threatened his companions. His hair was smoking, and his arms tingled as the magical lightning was unleashed.

"We're clear of the trees!" Ferran called from behind him.

Luxon gasped in relief. Sure enough, the group had cleared the dense forest to emerge into a wide clearing. His relief instantly evaporated at what he saw.

Scattered about the clearing were the rotting corpses of a dozen men in the livery of the Knights of Niveren. Weapons were scattered about, and blood was everywhere. Kaiden had halted his horse to stare in horror at the sight of his fallen comrades.

Ferran galloped up to the knight. "We cannot linger; the Pucks are too many. Your brother knights failed in their quest. Make sure we do not meet the same fate." Ferran grabbed Kaiden's arm firmly. "Come!"

The knight nodded, unable to hide the emotions coursing through him. The group rode on.

If they had lingered a little longer, however, they would have noticed that the dead knights had not been slain by Pucks but by assassins' blades. They were riding into even greater danger.

CHAPTER 24.

The tree was there, the one from his dreams. The moons shone dimly upon the hilltop, and in their faint glow there stood a twisted tree. In the distance, atop a tall outcrop of stone, sat the citadel of Tentiv.

They had lost the Pucks a few miles back, but still Ferran had insisted that they press on.

Luxon slowed his pony to a halt and stared at the tree. His stomach knotted with fear as the dream flashed before his eyes. Large and ominous black clouds were rolling in on the horizon, promising rain. He flinched as the clouds lit up brightly, the distant thunderclap reaching his ears only moments later.

"We have to keep moving," Ferran shouted over the noise of the thunder. "Tentiv is near. We can find shelter from that storm there."

A light rain began to fall, and the horizon lit as another bolt of lightning split the sky.

The others moved onward, but Luxon stayed rooted to the spot. He held the reigns tightly as his pony tried to move forward and follow its fellows. Luxon wouldn't let it. Something terrible was about to happen, he knew. He had seen it.

Yepert noticed his friend's apprehension. He turned his pony and trotted over to Luxon, whose face had gone a deathly white and whose eyes were wide with fear. Alira dismounted, her long hair blowing in the ever-strengthening wind.

"Luxon? What is the matter? We must keep up with the others," she said soothingly. She placed a hand on the pony's neck and whispered calming words into its ear. Even the animal could sense its master's worry.

"This place, I have seen it in my dreams. We must not go onward. Only horror await us, I know it," Luxon cried. He looked at his friends. They were looking at him as though he were mad. Sadness filled Yepert's eyes. Alira simply glared at him.

The girl took his hand in hers. "What do you believe is over that hill?" she whispered.

Thunder rumbled, causing them all to flinch.

Luxon glanced away and saw a shadow standing at the side of the road. He could see that it was a person; he could just make out the shape of a tall, robed figure. The figure raised an arm and pointed with a long, unnatural finger. It was the spectre from his dream.

Just like his dream, a menacing laugh came out of the darkness. Was it all in his mind?

That thought was put to rest when he saw a look of pure terror on Yepert's face. His friend fell backwards out of his saddle with a heavy thud and lay unmoving in the road.

Luxon was confused. That was until he realised that the laugh was not coming from the spectre. He followed the direction of the spectres finger, and looked straight into a set of black, evil eyes.

He screamed as the girl who he knew as Alira gripped him around the throat and flung him from the saddle. Her blond hair had turned black, her young face twisted into a maniacal and feral grin, and her eyes ... her eyes were now full of malice and hate.

With impossible speed she was upon him. Her hands, that had only moments before been slim and delicate, were now like talons. He screamed for help, but no one came to his rescue; not this time. The sharp nails raked across his chest as she savagely clawed at him.

"You are mine! You will not ruin my plans!" Alira screamed into his face. Spittle covered Luxon as her insanity-strengthened limbs threatened to tear him asunder.

In reflex, he focused and pushed. Magic flowed through him once again.

"Get off of me!" he yelled in rage. The telekinetic blast knocked Alira away, sending her sprawling in a tangle of limbs.

"What are you?" Luxon screamed as he scrambled back onto his feet. He whipped his robe open to free his arms and settled into the fighting stance taught to him by Master Ri'ges.

Instead of standing, the thing that had only moments before been a beautiful girl rose from the ground to float ghost-like before him. Her torn black hair radiated around her like some corrupted halo. Her features were of an old hag instead of a young woman.

Luxon flinched as he heard pained cries coming from over the hill. The thing that had been Alira turned to look and cackled wickedly.

"Your friends are now mine. You are mine. Your quest is over. Everything has gone according to plan."

Luxon stared at the thing. He gulped as he realised what she was.

"You're a witch ... the witch the Baron of Retbit mentioned in Caldaria. You were behind the attack on the city ... You ... You ...Why?" he shouted. Anger filled him. The witch had played them all for fools. But for what purpose, he had no clue.

The witch raised her arm and screamed. A blast of powerful magic slammed into Luxon, knocking him down once more. A wave of dizziness threatened to send him crumpling to the ground, but he focused and regained his footing.

The witch appeared surprised.

With a shout, Luxon retaliated with magic of his own. Fire erupted from his palms to engulf the witch and the nearby foliage. He fell to his knees in exhaustion, his energy depleted. He groaned when the cackling laughter mocked him. The witch floated above him; not a hair on her head had been harmed.

Again, the witch raised a hand, and this time she sent Luxon to oblivion.

Pain was in every inch of his battered body. Luxon groaned as he regained consciousness. Had it all just been a bad dream? He hoped that he would open his eyes and find himself in a nice warm bed back in Caldaria. His hopes were raised when he felt a hand brush his cheek gently.

"Hannah?" he muttered deliriously.

He opened his eyes and wished he hadn't.

Sophia was kneeling over him. Her face was a patchwork of bruises and her lips were bloody. She looked like hell.

"Thank Niveren you're alive," she sighed in relief.

She helped Luxon into a sitting position before pulling a dirty rag from her belt. Tentatively, she pressed the cloth to the back of his head causing him to cry out in pain. The rag came away bloody.

Luxon looked around. They were inside what appeared to be a small prison cell. A row of iron bars blocked any chance of escape. Beyond the cell was a single flickering candle placed upon a wooden table.

"Where are we?" he asked. He knew he wouldn't like the answer.

Sophia frowned.

"We are inside Tentiv. Prisoners of the witch," she replied. Her eyes were ringed with bruises. She took his left hand and put it over the rag. "Hold it to the wound; it should stop the bleeding."

"Alira is the witch," Luxon said simply. He couldn't believe it; he hoped it was all just some trick.

Sophia nodded. A look of anger crossed her battered features.

"She said she had a plan. That I was a part of it," Luxon went on miserably. Surely he should have known; the old pedlars they had met on the road had known something was amiss with Alira. Did they know what she truly was?

"We heard your cries for help, but we were ambushed by dozens of Crimson Blade assassins. Whoever she is, she is in league with them," Sophia said angrily. The witch hunter paced the tiny cell like a caged animal. Her hands clenched and unclenched.

"I should have seen through her. I am a witch hunter – killing bitches like her is my job. If she has hurt the others ..." She didn't need to finish that sentence; Luxon knew what she was going to say. He felt the same.

"We need to get out of here," Sophia growled.

"What about the Diasect? Where are they?" Luxon asked, gingerly dabbing his head with the rag. The bleeding appeared to have stopped for now. Slowly, he got to his feet. Dizziness washed over him, but he leaned against the cell's cold stone wall to save himself from falling over.

"They dragged us through the citadel," Sophia explained. "The bodies of the monks tasked to defend this place were everywhere. Most had rotted to skeletons. The Diasect ... they're gone. I think the witch took this place a long time ago."

"Who is she?" Luxon asked. In all his reading at Caldaria, he had never heard of a witch so powerful. He had used all of his magic and she had laughed it off. In all the history books, only Danon had been so strong.

Before Sophia could answer, the sound of a heavy metal door grinding open reverberated throughout the dungeon. Footsteps approached their cell, causing Sophia to back away from the bars to stand protectively over the wounded Luxon.

A crimson-robed assassin stood before the cell; their features hidden in the shadow cast by his hood.

"She will see you now," the assassin said, his voice barely higher than a whisper. It didn't sound like a voice from this world but from some distant place. The Crimson Blades had long been a mystery to the peoples of Delfinnia. Legend and myth surrounded them.

Some said that they were just mortal men and women that killed for coin, whereas others believed that they were from the Void, while others said that they served the N'gist cult. From all he had experienced of them, Luxon believed the latter. What they actually were, he hadn't a clue. They did not move and speak like normal men. Perhaps they *were* from the void.

The assassin pulled a large iron key from out of his sleeve and unlocked the cell door. It swung open slowly with a creak.

Sophia wasted no time. She charged at the assassin with a shout. She swung a fist at the robed figure, who casually ducked out of the way. When she swung again, the assassin's own hand shot out, grabbing hold of the witch hunter's fist. Sophia cried out as she was sent to her knees by the assassin's powerful grip. Tears streamed from her eyes as more pressure was exerted.

"I could snap your arm clean off, witch hunter!"

Sophia cried out in relief as the assassin released his grip. Sophia protectively clutched her arm close to her body. Casually, he pushed Sophia aside to lean over Luxon. With no effort, Luxon was lifted into the air and placed over the assassin's shoulder. Luxon tried to struggle, but the wound to his head caused the world to spin. He tried to use magic but found that he could not concentrate.

With Luxon over his shoulder the assassin grabbed Sophia and hauled her onto her feet.

"Come. She is waiting."

CHAPTER 25.

As he was carried, all Luxon could see was the stone floor. He lost track of the layout of the place as the assassin turned left then right numerous times. At one point, they ascended a flight of wide stone steps upon which lay a skeleton still wearing the blue and gold robes of the monks who had been tasked with protecting the Diasect.

Finally, they reached a large chamber. Flickering candles gave off the only light, casting eerie shadows upon the high-vaulted walls and arched ceiling. Upon the walls were tapestries depicting events from Delfinnia's history. Intricate runes were carved into the stone walls and precious gems glimmered in the candlelight.

The assassin dumped Luxon onto the ground with a thud and shoved Sophia down onto her knees. Luxon sat up to see the others. They too were on their knees, their hands bound behind their backs.

Ferran's face was pale, and like Sophia's, bloody and bruised. Around his neck hung an N'gist amulet like the one used by the baron of Retbit during his raid on Caldaria. Luxon could sense the amulet's dark power sucking the magic out of the beaten Nightblade.

Next to him was Kaiden. His face was one of pure misery. His right eye was wounded and bleeding, the crimson dripping onto the floor. His mantle had been stripped from him and his armour taken so that he shivered in the coldness of Tentiv.

Luxon paused. He couldn't see Yepert. A knot of terror wriggled in his gut. Where was his friend? Had he been killed?

"Ah, you're all here. Delightful," the witch cackled as she entered the chamber through a large metal door in the far wall. Two long crimson banners hung from the ceiling on either side of the doorway. A faint image of a black dagger was emblazoned on each.

Luxon gasped. The witch was no longer the hag that had thrown him from his pony. She once again looked like a young girl. He glanced over to see Kaiden struggle against his bindings as he saw her.

"Show your true self, witch!" the knight cried out, pain evident in his voice.

Alira laughed cruelly. She sauntered over to him and placed a finger under his chin. She raised his head so that he could not look away.

"You have feelings for this body ... I have surpassed even myself," she laughed, "to have a noble Knight of Niveren fall for me. Oh, this is perfect."

She released Kaiden's head and spun away happily her long dress whirling around her. Luxon could feel the knight's pain. Kaiden's expression was one of desolation, and tears threatened to fall from his eyes.

"Stop toying with us, you bitch, and kill us already!" Ferran snapped. The Nightblade was a mass of bruises, but defiance radiated from him like a beacon.

Alira stopped her joyful dance and glared at him. Her eyes narrowed to slits. In the blink of an eye, she crossed the chamber and put her hand tightly about Ferran's throat. With apparently no effort, the man who was a whole head taller than the girl was lifted into the air, his legs kicking as he battled for breath.

Sophia cried out. Ferran's face began to turn blue, his struggles weakened. Luxon looked away; he couldn't watch someone die.

Alira smiled wickedly before tossing the Nightblade across the room like a rag doll. Ferran crashed to the ground, gasping for breath.

"Now is not the time to kill you, Nightblade," she said softly as her gaze settled upon Luxon.

"What do you want with me?" Luxon stammered. Any pretence of defiance had left him. Fear was all that remained. He knew she was more powerful than him. He was no match for her and he was terrified about what she had in store.

Alira laughed mockingly.

"You are the key, Luxon. For many years I had visions of you. Then I set events in motion. The assassination of the royal family, the war – I did it all to lure the one from my visions out into the open, and I did!" She laughed happily, clapping her hands together like a lunatic.

"With magic outlawed, there was only one place you could be: Caldaria. The one place that I couldn't get into. The mages, despite their pathetic powers, would have detected me instantly." She paused and then skipped over to stand in front of Kaiden. "That is why I found this girl," she said as she ran her hands down her body seductively.

Kaiden raised his head to stare at the witch.

"What do you mean?" he growled.

"The girl Alira, she is my vessel. She provides the body that allows me to pass unseen through this world. It is a strategy that has served me well for eons. Do you really think that one as powerful as me would have gone undetected for all this time otherwise?"

Kaiden's eye widened at the revelation.

"The girl tries to struggle," the witch muttered. "Her incessant whining, and her pleading irritates me, but alas I do what must be done."

"Who are you?" Sophia shouted. The revelation had visibly shaken her.

With supernatural speed Alira flitted from the knight to appear before the witch hunter. A look of pure loathing was on her face. It didn't look natural on so pretty a girl.

"I am the first. The bride of he who embraced the darkness at the dawn of time," the witch boasted, raising her arms high into the air for dramatic effect.

"It cannot be ..." Sophia whispered in stunned disbelief. "The bride of Danon himself ..."

Alira lowered her arms, pure malice emanating from her.

Luxon could sense the dark power radiating from her. He found himself short of breath as it threatened to devour them all. The candles in the chamber seemed to fade into shadow, until everything was engulfed in darkness.

"Say ... my ... name!" the witch bellowed. Her voice was unnatural, rasping and tormented, like something from a nightmare.

Sophia stared at the witch unflinchingly. Tears ran down her face as the magnitude of her failure as a witch hunter hit home.

"You are Cliria. The first witch," Sophia whispered.

Cliria smiled and the darkness retreated; the flickering candles once more cast their light across the chamber.

Luxon stared in stunned disbelief. He had read the tales of Danon and of his wife. If true, she was one of the oldest living things in the entire world – tens, if not hundreds, of thousands of years old. His head spun at the revelation.

Time and again, she and her dark lord had threatened the world, and each time they had been bested by heroes. Each victory for the Light however came at a terrible price. Millions had perished in the wars of old, and whole continents had been engulfed in the flames.

His mind raced. He remembered reading a tome about Danon's last appearance in the world.

It had been Zahnia the Great who had ended the thousand year long Dark Age and cast Danon into the Void. His followers had fled into the mountains of the north, where they had skulked and bided their time. Then the Golden Empire had been created. It prospered for centuries until the Magic Wars, and Danon and his kin were forgotten as they faded into myth.

"Now, Luxon. Do you want to know what I have in store for you?" Cliria asked sweetly. She snapped her fingers. A Crimson Blade assassin stepped forward. In his hands was a long golden rod. Cliria carefully took the rod from the killer's hands.

"Do you know what this is?" she asked.

Luxon shook his head. He hadn't a clue.

"Well," the witch said as she tugged on one end of the rod. With a click the rod extended until it was over a meter in length. Luxon could now see that it was a staff, similar to the ones he had seen in books. It was a wizard's staff.

"This staff belonged to the first wizard, Aljeron. I'm sure you've heard of him. It is called the staff of the Void, and it needs powerful magic to charge and to reinvigorate its power." She twirled the staff above her head as she spoke. "And that's where you come in. You see, only you have enough of the magic I need."

Luxon tried to move, tried to struggle against his bindings – anything to escape.

"Why me? What makes me so special?" he cried.

Cliria laughed piteously, revelling in the young mage's terror. Luxon looked to his companions desperately, hoping that one of them had a plan to escape, that he would not befall the fate the witch had planned for him. All he saw was Ferran struggling against his bindings, Kaiden shouting at the witch, and Sophia trying to stand.

"You do not know? Oh, even better!" the witch cackled. She pointed the staff at him and touched it to his forehead. He tried to escape, but two assassins held him firmly in place.

"With this sacrifice, I imbue this staff with the power of old. With this staff, I open the Void between worlds and set free my beloved. With this staff I will unleash untold horror upon this world, and no one will stop us. Once again, the N'gist will thrive and I will take my rightful place as Queen of the World,"

"What of the heir to the Sundered Crown!" Kaiden shouted.

Cliria stopped her incantation. She spun around to glare at the knight.

"Have you forgotten, Alira? Have you forgotten your vision? In it, there was a light that pushed back the darkness ... pushed you back. As long as he lives you will not have victory," Kaiden growled.

The witch hesitated. Doubt was in her eyes.

A woman, scared and alone, clutches a small child to her chest. A blinding light: a halo of fire surrounds the child, casting back the darkness.

She shook the vision from her thoughts.

"You try to distract me, knight. The child is of little importance," Cliria said dismissively.

Kaiden stared unflinchingly.

"Then why go to all of the trouble of killing my contact at the Sundial? You knew my order had learned of his location."

The others gasped at his revelation.

"When were you going to tell us?" Ferran growled.

The witch cackled again.

"You failed, knight. I have your note." She snapped her fingers at one of the assassins, who pulled a sealed envelope from his tunic. It was the one Kaiden had received at the inn. Cliria broke the seal. As she read, her face grew red in fury.

"This is a recipe for Plock stew!" she screamed in rage.

Luxon could have laughed. It was one of Yepert's recipes from his notebook. The knight must have swapped the note with it. His glee at Kaiden outwitting the witch faded however when he realised that now she must surely notice that his friend was not here. And sure enough, she did.

"There is one missing ...the fat, stupid boy!" Cliria shouted. She smashed the staff over the head of the nearest assassin, who crumpled to the ground.

"There was no other when we reached you, mistress," hissed one of the assassins.

"He must have crawled away and fled into the forest; you fool!" Cliria snapped.

"You're not so powerful. Silly bitch, can't even count!" Ferran chuckled. His laughter was cut short by a savage blow delivered by the assassin standing nearest to him. The blow knocked the Nightblade unconscious.

"Find the boy! Kill him, and take the note he carries," Cliria ordered.

CHAPTER 26.

The stench of decay was almost overwhelming in the tiny cell in which Luxon found himself. The chains holding him up off the ground were biting into his wrists and ankles. His body shivered against the cold.

A rat squeaked as it scurried around his feet. Its beady little eyes regarding him for a moment before it resumed its circuit of the cell. He looked at it with tired eyes, envying its freedom.

A pained scream emanated from deeper within the dungeons. He flinched at the tortured sounds. The rat stopped, sniffed the air and ran off back through the small hole it had emerged from.

For hours, the cries had come. He wasn't sure whose turn it was, but all of them had endured the rack, the whippings, and the thumbscrews. The scream grew in volume until it ceased suddenly. He winced. What new torment had Cliria devised for them now?

Their torturers had only asked one question: where would Yepert be heading?

He had not said a word, but only screamed in pain. He hoped his friend was safe, but it was doubtful that he would have escaped the Fallen Wood by himself. Pucks and other foul beasts stalked those lands. One comfort he had was that the note Yepert carried had scared the witch. Her thoughts were hell bent on finding the child. Kaiden was right: she feared the prince.

Footsteps and the sound of something being dragged came from down the hall. Two assassins walked past his cell. Being dragged between them was Kaiden. The knight's body was a mass of bloody cuts and bruises. His head flopped loosely so that it almost hit the floor. He was out cold.

Luxon would have called out, but only a fist would have been the prize for his trouble. Instead, he shut his eyes and delved into his thoughts. He smiled as he thought of Hannah but felt sadness as well. It was a sadness which came from his fear that he would never see her again, that he had broken the promise he had made at the city gate in Caldaria.

For the first time in a long while, his thoughts flitted to memories of his mother. He hadn't seen nor heard from her in three years and he wondered where she had gone. She had been tall and fair, with an elegance that most of the women in the royal court envied.

He remembered walking through the high market of Sunguard, smiling as he noticed the jealous looks coming from the highborn ladies. His mother always smelt of lavender petals and her long brown sandy hair of jasmine. Around her neck, she always wore a silver pendant, with a golden serpent embossed on a blue background engraved upon its surface.

"No way!" Luxon blurted out. He instantly shut his mouth, not wanting to attract the attention of his jailers. His eyes were wide as his brain raced a mile a minute.

The pendant she had worn ... the symbol was the same he had seen on the robes of the dead Diasect monks. He shook his head. No ... it couldn't be. She was just the wife of a courtier, not some mysterious figure. Doubts crept into his conscious. Why had she abandoned him at Caldaria? Where had she gone? And how did she know that he had magic?

Before that fateful night when the royal family was murdered, he had just been a normal boy, completely oblivious to his powers. Only when he had arrived in Caldaria had he learnt what he was.

His thoughts were cut short by the sound of approaching footsteps. He moaned as the witch, and two of her assassins stepped into the candlelight that flickered away in front of his tiny cell. She had changed out of the clothes that Alira had worn. The long dress and travel tunic had been replaced by a long tightly fitting dress of pure black, which accentuated every curve of her lithe young body. Her hair hung long and loose about her shoulders. If he didn't know what she was, he would have thought her beautiful. Instead, all he felt was fear and loathing.

"Your friend will not get far," she mocked as she twirled a strand of her hair with a finger. "I will learn of the little prince's whereabouts, and I will kill him. And as for you; now is the time for us to resume where we left off."

He was too weak to struggle. The two assassins opened the cell door and unlocked the chains on his wrists. He cried out as the blood rushed back into his numb limbs. He was roughly pulled from the wall and dragged out into the dungeon's hall. Even the dim light of the candle hurt his eyes as they adjusted from the darkness of the dank cell.

As he was being dragged, he looked to his right to see other cells carved into the stone. Several were empty; others had skeletons still hanging from their chains. Despite his predicament, he could not help but wonder about had happened to the Diasect and the monks that guarded the sacred fortress.

As if hearing his thoughts Cliria spoke. "The Diasect have long been an enemy of mine. It was such a good feeling to come here and take this place as my own. The long years of isolation made them weak, and their attitude of self-importance had left them cut off from the realities of the world. Instead of watching, they were too busy counting their coins – a pathetic end to such a powerful group. They thought themselves so wise, the council that guarded the world. Ha!" she laughed mirthlessly.

Luxon glanced at her. So, the Diasect were people after all, flaws and all.

"What did you do?" he asked, wincing as his foot was dragged over a sharp stone.

Cliria slowed her stride so that she was walking just in front of him.

"My servants here," she said, gesturing to the assassins as if that would explain everything. In some ways it did. Luxon shuddered.

"The Diasect councillors were here ... all save one, who escaped. Each one was the descendant of the wizards of old. Ironic isn't it? Your kings outlawed magic, and yet they took advice and guidance from those whose bloodlines were full of the stuff. I strung them up, one by one until they told me what I wanted to know."

"And that was?" Luxon asked. Despite his weariness, he was interested in what the witch was saying. His inquisitive nature was getting the better of him.

"The knowledge I needed to bring back my beloved," she replied. In her left hand was the staff of Aljeron in its shortened form. She lifted it to show her prisoner.

"They told me where to find this, what it will do and how to recharge its power. Only after I flayed them alive of course," she added with a cruel laugh.

"And that's where I come in?" Luxon guessed.

They reached a large stone door which one of the assassins pulled open with little effort. A set of stone steps led upwards. Cliria didn't reply until they had crested the steps. Now they were back in the main chamber.

"You are of his bloodline," Cliria explained with a smile, "and the son of the one Diasect councillor who I could not find – the woman that hid you from me for all this time, your mother." She was relishing the shocked expression that crossed Luxon's face. His mind reeled. His wild suggestion was right? His mother had been one of the Diasect! He closed his eyes. Tears fell. It answered so many questions and mysteries. All of those times when he was little that she was absent. For months at a time, his mother was not there, his father being the one to care for him. This explained why she had fled, why she had abandoned him at Caldaria, and how she knew of his powers. They were the descendants of the first wizard, the one who had sealed the rupture to the Void aeons ago.

"A wizard's staff only works when it detects the power of its creator. Magic is like blood; it is passed on. And so only a descendant of Aljeron will power his staff. I would have used your mother, but she eluded my grasp. You will do very nicely instead. You have a unique gift, the blood of a wizard and powerful magic. Yes, you will do very nicely," Cliria mocked.

With a gesture, the two assassins shoved Luxon to the ground, grabbed his arms and held him in place. Cliria took the rod and once again extended it until it became the staff. She touched it to his forehead again.

"Now, we shall see if all my trials were worth the risk ..." the witch muttered to herself.

She gripped the staff with two hands and pushed it firmly against Luxon's head. He tried to struggle, but an assassin gripped him firmly about the neck, holding his head in place.

Once again, she spoke her dark incantation.

"With this sacrifice, I imbue this staff with the power of old; with this staff, I open the Void between worlds and set free my beloved. With this staff, I will unleash untold horror upon this world, and no one will stop us. Once again, the N'gist will thrive, and I will take my rightful place as Queen of the World."

A light began to emanate from the staff as it drained the magic from Luxon's body. He screamed as he felt his magic being torn from him. It felt like he was on fire; every fibre of his being burned. The light grew more and more intense until the chamber was filled with white light. The assassins released their grip on their prisoner as the light burnt their eyes from their sockets.

Cliria laughed manically as the power of the staff was re-forged. Finally, the light began to fade. Luxon had disappeared. In his place there existed a tear in the fabric of the universe. It was as though someone had punched a hole through a piece of paper. The hole floated in the middle of the chamber.

"Come to me, my love!" Cliria called into the tear, hoping that her voice would be heard in the Void beyond. Nothing happened. She called again, frustration in her voice. A few moments passed until the tear exploded outwards in a blinding flash, sending the witch flying backwards. She controlled her landing with magic to float gently to the ground.

"Nooooo!" she screamed.

The tear was gone.

Nothing had come through. And Luxon was gone.

CHAPTER 27.

The night descended quickly in the forest. With no source of light save for the waning moons, the Fell Forest was a terrifying place. Every tree looked like it was alive as their branches reached outwards like grasping talons.

Yepert walked slowly, being careful not to make any noise or trip on a root. The sounds of nighttime creatures made his imagination race. He couldn't help but wonder what fell beasts were stalking him?

The night was cold, and his breath exited his lungs in a plume of steam. He rubbed his body with his arms, hoping to keep the cold at bay. It was still summer, but an unnaturally cold wind had begun to blow from the north. Now he knew what Luxon had talked about back in Caldaria.

He shut his eyes to fight back the tears. He longed for the safety of the city and the days when he and his friend were safe and warm. He dreaded to think what had become of the others. A part of him wanted to go back, but a bigger part told him to run as far away as he could.

He thought back to the night when Kaiden had given him the precious note that felt like a boulder in his pocket. They had been fleeing the assassins and rest had been rare. When they stopped for some sleep, Kaiden had approached him.

"I have a special task for you, Yepert; one that is of the utmost importance," the knight had said when the two of them had gone to gather firewood. Yepert had been eager to prove that he could be trusted. The shame of almost being killed by the banshee had made his cheeks burn red with shame and embarrassment. He'd been eager to rip a page from his notebook and swap it with the note the knight had been carrying – anything to prove that he could be trusted. What the knight had said next, however, had caused him to doubt his courage.

"If anything happens to me, take that note and run," Kaiden has said sternly. "Take it to Sunguard and give it to Archbishop Trentian. Do not let it fall into the wrong hands."

Now he was fulfilling the knight's demand. Lost and alone in the huge forest, he doubted anyone would find him, let alone the witch and her assassins. He reached into his cloak and pulled out the note.

"I could destroy it ..." he muttered. He placed the note on the ground and focused. He whispered an incantation, raised his hands, and stopped. He tilted his head as he heard voices coming from deeper in the forest. They were drawing closer.

Quickly, he scooped up the letter, put it into his cloak's pocket and dashed behind a tree.

Two men pushed their way through the undergrowth. One was tall with short, cropped hair. The other was shorter and broader in build. He too had short hair. Yepert narrowed his eyes. The two men were wearing matching sets of armour. The dim moon cast just enough light to reveal the symbol of a crown emblazoned upon the breastplates.

Legionaries!

"I'm telling you I heard something," said the taller of the two.

"And I'm telling you you're imagining things," rebuked the other. "There's enough creepy stuff in this forest already without you dreaming up new stuff."

Yepert stepped out from behind the tree he had hidden behind. The soldiers of the legion would help him. Perhaps there were more nearby, and they could launch a rescue of his friends.

"Hello," he said.

The taller legionary spotted him and cried out in surprise.

"By Niveren! You scared me half to death."

The soldiers approached Yepert, their hands instinctively reaching for their swords.

"Who are you?" the shorter man said. "What's a lad your age doing in this place? Don't you know how dangerous it is here?"

The taller man hit his friend lightly on his chest. "Ease up, Kik. The lad looks like he's gone through the Void itself."

If Yepert had a mirror, he could have seen just what a state he looked. His hair was tousled, and his face and hands were covered in dirt. His cloak, too, was torn and ripped from all of the branches he had caught it on.

"My name is Yepert. I need your help ... My friends have been captured by a witch, and assassins are hunting me and ... and ..." Yepert's words came out in a rush. He desperately wanted the men to help him.

The two soldiers glanced at each other. Kik raised his eyebrows. "Easy, Yepert. We can take you to safety. Come with us, and we will take you to our general. I'm sure he'll be interested to hear about this witch and ... assassins, was it?"

"I don't have time for that! I have to rescue my friends," Yepert pleaded as the two legionaries grabbed him by the arms and pulled him along.

"I reckon this is the thief we were sent to find don't you, Jovi?" Kik said, laughing.

"Aye, I think he is," Jovi replied. "Anything to get out of this god-forsaken forest."

Yepert looked from one soldier to the other in shock.

"Thief? Who are you calling a thief? Where are you taking me?" Yepert tried to escape, but the soldiers were too strong.

"Stay still, you little git," Jovi snarled.

Yepert shut his eyes and muttered under his breath. With a surprised shout, the two guards were sent sprawling to the ground. Yepert rounded on them, his hands raised. He didn't want to hurt anyone, but these two were not going to help him.

"Let me go or else!" he shouted, doing his best to sound intimidating.

"He's got magic! The little shit is a mage! Don't you know your kind aren't allowed in this part of the realm," Kik growled. The two soldiers staggered to their feet and drew their swords. Jovi circled behind Yepert, whilst Kik advanced from the front.

"The general's definitely going to want to know about you, boy," Kik said menacingly. "No doubt we'll get some gold as a reward. Catching a mage ... hmm, should get us a nice big bag of delfins ..."

"I'm not your enemy. Please, just let me go!" Yepert pleaded, desperation creeping into his voice.

The soldiers laughed cruelly. Suddenly, Jovi lunged forward. The big man wrapped his powerful arms around Yepert, who screamed. With his arms pinned to his sides, he couldn't cast any spells.

Kik chuckled as he approached the struggling boy. He pulled a pair of manacles from his belt and strapped them to the boy's wrists. "Well, that was easy. I thought your kind would put a better fight than that," he mocked.

Yepert tried to struggle, but Jovi was too strong. His cries echoed into the night.

They had walked for most of the night, stopping only once when they heard the scuffling sounds of a pack of Pucks moving loudly through the forest. The two soldiers had drawn their swords, but they had remained undetected.

Eventually, they reached a large clearing with a rune stone standing tall and proud in its centre. Built around the stone was a wooden fort which had been constructed by the legion when they halted for the night.

Yepert's eyes grew wide as he recognised where he was. He was back on the Balnor Road.

The two soldiers roughly shoved him along until they reached the fort's gate. A legionary stood atop the gateway with a flaming torch. He barked an order to someone unseen, and the gate swung slowly open.

Yepert was pushed through the gate and into the fort. Rows of tents filled the space between the fort's wooden walls. He could smell meat cooking and the sounds of a blacksmith's forge rang out into the night.

Eventually, they reached a large tent with two stern looking legionaries standing guard outside. The right-hand guard frowned as he saw them approach. He raised his spear.

"Halt."

"C'mon, Odrin we've been travelling all night," Kik moaned.

The guard called Odrin scowled before he swung his spear and smacked the taller soldier across the face, sending him clattering to the ground.

"That is *Captain* Odrin to you, worm," the captain growled. He composed himself by tugging his blue tunic straight and adjusting his armour.

"Now then," he went on. "Did you two catch the man who stole from the stores?"

The captain glared at Yepert who shrank back under his intense gaze.

"This is a boy," Odrin said. "The thief who stole those supplies was a man. I know he was a man because he was a legionary, now a deserter. So, tell me why have you brought a boy to the general?" He spoke as though he were addressing a small and rather simple child.

"He's a mage!" Kik cried as he staggered to his feet. "He had this on him," the-red faced soldier added, passing the captain the note he had taken from Yepert's cloak pocket.

"He was in the forest, not far from Tentiv. We thought the general would want to know why" Jovi added.

Odrin raised his eyebrows in surprise. He regarded Yepert for a moment. A hint of sympathy flashed in his eyes.

"Is that true, boy? Are you a mage?" Odrin asked quietly.

Yepert nodded his head in the affirmative. There was no point in lying. Adults almost never believed the words of children.

"Leave us," Odrin ordered Jovi and Kik. The two men opened their mouths as though they were about to protest, but one look from the captain sent them on their way. Yepert wasn't sorry to see them go.

The captain's harsh expression softened as he unlocked the manacles around the boy's wrists.

"Now then lad, time to meet the general."

Rason looked up from the papers on his desk as the flap to his command tent opened. A brazier stood in the corner, giving off the only source of light. He rubbed his eyes tiredly and sat back on his canvas chair. Waging war was a tiring business.

"What is it, Odrin?" Rason asked. The general stood and stretched his aching back, grunting in satisfaction as he felt it click. He glanced at the map hanging by two wooden pegs sewed into the canvas of his tent. The realm of Delfinnia was upon it, regions controlled by his enemies shaded in varying colours.

The legion's push east had met little resistance so far, but his spies had revealed that the Baron of Balnor was mounting a defence at the Zulus Bridge on the Zulun River. It would be a tough battle. Many of his men would surely die.

"The men we sent after the man who was stealing from the baggage train found this young man deep in the forest," Odrin explained. "He claims to be a mage." The captain nudged Yepert forward and handed the note to his general.

"A mage you say," Rason said, taking a fresh look at the bedraggled youth fidgeting before him. He opened the note and walked over to the brazier to read it.

He froze as he read the contents.

"Leave us, Captain," Rason ordered. Odrin hesitated for a moment, before throwing his commander a salute and leaving the tent.

Rason waited for a moment, his eyes boring into Yepert.

"Who gave this to you, boy?" he demanded. His arm shook with excitement, and his eyes were wide. Yepert stepped back. The general was making him feel uneasy.

"A Knight of Niveren gave it to me; he was one of my companions. Please, sir, you must help my friends. They're all in terrible danger! A witch took them!"

Rason glared for a moment, before starting to chuckle.

"The Witch? Oh my, Cliria has been busy. Her little trap worked then," Rason muttered to himself.

Yepert stepped back in horror.

"You know the witch?"

Rason laughed humourlessly, before lowering his voice conspiratorially.

"Of course. It was she who encouraged me to fight for the crown. She promised me such power that no man could refuse her, and now ..." He smiled, waving the note. "And now, thanks to you, I know where the little bastard prince is hiding. I'm sure she'll be pleased to know as well."

The general banged a fist on his desk. The tent's flap reopened and in walked captain Odrin, who stopped and saluted his general.

"Bind this mage in chains and assign a detail to take him to Sunguard. Then summon the officers. We have a new destination."

Odrin hesitated. He looked at his general in disbelief. He glanced at the boy who looked as though he had seen a ghost and who was now on the verge of tears.

"Begging your pardon, sir, but where is this new destination? The Baron of Balnor's forces are only a day's march to the East ..."

Rason had his back to the captain and was studying the map of the kingdom intently.

"Eclin captain," Rason replied, his voice sounding distant. "We will march to Eclin."

Odrin frowned in confusion. Eclin was two weeks away to the north. Even at a forced march, the mountains would take a week to reach, barring any ill weather or other incidents.

"May I ask why Eclin, sir?" the captain asked, confusion evident in his tone.

Rason turned to face him.

"Because that is where the heir to the Sundered Crown is hiding."

CHAPTER 28.

Eclin

The sound of the drums was unnerving. All through the day and the long cold nights, the sound of the drums reverberated off of the surrounding mountains. For over a week the noise had persisted, but only now had they become so loud.

Woven watched from one of the high towers on the city of Eclin's battlements. Finally, the undead horde had arrived at the gates. Woven's thick grey cloak hid his face in shadow, and also from view of the nervous soldiers and citizens who had gathered to watch their doom form up in the snow.

Rank upon rank of undead had poured through the mountain pass, the ruins of the fortress of Ruion standing as a mocking reminder of the Rangers' failure to halt the lich's relentless march. Fire still flickered in the distance, casting eerie shadows of beasts upon the snow dusted mountainsides.

"They will attack soon?" Briden asked nervously. The younger ranger hopped from one foot to the other to ward off the night's cold.

"Probably at dawn. The ghouls have yet to come through the pass," Woven replied. He narrowed his eyes as he watched an archer on the battlements loose an arrow at the horde below. He shook his head. It was a waste of good iron and fletching.

"Surely the baron will order the retreat. We've done all we can to slow them down," Briden said, a hint of hope in his voice.

Woven snorted derisively. He could understand the man's fear, but he understood Lido more. The baron would never surrender his city without a fight, even if it was against a seemingly undefeatable foe.

"I wouldn't count on it," he growled. "The baron sent riders south months ago to beg for reinforcements, and still we stand alone. He's a prideful man and not one who ever gives up without a fight."

The stubborn baron would get them all killed.

The low note of a horn blast sounded in the distance. Woven turned to face the southern part of the city. That was where the call had come from. He felt a brief pang of excitement.

"Come on, lad. Sounds like some help has come after all!" he cried as he ran towards the southern gate with Briden hot on his heels. He bounded down the tower's stone steps and crossed an open courtyard. As he went, he noticed that other folk were also heading in the same direction.

"What's going on?" he asked a young woman who carried a small child in her arms. She too was hastily making her way to the south gate.

"The Knights! The knights are here!" she replied with a faint smile. Her accent was not of a commoner, but of someone who came from a regal family.

They made their way through the large city's streets, taking shortcuts that only a local who had spent their entire life living in a city would know.

Finally, they reached the wide avenue that led to the southern gate and pushed their way through the rapidly growing crowds. The large wooden gates were open, the iron portcullis raised.

"Thank Niveren," Briden whispered in awe.

Coming through the gate was the Order of the Knights of Niveren. Thousands were streaming in. Noble warriors astride their powerful warhorses, sergeants wearing the white livery and gold star of the Order following them. Archers, crossbowmen, and swordsmen all followed, and every man was dressed in bright white.

The citizens of Eclin cheered at the sight. Women raised their screaming children onto their shoulders so that they could see the warriors.

At the head of the army was an elderly man dressed in plate armour. He wore a long cape the colour of the sea and a silver open-faced helmet. Woven recognised him as the grand master of the Order, Sir Thondril.

A trumpet blast quietened the crowd. Woven strained to look up the road. Marching rapidly towards the gate was a contingent of the Eclin guard, their blue and gold mantels adorned with the city's sigil of the mountain bear. Riding at their head was Baron Lido. At his side was Sir Grandir.

Lido checked his horse bringing it to a halt before Thondril. The crowd fell into a tense silence as everyone strained to hear. Woven pushed his way closer so that he stood within earshot.

"Baron Lido," Thondril greeted warmly a smile on his elderly face. 'We come to you in this darkest of hours to offer you aid in your struggle against evil. We would have come sooner but, alas, the roads are dangerous, and the going was slow."

Lido sneered. He reigned in his horse which stepped from hoof to hoof as it sensed its owner's anger. A look of rage crossed the baron's face. His grey eyes were haggard, and his once-brown hair had greyed. The months of constant battle and watching his lands succumb to evil had taken their toll.

"I sent word for aid months ago! Months!" Lido bellowed. Sir Grandir moved to stand beside the Baron and placed a calming hand on the horse's reigns. Lido glared at the big knight, before staring daggers at the grand master.

"Since Sir Grandir sent our request, not one baron has marched to our aid," the baron raged. "The legion has not come and now, on the verge of our annihilation, you arrive. Why should I accept your aid when you left us to our fate!"

Thondril looked aghast at the Baron's words.

"Baron," he replied, bowing his head, 'we came as soon as we could. No riders came to us; no word has come from Eclin save for the rumours carried on the breeze by merchants and the like. Our journey took so long because the pass to the Delfinnian plains over yonder was blocked by huge boulders. It took us a week to clear them."

Lido glared disbelievingly at the knight.

"No messenger made it south?" Lido muttered despairingly. The fire in his eyes left him, and he slumped in the saddle. He had fought on with the belief that the armies of the south would come to his aid, and now that belief had been shattered.

Sir Grandir, too, looked pale at the news. Woven, though, shook his head in disbelief. "Impossible" he shouted. "I scouted the pass to the south but a day ago. Nothing blocked the way."

"Then your eyes were deceived," Thondril said soberly.

The Knights of Niveren made themselves at home in the city. Knights and retainers took up lodgings in many of the city's homes, or pitched tents in any scrap of open space they could find. The tired defenders of Eclin were pleased to see them, and most were happy to swap places on the walls with the holy warriors.

The white-mantled knights now manned the walls, making for an impressive sight. Thousands of bows and quivers of arrows were lined up against the stone parapets of the wall's crenellationscrenellations. The Knights also dragged braziers onto the walls; they would be vital to fending off the horrors that continued to pour through the mountains. Fire was the only thing that truly destroyed the dead.

The citizens of Eclin felt hope for the first time in a long time, the tales of the knights' battles against the undead and fell beasts stirring their hearts. No other fighting force in the realm was better at vanquishing the evil remnants of the Magic Wars and servants of Danon.

Woven watched the bustling activity from a high window in Baron Lido's private rooms. As senior ranger, he had been invited to attend the war council.

Sitting around a large round table were the Order's commanders, the baron's generals and representatives of the city guard.

"Magic can do terrible things to a man," the elderly Thondril preached. "It can make you see things that are not there; it can give you hope where there is none and it can destroy all you hold dear."

"This we have learned all too well," Sir Grandir said as he gulped a cup of wine. Baron Lido huffed.

"The lich that assaults this land was unexpected," Thondril went on, a slight frown on his face as he tried to ignore the Baron. "If we had known such a thing still existed, we would have come here sooner; we would have launched crusade after crusade until it was destroyed."

Woven shook his head. Lido was a good man, but he was also prone to being pig-headed or foolish. For a long time, the Rangers had warned that things stirred in the mountains, and yet Lido had dismissed those fears. His pride and desire for independence clouded his judgement until now when a creature the likes of which had not been seen since the last days of the Magic Wars was assaulting the kingdom.

"Who is the lich?" Woven asked. The question silenced the others.

"Every lich in history has had a name and was once a powerful magic user. The last had been the dark wizard Sivion if I remember correctly. So, who is it this time?"

The men sat at the table looked at him in surprise.

"You are very well read for a ranger," Thondril muttered. The elderly knight pushed back his chair and began to pace the room. He stopped to regard a portrait of one of Eclin's former rulers.

"It is true that the three liches that have appeared throughout history were all once men. Mages and wizards corrupted by dark magic. Necron, the first lich and master of the N'gist, was one; Rigonin the Failed, who became a monster to save his beloved, was another; and as you say, the last was Sivion, the dark master of the black mages in the Magic Wars."

The grandmaster stopped at the window to look out over the battlements.

"The one threatening us now must have been hiding for centuries in the depths of the mountains ... for no mage or magic user has been legally allowed to live outside of Caldaria since the reign of King Riis."

Lido chuckled humourlessly.

"Perhaps your order hasn't been as thorough with its purges as you believe," the baron sniped.

Woven shook his head and gave the baron a look of warning; they could not risk insulting the knights and losing their support. Something strange was happening, something that he did not understand.

"We can speculate over the lich's identity until the cows come home. We need to plan a defence of the city before it strikes," one of the commanders interrupted impatiently, stifling Thondril's angry reply.

"Of course. Shall we?" Lido said, gesturing to one of his stewards to bring in some refreshments. Woven took his seat. With the baron and the knight masters constant bickering, it was going to be a long day.

The sun was setting by the time the war council ended. The knights and Eclin commanders quickly set about getting their plans into place. The baron retired to his chambers, leaving Woven alone with Master Thondril.

Woven rubbed his eyes and stifled a yawn with the back of his hand.

"So," he said, looking at Thondril, "why exactly did your order come here? And do not try and lie to me. I may be a ranger, but I'm not a fool. You would not have marched all this way just on hearsay or rumours. There is another reason why you're here."

Thondril poured himself another cup of wine before sitting back in his seat. He appeared to think hard before replying. "You are smart," he told Woven, "and you seem to be a trustworthy sort. The Order needs someone who knows this city."

He sipped his wine before continuing. "What I am about to tell you must not leave this room. Do you understand?"

Woven raised his eyebrows in surprise at the master's serious tone. He placed his right hand over his heart.

"I swear." The ranger answered solemnly.

Thondril smiled.

"A man came to us. A man named Davik. He was there the night the royal family was murdered. He told us that an heir had survived … That a child, a boy, had been taken to safety far from the intrigues of the capital and those who would seek to harm him."

Woven whistled in surprise.

"This child is here in Eclin I take it?" he asked.

Thondril nodded in the affirmative.

"We did not know what to expect. I believed that the child could have been the prisoner of Baron Lido. I mobilised the Order in case we had to force him to hand the boy over to us.

"Instead we find a land under attack and in need of assistance. If I had known of the lich, I would have told the entire realm to march north. The threat posed by the lich and his forces is far greater than the squabbling of the barons. Why did it attack? I do not know, but something doesn't add up. Someone, or something, stirred it from its slumber."

Woven slumped into his seat, his stomach knotting in dread. He hated the idea that someone out there had the power to control such a beast. He reached across the table for the wine pitcher, poured himself a cup and quickly downed its contents.

"I need someone who knows the city, Woven," Thondril said. "Someone who could help us find the boy. I don't want anyone else to know of our true purpose here. If they did, I would fear for the child's safety."

Woven nodded. The sound of the drumming continued to sound from beyond the walls. Braziers lit up the crenellationscrenellations and revealed soldiers running to and fro.

"If his guardian is smart, they would have left the city when you cleared the road south," the ranger surmised.

Thondril shook his head.

"No, they are still here. Davik told me that the boy's guardian would not leave until they received this." The grandmaster reached into his tunic and pulled out a gold ring.

Woven gasped as he recognised the piece of jewellery. Everyone in Delfinnia knew the jewel of the king.

"This jewel was smuggled out of Sunguard by Davik on the night of the last king's death. This jewel will let the boy's guardian know who to trust."

Thondril slid the jewel across the table's smooth surface towards Woven, who picked it up and quickly stuffed it inside his cloak. As he put the jewel into his pocket, his fingers brushed against the strange stone he had taken from the Sigil Caves.

One mystery replaces another, he thought.

"Very well, Thondril. I'll look for this child and his guardian. There are a few places one can hide in this city. Before we go our separate ways, however, what happened to this Davik you speak of?"

A thoughtful expression crossed the grand master's face.

"The last we heard; he was making his way to Tentiv to find the Diasect."

CHAPTER 29.

Davik hid in the shadow of a large tree as the procession of crimson-robed killers marched past. At their head, astride a black horse, was a young woman with long blond hair.

He ached to draw his sword, but the wound to his side – still not fully healed – gave him pause.

Finally, the group passed, and he continued on his way. The broadsword on his hip weighed heavily as he limped down the road towards the citadel at Tentiv. Seeing the Crimson Blades coming from its direction, he knew that he would not find those he sought. Nonetheless, he had to see for himself.

Davik winced as the staff he used to help walk slipped in a patch of mud, almost sending him tumbling to the ground. Tentatively, he put his other hand on the bandage on his side. It came away bloody.

He recovered his composure and resumed his slow hobble down the road towards the citadel. The Fell Forest was eerily quiet; he had not seen nor heard any fell beasts.

The walk had been exhausting, and that was despite him catching a ride with a group of travelling merchants on the Balnor Road. He'd been forced to leave the kindly road folk behind, however, once they ran into the rear guard of the Sunguard Legion. A group of six legionaries had marched up the road with a young, podgy boy dressed in a blue cloak, similar to the ones the mages wore, in between them. The lad's hands had been bound.

After the showdown at the old king's palace, he had done his best to spread disharmony amongst the city's populace. Chances were that Rason's men were looking for him.

He had underestimated Rason's ability to win hearts and minds. Or was it that the people were simply desperate to see an end to the conflict?

Wounded and close to death, he had been unable to do no more than spread rumours. He had been fortunate to find safety within the Knights of Niveren's outpost in the city.

The sun was hanging low in the sky by the time he reached the citadel. The ancient fortress' towers cast long, ominous shadows over the forest below.

He paused and listened. The only noise was the distant squawking of a crow on one of the high towers. Satisfied that there was no danger, Davik hobbled across the road towards the gatehouse. His spirits sank as he saw the skeletal remains of one of Tentiv's monks lying at the top of the stone steps which led up to the gate.

He was surprised to see the iron portcullis was raised. His only obstacle now was the large wooden doors.

As he reached the doors, he placed his walking staff against the stone wall. He leaned against the gate and pushed with all of his strength. Pain emanated from the wound in his side, and his legs burned, causing him to cry out. After a few moments of straining, the gate creaked open.

He leaned heavily against the wall, his head between his legs, his breaths coming in ragged bursts. The pain caused stars to whirl in his vision.

He stopped and listened again. He tried to control his breath.

"What was that?" he panted. He hobbled through the doors to find himself in a large hallway. More skeletons were scattered about. Blood smears ran down the stone walls, and the banners of the Diasect were ripped and torn. Burn marks ran along the left-hand wall.

"Magic ..." he muttered under his breath. He'd seen what magic users could do when he had been one of the king's bodyguards. Being so close to the former king, he knew of the royal family's clandestine ties to the mages and Nightblades.

The noise came again. It was coming from one of the arched doorways cut into the stone wall. He hobbled to the arch and waited. A flight of stone steps led downwards into a maw of darkness. A cool breeze brushed against his cheek, and the smell of damp and decay filled his nostrils. He knew that smell.

"Dungeon ..." he growled. He had always hated them. As captain of the king's bodyguard, he'd had his fair share of watching torture. Defending a king often meant getting your hands dirty.

"Help!" came a voice from down in the dark. A quieter voice replied, it didn't sound friendly.

Carefully, Davik drew his sword and crept down the stone steps into the darkness. The staircase curved steeply to the left as he went. As with most castles, Tentiv was designed to favour a defender; with the steps spiralling downwards, a right-handed swordsman coming down would have the advantage.

He slowed as a flickering light came into view at the base of the stairs. With his back to the wall, he took a quick peek. Sure enough, he saw a long corridor with barred cells running down either side, a single candle giving off the only light. He tightened his grip on his sword. Sitting on a rickety looking wooden stool was a Crimson Blade.

"Help us!" cried someone from within one of the cells. It was a woman's voice.

"Quiet! You call out again, and I will gut you like a fish," rasped the assassin.

"Go to the Void, scum," replied the woman defiantly.

With a speed that startled Davik, the assassin was on his feet, his face pressed against the bars of the cell, a dagger in his hand which he waved menacingly.

Davik saw his opportunity. As stealthily as his wounded legs would allow, he crept up behind the robed killer. He raised his sword to deliver a killing blow.

He swung the blade, but to his amazement, the assassin was gone. Only his instincts saved his life. He whipped his staff upwards just in time to deflect the dagger aimed at his heart.

"Nice trick," he panted to the assassin. "My turn."

He lashed out with his own sword, causing the Crimson Blade to take a step back. Mistake. With his other hand, Davik flicked out low with the staff, causing the assassin to trip backwards. Instead of falling, however, the assassin steadied himself. He contorted his body in a way that no normal human being could.

With a shout, Davik pressed home with his attack. He lashed out with his sword, parrying any dagger thrusts with the staff.

Sweat poured into his eyes as he fought. Thanks to all of his years training with the sword, and the many battles he had fought in his life, he was able to match the assassin blow for blow.

Despite that, his legs burned and the sensation of warm blood oozing from the bandaged wound at his side made him wince. If he didn't end the fight soon, he would die.

Something out of the corner of his eye caught his attention. Standing behind him and close to the bars of a cell was a man with long black hair and dark eyes. The man was naked, and his body was covered with bruises. The man nodded to him.

Davik smiled. He pivoted on the balls of his feet using the staff to help him along. Now the fight had spun in the opposite direction. Now the assassin had his back to the caged man.

Gradually Davik slashed and shoved the assassin backwards until, with a kick that caused him to cry out in pain, he sent the robed killer flying backwards. The assassin crashed into the metal bars of the nude man's cell.

The man reached through the bars, wrapping his strong arms around the assassin's throat. With a shout, the man squeezed hard. The assassin desperately struggled to free himself but to no avail. With a sickening snap, the assassin went still.

The body slid to the cold, damp floor where it lay unmoving.

"The keys are in his robe pocket," the woman in the cell across the hall cried in relief.

Davik rooted through the dead killer's robes. He grunted in satisfaction as he found a bunch of iron keys. The pain in his tired limbs almost made him collapse as he stood, but he caught himself by placing a hand on the cold stone wall.

"I'm getting far too old for this nonsense," he muttered.

Davik was resting on his back in the courtyard at the centre of the fortress when Ferran, Kaiden and Sophia joined him. Each looked exhausted, but they were all happy to be free.

"We owe you our lives, old man," Ferran said offering his hand to Davik, which the old warrior shook.

Davik chuckled. "Less of the old if you please. I see you've found some clothes," he said, gesturing to their attire.

"The bastards left our gear just out in the dungeon's hallway, right where we could see it," answered the taller of the two men. Kaiden sighed and muttered a silent prayer as he pulled his knight's mantle over his head.

"A Knight of Niveren ... are you Sir Kaiden by any chance?" Davik asked.

Kaiden's eyes went wide in surprise.

"You know me? Did the Order send you?"

"Aye, I've heard of you. But no, your order did not send me; I came here of my own volition. I had hoped to find the Diasect and gain their support against Rason, but it seems that events have taken a darker twist. The Crimson Blades presence here confirms that evil befell this place." Davik tried to stand but winced in pain. Sophia offered him her hand which he took gratefully.

"You don't know the half of it, friend," Ferran said, pulling his leather armour on. "Two of our company are missing. And the witch has escaped."

"Witch? What witch?" Davik asked, genuinely confused.

"Cliria, the first witch and the one who is behind all of the ills that have befallen the realm," Sophia sighed as she shouldered her bow.

"It does not matter," Ferran interrupted. "We should return to Caldaria and inform Thanos what we have learned. It's high time the mages got off of their collective arses and stopped cowering. Only magic can best Cliria's power."

Davik held up his hands. "Wait just a minute. You're telling me that the first witch, the bride of Damon, is real?"

"Yes. She was the one who ordered the deaths of the king and his heirs. It was all part of her plan to lure Luxon ..." Ferran faltered as he mentioned the boy. He had failed to protect him and Yepert.

"Luxon?" Davik asked. His head was spinning. All this time he had believed that the Baron of Retbit had ordered the king's death. And now he had learned that a witch he thought just a fairy tale was real and behind everything.

"A young mage who travelled with us ... we walked right into the bitch's trap," Ferran growled.

Sophia walked over to the Nightblade. She could see the pain in his eyes. She placed a hand on his shoulder. For a brief moment, she saw the man she had once loved: a man who cared; a man who wasn't distant.

"There was another boy with us, a mage. A lad named Yepert. The witch hadn't caught him; he's probably lost in the Fell Forest somewhere," Sophia added hopefully. If they could just save one of the boys, she thought, then Luxon's death wouldn't have been for nothing.

"This other boy. Was he on the chubby side?" Davik asked remembering the group of legionaries he had encountered on the Balnor Road.

Sophia nodded.

"Yes, he did look as though he'd eaten one too many pies," Kaiden answered.

"I saw him. No more than a few hours ago on the Balnor Road," Davik said. Sophia's eyes went wide with happiness. "He seemed to be the prisoner of some of Rason's legionaries, however," he warned.

"We must rescue him," Kaiden said firmly. "He carries something very important. I just pray he destroyed it before he was captured."

They gathered their gear quickly and hastened out of Tentiv. Luckily, the assassins had left their mounts tied up in the dilapidated stables.

CHAPTER 30.

A vibration ran through the ground, causing Luxon to stir. Slowly, he opened his eyes. He was lying on his back, and the citadel was nowhere to be seen.

Where he had expected the high stone ceiling of Tentiv, there was instead open sky. Except it wasn't blue; it was a dark purple streaked with wispy black clouds.

The ground shook again. It hadn't just been his imagination. He sat up slowly, stifling a cry as he took in the sight before him. He was on a hill overlooking a vast plain which went on for as far as the eye could see.

A vast forest of black menacing trees covered every scrap of ground all the way to the horizon, which was lit up with distant flashes of what appeared to be lightning.

He wasn't in Delfinnia anymore.

His mind raced at the possibilities.

Looking over his body for injuries, he was surprised to see he was clothed. He was in his favourite blue cloak and comfortable tunic and breeches.

"Wasn't I just in my trousers?" he mumbled to himself in confusion.

Something shiny caught his eye amongst the clouds. The purple sky was awash with glittering streams of silver dust which flowed in dazzlingly beautiful patterns. The dust streams twisted and turned in the warm breeze that was flowing up from the plains below, arching and diving through the air, pirouetting and moving with a purpose that made it seem alive.

Luxon stared in wonder at the sight. The beauty of the spectacle made his heartache. To his surprise, he felt warm tears running down his cheeks.

He watched the spectacle for a good hour before his attention was caught by a rustling in the forest below. He got to his feet, ready to run.

A massive creature was bulldozing its way through the trees. Even from his high vantage point, he could hear their trunks snapping like twigs. The vibration he had felt resumed as the beast drew nearer to the base of the hill upon which he stood.

"You've suffered a terrible fate, haven't you?" whispered a voice on the breeze.

Luxon froze.

"Do not fear me ... Luxon," the voice whispered again. This time it was close behind him.

Luxon turned, his hands held high ready to defend himself.

There standing behind him was a cloaked figure. It was tall, and the person's features were hidden in shadow. Yet he couldn't shake the feeling that he had seen the figure before.

"Who are you?" he asked. His head ached; he couldn't remember much of anything aside from flashes of people's faces and voices.

"I have watched you for a long time, Luxon," the robed figure said. "Your memory will return in time. Come we must leave this place." The figure's voice sounded as though it came from far away instead of close by. Luxon hesitated before following. He was so confused. The world around him had changed. He felt half empty, as though he were not all there ... that a part of him was missing.

"What is this place?" he asked as he jogged to catch up with the figure, who was moving fast. He skidded to a halt as he realised that the person was floating.

The stranger stopped.

"This is the Void – the realm of the fell; the universe made by the forgotten god. Come. We must hurry."

They went down the other side of the high hill to find themselves at the edge of another dark forest. The robed figure drifted into it, urging Luxon to follow.

As they went, Luxon couldn't shake off the feeling that they were being watched by many eyes from within the forest's dark depths.

Flowers the likes of which he had never seen before grew at the base of the trees. Luminous yellows, greens and violets gave the place an eerie beauty. The gurgle of fast-flowing liquid filled the air as they went. Finally, they came to a clearing which overlooked yet another vast plain. This one, however, was covered in lakes of gold and silver which glowed in the strange starlight.

Another hour or so passed by the time they reached their destination. A small cottage was built into the side of a massive tree of the like Luxon had never seen before. He had to crane his neck back to see the top leaves, but even those were so high that they were lost in cloud.

The robed figure opened the cottage door and gestured for him to go inside.

Cautiously, he stepped through the door and was surprised to see the room he had lived in at the mages' college in Caldaria. He held his head and cried out as memories of the mage city flashed back into his mind. He staggered and fell onto the bed. It even smelt like the one from his dorm, he thought, as he drifted into unconsciousness.

Luxon awoke to find himself still in what looked like his dorm room. Only the purple sky and strange silver starlight betraying the fact that he wasn't really there. Standing next to the room's fireplace was the robed figure.

"I have long forgotten the confusion and the effects of first entering this place," it said in its eerily distant voice. "I have been here for far too long."

Luxon plumped up the pillows on the bed before leaning against them heavily.

"Who are you? I feel as though I know ... But so much seems strange here," he said.

"I suppose it is time for me to reveal myself. I have appeared to you many times in dreams and at times of danger. I did my best to guide you, but alas here you are all the same." The robed figure moved closer to the bed. Its long arms reached up and pulled back the hood of the robe, revealing an elderly man with long grey hair. His eyes were blue, and kindly, his nose was long and proud, and his mouth was small and serious.

"I am Aljeron, the first wizard of Esperia and your ancestor. I have been here for aeons and yet I linger. For all of my faults, I did not deserve what happened to me. I stopped Danon's plan and was trapped here for eternity. My only solace is that he was trapped here also. But that may change, and the world may fall."

Without another word, Aljeron pulled up his hood, took Luxon's hand and took him back outside.

"Hold on."

Aljeron lifted his right hand into the air. He tightened his hold on Luxon's hand with his left and uttered an incantation. The two of them shot off from the ground and soared into the sky.

Luxon screamed out. The world below shot past in a dizzying blur as they flew. Down in the forest, he saw packs of Pucks running, and banshees drifting along the golden riverbanks. Beasts and monsters of all descriptions: he saw them all as they flew.

Rapidly approaching was a line of tall mountains. Luxon shut his eyes tightly, expecting them to smash into them. Instead, Aljeron changed course, and they shot upwards to pass over the peaks. If Luxon lowered his feet, he was sure he would have been able to touch the mountain tops with his toes.

They flew onward, crossing a sea of gold to reach another land mass. As they approached, the air grew thick, and the smell of decay and rotting flesh threatened to gag Luxon.

"We are here," Aljeron said in his wraith-like tones.

They drifted downward. Luxon staggered as his feet touched the ground, and he fell onto his face with a cry. The world spun, and his stomach fluttered. He was going to be sick.

"There are things you must know about this place, Luxon. You feel dizzy and sick; yet how can that be when your body is not here?"

Luxon wretched. He stood upright and stared at Aljeron as though he was mad.

"What do you mean my body is not here?" he asked slowly. He looked over his limbs. He felt like he was all there. He wiggled his toes and stretched his fingers.

"Only things created in the Void can exist here physically. Things from your world that enter here ... only their spirits can exist here. The body itself, however, remains in the other place."

Luxon blinked a few times as he processed what he was being told. Was he just a spirit? Panic filled him. If that were true, then where was his body?

"Your body could be next to where you entered the Void or, it could have been sent through one of the many tears spread across the world. It could be thousands of miles away from where you think it should be," Aljeron explained sympathetically.

"You must also know that time flows differently here. An hour in the real world is like a year in the Void. I have been here so long ..." Aljeron's voice drifted off.

Luxon looked at the wizard in sympathy. He was terrified, but the spirit before him had been trapped in this strange place for thousands of years. To Aljeron himself, that time would have felt like millions.

Aljeron drifted forwards and pointed. A vast crater surrounded by steep, jagged cliffs lay before them. Blue flames surrounded the crater, and at its centre lay a massive tower. The structure itself appeared as though someone had stabbed the very surface of the world from underneath so that the tip of a spear had ripped through flesh to protrude out the other side.

Luxon could now see what was causing the awful smell. Between the flames were three gigantic creatures surrounded by carrion. Each was the size of a castle. Their bodies were long and scaled. Massive, clawed talons were attached to their four long limbs. At the top of their long necks was a snouted head with a mouth full of sharp teeth. Upon their backs were massive leathery wings which they splayed open as they squared up to one another.

Luxon narrowed his eyes.

"What are they? What is this place?" he asked in awe.

Aljeron stood next to him. He raised his hand, gesturing towards the tower.

"That is where Danon resides. Like us, he is a spirit only, but even here his dark will twists and corrupts. Those creatures are dragons. Noble creatures that once walked our world in the days of creation, banished here when men appeared in Esperia. They were the favoured creations of the goddess of creation, Aniron, but were deemed too powerful to share the world with men. Now they are servants of Danon. Slaves to his will in this place."

Luxon sat back on his heels. Danon himself was down in the crater. He would have laughed if it weren't for the fear in his heart.

"He resides in his fortress waiting for his chance to return to the world," Aljeron muttered.

"Cliria ..." Luxon growled. Memories were coming back to him: the witch, Tentiv – all of it.

"The witch hoped to use you to free him. Instead, she made a mistake, and now we have a chance," the old wizard said. "You are here with me – something she did not expect. We have time on our side. Time enough for me teach you."

Luxon looked at the wizard in confusion.

"I will teach you to become what you are destined to be," Aljeron said, a faint smile on his lips. "A wizard."

CHAPTER 31.

Luxon's palms were sweating. At least, they *would* have been if he were actually in his body. Despite being a spirit in the Void, he felt all the same things he did when back home. He got tired, hungry, thirsty, and everything else besides. Aljeron had chided him for it, saying that he himself had long given up those mortal sensations. Luxon had simply scowled at the wizard.

Aljeron hadn't lied when he'd talked about teaching. Three days had already passed since Luxon's arrival, and each had been filled with sermons. The first day had seen him learn and master the lowest ring of magic. To Luxon's surprise, it had been incredibly easy. Now though, Aljeron was teaching him the middle ring. Spells such as healing, transmutation and divining were proving tricky to master.

"No. You must see the object in your mind, Luxon. Stop letting your thoughts wander, and focus," Aljeron infused from his perch in a nearby tree. The wizard had been using the small clearing outside of the strange cottage as a training ground, and he liked nothing more than to drift lazily from tree to tree. Aside from being hugely distracting, Luxon found himself more than a little jealous of the wizard's control of levitation. His cheeks flushed red as he remembered his own near-disastrous attempt at such a spell.

"It's a bit hard to focus with you flittering about," Luxon muttered under his breath. He narrowed his eyes and concentrated, picturing the object Aljeron had described in his mind.

The pebble with a blue streak.

He focused as hard as he could until his mind's eye flashed away from the clearing. He almost cried out but refocused. He wouldn't fail again. The spell was surreal in that it made him feel as though he had left his body entirely to fly through the forest. He could see trees, rocks and a small group of Pucks squabbling. He almost shouted out in joy when he saw the stone lying amongst a pile of other stones of similar size.

"Found it!" he said triumphantly. He shook his head to release the spell and once more the clearing came into view. Aljeron didn't look impressed.

"Well. Where is it? You found it with your sight. Now summon it here," the wizard said with his arms crossed. "A wizard can summon what he needs into his hands at a moment's notice."

Luxon sighed. He took a deep breath and focused. It felt easier this time as within moments he had once again found the stone. Now he just had to call it to him.

How do I summon a stone? he thought. An idea popped into his head. He focused away from the stone but kept it at the back of his mind. He drifted back through the forest until he found the group of Pucks. Concentrating again, he aimed his power at the creature.

"Find this stone and bring it to me," he muttered through gritted teeth. His mind was now in three separate locations, and he was growing tired as he focused. He muttered the words again, trying to plant the suggestion into the Puck's mind. The Puck looked around as though it had heard something. It sniffed the air and scratched at the ground before returning its attention to the other Pucks that were moving through the forest.

"Don't understand words, eh ..." Luxon grumbled. He focused on the Puck again, only this time he turned his words into pictures. His head was damp with sweat as he tried to maintain control.

This time the Puck spun around on the spot before running off into the forest.

Luxon gasped as he released his link with the beast. Now all he could do was wait.

Just as Aljeron was about to mock him again for his failure, the sound of the Puck sneaking into the clearing caught his attention.

The normally vicious creature was acting like a puppy returning a stick. Slowly it crept closer until it gently placed the blue streaked stone at Luxon's feet. The young mage smiled in triumph as the Puck scampered off back into the trees.

Aljeron raised an eyebrow.

"Very clever. Wasn't exactly what I had in mind, but it was effective," the wizard chuckled. He raised a hand, and the stone flew into the air to hover around his head like some sort of insect.

A loud crash came from the forest. Aljeron cried out in alarm before drifting down to the ground to stand protectively in front of his young pupil.

Luxon was about to ask what was going on when he felt the ground shake. The sound of distant trees crashing to the ground roared through the forest and into the clearing. A booming noise drew nearer, and each sound was quickly followed by the shaking of the ground.

"Stay still, Luxon. We have a guest," Aljeron said seriously.

The booming drew nearer and nearer until the trees at the edge of the clearing toppled over like dominoes. The sound was deafening, and the vibration ran up Luxon's legs and into his head.

Emerging from the forest was the biggest creature Luxon had ever seen. The beast's massive head swayed from side to side, its large snout sniffing the air. It was a dragon.

The dragon stepped into the clearing, but due to its enormous size, only its head and long, scaled neck could fit. The rest of its mountainous body stayed among the broken trees. It turned its head so that it could see the two magic users.

An eye the size of a wagon affixed its gaze upon them. The pupil alone was the size of Luxon. It blinked a few times as it focused. Huge leathery eyelids closed over the yellow-tinged eyeball before it regarded them again.

Luxon couldn't help but take a step back. The creature was overwhelming.

"So ... Aljeron, this is the one who came through the portal," it said in a voice that sounded like thunder. "I had hoped to reach him before you did, but alas in my old age I'm not the dragon I used to be."

Luxon froze in amazement. The dragon could talk!

The wizard stepped forward and affectionately rubbed the creature's snout. A thin puff of red flame shot out of one of the nostrils as the dragon purred in pleasure. Luxon almost laughed. It reminded him of a giant cat rather than some ferocious beast.

Aljeron waved Luxon forward so that he stood in front of the dragon's huge eye. It blinked again, and the pupil widened. Standing so close to the beast, Luxon could feel heat emanating from it. He could also sense powerful magic, the likes of which he had never sensed before.

"So ... You are Luxon. Aljeron has told me a lot about you. Even his long years of peering into your world, he sees something in you which he has not in any other," the dragon rumbled.

Luxon looked away in embarrassment.

"I wouldn't know. All I know is that I have to return to my own world," he replied. "My friends need me."

The dragon chuckled, shaking the ground with its deep rumble.

"We all dream of returning there, boy. Even I who have been here for time immemorial still dream of the blue skies and warm sunshine of Aniron's creation. Alas, it is something that even we dragons have been unable to do." There was a hint of sadness in his voice.

"Now, now, Umbaroth, not all hope is lost, my friend. Luxon here still has a chance. I am sure that together we can find a way," Aljeron said reassuringly.

The dragon lifted its head with its long neck. Luxon stepped back as the dragon stood to its full height. Trees snapped, and the ground shuddered as it moved. The beast was massive, taller than a castle. Now that it was clear of the trees, Luxon could see that the dragon was covered in large thick white scales. Its belly was the colour of silver, and large spines ran down the length of its muscular back. Its vast wings splayed outwards, covering the light cast by the stars.

"Danon knows a way!" Umbaroth snarled. "Do not think the dark one has been idle these millennia, wizard. He seduced my brethren with promises of power and freedom. I can feel that he draws closer to escaping here, and the boy ..." The dragon paused as it raised a massive talon to point at Luxon. "The boy is the key. If he takes the boy's power and combines it with the dragons' and his own, he will have more than enough magic to force a way out of the Void."

Luxon shook his head.

"No. Aljeron's staff was the key!" he cried.

The old wizard placed a hand on the boy's shoulders. "No Luxon. The staff only opens the way into the Void. I made it that way so that it would only allow things in. Not out. Otherwise, countless evil folk would have abused its power. The witch believed that it would allow Danon to escape. The dark lord knew better. He sensed your power just as Cliria did. You have the power he needs to escape. The nightmares you had were caused by him. Only a wizard can oppose him, which is why I will teach you."

Luxon slumped to his knees. He was just a pawn for powers far beyond himself. He was afraid. Danon, the scourge of all things was coming for him. He wanted to cry. He didn't want any of this. He just wanted to be safe in Caldaria with his friends.

CHAPTER 32.

Eclin

Woven paced the city walls nervously. A tension was in the air that was near unbearable. The lich's forces had finally finished pouring through the mountain passes earlier in the day; the moans of the undead were almost deafening. Fear had spread through the now trapped populace and soldiers like a wildfire. Woven had already had to order his rangers to shoot down any man who tried to flee the walls. Everyone would be needed, every blade.

He wore a chainmail cuirass under his grey ranger's cloak. His hands were covered in leather gauntlets, and his knee-high boots were made of leather lined with iron. His black beard was slicked with oil, and his long hair was tied in a knot under his hood.

Around his neck, he wore the amulet that identified him as a captain of his Order. The young men at his command all looked to him; he just hoped he looked the part of the warrior. Many of them would not survive the coming days. He did his best to hide the fear in his own heart.

Looking out over the wall did little to ease his terror. Swarming just out of range of bowshot were tens of thousands of the enemy. The zombies shambled, the werewolves howled and, as usual, the ghouls, the deadliest of the lich's forces, stood ominously quiet in their black armour.

"What are they?" asked the young ranger standing next to him. The lad was no more than nineteen years of age, and his eyes were wide with panic.

"They were once men; warriors that fought in the wars of old. Their bodies and their souls became the playthings of the foulest magic," Woven replied, his eyes shut as he remembered the tales his grandfather had told him around the fireplace in his youth.

"The legend is that at the final battle of the Magic Wars, the dark mages unleashed their full power against their enemies. They cursed them to forever serve them in death. As the battle raged and more warriors fell, the ranks of the dark mages swelled. Only the defeat of Sivion had saved the day and sent the ghouls and other foul abominations fleeing into the depths of the mountains."

He patted the young man on the arm and squeezed it reassuringly.

"Do not let fear overwhelm you. Be strong. Let your arrows fly true and your sword cut deep," he said evoking the battle words of the rangers.

He walked along the wall, past the soldiers of Eclin who stood with crossbows and longbows at the ready. He could almost smell their fear. The whole city stank of it, for now, the city of Eclin was completely surrounded. The pass south had been cut off by a horde of zombies. The last group of escaping refugees had not stood a chance. Even the knights sent to escort them had been overwhelmed. Pulled from their mounts and devoured alive, their screams were heard from the city walls.

Woven bounded down a flight of stone steps and made his way through the narrow streets. The jewel in his cloak pocket felt heavy. He was running out of time. Preparing his men and aiding with the city's defence had taken too much of his time already. He had to find the child and get him to safety.

He rounded a corner and entered a tavern. It stood eerily silent. With a city full of soldiers, he had expected that most would be seeking to get blind drunk before the siege truly began in earnest.

Sitting at a table close to the door was Briden. The young ranger was staring into a mug of ale. His bow was leaning against the table and his quiver of arrows lay on the ground at his feet.

"Drinking alone? Never a good sign," Woven chuckled, trying to lighten the taverns gloomy mood. He looked around and could not even see the tavern keeper.

"The tavern keeper went back into the cellar. He thinks he and his wife will be safe down there if the walls fall," Briden said, waving a hand in the general direction of the bar. "If you want drinks, just help yourself."

Woven was sorely tempted to down a few pints but resisted the urge. Being drunk wouldn't change anything. He placed his own bow next to the table before pulling up a stool and taking a seat.

"So ... any luck finding the boy?" Woven asked.

The young ranger nodded in the affirmative. "Aye. I asked around all of the major housing districts. The boy's guardian is a clever one. She's kept to the poorer areas of the city, the places where people don't tend to talk to figures in authority." Briden smiled as he gestured to himself. Woven snorted.

"She did, however, make one mistake."

"Oh?"

"She didn't change her accent," Briden smiled. "The folk living in the old town told me of a girl whose voice was distinctly southern. 'As though she were from the capital or something,' was how one old sod put it. He also said that she looked a little too young to be the mother of a toddler, like the lad she looks after."

Woven felt a pang of excitement.

"Do you have an address?" the ranger captain asked as he pushed his stool backwards and rose to his feet. He picked up his bow and slung it over his shoulder.

"I do indeed, sir," Briden said proudly. He rooted about inside his cloak pockets until he pulled out a scrap of paper. He handed it to his superior.

Woven unfolded the paper. A name was written on it; the name of a house: *Torvig Folly*.

"Well done, Briden," Woven said. He turned to leave, before facing the younger man. "Get to your post. Getting pissed in the local tavern isn't going to do anyone any good."

The ranger captain left to leave Briden staring into his empty mug of ale.

"Would have made me feel better ..." he muttered under his breath.

Woven hurried across the city. He was delayed several times by panicked civilians pleading for help. All he could do was point them in the direction of the baron's castle sitting on the bluff overlooking the city. Lido had been generous enough to open the gates to the populace. If things did turn ill, however, then it would be at the castle where things would come to an end.

He walked down a narrow lane that ran between two stone buildings until he reached a bridge that crossed a gently flowing stream. On the opposite bank was the old town with its wooden houses and thatched roofs. Woven glanced at the scrap of paper again and read the name out loud. He closed his eyes to get his bearings before heading across the bridge and down one of the narrow streets. He had lived in Eclin all his life and knew the city's streets like the back of his hand.

As a lad, he'd been an urchin working for the city's Fleetfoot chapter. Many a time he and his friends had fled through the winding streets from the city watch. A stolen necklace here, a coin purse there – he had lifted the lot until he had been captured. The city's watch captain, a vile man, named Grundil, had wanted to take his hands. Only Baron Lido's clemency had spared him.

The baron had been a generous man in his youth and, instead of punishing him, he had ordered Woven to be taken into the care of the rangers. From that day onward, his life was full of training with the sword and bow. He had learned the lay of the land, survival skills and the ability to track virtually anything through the mountains. It had been a tough life, but it was far better than being a dishonourable thief.

The muddy streets were quiet as he walked. Most of the houses lay dark and empty, but a few brave souls had chosen to stay. Grim-faced men were armed with shovels, their wives with knives. Children were hidden from view, probably hiding in basements or roof spaces. They didn't bother the ranger as he passed by, although some called out encouragements.

He was nearing the street on which *Torvig Folly* was located. At the end of the street was a tall wooden structure which housed over a dozen families. Etched onto a plaque of bronze was the building's name, nearly unreadable thanks to the dirt which covered it.

Woven knocked on the door. If Briden was right then, the girl and prince would be inside.

The door creaked open slowly to reveal a young woman. Her long brown hair was tied back with a red bow, and her eyes were wide and blue. But her most distinctive feature was her small nose and soft lips. The girl was defiantly not from Eclin. She had a softness about her that the women of Eclin didn't, but he could tell she could be feisty from the fire in her eyes.

"Miss," Woven said with a bow. "I have been instructed to bring you to safety by the Knights of Niveren."

The girl narrowed her eyes. She had one hand on the door, the other behind her back. Woven smiled. He knew she had a knife in her hand.

"I was told to show you this," he said as he reached into his cloak and pulled out the glittering king's jewel, "as proof that I am a friend."

The girl gasped at seeing the stone. Tears sprung from her eyes. She opened the door.

"I'm sorry," the girl wept. Relief was obvious on her face. "We have run for so long ... forgive me. My name is Elena," she cried, her words coming out all at once. She held up her concealed hand and turned red. In it was a dagger. "Sorry," she mumbled.

"No harm done," Woven said reassuringly. He stepped inside the house. It was a simply decorated place with wooden walls that smelled vaguely of damp. A picture was nailed to the wall at the base of a small staircase which led upwards to the roof space. The picture was of a distinguished-looking man with a neatly trimmed beard.

"My father," Elena explained when she noticed him looking at it. "I haven't been able to see nor speak with him in three years. I couldn't risk it."

A giggle came from the top of the stairs. Woven looked up to see a small boy with blond curly hair and big blue eyes.

"Alde," Elena scolded, "get back to your room; you know you have to stay out of sight." She sighed. "I guess it's too late now. Pack your travel bag and come downstairs."

The boy smiled, clapped his hands, and disappeared out of sight. The sound of him rummaging about as he sang some shanty caused Woven to chuckle.

"The prince, I presume?"

Elena smiled sheepishly. "Yes. He's a very willful little man."

A few moments later, Elena and the prince were dressed for travel. The girl was struggling to put the prince's boots on, but he was resisting.

"No Lena don't want to go!" he cried.

Woven knelt down in front of his future king. Just as he was about to try and distract the boy, he felt a warm sensation in his cloak pocket. Curious, he reached into it and pulled out the stone he had found in the Sigil Caves.

To his amazement, the stone was glowing brightly, as it had done when he had first found it. He looked from the stone to the boy. The child was staring at it, his eyes wide in wonder. He reached for it, and as he did so, the stone grew hot, so hot that Woven dropped it with a cry. The boy ignored the ranger and went to pick up the stone which was now shining brightly.

"Alde!" Elena shouted. The prince ignored her and wrapped his small hands around the stone.

It didn't burn him.

CHAPTER 33.

Woven gawped at the boy. The stone was shining brilliantly in his small hands; the picture of the sword manifested itself as it had done in the Sigil Caves.

Elena went to take it from the prince's hands, but to her amazement, she couldn't bring her hands close due to the fierce heat that radiated from the stone. She looked to Woven, a look of fear on her face.

"What is that?" she demanded of the shocked ranger.

"I ... I found it in a cave in the mountains. It hasn't glowed like that since I first found it. It didn't give off any heat then, though," he replied, scratching his head.

"Pretty" Alderlade giggled as he placed it on the floor. As the stone left the prince's hands, the light faded once more. The little boy looked at the stone with his mouth agape. When the light didn't return his bottom lip trembled. "Where it go?"

Elena scooped the boy up into her arms, thankful that he had let go of the mysterious stone. Woven knelt down and tentatively touched it. It was no longer hot, just cool like any normal stone.

"Whatever that thing is, it's magical. I don't want it anywhere near Alde," Elena scolded as she tried to soothe the upset boy who was struggling to get out of her arms and back to the stone.

Woven scooped it up and tucked it back into his robe pocket.

"It seems to like the boy ..." he muttered. If he survived the coming days, he would be sure to seek answers. An idea popped into his head: perhaps the Knights of Niveren would know what it was.

A loud blast from a horn came from outside the house, then another.

Woven took the girl's hand. "We have to get you to the baron. The attack has begun."

Woven, Elena and the little prince moved quickly through the streets. In the distance, they could hear the sounds of soldiers running to their posts on the walls. Terrified civilians were all fleeing towards the baron's castle.

Woven led them through back alleys and took shortcuts to avoid the panicking crowds.

Finally, they reached the base of the hill which led up to Lido's castle. A throng of men, women and children were all jostling to get through the large metal gatehouse before the soldiers dropped the portcullis.

Woven tightened his grip on Elena's hand. He pushed and threatened his way through the crowd. The prince was tucked tightly to the girl's chest; his muffled cries could just be heard over the din.

Woven drew his sword and used it to shove his way to the front of the crowd. People recoiled from the cold steel, making the passage easier.

A nervous, angry looking soldier was barring the entrance to the courtyard beyond the gate. Standing behind him was a line of other nervous troops, their kite shields locked together, and their spears pointed towards the crowd.

"There is no more room!" the soldier bellowed. "Seek shelter in your homes or at the barracks. Keep off of the streets if you value your lives."

The crowd roared in protest and surged forward. Woven pulled Elena to the side to avoid being trampled. If he didn't get her and the boy inside the walls soon, they would be caught up in a riot. The people's mood was growing darker by the second as desperation filled them. The moans of the undead being carried on the wind did little to ease their fears.

"Soldier. Get these two inside now!" he shouted in his most authoritative voice.

The soldier hesitated. He recognised the ranger.

"I have my orders from the baron himself. There is no more room, sir," the soldier replied with a shout. The angry yells from the crowd were growing in volume.

"Why should his strumpet and bastard be let in?" screamed an elderly man in the crowd.

Others took up his cries of protest. Woven was quickly losing his temper. He grabbed the soldier by his mail shirt and hauled him close so that their faces were mere inches apart.

"The boy is the prince and heir to the crown. Let them in," he said angrily. The soldier's eyes widened at the ranger's words.

Woven gestured to Elena; the girl pulled out the king's jewel which shone in the sunlight.

"The jewel of the king," the soldier gasped. He pulled away from Woven's grip. The ranger let him go.

"Let these two inside. Make sure they are protected," the soldier ordered his men.

"Thank you," Elena cried. The soldiers opened up their shields to allow her and the child to enter. Woven sighed in relief and nodded to the soldier in thanks. He had to reach the walls and the other rangers.

The angry crowd, however, had other ideas.

"Bastards!" cried a woman who held her crying baby into the air. "Let my son in too. He's just a baby."

The crowd surged forward drowning out her pleas. Upon seeing the crowd charge, the soldier grabbed Woven and hauled him into the castle courtyard and behind the line of soldiers.

"Drop the portcullis," the soldier cried. Another soldier ran forward, drew his sword and cut the rope which held the large metal gate aloft. The portcullis slammed shut crushing several members of the crowd beneath it. Pained screams and the sickening sound of bodies being crushed under metal filled the air. Blood sprayed the soldiers, some of which vomited at the sight of the broken bodies.

Woven stared at the scene of carnage. The siege of Eclin had just begun, and already hell had arrived.

Master Thondril watched the attack from the top of one of the many turrets that lined the city walls. Behind him was a rather nervous looking ballistae crew. The team of four were all young men of the Eclin watch. None of the deadly weapons had been fired in anger for over a hundred years. Today that would all change.

The white-mantled knights and sergeants on the wall below loosed arrow after arrow into the oncoming horde. Tens of thousands of zombies shambled towards the walls, their moans echoing off of the surrounding mountain peaks.

"They will never get up the walls," the knight standing nearest to Thondril said in amazement.

"They aren't supposed to," The grand master muttered. He had seen such a tactic used before in the last crusade he had led into the mountains. On that occasion, he and a hundred of his men had sought shelter in a ruined tower, a relic of the Golden Empire when the weather had turned. Out of the snow and darkness, the enemy had attacked.

"The zombies are to probe for weaknesses in our defence. Do not be fooled into thinking that there is no intelligence behind this, Sir Fronti," Thondril explained to the younger knight.

Amongst the zombies, werewolves charged forward. Some reached the bottom of the walls and began to climb. Their razor-sharp claws acting like climbing picks. The archers on Thondril's tower shifted their aim and loosed. The volley slammed into a dozen of the beasts, sending them tumbling into the mass of undead below.

Volley after volley of arrows lanced downwards into the packed ranks of the enemy. The men on the walls used the flaming braziers to set their arrows aflame and send fiery death into the zombies. The knights had learned long ago that only fire destroys the undead.

The smell of cooked, rotten flesh was carried on the breeze, causing the defenders to gag. Some covered their noses with strips of cloth to filter out the foul stench.

Thondril was on the eastern wall facing the mountain passes. From his position, he could see that the enemy was slowing in its assaults. He smiled softly to himself. They couldn't find a weakness there. For a brief moment, he thought that the city could hold.

Those hopes were dashed when he heard screams coming from the southern walls and the road leading into Delfinnia itself.

He rushed over to the crenellations which faced south to see a huge billow of smoke pouring skywards. He narrowed his eyes. A bright flash struck the gatehouse, and a moment later the sound of thunder reached his ears.

"Magic ..." he muttered when he understood what he was seeing.

He turned to face Sir Fronti, who also was watching the carnage on the southern wall. "Tell half the men on this wall to reinforce the south," Thondril yelled.

Fronti ran over to the wall and bellowed orders at the men below. Within moments, half of the defenders on the eastern wall were running to the south.

"Sir!" Fronti shouted, a tinge of panic in his voice. Thondril ran back to the other wall. He swore under his breath. The enemy had been waiting for such a move. Out of the mountain pass charged the implacable ghouls. Thousands of them marched forwards. In their midst were tall towers made of iron and wood.

"Siege towers!" Thondril bellowed, drawing his silver sword. The towers rumbled forward from their hiding place in the pass. Fronti ran down the steps of the tower, desperate to catch up with the men he had just ordered to the other wall.

Thondril followed, but instead of heading to the south he took up position on the wall. His nervous men looked to him for courage. The knights drew their silver blades while the sergeants continued to rain arrows and crossbow bolts upon the approaching ghouls. The stamping of their armoured feet sounded like distant thunder as they drew nearer. Thondril narrowed his eyes, trying to measure distances in his mind.

"Ballistae!" he ordered with a shout. The young sergeant standing nervously at his side raised a blue-and-red-crossed flag, the signal to the ballista crews stationed on the towers lining the walls. A similar flag was raised as the crew acknowledged the order.

Seconds later, a bolt the length of a man was launched from atop the nearest tower with a deafening twang. The crossbow-shaped ballista lurched in its iron frame as the deadly metal bolt flew.

The men roared as the bolt smashed into one of the approaching towers. The bolt decapitated the top of the wooden structure sending debris flying in all directions. As the order spread down the line, more ballista bolts were launched.

One flew wide of its mark to plunge into the horde below. The bolt carved a huge furrow into the earth, vaporising zombies and ghouls alike. Another bolt struck another tower, but instead of breaking it in two like the other had done, it embedded itself deep into the wood.

Thondril wiped his brow of the nervous sweat which was threatening to drip into his eyes. The ballistae were powerful weapons but would take precious minutes to reload. For a brief moment, he wished that the legion were manning the wall with his men, rather than the less-skilled soldiers of Eclin. *Use what you are given*, he scolded himself.

He turned to look at the southern wall. Smoke continued to rise, and the sound of clashing steel could be heard faintly over the stamping feet of the armoured ghouls.

He closed his eyes and offered a prayer to Niveren that the city would hold.

CHAPTER 33.

Woven left Elena and the boy at the baron's castle; then he snuck back out into the city. His men were fighting for their lives, and he would be at their side. To avoid the angry crowd at the castle gates, he had used one of the baron's escape tunnels which ran under the city streets. If the city fell, then the prince and baron would be smuggled out of the castle.

Unfortunately, the escape tunnels were also used as the city sewers, and the smell was foul. After ten minutes of running through the maze of tunnels and through who knew what, he came across a metal runged ladder which led back up onto the streets. He lifted the manhole cover and gasped as he breathed in the smoke-tainted air.

He looked around to get his bearings and realised he was on the main thoroughfare which led from the southern gate to the market district. A scene of utter carnage lay before him. The stones of the south wall were blackened by fire, and the charred corpses of dozens of soldiers were scattered nearby like broken toys. The gate was still standing, but every now and again it shuddered as something large and heavy smashed into it from the outside.

He narrowed his eyes to see rangers rushing towards the gate. Clambering over the walls were werewolves, their teeth bared and ready to kill. The Rangers shot a volley of arrows, which sent some of the beasts falling back from whence they came. Other werewolves evaded the deadly maelstrom, so the rangers drew their swords and charged into the fray.

Woven took his own bow from his shoulder and placed an arrow on the bowstring before running towards the fighting.

He dove for cover as the body of a ranger smashed into the ground. A werewolf had its jaws clamped tightly around the dead man's throat. Woven didn't hesitate; he loosed his arrow. It struck the monster in the eye. The beast howled as it reared back in pain. Woven drew his sword, pulled back his arm and hurled the blade. The sword spun as it flew. It punched through the wolf's chest with a satisfying *shlick* sound.

He darted forward, pulled his sword from the wolf, raised it high and cleaved the beast's head from its body. He did the same to the body of the ranger. The werewolves' curse was highly contagious; it was a well known fact that even the recently deceased could return as one of the beasts.

A horn sounded back up the road. Riding hard through the smoke were two dozen heavily armoured Knights of Niveren. They dismounted before quickly heading into the nearest tower to scale the stairs upward and join the fray. Woven was right behind them.

After a tiring climb, they burst out onto the walls. The knights ploughed into the beasts, their silver swords glinting in the sunlight as they cleaved their way into the enemy ranks. Woven let the Knights lead the way. He could see that they would secure the walls. Further down, he could see the rangers advancing steadily until with one last swing of a sword; the last werewolf was thrown from the wall. The rangers cheered at their victory.

"We were told the lich was here. Where is it?" one of the knights said sombrely.

Woven looked out over the wall. The ground was littered with arrows, broken bodies of defending soldiers and the corpses of zombies and werewolves. The lich was nowhere to be seen. He frowned as he noticed the burning gatehouse.

"It was here. It tried to destroy the gate," he said quietly. A nagging feeling wormed its way into his gut. Why had it stopped its assault? Was it toying with them?

Cheers went up from the other walls. He could see Eclin troops raising their weapons into the air in celebration on the western flank.

The Knights to the east, however, were quiet. A flaming arrow was shot high into the air from their position.

Woven sheathed his sword. That was the sign for the all clear.

"Have we won the day?" the knight asked, hope evident in his voice.

Woven shook his head.

"This was just the first day. The lich won't stop until we are all dead, or *we* kill *it*," he said as he clapped the knight on the shoulder. "If I were you, I'd prepare for a long siege."

CHAPTER 34.

Yepert tripped as the grim-faced legionary captain shoved him forward for the tenth time in as many minutes. With his hands bound, he was unable to keep his balance and fell face first onto the road. The three other soldiers laughed at the mage's plight. Yepert had been shocked at the hate the men directed towards him. Having spent much of his childhood safe in Caldaria, he'd had little knowledge of just how hostile the normal folk were to those with magic.

"Get up," the captain growled. A pair of big hands gripped his arm painfully and hauled him back onto his feet.

"Please. You have to listen to me!" Yepert pleaded.

"Don't! Cover yer ears less the mage puts a curse on us," another of the legionaries said. Genuine fear was in his tone.

The soldier squeezed Yepert's arm painfully.

"Shut up. You're gonna find out what happens to mages who break the law when we get to Sunguard. You'll probably be burnt alive on a pyre, or perhaps pulled apart by horses," the captain chuckled, licking his lips in glee.

"I think not," said a voice from ahead of the group.

Yepert's eyes widened, and a smile creased his lips. Standing in the middle of the road were two men. One clad in black, the other in white.

The black clad man was Ferran. At the Nightblade's side stood Kaiden; the knight had his silver sword resting casually on his shoulder.

"Who the heck are you? You dare interfere in legion business?" the captain snarled. He tightened his grip on the mage and unsheathed his sword. The other three soldiers did likewise.

"I am Ferran, Nightblade and defender of the realm. This," he said, gesturing to Kaiden, who flashed a smile, "is Sir Kaiden, a Knight of Niveren, and we are here to rescue our friend."

The legion captain spat.

"I don't care who you are. My orders come from General Rason, the true king of Delfinnia. Stand aside, or I'll order my men here to gut you like fish. You understand?"

Kaiden lowered his sword and pointed the tip of the blade at the captain.

"We will leave you till last," the knight said darkly. "You can tell your false king that we will stop him."

The captain chuckled humourlessly. He hauled Yepert backwards and threw him heavily into a bush at the side of the road. He pointed at one of his men.

"Make sure he doesn't move. Me and the lads have some killing to do."

The captain and two of the legionaries stalked towards Ferran and Kaiden, their weapons drawn.

"You take the goons, I'll take the captain here," Kaiden said to the Nightblade at his side. Ferran smiled and nodded in agreement.

Kaiden dashed forward and swung his sword in a wide arc. The sound of clashing steel rang out through the silent forest. The legionary captain blocked the attack with ease and countered with a thrust of his own. With lightning fast speed, Kaiden parried the blow and countered with a quick jab aimed at the captain's throat. The captain arched backwards. The tip of Kaiden's sword missing its target by mere inches.

The two men circled one another. Both were skilled; both were quick.

Kaiden feinted with a shift of his shoulder. The captain read the feint and forced him back a step with a lunge of his own sword. The blades clashed, and the fight began in earnest.

The captain bellowed as he swung his sword, narrowly missing Kaiden's chest. Kaiden parried another blow and launched a series of quick thrusts and cuts. They struck, coming together in a twist of sweat and straining muscle.

Kaiden took two quick steps forward forcing the captain off balance, and brought his blade up in a neat slice, breaking the captain's defence and cutting deeply into the growling man's chest. Only the captain's armour had saved him from a mortal wound.

The captain grunted in surprise as Kaiden pressed his attack without pause, slash after slash. Each was parried by shifts of weight and movements of the legionary's blade. Sweat poured into Kaiden's eyes.

Desperation filled him as he tried to think of new moves to break his foe's defences. He disengaged with a quick step backwards. Both men were panting and covered in sweat.

They stood glaring at one another. Both were skilled in the art of swordplay. For a heartbeat, neither man moved, then suddenly and with explosive force the two fighters smashed into each other again.

Kaiden darted in past the captain's guard with a twist of his body and was out again before his opponent could react. He buried his sword deep into the man's chest plate, piercing the armour as well as flesh and bone. Blood burst from the mortally wounded man's mouth before he crumpled into the dirt, blood pooling under his corpse.

Kaiden planted his sword into the ground and leaned heavily on the hilt, his breath coming in ragged gasps. He glanced behind him to see Ferran standing over the bodies of the other two legionaries. The Nightblade flashed him a cocky smirk. He had dispatched his foes without breaking a sweat. They had been no match for his magic.

"Good work, sir knight. These two," Ferran said gesturing to the bodies, "weren't all that good."

He whistled sharply. A few moments later, Sophia and Davik emerged from the trees. The Witch hunter had her bow ready and aimed at the remaining legionary, who now had his arms held high in the air in surrender.

"Please. Please don't hurt me. Don't turn me into anything unnatural, I beg you!" the soldier cried as Davik helped Yepert to his feet.

Yepert glared at the soldier. He felt sad that just because he was a magic user, the man was terrified of him. He was just a boy, after all. Davik disarmed the pleading man and shoved him to his feet.

"On your feet, son. Where were you heading?" the old warrior asked the soldier softly.

"S-S-Sunguard," the man stammered. "We were ordered to take the mage to the capital to stand trial. Please, I was just following orders."

Davik drew his sword and pointed it menacingly at the man's throat.

"We're letting you go. I suggest you run home, cast aside your weapons, and lay low. Now go," he said. The soldier sighed in relief and scurried off up the road.

"Are you alright?" Sophia asked Yepert. She hugged the boy tightly, causing him to blush. "They didn't hurt you, did they?"

"No. I'm fine, really," Yepert said. "How did you find me? I thought Alira had you all."

"As a Nightblade, I know some shortcuts through the wilds," Ferran explained. "The Golden Empire's engineers may have been brilliant, but they weren't very good at making their roads the shortest route."

Yepert then described all that had occurred since that night in the forest, and of what Rason had told him. Finally, he finished his tale. He noticed something. Someone was missing.

"Where's Luxon?"

Sophia looked away, tears in her eyes. Ferran looked away too, unable to meet the boy's concerned gaze. Kaiden, however, placed a hand on Yepert's shoulder.

"The Witch. She did something. Cast a spell, I think. She mentioned something about the Void ... that Luxon was the key." Kaiden sighed heavily. "He never returned, and we couldn't find him after Davik here freed us. I'm sorry."

Tears threatened to fall from the lad's eyes. His best friend in the world was gone. The knight squeezed his shoulder.

"What do we do now?" Davik asked tiredly. The old man was leaning against a nearby tree and rubbing his wounded leg. The speed at which they had crossed country had taken its toll on his body. Every part of him ached. When they had found the boy, he had been in no state to fight.

Ferran rubbed his chin, deep in thought.

"Rason is heading to Eclin," Sophia offered. "We know that Cliria and the general are allies in some way. Could she be looking to join him?"

"The legion ally with a witch? Never," Davik replied. "If his men knew that he was in league with one, they would stop following him in a heartbeat."

Before being made the king's bodyguard, Davik had been a commander in the legion. He knew how legionaries thought, and what they believed in.

"It's all for nought," Ferran said. "Even if we do find her again none of us have the power to oppose her. I say we return to Caldaria and get help from the mages. What do you say, sir knight?"

Kaiden was sitting on the ground; his eyes closed in prayer to Niveren. "My order went to Eclin," the knight said slowly. "The Heir is there. I will not speak for you all, but I am heading north. Balnor is a few miles to the east," he said, pointing down the road. "There we can resupply, get fresh horses and maybe even some allies. I feel that much will be decided in the mountain realm."

"I will go with Kaiden," Sophia said. "It is my sacred duty as a witch hunter to put an arrow in that bitch's black heart."

"I too will go with the knight. I have unfinished business with the general," Davik said as he limped over to stand beside the knight and witch hunter.

Ferran nodded in understanding. "Very well. The boy and I will return to Caldaria. I will bring as many Nightblades and mages as I can muster and hasten to Eclin. The priority is to safeguard the heir and destroy the witch. If we succeed, we can end the war."

CHAPTER 35.

Umbaroth soared over the strange world of the Void. Holding onto the mighty dragon's neck for dear life was Luxon.

Despite Aljeron's insistence that he wouldn't fall, he clung on tightly. The wizard was standing next to his young pupil, an amused expression on his face.

Passing below at an astounding pace were vast black forests and purple seas full of bizarre life forms. They had passed over a gigantic plain which was covered in huge luminous mushrooms, through which monstrous six-legged creatures ploughed.

The Void was an entirely different world and one that Luxon was finding stranger and stranger by the day. He had lost all track of time but knew that he must have been in the Void for over a decade. Time flowed differently in this strange place, and his worries for his friends had faded to a faint memory. But Aljeron assured him that in the real world, only a day or two had passed.

The dragon's massive wings cast a shadow on the lands below. Upon seeing the dragon, most of the creatures turned tail and fled. A huge host of Pucks had caused a stampede as they ran back into the forests of black trees.

Luxon was realising how much of a danger the Void posed to his home. If Danon or his followers ever succeeded in opening the rift as he had done thousands of years previously, then the beasts would flood through. He remembered the history classes taught by Master Ri'ges back in Caldaria.

The creatures of the Void had poured through the rift, their numbers beyond counting. In the days that followed, entire towns and cities were overrun. Countless men, women and children had perished.

"We're almost there," Umbaroth said in his deep rumbling voice over the sound of whistling air. Luxon almost heaved as the dragon began to descend. Even though he knew he was just a spirit in this place, his mind still held on to the belief that he was there physically.

After a quick descent, the dragon landed with a slight thud. Despite his huge size, Umbaroth was surprisingly light-footed when he wanted to be.

Luxon slid off the dragon's back. Using magic, he slowed his descent. The dragon was the height of a two-storey house after all.

His powers were growing by the day. Already he had mastered the lower and middle rings of magic. Today he would be taught the upper ring.

His feet touched the ground softly. Aljeron applauded his skill at levitation.

"Well done. Remember that magic can be used to enhance your body. The upper ring will grant you the power to increase your speed and even your strength. Be warned, though, that such spells are immensely tiring." The wizard, too, floated down to the ground. "The Nightblades specialise in such magic. They make it look easy," he added.

Luxon looked around. They had landed on a small island in the middle of a vast lake. Strange purple water lapped gently upon the shore. He could see brightly coloured fish-like creatures swimming. They glowed in the twilight, turning blue, orange, and yellow. The Void was full of strange beauty.

"I wouldn't get too close," Aljeron warned, pointing at the brightly coloured creatures. "The Mokoin tend to drag their victims from the shore. Then they drown them and eat them."

Luxon stepped back from the water's edge slowly. Things were beautiful, but underneath it all everything could kill in the Void.

"Why are we here?" Luxon asked.

Umbaroth settled onto his haunches, placing his huge head on top of his front legs, folded his wings, and closed his eyes.

"I, for one, am here to sleep," the dragon muttered. In a few moments, the mighty creature was snoring loudly.

"We are here to teach you. Today, you will learn how to fight with magic. As a wizard you will face many challenges," Aljeron explained as he led the way through a copse of trees and into a clearing. Around the edges were bushes covered in sharp leaves.

Aljeron gestured for Luxon to stand in the middle of the clearing.

"I call these strange bushes razor plants,'" the wizard said. "It is here that you will learn to shield yourself from harm. I will also teach you the first of the four elemental upper spells. The first of which is wind."

Aljeron closed his eyes for a second. He opened them again and stared at one of the razor plants. He pursed his lips and blew. To Luxon's amazement, the plants began to stir. A soft wind began to blow through their leaves. Aljeron blew harder, and the wind picked up strength. The wizard kept blowing. With every puff, the wind grew in power until it howled like a gale. Luxon staggered under the wind's assault. The razor blade leaves of the plants began to snap off the branches and were hurled around in a vortex.

Aljeron stopped blowing and raised a hand at the swirling howling winds.

"Once the wind is strong enough, I can direct it and control it as though it were something solid and alive," he said, his voiced raised in order to be heard over the noise of the gale.

He gestured with his arms, and the vortex swirled along with them. Luxon laughed. He had never seen such a spell. He was beginning to realise the gulf between being a mage and being a wizard.

Aljeron lowered his arms and the wind dissipated. The razor leaves dropped to the ground like a deadly rain shower.

"Now for your test. I will use the wind to stir up the leaves. You must then use only magic to protect yourself. If you do not, then you will be cut to ribbons," the wizard said seriously. "As you are a thaumaturgist, you should instinctively cast the correct spell."

"That's reassuring," Luxon mumbled warily.

Aljeron smiled.

"Prepare yourself."

The wizard blew once more. The winds stirred again, and the razor leaves were lifted into the air.

Luxon set his feet and concentrated. A single leaf shot towards him, its jagged edges spiralling erratically as it was buffeted and rocked by the winds. It flew closer and closer. Luxon felt sweat break out on his forehead as panic threatened to overwhelm him. He cried out as the leaf struck; the pointed edge cut his cheek as it whipped past.

"You had best do better," Aljeron chided.

Luxon scowled at the wizard. He put a hand to his cheek; it came away bloody.

"If I am hurt here in the Void, what happens to my body in the real world, wherever it may be?" Luxon asked as he pressed his hands to his wounded face in an effort to stem the bleeding. He focused his magic, and a white light emanated from his palms. The cut was healed. He was glad he had mastered the healing spells of the middle ring before this little test.

"If you are harmed here, your body too is harmed. However, if you are hurt or die in the other world, you will linger here in your spirit form. My body perished countless aeons ago," Aljeron replied a hint of sadness in his voice.

"Oh great. Now you tell me!" Luxon replied sarcastically.

"All the more reason for you not to fail again," Aljeron scolded. "Now focus."

Again the wizard stirred the winds, but this time, instead of sending a single leaf Luxon's way, he conjured up a maelstrom that pulled the deadly leaves off of every razor plant in the clearing. Luxon gulped as the mass of dagger-like leaves swirled towards him.

"You have the power of a wizard within you, Luxon. Use it and prove your might," Aljeron shouted over the howling winds.

Luxon planted his feet and narrowed his eyes. He plunged into himself until he felt the warm sensation of the magic within. Slowly, he eased it outwards until it filled every part of his body. The power grew and grew until he felt the sensation he had felt in the Arch Tower when confronting the Baron of Retbit.

The first of the leaves soared towards him, but this time he was ready. He raised his arms and unleashed some of his power. The leaves struck the shield he had created and were vaporised into ash. More and more leaves struck until he was engulfed in them. The shield shrank under the onslaught. Sweat poured into his eyes as he maintained his concentration. He focused more and drew the shield into himself so that it shrouded his body like a second skin. The deadly leaves snapped and burned as they struck his body.

Luxon was revelling in the power he felt surging through him. He smiled. With a shout, he thrust his arms wide, sending the magical energy exploding outwards in a blinding flash which destroyed all of the leaves in an instant.

Steam poured off of his body. If he had been wearing real clothes, he was pretty sure they, too, would have been vaporised. He panted as he gazed around the clearing.

Where he was standing, the ground was blackened as though a hot flame had scorched it. The bushes surrounding the clearing were now just blackened stumps, and Aljeron was standing and smouldering nearby. He looked unimpressed. Luxon had to try his hardest not to laugh out loud.

"That was amazing!" he cried in excitement. The buzz of the power was coursing through him.

"You did well. You are indeed powerful, young one," the wizard said. Luxon frowned; something was off with the wizard's tone. It sounded like jealously was in the old man's voice.

"It won't be long before you're strong enough to stand against Danon!" the wizard exclaimed.

Luxon took an involuntary step backwards in surprise.

"Wh-what do you mean, stand against Danon? He'll destroy me in a heartbeat, surely," he stammered.

The ground shook as Umbaroth lumbered into the clearing. The dragon lowered its head.

"If you wish to return home, you will need his power," the dragon said. "Only immense magical energy is capable of opening a rift back there from here within the Void. It's what Danon has been trying to achieve for centuries. To get you home, we must follow his plan. I too will be needed, and that is why he had enslaved my kin."

Luxon slumped his shoulders. He was afraid, but he knew they were right. He couldn't allow his fear to overwhelm him. His friends needed his help. He straightened his back again and set his jaw in determination.

"If it's the only way for me to return, then so be it. Teach me everything I need to defeat Danon; teach me to be a wizard."

The girl was happily walking along the sandy shore. Her long brown hair was tied up into a knot – a common style among Yundol women – and her clothes were brightly coloured and loose, as was the Yundol tradition. She hummed a song of her tribe as she dipped her toes into the gently lapping sea. The cold water was refreshing compared to the harsh heat of the scorched land which made up much of the Yundol continent. Her tribe lived on the cliffs above the coast and made their livings as fishermen or pirates. The kingdom of Delfinnia across the sea was wealthy, and her merchants made easy prey since the royal fleet had disbanded at the outbreak of the civil war.

The girl lazily stretched her limbs and yawned. It had been a good day. The sack at her feet was full of shellfish which she had plucked from the nearby rock pools. She frowned as a dark shape in the sand further up the beach caught her eye. Things were often washed ashore; sometimes barrels of Delfin ale or other valuables made it onto the beach. There was good coin to be had from the selling of such things.

She picked up the sack of shellfish and slung it over her shoulder. The sun was going down, but she had time to investigate the shape.

As she drew nearer, she could see it was covered in something blue. It was a cloak, she realised, as the blue material fluttered about in the breeze. Underneath was a body. She cried out and ran towards the figure. Sure enough, the object was, in fact, a person – a young man, in fact. A boy who had seen no more than fifteen summers, with a head of sandy blond hair. She dropped her basket and ran back up the beach to her village for help.

CHAPTER 36.

Balnor

The city of Balnor stood proud and strong, nestled among the hills that had given the empire its name. It was also known as the City of Gold. The banners of the Baron of Balnor fluttered in the breeze. The emblem of the eagle with a bar of gold in its talons flew proudly.

Kaiden halted Herald with a tug of the reins. The white stallion whinnied and stamped the ground, kicking up tufts of dirt and dust. Kaiden patted the beast's neck fondly.

"Easy boy," he soothed. Sitting behind him was Davik. The elderly warrior had no horse of his own and had been forced to ride with the knight. His pleas to ride with Sophia had been met with humorous scorn by the witch hunter.

"Do you think the baron will be here? If Rason's legion took the road north, surely Balnor scouts would have spotted it," Davik surmised.

"Even he's not here, as a Knight of Niveren I can evoke conscription. The men of Balnor will eagerly march north in order to save the rightful heir," Kaiden said certainly.

Sophia didn't look convinced.

"Balnor was one of the first barons to declare that the crown was his, and his forces have seen the fiercest fighting. He's probably still licking his wounds from his defeat at the Golden Hills," she said.

Davik flashed her a smile. "That, my dear, is why he's more inclined to help us. He'll want revenge on Rason after that little debacle. I saw the battle with my own eyes. Despite superior numbers, Balnor was routed by the legion. Some of the tactics Rason used were simply brilliant."

The fading sun caused the tower's shadows to stretch across the surrounding landscape.

"The sun's going down, and I need a drink. Shall we?" Kaiden said spurring Herald into a trot.

The group entered the city without any fuss, something that surprised Davik. The city was at war, and yet the gates were open. The guardsman watching the road and questioning new arrivals seemed tense. The travellers passed under the gatehouse and into a wide avenue that stretched for over a mile. Along both sides were buildings, taverns, shops, and houses. True to the city's name, many of the buildings were painted gold, and some even had the precious metal engraved upon their walls. The stone slabs of the road were also painted gold, giving the city a sense of wealth and cleanliness not common in Delfinnia.

Most towns had mud roads with waste lying in the streets. Only the major cities had any form of sanitation. The vast sewer systems built by the Golden Empire were now mostly just ruins, the relics of a bygone age.

"If I remember correctly, the baron's castle is along the avenue and then up a steep incline," Kaiden explained as he pointed to the castle, which stood higher than the surrounding buildings.

"Ye searching for the baron?" Came a voice from a nearby doorway. A man dressed in simple clothes stepped out of the shadow of the doorway. He was bald with a bushy beard that covered much of his face. His eyes were blue, but his most distinguishing feature was the tattoo that covered half of his face.

"We are," Kaiden replied cautiously. He glanced around. The street was quiet; even the taverns were not giving out the usual sounds of minstrels or raucous laughter.

The man looked around shiftily.

"You should come with me. These streets aren't safe anymore. Not since the baron ... well, not since he changed."

Davik slid off of the back of Herald and drew his sword.

"Who are you? Talk, or I'll run you through," the warrior snarled. He was tired and in no mood for games.

The man raised his hands in surrender.

"Easy, old man. I was just offering ye shelter. When the sun goes down, the streets are far from safe. This city is cursed," the man said conspiratorially.

Kaiden frowned. The silence of the city, the fact that the gate was wide open, and the vacant look in the guards' eyes: something was wrong in Balnor, he knew it. Looking at Sophia, he could tell that the witch hunter could sense it, too. He put a calming hand on Davik's shoulder.

"I think we should go with our new friend here," he said gently. The sun was dipping below the walls, causing shadows to spread like spilt ink across the cityscape.

"My name is Thrift," the man introduced himself.

Sophia stared at him. "Thrift? As in Thrift from Ridderford?" she asked, her hand reaching for the dagger tucked into her belt.

"You know this man?" Kaiden asked. He too rested a hand on the pommel of his sword. The look on the witch hunter's face did little to ease his nerves.

Sophia nodded. Thrift squinted his eyes to study her.

"He's a thief. Last time I saw him, he was the leader of the Fleetfoot guild in Ridderford," she explained as she stepped closer menacingly.

Thrift threw his hands up.

"Hey, I ain't no thief. I've lived 'ere all my life, I swear it!" the bald man said defensively. "We ain't got time for this nonsense. The sun is going down."

Sophia grabbed the man roughly by his collar and hauled him close, her dagger pressed against his chin.

"You know Ferran of Blackmoor," she said quietly. Upon hearing the name, Thrift's eyes widened. "You were his friend and source of information if I remember correctly. I also seem to recall that it was you who helped the Nightblade murder, my father," she snarled.

Thrift struggled against the witch hunter's grip. She let him go, causing him to fall backwards into the doorway from whence he had appeared. He clambered to his feet. His eyes darted from Sophia to the two armed men, both of whom had now drawn their swords.

"You're Sophia Cunning- the witch hunter general's daughter? The one who came to me all those years back for help," Thrift gushed, his words coming out quickly. "You've aged very well; I must say," he added weakly.

Sophia pointed her dagger at the thief's throat. "That's right. You owe me, you whoreson. You left me to die in that N'gist tomb," she snarled as dark memories came flooding back.

Kaiden placed a hand on the witch hunter's arm and squeezed gently. He could feel it shaking with anger.

"Sophia," he said softly. "If what this man says is true then we must get off of the streets."

With a deep sigh, Sophia reluctantly released her grip on the thief. She glared at the man for a moment before turning and walking away.

Thrift adjusted his collar.

"Thank you," he said to the knight. But he would not find any sympathy from Kaiden, who gave him an icy look.

"Just take us to this place of yours and tell us what evil has befallen this city before I change my mind and let her have her way with you," he threatened, pointing at Sophia. "Somehow I doubt it will be a pleasant experience."

Thrift led them through a warren of back streets and side alleys until they reached the door of a rather innocuous-looking building. Unlike the other buildings in Balnor, not a trace of gold leaf decorated the walls. Instead, it was covered in ivy and mould-darkened plaster. The sunlight finally faded as they reached it.

Just as Thrift was fumbling to unlock the door, a gut-wrenching scream emanated from somewhere deep in the city. Kaiden and Davik instinctively reached for their swords.

"Those won't do you any good. C'mon, get inside quickly," Thrift said, shoving the heavy wooden door open.

They found themselves in a brightly lit hallway with a dozen doors lining either side. Small, dirty looking children stared at them as they walked deeper into the building. Men and women lived in cramped conditions, and all were curious about their guests.

As they passed the doorways, they could see dozens of children playing with dice and other games. Elderly women nursed infants, and men with missing limbs or other medical conditions limped around.

"Welcome to the Balnor Fleetfloots," Thrift said dramatically. He pushed open a pair of big oak double doors and led them into a high-ceilinged room.

Candles burned brightly, lighting up a large stone platform at the room's far end. A long table which could seat over forty people stood in the centre of the room. Thrift leapt onto the platform and opened his arms wide.

"This is my home, and the home of orphans, cripples and other unwanted souls. We take from the rich to feed our bellies and keep a roof over our heads," He exalted.

"Thieves' with honour- pah," Davik scoffed.

Thrift frowned.

"Who else but the Fleetfoots would take in and feed those folk? You lords and ladies are all too busy fighting your stupid wars and delving into intrigues whilst the common folk starve and are forgotten," Thrift snapped. The thief clapped his hands loudly.

A side door opened and out came a dozen young men and women. Each wore brown leather armour, and each had a dagger in their belt.

"The orphans are sheltered and fed. They grow up and join the Foots. Believe it or not, old man, we try to serve the realm just as much as you, knights and witch hunters do," he added, hesitantly glancing at Sophia.

"We just do it in the shadows. I bet I know more things that are occurring in the world at this moment than any of you lot do."

Sophia was about to snap off a snide remark, but Kaiden stopped her with a look. He opened his hands to put the thief at ease. In his travels as a knight of the Order, he had often seen the Fleetfoots. In every major town and city in the land, they had a presence. They were an intelligence network in all but name.

"I'm sure you do," Kaiden said slowly. "So, what is occurring in Balnor that leads the famous Fleetfoots to hide inside during their preferred hours of activity?"

Thrift looked away, his skin whitening. The other thieves also looked frightened.

"Death stalks the streets," one of them said, a young woman no more than sixteen.

"'Tis true. It comes from the baron's castle every night to feed on the living!" chimed in another, this one a boy.

Sophia glanced at Kaiden with a raised eyebrow.

"*What* comes from the castle?" Kaiden asked.

"It started a few days ago," Thrift explained. "A woman with long blond hair arrived in the city and met with the baron. That same night, a scream came from the castle, one that would have chilled you to your very core. Everyone heard it. The next day there were stories that people had vanished from their homes. Every night the same scream, and more folk vanished. People tried to escape the city, but none could."

"How come?" Davik said. The old man was idly fingering his sword's hilt. His eyes were tight with tension. He was a man used to fighting other men, not monsters.

CHAPTER 36.

"A spell!" the young woman cried. "Those who stepped through the city gate ... they ... they ... died."

"It can't just be me that's thinking that Cliria passed this way," Sophia muttered.

Kaiden wiped a gloved hand over his face. Just once he wanted things to go right. If Cliria was in the city, then they were all in grave danger. None of them were a match for the witch, not even the brave witch hunter, or tough old warrior.

"What purpose would she have being here? Why prevent the people from leaving?" Davik asked, scratching his chin.

"I guess we should find out," Sophia said fingering the hilt of her dagger, "and if the opportunity arises where I can put a knife in her blackened heart all the better."

CHAPTER 37.

Sophia knelt in the darkness. The shadow cast by one of Balnor's tall spires added to the depth of blackness concealing her. Crouched next to her was Thrift. The thief had insisted on leading her through the maze of backstreets leading to the baron's castle.

Their hiding spot was close to the gatehouse which barred the path leading up the hill to where the castle stood. A large square of open ground lay between them and it.

As they had crossed the city, they had heard panicked cries and the sounds of people cowering in their homes. Luckily, they had avoided whatever was stalking the streets.

"There are no guards," Thrift whispered, pointing to the gate. Sophia's gaze focused: sure enough, the gatehouse was dark and quiet. She grabbed Thrift's hand and pulled him after her as she sprinted across the square. It was eerily quiet.

With agile grace, the witch hunter climbed up the stone wall and leapt down to the other side. Thrift was close behind.

"Been awhile since I snuck into this place," he said, licking his lips at the prospect of the loot within the castle's walls. Sophia gave him a sour look.

"We're not here to steal," she growled. "We're here to find the witch and find out what she wants from Balnor. If I catch you inching a single candlestick, I'll put my dagger up your dung-hole."

Thrift's eyes went wide; even in the pale light cast by the moons, she could see his face pale.

Quickly, they moved up the hill. No guards were in sight. Whatever was terrorising the city had scared them off, too. They stayed close to the tall wall's shadow. Thrift avoided the main gateway and led them around to the base of the castle. Hidden in a small arched alcove was a wooden door.

Thrift pulled a small pouch of black powder from his belt and poured a small amount into the door's iron lock. Next, he took a piece of flint and struck a spark. With a smile, he placed a small piece of cloth around the lock and held the flame under it.

With a muffled cracking noise and a bright light, the lock was blown off.

"Very clever," Sophia said, genuinely impressed.

Thrift flashed her a toothless smile before slowly opening the door. The door's hinges creaked loudly, and dust fell as the heavy wood moved inwards. Quickly, they stepped inside.

"We're in the cellar. Up those stairs are the castle kitchens," Thrift said quietly. He hefted his dagger and Sophia likewise drew her blade. If they did run into trouble, they had to hope that being fleet of foot would save their hides.

The cellar was filled with large barrels full of ales and *Glog*, the favoured drink of the citizens of Delfinnia. Cobwebs covered every spare inch of space, suggesting that the room was rarely used.

"There's a newer, bigger cellar on the other side," Thrift explained. Crouching, he hurried to the base of the stairs. At the top was a door. No light could be seen shining underneath its frame. The thief reached into the pouch on his belt to pull out two small metal rods. He pressed his ear to the wooden door and placed the rods inside the lock. After a few moments of fiddling, the lock snapped open with a satisfying click.

Sophia smiled. She'd never seen a lock picked so quickly. She was skilled in the art, too, but she knew she was no match for the master thief before her.

Her smile faded as the memory of that dark day drifted into her mind. It had been Thrift who had helped smuggle Ferran into her father's stronghold. It was he who had helped the Nightblade find evidence of treason against her father – the catalyst for his death.

She shook her head angrily, wiping a tear from her eye with a gloved hand.

"You okay?" Thrift asked uncertainly.

"I'm fine. Let's get this over with," Sophia replied shortly.

Carefully, Thrift eased the door open. On the other side was a kitchen. It was dark and empty, save for the mouse scurrying across the surface of a table in the centre of the room.

A big iron pot sat in the centre of a long dead fire, and food lay scattered about as though the cook had suddenly vanished while preparing a meal. Whatever had occurred in the castle had happened quickly and with little warning.

"This way to the main hall," Thrift said pointing to an arched doorway at the opposite side of the kitchens. They slipped out of the room and found themselves in a long corridor. The braziers and candles which normally would have been lit by the castle servants lay dark and cold, casting an eerie feeling over the place.

Guessing that the place was deserted, they picked up their pace. They passed through what appeared to be servants' quarters. It, too, was dark and empty. Finally, they reached an open door which led into a long high-ceilinged throne room.

Sophia pressed her back against the cold stone wall and peeked around the door's frame. Her eyes widened, and her heart sank as she saw Cliria pacing the room. A single candle was lit, its light flickering and casting shadows along the walls. The opulent room was painted with gold leaf, and huge red and gold tapestries hung from a balcony high up on the walls.

Sophia narrowed her eyes. Sitting on a throne behind the witch was a man. He was no older than fifty, but his haggard appearance made him look far older. His beard was grey and unkempt, and his long hair was a tangled mess. From his clothes, she knew that the figure was the Baron of Balnor. He wore the clothes of a nobleman: a large golden chain was around his neck, and his purple shirt and blue trousers were inlaid with golden silk.

Deftly, Sophia slipped into the chamber. She rolled silently across the polished marble floor to take up a position behind one of the pillars that ran along the edge of the room. She wished she'd brought her bow, but the bulky object made moving stealthily near impossible. She held her dagger tightly.

"I tire of this game, Baron," Cliria was saying.

Sophia inched closer, straining her ears to hear what the witch was saying.

"You are broken, and yet you refuse to give me what I want," the witch snarled, pacing in front of the slumped baron. "Has it not been torture enough to see what I have done to your beloved wife? Do you wish her and your people's suffering to continue?"

"I will not tell you," the baron replied quietly, his voice breaking with emotion. "You have failed, witch. Unlike Rason or Retbit I will not become your puppet."

Cliria rounded on the baron and glared icily. She clicked her fingers and, seemingly out of nowhere, one of the crimson-clad assassins stepped out of the shadows. The killer pulled his arm back before punching the baron hard across the face. Blood sprayed, and the baron's head lolled to the side.

"Perhaps seeing your wife be turned was not enough," Cliria muttered, stroking her chin with a long finger. A vicious smile creased her lips, and she chuckled wickedly.

"Bring me his children."

The baron's eyes went wide. He struggled against the assassin who had pinned him into his throne. Tears flooded from his eyes.

"Please, no, not my children. You must not! Please!" the baron cried.

Sophia ducked back deeper into the shadows. She noticed Thrift slip into the room to hide behind a pillar on the opposite side. She was too busy focusing on the thief to notice the Crimson Blade sneaking up behind her from the darkness. Thrift did. He pointed wildly, causing her to turn.

The assassin was taken by surprise. He'd intended to snap her neck, and his dagger was still in his belt. Sophia's was not. Quickly, she spun to face her attacker, instinctively bringing her blade around in a slicing motion.

The metal caught the assassin in the throat, slicing it open. Before he could scream and give away her position, Sophia leapt on him and drove the dagger deeper into his mangled oesophagus.

Only quiet gargling and a spray of blood emanated from the killer. The two fell to the ground. Sophia sighed in relief as the thick red carpet muffled their fall.

She was breathing heavily and sighed. She could still hear Cliria tormenting the baron; they were still undetected. She scanned the shadows for any more of the assassins and was relieved to see no more on her side of the room.

Her thoughts were interrupted by the sound of children's cries. The baron wept.

Two small children, no older than eight years old, were shoved into the room. A boy and a girl, holding hands and crying. Both had curly blond hair and blue eyes reddened by tears. They were both in night clothes, the boy in blue pyjamas and the girl in a pink nightdress. Behind them was another of the crimson-robed killers.

"No!" cried the baron.

"Papa," the children cried. The assassin pushed the children forwards. Cliria clapped her hands, laughing with delight. Sophia tightened her grip on her dagger. Out of the corner of her eye, she could see Thrift shaking his head in warning. She eased her grip. If they were discovered, they all would surely die.

"Oh, aren't they just precious," Cliria cooed sickeningly.

"Please ... not my children," the baron pleaded weakly.

All pretence at being kindly vanished from the witch's features. She darted forward, roughly grabbed the bawling girl by the arm and dragged her towards her father.

"Tell me what you know of the sword. Tell me or this mewling brat will suffer the same fate as your wife," Cliria snarled. The girl struggled against the witch's powerful grip and cried out for her father. The baron glared at the witch, his eyes full of hate.

Sophia tensed. Her mind raced. What sword did Cliria want to learn of?

The baron hesitated; his eyes raw from the tears streaming down his distraught face. He closed them and firmed his mouth shut. He turned away, unable to look at his daughter.

"You think your silence will spare them? You think that it will save you? Nothing can stop our plans!" Cliria screamed.

Enraged, she shoved the girl to the ground. One of the assassins held the girl still whilst the witch stood over her.

She closed her eyes, summoning the dark powers. Her skin faded to a sickly white, and black veins appeared on her hands and face. Her voice turned deep and unnatural. She spoke strange words ... words of the N'gist cult.

Dark energy swirled around her body as an unnatural wind swept the hall. The large tapestries swayed and rocked and the ground itself shuddered. The candle went out, plunging the room into deeper darkness.

The girl began to scream. Her small body contorted, the bones snapping sickeningly. Her skin tore and split as the summoned abomination clawed its way out from the terrified child.

The winds faded. The candle burst back into life. Sophia clamped a hand over her mouth to stifle a scream.

Standing where the child had once been was a monster from the worst of nightmares.

"Behold, Baron," Cliria chuckled cruelly. "Both of the women you love are now Necrist. Is it not an improvement?"

The beast was the height of a man, and it stood on two muscular legs, but that was where the similarities ended.

Its arms were long and covered in spines; its hands were talons, the nails like razor blades. The colour of its skin was a dark grey, and its torso was thick with muscle and covered in sharp black hairs.

Most disturbing of all, however, was the face. It bore the features of the little girl, but instead of her dainty mouth, there was an open maw filled with sharp teeth.

"Thanks to you, Baron, Balnor will now be terrorised by two monsters," Cliria said. "I wonder how many of your people will be left alive by the time you tell me what I need to know." The witch stroked the slavering monster like someone would pet a dog or cat.

"Go outside and have some fun, my dear," she whispered into the beast's ear. With a snarl, the Necrist turned and bounded out of the room.

Cliria turned her attention back to the baron. She clicked her fingers, and the assassin shoved the terrified boy onto the floor. The witch draped an arm over the lad's shoulders.

"Look at your boy, the heir to your lands. So scared, so afraid. All noblemen love their sons, for they continue your legacy. Tell me what I wish to know, and I will spare him."

The baron looked at his son. His lips quivered. He was a broken man.

"The Sword ... it lies hidden. Safe. Only the one destined to wield it can find it. All I know is where the key is," the baron answered weakly.

"Key? If I have the key then the one meant to wield it can never find it," Cliria said thoughtfully. She stroked the boy's cheek threateningly. The baron held a hand up.

"The key was crafted by mages and hidden. The companion of King Markus the Mighty, the first king of Delfinnia, hid it in the north. It lies within a cave nestled high in the Eclin Mountains. It is a place known as the Sigil Caves."

Cliria clapped her hands in delight. She spun around, her arms open wide, her long dress twirling as she pranced.

"Oh happy day!" she cried. "I will find the key, and the threat to my beloved will be gone forever. His return approaches. He told me so in my dreams. Soon he will have all the power he needs to return to me."

"Kill me, witch, for I have doomed the entire world," the baron sobbed.

Cliria stopped her twirling to skip over to the broken baron. She put a finger under his chin and kissed him on the lips. A red glow appeared around the baron's face. She kissed him harder, and the light intensified until it was blinding.

Sophia looked away. The boy screamed. The flesh on the baron's face had been burned away. Only his charred skull remained.

Satisfied with her handiwork, Cliria turned and tousled the boy's hair before striding out of the chamber, her assassins at her back.

Sophia fell to her knees. The horror she had witnessed overwhelming her. Tears streamed down her cheeks as she stifled sobs. Thrift emerged from the shadows after hearing the large doors close deeper from within the castle.

"Niveren save us ..." he uttered in stunned disbelief. He'd heard tales of the N'gist cult. Hell, he'd even helped Ferran destroy a sect of the cult years before, but never had he seen such terrible magic in action. He felt sick.

Cries brought him back to reality. He turned to see the baron's son hugging the legs of his dead father.

"The sword she was asking about. I think I know what it is," Thrift said, staring at the baron's body. The charred skull stared back at him with holes where his eyes had been. Sophia stepped out of the shadows, her emotions once again under control.

"What is it, Thrift? What is so important for her to have done this?"

The thief swallowed hard.

"I think the sword she was talking about is *Asphodel* – The weapon used by Zahnia and Niveren himself to destroy evil. If she gets her hands on it; the world is doomed."

CHAPTER 38.

"It's funny how old stories get forgotten or twisted. Details which should never be forgotten sometimes are, and the more fantastical aspects are wrongly elaborated upon.

"The fall of Danon is such a tale. Most believe that at the end of the Age of Darkness, Zahnia the Great beheaded the enemy and cast his body into the Void. This is not so. For how could it be that over a thousand years later, Danon came close to returning to the world in the final days of the Magic Wars?

"No. Danon's body was never destroyed. There is a myth that only a few now recall. In this version of events, the followers of the N'gist cult recovered their master's body and hid it deep within the mountain lands beyond the boundary of the empire. In the deepest cavern of the tallest mountain, Danon's tomb was made. His soul was cast into the Void, but not his body.

"Instead it was hidden and kept for his return. Thousands of years have passed since those days, but still, his immortal bride continues her quest to restore her beloved."

As Aljeron spoke, Luxon sat cross-legged on a patch of purple grass, his eyes closed in concentration. He had lost track of how long he had been in the Void. In the outside world, only a few weeks had passed, but to him every hour felt like a year of time. He felt old.

"Why are you telling me this?" he asked the wizard irritably. His powers had grown beyond his imaginings. There was nothing more the old wizard could teach him. He was losing patience.

Aljeron stroked his beard, a faint smile on his lips.

"I tell you this, Luxon, because it is important. I have taught you for years, and still, you do not understand."

Luxon opened his eyes, frowning. "What am I supposed to understand? I am ready. The longer we waste our time here, the more danger my friends are in, and the more mischief the witch can do. I am strong enough to face her. I know it."

Aljeron chuckled, infuriating Luxon even more.

"Very well. So be it," the wizard said. He walked forward a few paces and raised his staff high into the air. With his free hand, he cupped his mouth.

"Umbaroth summoni," his voice boomed. The sheer volume caused Luxon to clasp his hands over his ears. He hated it when the wizard did that.

Aljeron's voice echoed off of the nearby hills, and a flock of the strange lizard-like birds native to the Void launched themselves from the trees in terror.

A few seconds later, the familiar sound of large flapping wings could be heard approaching. Luxon looked to the sky. Umbaroth soared over the mountaintop; his massive wings opened wide as the dragon glided down the other side.

With agility that always surprised Luxon, the massive beast landed gracefully into the clearing.

"You summoned me, Aljeron? It has been a long time since last we met. I was busy eating some Pucks when you called. I still have some bones stuck in my teeth." The dragon used one of his huge talons to pick his equally massive teeth.

"Yes, my old friend. Luxon here says that he is ready," Aljeron said.

The dragon arched a scaly eyebrow. He lowered his huge head to look at Luxon.

"You look old, boy. But I do sense the power within you." Umbaroth glanced at Aljeron questioningly. A look passed between the two.

Luxon frowned. *What was that about?* He wondered. For the first time since his arrival in the Void, he felt something – a nagging sense that something was wrong.

He doubted Aljeron.

Over the past few years, the old wizard had become strange. He'd vanish for long periods of time to places Luxon knew not where.

Something else nagged at him. He'd been trapped in the Void for what felt like decades, and yet not once had he encountered Danon or even his minions. He'd had a few close encounters with Pucks, redcaps and banshees for sure, but nothing sent by the Dark One.

Aljeron looked at the sky.

"It is late in the day. Tomorrow we will go to Danon's tower, and together we will send you home."

Ominous dark clouds filled the northern skies. Bright flashes of lightning illuminated the distant mountain peaks before leaving them to fade back into shadow.

The Sunguard legion trudged its way along the Eclin road, their feet sore from the long march north. Legionaries supported their comrades as they succumbed to agonising blisters that slowed down the column's steady march.

Captain Odrin watched the men go past. He was sitting upon his grey mare, eating a slice of rock-hard cheese and frowning all the while. He had followed general Rason into more battles than he could count.

They had fought side by side on the Marble Shore against the Yundol invaders years earlier. The battles fought deep in the jungle lands of Zahnia, and the marshlands of

Retbit had been like hell, but together they had come through it all. Rason had got them through it.

Now, however, for the first time in his long career, Odrin doubted his general. Ever since that terrible night in Sunguard, the general was changed. Any shred of mercy or kindness that had been in his soul was lost, replaced by a blind ambition and a dark ruthlessness.

His mind drifted back to the night when the royal family had been murdered.

Before the alarm bells had begun to toll their harrowing sound across the capital, he had been playing a card game with the general and other officers.

A knock at the barracks door had paused the game, and he himself had opened the door ...

Odrin glanced to the horizon. The storm raged on just like it had done the night Delfinnia went to shit.

The caller had been a young woman. Her face had been hidden by a cloak. She had specifically asked for Rason. As men often do, they wolf whistled and leered and even congratulated the general on his good fortune. Odrin hadn't seen Rason again until the legion was ordered onto the streets to hunt for the assassins. It was after that woman's visit that his old comrade had changed.

He closed his eyes, wishing he could shake the horror of the following night out of his mind. The Night of Tears they called it. It had been the night that Rason lost his mind, and the legion lost their sense of honour. They had butchered men, women and children until the capital's streets had run red with blood.

A distant thunderclap made Odrin open his eyes.

"Riders incoming," yelled a legionary scout galloping up the column.

Odrin looked down the line of marching men. Sure enough, four cloaked riders thundered past him to head towards the front of the column.

"Scout!" he bellowed, causing the rider to turn his horse and trot back down the line to his captain.

"Sir!" the scout greeted with a smart salute.

"Who are those riders? Why didn't the rearguard hold them?" The men were tired, but they weren't stupid.

"The rider gave the password, sir. It was a pretty lady and three blokes. Their faces were hidden by their hoods. She said that she was a friend of the general," the scout explained in an oddly monotone voice. The man's eyes were strangely vacant, as though his mind was someplace else.

Odrin narrowed his eyes.

"Are you alright, soldier?" he asked.

The scout simply smiled dumbly.

"Her voice is like music," the man said in a sing-song tone.

That was it. Something was definitely afoot. With a salute, he dismissed the scout, turned his horse, and shot off up the line to see the general.

As he approached the head of the column, Odrin noticed the legionaries throwing him looks of concern. Some of the grim-faced veterans were muttering to themselves; others made the sign of Niveren as though warding off evil.

Up ahead he could hear a woman laughing in delight, the general's deep laughter accompanying it. Odrin scowled deeper, his hand reaching for his sword. He rode closer to the general.

Sure enough, a young blond-haired woman was with the general. She was a beauty and no mistake. He would have dismissed her as just one of Rason's many mistresses, but the silent, crimson cloaked figures riding at her side emanated menace.

"Ah, Captain. The lovely Cl— er, I mean Alira here has just told me some fantastic news," Rason smiled happily.

Odrin saluted smartly, throwing the woman a cautious look.

"What news is that sire?" he asked, careful to use the title Rason enjoyed. His pledge to earn the crown may have won the support of Sunguard and the legion, but in secret most resented his use of the title.

"The Baron of Balnor is dead; apparently a beast of the Void or something got into the city and killed the bastard. It happened not but three days past," Rason chuckled. "A shame. I had hoped to whip his hide again like at the battle of the Golden Hills."

Odrin's mouth opened at the news. One of the most powerful men in the realm was dead. A claimant was dead. The war was one step closer to being over.

"That's ... that's great news, milord. Sire, could I have a word in private," he asked, flashing the strange woman a pleasant smile.

Rason looked aghast at the request. "Whatever you have to say you can say in front of my lady here," he snapped. The lady laughed, placing a hand upon the general's arm.

"Do you not trust me, captain?" she said, gazing deep into Odrin's eyes.

Odrin stared back, unable to look away. He could feel sweat breaking out on his forehead. For some reason he wanted to run, to scream. The young woman's blue eyes bore into his very being. He tried to scream as her eyes turned black, her skin wrinkled, and her hair turned black like the veins on her twisted face and limbs.

"You are mine, captain. Just like your general, you are mine. And I have a very special mission for you," a rasping female voice boomed inside his head.

Odrin tried to scream, but his body was not his anymore. He just nodded his head and smiled instead.

"I will do all you command, my lady," he heard himself say. His voice was monotone like the scout's had been. In his mind, he was screaming. He was a prisoner in his own body.

"Ahead lies the city of Eclin and beyond that the mountains," the voice in his head rasped. "You will lead a cohort of your best men into those mountains and find a place called the Sigil Caves. Within you will find a key which you will then bring to me."

"So, general ... or should I say, my king?" laughed Alira. Odrin shook his head. She looked young and beautiful again, her voice soft and ladylike once more. "You will lead your army to Eclin and there what will you do? I have a friend ... shall we say ... who is already at the city's walls. I do hope you will aid him in his quest to massacre every living soul inside, and of course, kill the Prince hiding there."

Rason took her hand in his.

"For you, I would burn the entire world," he replied, smiling.

Woven parried the claws of a snarling werewolf deflecting, the iron-like talons just as they were about to plunge deep into a knight's back. The beast roared in frustration as the knight jumped backwards, a look of thanks on his face. Sweat poured into Woven's eyes. All day long the monsters had been assaulting the city walls. He'd lost count of the number of men who had fallen in the desperate defence.

He feinted low with his blade, causing the wolf to flinch and raise its thick arms. It was the move he wanted it to make. Rotating his wrists, he lashed out with his sword to stab deeply into its underbelly. The wolf roared staggering backwards. The knight stepped in, dispatching the foul creature with a savage blow to its neck. With a mewling howl, the wolf crashed to the blood-stained ground.

Woven placed his hand on his knees. He was exhausted. They all were. The siege was now into its second week, and still, the lich's forces attacked. It seemed hell-bent on taking the city. He sighed in relief as the *all-clear* horn blew. The monsters had retreated yet again.

He had been fighting on the east wall, as that was where the combat had been thickest. A small boy ran along the wall, careful not to slip in the blood or trip on the bodies. Over his shoulder was a large bucket sloshing with water.

Woven stood and gratefully ruffled the boy's hair before drinking. His throat was parched from the smoke caused by the fires burning inside the city walls. Thatched houses were ablaze, the victims of the lich's latest magical assault.

"We can't take many more days like today," Master Thondril said tiredly as he walked along the wall, bloody sword in hand. "We're down to just a few hundred men. It won't be long before disease does for us what the lich cannot. We're running out of kindling to burn all the bodies."

The old warrior's face was streaked with dirt and blood. A livid wound ran across his right cheek, down to his jawline. A ghoul's axe had been the cause.

"Now that the ghouls are being sent against us, we're getting a pasting," he said gesturing to the wound. "Even our silver weapons are having a hard time killing them. It took six knights working together and the use of fire to just kill the one that did this."

Woven leaned wearily against the wall, his sword now back in his sheath. He put his forehead upon the cold stone. He was so tired.

"I give us another day or two before we have to abandon the walls. Then it will be a last stand at the baron's castle," he groaned. Tiredly he stretched his limbs, grunting as his shoulders clicked.

Thondril leaned in close.

"I trust the prince is safe?" the knight master whispered.

"Aye, he's safe. I moved him and his nanny to my private rooms in the castle. I assigned Briden to be their bodyguard. If the city falls, I told him to try his luck in the underground caverns."

Thondril leaned heavily against the wall. The man appeared as though he was older than his already advanced years.

"We've held our own these past weeks. If only we had known of the lich before we arrived. I would have summoned every warrior in Delfinnia to march," he said despairingly.

"Word will have reached the rest of the kingdom. A whole barony going silent is sure to have drawn attention. There might be an army already on its way here ..."

Before Woven could finish his reply, a horn blast wailed from the direction of the south gate. Both men looked at the walls to see Eclin soldiers waving frantically.

A few moments later a red-faced young squire came bounding up the steps leading to the top of the wall.

"Commander Thondril! I have word from Sir Grandir on the south wall," the lad panted breathlessly.

Thondril threw a cautious glance to Woven. The ranger shrugged his shoulders in reply.

"Whenever you're ready, lad," Woven said impatiently.

The squire shot him a frown before facing his commander.

"Sir. Sir Grandir says that an army is approaching from the south. He spied a sizeable force of men advancing through the mountain pass."

Thondril smiled at the news.

"It looks like my prayers have been answered," he laughed, clapping his gauntleted hands.

Woven shook his head in caution.

"I'll share your joy once we know if they are friendly or not. In case you had forgotten, Commander, the realm is still in the midst of civil war. If it's an army from Retbit or one of the other claimants ..."

Thondril's smile faded as the truth of the ranger's words sank in.

"Surely they would not abandon us to the lich. Even a claimant would not tolerate a force of evil such as this," he said, gesturing to the horde snarling at the walls.

"Let us hope you're right."

Rason crested the small hill which overlooked the city of Eclin. His legion marched through the pass to form up ranks. They were still a mile from the city walls but, could clearly see the army besieging it.

"By Niveren ... that's an army of the undead!" Cried out one of the legionaries standing in the front ranks. A ripple of concern spread down the lines.

"We have to aid them," cried another soldier. Soon, much of the army was bristling to advance and save Eclin from the ancient foe.

Rason rode his horse along the front rank. He raised his voice. "We are not here to destroy the undead. We are here to destroy Eclin, my foe for the crown!"

The Legion roared in protest.

"Are you mad? The old foe is there. What about those poor people? Our oath is to defend Delfinnia from all foes, especially the Old Enemy!" shouted one of the centurions.

Rason scowled in annoyance at his men. Why were they so eager to save his enemy? Why didn't they share his desire to end the war and win the crown?

"They will not follow me," he muttered to Cliria who trotted her horse next to his. "They swore oaths to me, their general and king, and yet they will not follow."

Cliria smiled.

"They will follow you. You have a glorious task to perform."

She slid from her horse to stand in front of the legion. One of the centurions stepped forward, his hand reaching for his sword.

"I knew he was bedevilled. You've put him under some spell." The centurion turned to face his men. "She is a witch!"

Angry yells came from the ranks. Others had noticed their general's strange behaviour.

"The Rason I bled with on the Marble Shore would never have allowed a witch to march with the legion, and he would not leave a city full of innocent women and children at the mercy of monsters!" the centurion continued. Other legionaries drew swords; some raised their spears.

The centurion charged at Cliria. She stood still, an amused smile on her face. Just as the centurion got within striking distance, she casually flicked her wrist. The big man was sent flying backwards by a burst of magic to crash heavily into his comrades.

Cliria raised her hands in the air. An unnatural wind began to swirl about the now terrified legion. Then, to their horror, they watched as the witch rose into the air. Her long hair radiated around her, her eyes were black, and her face was hideous. Black veins spread across her skin.

"You are mine!" Cliria screamed. "You will serve Rason until your last breath! You will serve me!"

The unnatural wind grew in strength. Dark energy crackled and fizzed as the legion was engulfed by it.

"What was that?" Woven cried as he watched the distant army being engulfed by the black wind. The other knights and warriors stood in stunned silence.

Thondril leant heavily against the wall, his earlier smile replaced with a look of horror. The black wind faded to reveal the distant army once more. The legion began to chant and stamp their armoured feet.

"Magic," the knight commander uttered under his breath. "Help has not come. Instead, it is our doom."

Woven stared at the now advancing army, a fresh knot of fear worming its way into his guts.

CHAPTER 39.

The tower of Danon stood black and menacing over the ravaged plain. The bones of the mighty fell beasts and the twisted dead hulk of an ancient forest spread for miles around.

Luxon and Aljeron quickly but carefully made their way through. The old wizard moved fast, sure of the path through the maze of death. Amongst the dead forest were razor leaves which they avoided.

Somewhere behind them, the dragon Umbaroth waited, ready to come to their aid if he could. Aljeron slowed as they came to the edge of the dead forest. A large clearing lay between them and the tower. Outside were the three dragons which Luxon had seen the last time he had set his sights upon the place.

Each appeared to be asleep. Aljeron placed a finger to his lips as he slowly stepped out into the clearing. Luxon followed, keeping low.

They hurried across the open space. One of the dragons raised its massive head, causing them to freeze.

The beast opened its cavernous mouth in a wide yawn before setting its head back down upon its talons. It closed its eyes and began to snore loudly.

Luxon sighed in relief. He opened his hands which had clenched into fists. He was ready to fight if necessary, confident in his power. He paused as he realised, he was eager.

He set his jaw, took a deep breath, and followed the wizard into the heart of Danon's lair.

At the tower, Aljeron raised his staff, muttered an incantation, and thrust it at the massive doors. To Luxon's surprise, the doors creaked open to reveal a vast space beyond. No light was visible, just inky darkness. He frowned at the wizard. He was about to ask how the wizard knew how to open the doors when Aljeron tapped his staff onto the black stone floor. A bright light flashed into life, illuminating the cavernous chamber.

The walls were black and lined with jagged spikes. Hanging from some were tattered banners, the images that had once been upon them now faded and worn.

Luxon nearly jumped out of his spirit as the doors slammed shut. He spun, panic rising within him. He turned back to see Aljeron watching him, a faint smile on his old lips. Something was not right. The old man seemed different, taller somehow, as though his soul was feeding upon the blackness around them.

"This way to Danon," Aljeron whispered, pointing deeper into the chamber. Luxon nodded and followed the old wizard. He frowned deeper as he noticed the wizard's stride was stronger than it had been. Before, Aljeron had walked with a stoop and a bit of a shuffle.

They walked deeper until the darkness felt like a smothering shroud. Aljeron cast a spell of light to guide their way. The place was eerily silent. So much so that Luxon felt the hairs on his neck begin to rise. A sense of dread was building within him.

Finally, they reached a huge chamber. At the far end, atop a flight of steep steps, was a massive throne.

"What the?" Luxon gasped.

Sat on the throne was a figure. Huge it was, twice the same size as Umbaroth. Only it wasn't a dragon. Instead, it looked like a man, an impossibly huge man.

Covering the body was a suit of metal armour the likes of which Luxon had never seen before. A black helmet hid its face. As he got closer, he could see that the armour had rusted. No sign of life stirred.

"Who is that?" Luxon stammered.

Aljeron ascended the steps to stand before the throne.

"That is Vectrix. God of the Void," the wizard answered simply.

Luxon staggered back a step in shock.

"How can this be? Why didn't you tell me about this?" Luxon demanded, his shock being quickly replaced with annoyance.

"It does not matter," Aljeron snapped "For you will share his fate." The wizard raised his staff, unleashing a bolt of lightning at his student.

The move took Luxon completely by surprise. He had no time to deflect the attack. Sheering pain lanced through his body as the lightning struck. He was sent sprawling backwards, landing heavily in a heap.

Luxon shook his head, desperately trying to shake away the stars that now swam before his eyes. Slowly, he stumbled to his feet.

Aljeron laughed, clapping his hands in delight.

"You *are* strong enough," the wizard cackled. "All of that effort paid off, it seems. All those years of putting up with your whining, your stupidity, your false hopes ... all of it will have been worth it!"

Luxon fell to one knee, the pain of the attack cramping his muscles painfully. He raised his head to watch the man who he thought was his friend, his mentor, his ancestor.

"Who are you?" he shouted, a part of him already guessing the answer.

Aljeron chuckled. He threw his staff away and cast off his robes. For a moment he faded into shadow before reappearing.

In place of the kindly old man who had taught him to harness his power stood a figure dressed in black. His skin was as white as snow. Thick black veins covered his face. His teeth were pointed and savage, and his eyes ... his eyes were as black as night.

Luxon closed his eyes. He understood his dreams now.

"You were watching me. All this time," he said miserably. He opened his eyes and glared at the smiling monster before him. "Danon. That was the name in my dream. The one that was always just out of reach. *Your* name."

"I have watched you since the day you were born, Luxon," Danon replied. "From this wretched place I have watched events for millennia, waiting for my time, waiting for the one with the right blood and power to get me out of here.

"You should feel honoured. I went to so much trouble to get you here to make you what you are. The right whispers into the right ears, the gentle nudges, the assassinations. Cliria followed my plans to the letter. She began the civil war to weaken resistance to my will. She stole Aljeron's staff and sent you to me. She didn't know at the time that would happen, mind you. And now here we are at the heart of the Void's power."

Luxon stood once more, wincing against the pain.

"What happened to him?" he said, pointing to the giant corpse upon its throne. His mind raced. It had all been a trap, and yet something nagged at him. A question was in his mind, one that he feared the answer to.

Danon pulled his hood down over his face before sitting on the armoured foot of Vectrix. Casually, he stretched out and put his hands behind his head, all the while with an amused expression on his lips.

"I drained his power," Danon answered simply as he checked for dirt under his claw-like nails.

"It was a hell of a scrap. Took thousands of years, but eventually, I bested him and took his power for my own. With it, I was able to control the dragons and also add their power to mine."

Danon slid off the dead god's foot like an agile cat.

"And yet with all that power, it still wasn't enough to escape from this place. It took me aeons to finally figure it out," he said bitterly. "Aljeron, the first wizard, sealed the first breach and made it so that only he or those of his bloodline could reopen it. That is why Cliria sent you here. The portal can only be traversed from one side. Now that you're here with me, I will use your power to open the breach from this side."

Luxon dropped his head. He had been nothing but a pawn. He knotted his hand into fists. Anger built inside of him. He couldn't let Danon escape. He had to try and stop him.

"Does Umbaroth know what you are?" he asked. He had to buy some time. His eyes darted around the room, desperately trying to seek out something he could use as a weapon.

Danon laughed wickedly.

"The King of Dragons? No, he does not know. I needed him on my side. By gaining his trust, I was able to learn of the other dragons, and over the centuries I claimed them one by one without his knowledge. Do not fear, Luxon. Now that I have you, the dragon will share your fate. I will need every scrap of power I can muster to open a way back home big enough."

"Big enough for what?" Luxon replied. If he could keep Danon talking, perhaps he had a chance. He slowly began inching backwards. He had to escape.

"To bring the Void to Delfinnia of course!" Danon boasted. "I will be master of all worlds, all plains of existence. Darkness will rule, and my brother, Niveren's failure will be complete!"

Luxon's blood ran cold. He imagined hordes of Pucks, banshees, goblins ... all the nightmarish creatures of the Void unleashed upon the kingdom. It wouldn't stand a chance.

He couldn't let the monster before him fulfil his plans.

"I will stop you," Luxon growled. He knotted his hands into fists and narrowed his eyes. He focused until he could feel the magic stirring within him.

Danon laughed dismissively.

Luxon raised his arms, focusing on the corpse of Vectrix. With all of his power, the body began to shudder. With a deafening screech, the god's body lifted from its seat like some ghastly puppet.

Danon stopped smiling. His face twisting in rage. He spun just as the heavily armoured Vectrix was pulled from his throne. The god seemed as though it were alive as it towered over them both.

With a yell, Luxon pulled his arms backwards. The telekinetic link with the corpse shifted. With a rumble, Vectrix fell forward.

Danon screamed as the behemoth fell towards him. Luxon released his spell to allow gravity to do the rest. He didn't wait to see the effects; He was already running towards the exit of the tower.

He slowed and then stopped. There had been no sound of the corpse striking the ground. His heart raced. A sinister cackling came from behind him. Slowly, he turned to find Danon standing tall, one hand held aloft, the massive corpse resting casually upon it.

"Really? I, who have existed since the dawn of time and been the master of the world – you really think you can best me with a cheap trick like that?" Danon said threateningly. "I could best you with my little finger, you fool."

Danon raised his other hand and pointed it at Luxon. With a cry, he was lifted off of his feet and sent flying back towards the dark wizard.

He crashed to the ground, sliding to a halt at Damon's feet.

"Ah, I do so love it when people are on their knees. Soon the whole world will be."

As though he weighed nothing, Luxon was hauled into the air. With his magic, Danon had him floating, unable to move.

Luxon had tried to fight, but he couldn't move. Danon's magic was too strong. Now he found himself at the top of Danon's tower. The view was spectacular. The vast plains and tumultuous purple sky spread out for as far as the eye could see. The jagged spires of the tower stood tall and dangerous, giving him a renewed sense of dread.

Danon stood in the centre; his arms held high and wide. Luxon felt his bowels loosen as Danon emitted a terrifying roar. Soon the sound of flapping leather wings approached. For a moment, Luxon hoped that Umbaroth would come to his rescue.

Those hopes were dashed when four dragons flew into view. The dragons were nothing like Umbaroth. Whereas he had a look of nobility, these looked sinister. Their scales were blackened, some had large scars running down their bodies, others had scales missing, and one even had lost an eye.

"Finally, the time has come, my pets. We will return to our rightful homes. You will fly the blue skies, and all men will run in terror from your flames," Danon cried.

The dragons flew in a circle above the tower, hissing their delight that freedom was so close.

Danon knelt over Luxon, a wicked smile on his nightmarish features. Luxon tried to move, but the spell he was under was too strong.

Danon placed a hand upon Luxon's head.

A searing pain lanced through Luxon's body, causing him to scream out in agony, his body twisting and contorting. His skin felt like lava, and his veins felt as if they were being sucked dry. A bright light began to shine around Danon's hands. He looked to the sky to where the dragons flew. He thrust his other hand towards them. Light began to emanate from the dragons until they, too, roared in agony. Danon was draining them of their power as well.

The light grew in intensity as the power was absorbed by Danon. Luxon had to shut his eyes as it became too bright to look upon.

The sound became deafening. The dragons' roars mixed with Luxon's own cries and the roar of energy. The tower itself began to shake until a loud cracking sound could be heard over the other din. Luxon opened an eye to see a large crack shooting up the tower; even the ground far below was splitting apart.

"Free at last!" Danon cried.

He raised his hands skyward once more. The sky itself ripped apart. Luxon cried out as he could see his homeland through the tear. The green grass of the Bison plains, the high towers of Sunguard, the crystalline walls of Caldaria: all flashed into view.

Then a city, aflame and under siege, appeared through the tear.

Danon smiled. With a shout, he summoned one of the dragons to him. The black-scaled beast broke free of the swirling energy to land with a thud on the tower, which swayed and rocked dangerously under the extra weight. With horror, Luxon realised that the structure was on the verge of collapse. He had to escape.

Danon leapt onto the dragon's back. He threw a look at Luxon.

"I must thank you, Luxon. You've set me free ... and now I will kill everyone you know and love!" With a mocking salute, he kicked his heels into the dragon's flank. The beast flapped its huge wings and, with a roar, shot off into the sky.

Luxon gasped as the invisible grip that had held him down vanished.

Slowly he sat up; the world swam before him, and his body felt numb.

He shielded his eyes as, with a blinding flash, Danon and the dragons vanished through the swirling portal above him.

Lightning lanced out as the Void itself appeared to tear itself apart. Luxon got to his feet but was sent sprawling again as the tower began to collapse.

Instinctively he cupped his hands around his mouth. Using what magic he had left, he shouted.

"Umbaroth summoni!"

With the last of his magic spent, the world went black. The last thing he remembered was the roar of the collapsing tower and the sensation of tumbling to his doom.

CHAPTER 40.

Yepert threw himself to the ground. His face was red and flustered, his breaths coming in gasps. Around him, a hundred black-garbed figures went prone as well. In front of him, also on his stomach, Ferran raised a fist into the air before pointing to the right. A group of a dozen of the figures sprung to their feet, before quietly scurrying off through the undergrowth.

"What is it?" Yepert asked quietly. He looked to the sky to see the twinkling of the stars and the brilliance of the moons.

Ferran turned, his white teeth visible in the darkness.

"We're close. Are you ready?" the Nightblade replied.

Yepert nodded in the affirmative, gritting his teeth in determination. He wasn't going to let himself or his friends down.

After departing from Kaiden and Sophia, Ferran and Yepert had travelled back to Caldaria. The journey had taken less than half the time that a normal traveller would have taken, as the Nightblade used paths long hidden or forgotten by most folk.

In less than six days they had arrived, but no rest was to be found. Immediately upon their arrival, Ferran had demanded an audience with Grand Master Thanos and the other mages. After a heated debate, the mages had agreed to finally choose a side. Now a hundred Nightblades were creeping through the mountain woods towards the city of Eclin. Not far behind them was a small contingent of volunteer mages.

Not since the days of Aljeron had such a large number of Nightblades acted in consort. Yepert was excited to see what they would be capable of. Despite Ferran's concerns, Yepert had insisted on coming with the Nightblades. He was eager to avenge his lost friend and get a little payback on Rason.

Yepert flinched as a mighty boom came from somewhere ahead. A series of smaller bangs and twangs followed.

A few moments later the small group Ferran had ordered ahead returned.

"We crept up to the edge of the forest. Between us and the city is a legion," the lead Nightblade said in hushed tones. "Those sounds were their siege weapons being fired. The main gate of the city seems to be holding, but a few more volleys and it will be turned into splinters." He pulled down his hood. Yepert smiled as he recognised Welsly.

"You did well, Welsly," Ferran, said patting his fellow Nightblade on the shoulder.

"There's more ...' Welsly said hesitantly. "Something is happening in the sky. Where the undead horde is amassed ... I have never seen anything like it. It looks as though the sky itself is being pulled apart. It is a magic the likes of which I have never seen before."

Ferran frowned at the revelation. Something else was occurring in Eclin. The witch wasn't just there for the heir. He chewed his lip in thought.

"We have to take out those siege weapons," Welsly whispered. "If we can, then we can buy the city's defenders more time."

"Time for what?" Ferran replied, stroking his trimmed beard. "The undead will breach the walls before long. We have to get inside the city, find the heir and get him out alive. Even we Nightblades won't be able to take on the witch, the legion and whatever else is against us."

"We have to try," Yepert chimed in. Welsly smiled at him.

"Yepert is right. If the heir is lost, then all hope is lost. We must try," Welsly implored.

Ferran's frown turned into a roguish grin.

He stood and drew his tourmaline blade, willing it to life with magic. All around, the other Nightblades rose and ignited their blades.

"Well then, if you put it that way, let's have at them!" he shouted as he began to run through the trees towards the waiting enemy.

"Brace!" roared Woven as he joined the other rangers in throwing their weight against the city gate. A few seconds later, they were sent flying backwards as a heavy boulder launched by a legion catapult smashed into it. Splinters flew outwards, cutting down a number of the defenders, their screams adding to the din of the battle raging all around them.

As soon as the legion had begun firing, the horde had launched a full-scale assault against the walls. Werewolves, zombies, and ghouls were pouring over the top. The Knights of Niveren and soldiers of Eclin were fighting bravely but were quickly being overrun.

Men wearing the white mantle of Niveren lay dead alongside those in the blue of Eclin, their spilt blood joining them as brothers in the afterlife.

Woven staggered to his feet, his head ringing from the impact. All around was fire and death. The city was burning. An incendiary round from a legion catapult had struck one of the city's many thatched roofed buildings and the blaze had quickly turned into an inferno that threatened to devour them all. Smoke swirled, blinding and choking the defenders.

He looked to the walls to see Master Thondril and a dozen knights desperately trying to prevent ghouls from climbing over the crenellations. Their silver swords had little effect on the undead monsters. Only fire seemed to be effective.

"Sir!" cried a ranger. Woven looked up to see the man waving frantically to get his attention. "There's something in the forest to the south," the ranger cried in panic. The man was covered in blood and dirt. Woven noticed that his arm hung loosely at his side, no doubt broken by the siege weapon's impact.

Woven shook his head to try and clear it. He ordered his men to brace the gate once again, before staggering through an archway and up a flight of stone steps which led to the top of the wall.

Once at the top of the wall, he gasped as he saw dozens of light sources moving quickly through the nearby woods. He narrowed his eyes and could make out that the shapes were people clad in black.

"Nightblades ... It can't be ..." he muttered to himself, a sense of hope springing in his heart. His guess was realised when the first figures leapt from the trees to fall upon the rear of the attacking legion. Tourmaline blades swung, cutting down a number of legionaries.

"Get to the walls and help the knights!" Woven yelled at his men. The legion would be kept busy by the Nightblades, and now he could free his men to aid the beleaguered defenders on the wall.

The rangers and Eclin soldiers under his command ran toward the walls, a sense of renewed determination in their ranks. Help had arrived; not all was lost.

Ferran ducked under the steel sword of a legionary and lashed out with his own. The magic blade punched deep into the man's armour and lodged into his heart. All around him, his fellow Nightblades were taking the fight to the legion. He frowned as he pulled his sword from the dead man's chest. The soldier hadn't screamed in pain – in fact, none of the legionaries were making any noise at all. They fought hard, but they did so in an eerie silence.

Another legionary ran towards him. Ferran stepped backwards, lithely bringing his blade down to parry his attacker's. Again, the man attacking him did so in silence, a blank expression on his face. Ferran dodged another attack. He raised his free hand, sending the legionary sprawling with a blast of telekinesis. He followed through by kicking the dazed legionary's weapon out of his grasp and pulled off his helmet.

The legionary stared at him. Ferran stepped back in shock. The man's eyes were black; the whites could not be seen at all.

A deafening boom caused him to look away. The sky above the city looked as though it was on fire. A tear was forming, pulling it apart.

The legionary saw his opportunity. Pulling a dagger from his belt he lunged. The steel blade stabbed deeply into Ferran's leg. The Nightblade cried out, collapsing into a heap as pain lanced its way up his thigh. The legionary staggered to his feet and raised his blood-soaked dagger high.

Ferran shut his eyes tightly, expecting death.

It didn't come.

He opened his eyes to see the legionary lying in a smouldering heap. Behind him stood Yepert. The lad had steam pouring from his hands.

The boy ran over to Ferran and offered him a hand up. Ferran took it, a grin on his face.

"I never thought you'd save me, lad," he said, roughing up Yepert's hair affectionately.

"I figured I owed you one," Yepert replied. "If it weren't for you, that Banshee would have sent me to the Void."

As Ferran was about to reply, the ground shook, sending Nightblades and legionaries sprawling to the ground. Ferran leaned on Yepert to stay upright.

The tear in the sky was widening. Lightning flashed out of the tear and the night sky turned a fiery red. Two blindingly bright flashes caused them to look away. A shard of light lanced downwards towards the horde at Echlin's walls; another shot off far to the south.

"What was that?" Yepert cried.

Ferran's answer was drowned out by a deafening roar. Three massive black shapes emerged from the tear. Instead of falling they unfurled huge leathery wings. Their long necks swayed from side to side and fire poured from their mouths.

"Niveren save us!" Ferran cried.

"What are they?" Yepert asked his voice cracking in panic.

"Dragons! Those are goddamned dragons," Ferran answered in disbelief.

The battle had been forgotten as all eyes stared at the now soaring beasts. The biggest of the three flew high into the sky before diving down towards the ravaged city. It opened its cavernous mouth, and dragon's fire poured forth to set Eclin ablaze.

CHAPTER 41.

Panicked screams drifted into his consciousness, stirring him. He felt as though he had been gone for years like he was returning to his body after a long terrible dream. The screams were the first thing he was aware of, adding to his confusion. The next sensation to come was the heat. Dry and yet comforting, it made him feel safe. So why the screams?

Luxon opened his eyes slowly. He was in a bed of soft feathers and sheep wool. The room was round, the walls made of mud brick, and on the reed-strewn floor was a simple red and gold rug. Various pots and urns of a design that he did not recognise were standing against the far wall.

More shouts and cries could be heard coming from outside. He pulled back the thin blanket which covered his body and swung his legs out of the comfy bed. To his surprise, he was wearing a simple brown robe. He looked about and saw his blue mage's robe hung on a wooden peg next to the room's arched doorway. His boots, trousers and shirt were laid neatly next to it on the floor.

Cautiously, he crept to the doorway and peeked around it. A larger open room lay beyond. A simple mud-brick fire pit lay at the centre, deep in the floor. Large cushions were arrayed in a circle around the fire. A long wooden pipe was propped up against a wall. Luxon walked over to it and ran his fingers down its length. Small holes ran down the side. It was an instrument of some kind, he realised.

The sound of someone running into the house caused him to spin around. He raised his hands to defend himself. Was he still in the Void? Was he dead?

A young girl stood before him. She wore a dress of a style not of Delfinnia. Her skin was dark, and her hair was tied up in a long braid. Her large brown eyes widened as she saw him.

She began to speak, but Luxon didn't recognise the words. He held up his hands to try and put the girl at ease as her voice grew increasingly panicked. More shouts came from outside.

"Where am I? What is this place?" Luxon asked slowly. The girl screamed.

"Delfin! Delfin!" she yelled, turning, and fleeing the room. Luxon rushed after her. He pushed a curtain out of the way to find himself outside. He had to shut his eyes as the glare from a staggeringly bright sun blinded him. Heat struck him; it felt like he was in a furnace.

He held a hand up to shield his eyes.

The sky was blue!

He was home, but where. He looked around to see that he was in some kind of village. A dozen mud-brick houses were arrayed in an oval pattern, but the most surprising thing was the hot sand that covered everything. He was in a desert. He wracked his mind. To his knowledge, only the land of Yundol had deserts. Was he so far from Delfinnia?

The girl who had screamed was standing a few feet from him, a group of men covered in long robes and tribal clothes standing protectively at her side. Each brandished a long spear which they pointed at the house menacingly.

A shout came from somewhere out of view, causing the men to glance nervously in that direction. Luxon looked that way too and laughed. Standing tall and powerful on a nearby dune was Umbaroth. The mighty silver dragon had his wings spread wide. Around him were a hundred or so Yundol warriors, unsure how to deal with such a massive beast.

"You know of this beast?"

Luxon spun back to face the girl and the ever-growing group of scared villagers. An elderly man with dark skin and a long silver beard pushed his way to the front. He spoke Delfin with a fragmented tone.

The old man stood before Luxon. As the man got closer, he could see that the old man had kindly blue eyes and skin so weathered and worn it looked like old parchment. He could see in the way the old man stood that decades of living under the harsh sun had made him tough and proud. His head was held high, despite the slight hunch of his old shoulders.

"I do. He means you no harm, and neither do I," Luxon said, trying his best to sound friendly.

The old man frowned for a moment as he looked over the strange young man.

"For someone so young, your eyes look so old," the old man said in wonder. He reached out and ran his rough hands over the lad's face.

"I am Suabei, the elder of this village. You have been a great mystery to us ever since Sasa, my granddaughter –" the elder gestured towards the girl who had been in the house "– found you on the beach. She thought you had come from the gods. Instead, you are one of the white folk from across the sea." He almost sounding disappointed.

"I am Luxon, and that," he said, pointing to the dragon which had sat on its haunches, "is Umbaroth. He is a dragon."

Suabei's eyes widened.

"A dragon? Were they not sent to the Void long ago?" His eyes grew even wider as a realisation struck him. He stepped back and made a strange sign with his hands, no doubt a way to ward off evil.

"You are from the Void. The bright light that fell here was your spirit returning ... You were found weeks ago." Suabei looked at the strange boy in a new light and felt pity.

"That is why your eyes are so old. I am sorry," he said with a bow.

Luxon scratched his chin unsure what to say. To him, it felt like a bad dream.

"I have to get to Delfinnia, Suabei. I have friends who are in grave danger. Danon has returned."

Suabei made the sign yet again.

"And you are sent by the god of balance to stop him, you and your dragon?"

"I don't know about that," Luxon said, "but I know I have to try."

Luxon was once again dressed in his normal clothes and blue mage's cloak. He felt weary; his reserves of magical energy had been drained by Danon. Even so, he had to try and to stop him. A crowd of Yundol had come out to watch him leave. Learning that Umbaroth was not to be feared the villagers had given the dragon gifts of food and gold. Children clambered over his huge claws; one even climbed as high his snout. The dragon had then carefully plucked the giggling child off with his talons and lowered it gently back to the ground. Luxon couldn't help but smile at the joy evident in Umbaroth's eyes. The great beast had waited since the dawn of man to return to the world.

Sasa stepped forward and looked at Luxon shyly. In her arms was a long stick capped with the figure of a dragon. She held it out for him and smiled. Luxon took the stick and looked it over. He hefted the weight and marvelled at the detail of the figure and the runes engraved along its length.

"It is a mage's staff," Suabei said as he put an arm around the girl. "I recognised your blue robes and told her that you must be one. She spent the weeks whilst you slept carving it. I think she has taken a shine to you," he added with a twinkle in his eye.

Luxon blushed. He bowed to Sasa. "Thank you; it truly is a thing of beauty." He felt around inside his cloak for something to give her in return. His pockets were empty save for the dagger that Grandmaster Thanos had given to him. *Won't do me much good against Danon,* he thought. He pulled the weapon from his cloak and held it out to the girl, handle first. The blade was Delfin steel, far superior to the iron weapons many of the Yundol warriors carried. It would fetch a tidy sum of gold.

Sasa took the dagger and smiled. She bowed in thanks before scurrying off to show her gift to her friends. Suabei placed a hand on his shoulder.

"Good luck. May Niveren guide you. You and your dragon are always welcome here."

Luxon bowed in thanks. The kindness shown by the Yundols warmed his heart. The Delfin people and the Yundols had been enemies for centuries, ever since the days of King Marcus and the founding of the kingdom of Delfinnia.

With a wave goodbye, Luxon walked away from the village towards Umbaroth, who had retaken his place on top of the nearby dunes. The dragon raised his head to point at the staff in Luxon's hands.

"A staff? You truly are a wizard," he chuckled. "Although you're not much of one with no magic," he added.

Luxon shot the dragon a look of annoyance.

"I have to try, Umbaroth. We both do. Those other dragons are no doubt free and wreaking havoc." He sighed and shook his head. "I'm sorry. I guess I should be thanking you. I assume you saved me at Danon's tower?"

The dragon lowered his head to rest it on the ground.

"I did. I saw you fall and heard your summons. I caught you and flew through the tear. There was a bright light, and we ended up here. You back in your body, and me in the sand. I am sorry too, my young friend. Now is not the time for jokes or snide remarks. I can help you if you would allow me too. Stand before me."

Luxon raised an eyebrow before stepping in front of the dragon.

"Close your eyes. This may tickle a bit," Umbaroth explained.

Luxon did as he was told and closed his eyes. Umbaroth rose to his full height. He opened his mouth and breathed. Instead of fire, pure magic came out. The energy flowed from the dragon into Luxon, who gasped as he could feel power and strength return to his body.

He opened his eyes and smiled. He felt fantastic; the tiredness was gone.

"What did you do?" he asked. He looked at a nearby stone and focused, causing it to rise into the air. He made a fist which made the stone explode into dust.

"I cast a spell which has bound us together. My strength is yours and vice versa. This is a sacred bond, one that is only usually done between dragons. Place your staff into the sand over there," Umbaroth said solemnly.

Luxon took the staff and plunged into the sand.

"Step back," the dragon commanded. Luxon did so, curious as to what would happen.

Once again Umbaroth stood to his full height. He took a deep breath. His stomach lit up, and light flowed up his body into his neck until finally, fire poured forth to envelop the staff.

As the dragon fire struck, the staff blackened, and the surrounding sand turned to glass. Steam erupted from the ground, almost blinding Luxon.

After a few moments, the steam cleared to reveal the staff. To Luxon's amazement, the wood hadn't turned to ash but stood tall and strong. An aura of pure magic radiated around it, sparkling in the desert sunlight.

"Take it. It will be quite cool. I have enchanted the staff with dragon's fire. It will make a mighty weapon for a wizard," Umbaroth said with pride.

Luxon gazed at the staff in awe.

Cautiously, he approached it. The carbonised ground crunched as he walked, but no heat save from the sun and sand could be felt through his boots.

He gripped the staff, expecting it to be hot. Instead, it was just warm. With a grunt, he pulled it from the ground and cried out as he felt power shoot from the staff and into his body.

"I will call it *Dragasdal*: The Dragon's fire."

CHAPTER 42.

Elena held the prince close to her chest as she watched in horror at the firestorm sweeping through Eclin's streets. From her vantage point in Baron Lido's castle, she had seen the dragons emerge from the tumultuous sky, which fizzed and sparked with unearthly power. She stifled a cry as the biggest of the dragons had dived down over the city, its cavernous mouth spewing deadly flame.

"It's over," a tired voice came from behind her. She jumped at the unexpected intrusion.

She held the prince tighter as she slowly turned to face whoever had come into the room. There standing before her was the baron. His face was white and haggard, and his eyes were bleary due to the influence of alcohol. His once regal clothes were stained with wine; in his hand, he held a half-empty bottle whilst in the other was his sword which scraped upon the floor.

"My ancestors kept this city safe for centuries, my own grandfather died protecting it, and now I will share his fate. Only this time there will be nothing to survive me," Lido sobbed.

Elena felt pity for the man. His spirit was broken. What chance had he had against such evil?

Now as the city burned and monsters from myth were raining death from above, she too felt the stirrings of despair. Only her love of the small child in her arms kept her from giving up. She frowned and firmed her lips. She would not let them die here. The baron had failed; he could wallow in his own self-pity if he wished, but she would live, and she would make sure the prince lived too.

Cries of the dying were carried on the smoke-filled air. Panicked shouts and screams from the terrified refugees hiding inside the castle walls added to the sounds of the apocalypse, and in the distance was the steady rhythm of the ghouls marching steadily through the city's streets.

Cautiously, she stepped past the baron and with a last look of pity left the room. Quickly, she hurried down the stone walled corridor and passed through an inner courtyard.

A terrifying roar caused her to find shelter in the shadow of an archway as the massive black dragon flew over the castle. Archers loosed their arrows with no effect. The beast would return, and the castle's fate would be sealed.

Panicked men and women ran past her, all heading for the cellars and the escape tunnels that Woven had mentioned before he had headed back out into the battle raging outside.

Elena pushed her way through the crowd until she found some room. The dark, cool cellar was filling up fast, and soon it would turn into a tomb. The grate that Woven had shown her hung loosely as people ripped it off its hinges. Eclin soldiers tasked with defending the grate were pushed aside by the crowd; some even put down their spears and joined the rout, each desperate to escape the burning city and the dragons.

Elena cried out as she saw a man pushing his way through the crowd. He was trying to get inside rather than flee. Finally, he broke free. It was Woven. The left side of his face was burnt terribly from his temple to his chin, and his clothes were blackened and singed. He staggered a few steps before collapsing onto the cold stone floor as the weight of the crowd gave way.

Elena rushed over to him. She placed Alderlade down and held his hand tightly before kneeling over the wounded ranger. His breaths came in ragged gasps.

"Woven, we have to flee," she cried. The man winced in agony. He reached up to take hold of her hand.

"There is nowhere to flee to, my lady," he said through gritted teeth. "The undead are everywhere, the city is lost and the dragons ..." He reached into his scorched tunic and pulled out the strange sigil stone. "Here ... in case you do escape ... Take it and keep it safe. It is important, I know it ..." With one last effort, he forced the stone into her hand and wrapped her fingers around it tightly.

"Woven," Elena sobbed, tears streaming from her eyes. The man had saved her life, had kept them both safe. Now she could see death coming for him. With a last gasp of breath, the ranger's grip loosened until his hand fell to the ground.

Elena wept with the stone held tightly in her hands.

Kaiden rode as fast as he dared. At his side were Sophia and Davik, who had now appropriated his own horse from the grateful citizens of Balnor. It had taken them three days to hunt down and destroy the Necrist. With the monsters destroyed and Balnor safe, the three had hurried north. At their back was the remnant of the army of Balnor. With their lord dead, the army had sworn fealty to his son, who had, in turn, ordered them north under the command of the newly named Heroes of Balnor. Also joining the army was Thrift and his two hundred Fleetfoot thieves. Each was skilled in the way of the bow and the blade.

With the force of five thousand warriors, Kaiden had led the march north. Every step of the way he prayed to Niveren that they weren't too late.

They had been marching quickly and with little rest for three straight days, stopping only at the town of Plock to pick up volunteers to fight. The panicked townsfolk had told tales of the sky turning to fire in the north.

Now as they approached the valley which led to the city of Eclin, their words rang true. The sky was indeed a violent cacophony of colours. It looked as though the world was ending.

They crested the small hill at the valley to be greeted by a scene of utter devastation. The city was burning. Ahead of them, they could see the flashing blades of battling armies. To the east, a horde of undead and other foul beasts swarmed over the battlements, while in the sky three huge winged dragons circled.

"By Niveren ..." Sophia exclaimed in awe.

"Looks like we arrived just in time. Look," Davik said, pointing down the road. Sure enough, they could see a group of mages lobbing fireballs and lightning. Next to them, in a defensive formation, were a group of Nightblades, their tourmaline blades active and held at the ready.

"Ferran?" Sophia said, hope in her voice.

"It must be. Looks like he managed to get the mages to help as well," Kaiden said, pointing at another group of mages. One of the dragons dived towards them, unleashing its fire. The mages cast a spell which caused a barrier of energy to deflect the fire. The dragon wheeled away in rage.

Kaiden kicked his heels into Herald's flanks. The horse surged forward; the others close behind. At their back, the army roared its anger at the scene before it.

As he approached the Nightblades, he was hailed in greeting.

Standing in the road was Ferran. A deep red wound was on his forehead, and his black armour was scuffed and singed.

"You're a bloody sight for sore eyes, Sir Knight," Ferran greeted tiredly.

Kaiden reigned in his horse. Thousands of bodies lay scattered along the road.

"What's the situation?" he demanded all business. He knew his order was in the city, but of the defenders, he couldn't see any. A sinking feeling knotted in his gut.

"Where to start? We've taken care of the legion's siege weapons," Ferran started. Kaiden held a hand up to interrupt him.

"Legion? Cliria turned them to her will?" the knight asked, his eyes scanning the battlefield. Thousands of ghouls marched through the city's broken walls. Standing behind them on horseback were a half dozen familiar, crimson-robed figures.

"Aye, she must have," Ferran replied. "They put up one heck of a fight, but as soon as the mages arrived, they were able to remove the spell. As soon as she saw that happen, Cliria did something which killed them all."

Kaiden closed his eyes and offered a prayer for the dead legion.

"That's not the worst of it. That portal in the sky," Ferran said, pointing to the swirling vortex, "is getting larger. I snuck closer. There are fell beasts pouring through it. Pucks, red caps, banshees; you name it, they're coming through."

Kaiden swore under his breath. He hadn't been expecting the odds to be so much against them.

Cliria wept with happiness. Standing before her in the ruins of Eclin was her Danon, her lost love. His plan had worked to perfection, and now his victorious return would be cemented by vanquishing the heir to the Sundered Crown.

Danon looked himself over. His hands were skeletal, the flesh tight and grey. His clothes were tattered robes, and he stank of death. He had returned but only returned to a corpse.

"Bring the one you deem suitable before me," he said, his voice a rasping whisper. His body had survived the centuries thanks to Cliria and the dark magic of the N'gist; without it, he would have been doomed to an eternity in the Void. Now that he had returned, though, he could not walk about as a walking corpse. A lich wasn't a very good vessel, but it had been vital to his plans.

Cliria snapped her fingers.

Two Crimson Blade assassins stepped forward. Between them, they dragged the body of a man in golden plate armour.

"Behold, my love," Cliria said sweetly. "The body of General Rason, a man of strength. I believe he will make a fine vessel for you."

Danon walked over to the body. With a skeletal hand, he lifted up the man's head. Rason's eyes were open wide. He wasn't dead, for a possession spell only worked with a living vessel.

"He will be perfect. Does his appearance please you, my love?" Danon asked, running his corpse like hands over the general's face.

Cliria smiled sweetly and twirled a strand of long golden hair with a finger.

"I do. He is handsome. How do you like *my* vessel, my love?" she asked.

A dragon roared from overhead as a volley of fireballs struck the beast. Cliria frowned.

"It seems the mages have decided to leave their self imprisonment," she muttered darkly. She pointed at the half-dozen Crimson Blades. "Find those mages and kill them. We are too close for victory for anything to challenge us now."

Danon chuckled, although it sounded more like wheezing.

"Do not fear the mages. The entire might of Delfinnia could have arrayed itself against us, and we would be victorious. The goddess of darkness favours us this day." He strode over to Cliria and took her in his skeleton-like arms.

"I like your chosen vessel very much," he said before kissing her deeply, his corpse like face meshing disgustingly with the young girl's. "Where did you find such a beauty?"

Cliria smiled lovingly at him.

"I found her wondering the Great Wood as she picked mushrooms for her grandmother. A simple, kind-hearted girl. She even won over a Knight of Niveren," she laughed cruelly.

In the distance, the ghouls had reached the castle, which still stood at the centre of the city. Immediately they assaulted the high stone walls, while the remaining defenders battled desperately.

CHAPTER 42.

Elena ran with the prince in her arms through the castle's escape tunnel. Dust fell from the rock ceiling, and the wooden supports screeched as the dragons continued their assault upon the city. She screamed as, with a deafening rumble and crash, the tunnel collapsed in front of her. Dust blinded her, causing her to cough uncontrollably. Alderlade clung to her tightly, his head buried tightly against her neck. She cried out in despair as the dust cleared to reveal a pile of rubble barring their escape route. Their last hope was lost. She clung to the boy, tears streaming from her eyes.

"I'm sorry, Alde. I'm so sorry," she wept. The sound of earth and rock moving above her made her look up. A large crack was spreading up the tunnel; in moments, the whole thing would collapse and bury them both.

Angrily, she wiped her eyes clear of tears, turned around and ran back up the tunnel. Other refugees saw the panicked look in her eyes, and they too turned and fled. With a loud crack, the tunnel began to cave in.

Elena picked up the pace, pushing aside those too slow to outrun the falling death; their pitiful cries were cut short or drowned out by the falling rock. She reached the entrance to the tunnel and cried out once more as strong hands reached for her and pulled them into the relative safety of the castle's cellar.

A young ranger steadied her.

"Are you alright, miss?" he asked in concern. More soldiers rushed forward to help the others who had managed to outrun the tunnel collapse. Elena nodded, thanking the man.

"What now? The tunnel was our last hope," she said tiredly.

"No, miss. Help has come," the ranger said with some hope in his voice. "Before we fell back to the castle, I saw an army flying the colours of Balnor. And there are Nightblades out there, too. Another bloke said he saw mages as well." He glanced at the body of Woven, which had been moved to one side of the cellar, his face covered in his cloak.

"My commander taught me well, miss. He never gave up hope and neither will I."

"What's your name?" Elena asked.

Before he could answer another ranger shouted, "Briden, we're needed back on the wall,"

Briden smiled at Elena and squeezed her shoulder.

"They still have to get through us. There is hope," he said before he picked up his bow and hurried after his comrade.

"Good luck," Elena whispered clutching the prince tightly.

The last surviving defenders of Eclin stood in the castle's courtyard. Three hundred were all that remained. A wall of spear points and sword blades were pointed at the heavy gate which shook with every impact of the ghouls' battering ram. What archers there were had their bows aimed at the sky.

Outside and in the ruins of the ravaged city was the enemy host. The zombies swarmed through the streets devouring anyone unfortunate enough to have been trapped in the dragon's firestorm.

Grand Master Thondril and the Knights of Niveren were all dead, their bodies now carrion for the horrors that stalked the city's streets.

Sitting on his horse, Kaiden could see the carnage brought upon the dying city. Next to him were Ferran and Sophia. Each drew their swords.

"The enemy is focused on the castle leaving the broken walls unguarded. We will punish them for their arrogance," the knight said to his companions. He turned his horse so that he could address the motley band of warriors that had marched north with them.

Standing side by side were Nightblades, warriors, mages, and thieves.

He raised his voice so that all could hear him.

"In that city is this realm's best hope for peace: an heir to wear the Sundered Crown and reunite our broken nation, a nation brought low by forces ancient and evil. They believe that they will win, that darkness will reign once more as it did in the days of old. I say never. I say the light will win the day! For Niveren, for Delfinnia!"

With a roar, he spurred Herald forwards, the five thousand warriors at his back.

CHAPTER 43.

The air whistled in Luxon's ears, and the sun was dazzlingly bright. Perched on Umbaroth's back, he could see for miles around and marvel at the sights. If he didn't know any better, he was the first man to ever take to the skies.

Below him and passing at startling speed was Delfinnia. Forests, rivers and villages flashed past beneath him. He shouted with joy as he recognised the city of Sunguard in the far distance, its high peak glistening in the sunshine. It felt good to be home.

His joy was short-lived, though, as thoughts of what was to come entered his mind.

Up ahead on the horizon he could just make out the rapidly approaching Eclin Mountains. In the sky was the widening vortex which he had to close. In his hands was Dragasdol. The staff offered some comfort.

As he looked the staff over for the umpteenth time, a thought occurred to him, a thought which manifested itself into a plan. He barked a laugh before leaning down so that he could shout to the dragon.

"Aljeron's staff!" he exclaimed excitedly, "If Cliria still has it, I can use it to seal the Void. I just need to get in close enough to take it from her."

The dragon turned its huge head so that it could look at the young wizard.

"A sound plan, but what about Danon? You may be able to best the witch, but not him. Even I could not hope to harm him."

Luxon gripped the staff tightly.

"I have to try."

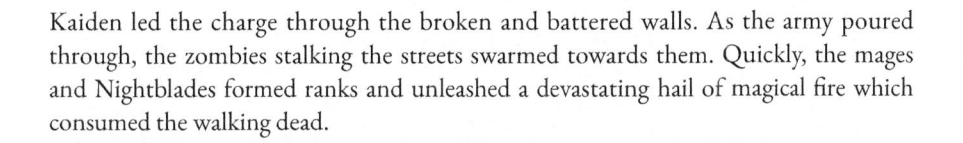

Kaiden led the charge through the broken and battered walls. As the army poured through, the zombies stalking the streets swarmed towards them. Quickly, the mages and Nightblades formed ranks and unleashed a devastating hail of magical fire which consumed the walking dead.

The army gathered behind the magic users as they slowly advanced up Eclin's main avenue. When the magical fire began to stutter, the Nightblades brought their magical blades to life and charged into the enemy. The tired mages stepped back through the ranks to regain their strength.

Kaiden glanced to his right to see Thrift and the Fleetfoots climb onto the city walls. With surprising skill, the thieves went to work unleashing arrow after arrow into the packed mass of undead.

Davik, who was leading the army on foot, shouted a warning. Kaiden looked to where the veteran warrior was pointing. Further down the street and rapidly approaching was a pack of snarling werewolves. Behind them were the sinister figures of Crimson Blade assassins.

The wolves clambered up the side of fire-damaged buildings, before leaping from rooftop to rooftop towards the army. The thieves on the walls loosed a hail of arrows, cutting a few down and sending howling corpses tumbling into the streets below.

Dodging the arrows with breath taking agility were the assassins who ran and leapt across the rooftops with majestic ease.

Kaiden glanced upwards just as a Crimson Blade leapt at him from a nearby roof. The assassin's foot connected solidly with his breastplate, knocking him from his saddle. Herald whinnied in fear. Just as the assassin was about to plunge his dagger downwards into Kaiden's chest, a silver-tipped arrow punched through the assassin's throat.

Sophia lowered her bow and jogged over, offering him her hand, which he took gratefully.

"Thanks," Kaiden said.

"Don't thank me yet," the witch hunter muttered.

He stood up to find that more of the assassins had leapt from the ravaged rooftops. Six of the killers now stood in a semicircle, surrounding them.

Kaiden raised his sword; Sophia readied her bow.

"C'mon then, you bastards. It's about time I had a little payback," Kaiden snarled.

As though some unseen signal had been given, the six assassins surged towards them. Sophia shooting her arrow, but her intended target cartwheeled out of the way with impossible speed. Discarding her bow, she drew her own blade. The two fought back to back, desperately parrying and blocking the assassins' dagger thrusts. Both we're quickly tiring and sweat poured into their eyes.

One of the assassins flew backwards as though punched by an invincible fist. Then another and another, until all six were lying in a heap of twisted limbs. Kaiden spun to see Ferran and two Nightblades running towards them up the avenue. They ignited their tourmaline swords before quickly dispatching the assassins.

They all looked up when a deafening roar pierced the air. Kaiden pulled Sophia to the ground as one of the black dragons swooped low over the army, its razor-sharp talons raking the ground to tear a dozen men to pieces. A volley of arrows from the thieves and magic attacks from the mages caused the dragon to shy away.

"We have to kill those things," Sophia cried. "They'll roast us all alive if we don't."

"Assassins, undead and fell beasts; we can handle. Those things, I'm not so sure," Ferran muttered.

Another roar came from the sky, causing them all to look upwards.

Coming in fast from the south was another dragon. It was bigger than the others, but its most distinguishing feature was its colour. It was silver.

The black dragon that had attacked moments before turned to face the newcomer. It spewed fire, but the silver dragon sped on through the flames, which seemed to part like waves when a ship passes through them.

Sophia cried out in joy and pointed to the silver dragon.

Sitting upon the great beast's back was Luxon, a staff held high in his right hand.

The silver dragon smashed into its black counterpart, its mighty jaws clamping down around the other's throat. For a moment the black dragon struggled and tried to claw at its attacker. Luxon raised his staff once more and lightning split the sky. The deadly bolt of light lanced down to stab through the black dragon's heart.

The army of Balnor cheered at the unexpected intervention, and none yelled with joy more than Sophia, Kaiden and Ferran.

The silver dragon shook its head savagely and released its grip on the now dead black serpent, sending its corpse smashing into the horde of ghouls and scattering them like dominoes.

It then flew low over the undead and unleashed its own dragon fire.

Only fire can kill the dead.

Instantly, the dragon fire swept through the thousands of ghouls, destroying them in the blink of an eye.

Kaiden raised his sword and leapt back into Herald's saddle.

"To the castle!" he cried.

The army advanced forwards quickly, cleaving their way through the now scattered and dying enemy. The stench of burnt flesh wafted in the breeze.

Ferran shook his head in amazement as he watched the silver dragon cartwheel through the sky. He could see the young lad on its back shouting in exhilaration. He couldn't help but chuckle.

"That boy is full of surprises," he said in awe.

Sophia smiled before hugging the Nightblade in a tight embrace and kissing him deeply. She let him go, a flustered look on her reddened face.

Ferran stared at her, a boyish grin on his face.

Luxon whooped in joy as Umbaroth rained destruction upon the horde of monsters below. The ghouls, zombies and other foul creatures were vaporised in a blaze of dragon fire.

"I see Cliria," Umbaroth bellowed over the din of whistling air. Luxon looked to where the dragon was pointing. Sure enough, he spotted the witch standing close to the besieged castle's gate. Her face was twisted in fury. At her side was what looked like a walking corpse.

Luxon's eyes widened as he realised that the corpse was Danon.

"Danon is there too. Be careful …" Luxon yelled in warning.

He was too late.

The Lich thrust an arm skywards. A flash of light lit up the sky, blinding him. Umbaroth roared in pain. Then they were falling like a stone towards the ruined city below.

Luxon held onto Umbaroth with all of his strength, the air ripping past him as they fell. He gritted his teeth and focused. Just before the silver dragon smashed into the ground, he leapt from its back.

The ravaged ground approached at a sickening speed. He thrust Dragasdol downwards and focused with all of his power. His fall began to slow as the levitation spell took effect.

Unlike when he had first cast such a spell, he could now control it. He landed gently on his feet.

Umbaroth wasn't so lucky.

The unconscious dragon smashed into ruined buildings, his great size demolishing them in the process in a great cloud of dust. The ground shook as the beast crashed to a halt.

Luxon called out to the dragon, but no reply came.

He shivered in fear as he spotted Danon and Cliria stalking towards him. In the witch's hand was the staff of Aljeron. He was no match for the both of them. He glanced about; they were on a wide avenue leading through the heart of the city. At one end was the besieged castle's main gate; to the sides were fire ravaged buildings, and behind him was the approaching Balnor army, which was battling its way through the remaining ghouls.

It was just him against them; the enemies of the world since the dawn of mankind against a boy who did not yet know what he was capable of.

His mind raced. No warrior or wizard had ever been able to defeat them both. Despair threatened to overwhelm him.

"Indeed, you are powerful," Cliria mocked. The witch twirled and skipped around her beloved dark lord. "My lord was right; you are the one. The one blessed with the powers of Niveren himself. I will enjoy cutting your heart out."

"You cannot hope to defeat us, boy," rasped Danon. "You have served your purpose."

"He's not alone, foul creature," a voice said.

Luxon spun around and sighed in relief. Marching quickly up the road was the army. At their head rode Kaiden, Ferran and Sophia. The three dismounted and drew their swords before taking their place next to Luxon. Sophia squeezed Luxon on the shoulder.

"We are with you," she said, her eyes narrowed and focused on the foes ahead.

"Time for some payback," Ferran added with a growl.

"How sweet," Cliria sneered sarcastically. She turned to Danon. "I will handle these fools, my love. You should have the honour of killing the brat."

Luxon tensed. The witch's overconfidence was her weakness.

Danon smiled, his skeletal face contorting into a nightmare.

"Make it quick but painful," He chuckled, before turning and striding towards the castle. The lich raised his arms once more. The ground began to shake, causing already damaged buildings to collapse and a crack to appear in the castle's wall.

"He's going to bring the walls down!" cried Sophia.

Cliria smiled wickedly. She clicked her fingers and stepped back. Luxon and the others looked upwards as the two surviving black dragons flew into view. The bigger of the two had an eye missing. It was the one at Danon's tower, Luxon realised. The two dragons landed on the road, blocking their view of the castle and shielding Cliria.

"Get behind me," Luxon yelled at the others. The dragons reared up on their hind legs and towered over the city. Light formed in their bellies and Luxon knew what would come next.

He raised his staff and channelled the magic within him. The dragons roared as they unleashed their fire. The inferno raced down the street. Sophia shut her eyes tightly, holding onto Luxon's cloak. Behind her were Ferran and Kaiden. Further back, the advancing Balnor army panicked and fled.

But the fire didn't incinerate them. Luxon cast a shield spell, the most powerful one he had ever cast. The dragon's fire crashed into the magical barrier and passed harmlessly around the huddled heroes. Once the smoke cleared, Luxon stepped forward.

"My turn," he whispered.

He pointed Dragasdol at the dragons and felt the magic course through him into the staff. His eyes shone blue as the magic engulfed him; the power he had tapped into in Caldaria now flowed easily through him. The time in the Void had taught him much.

A massive burst of fire exploded out of Dragasdol. The fireball flashed outwards to strike the smaller of the black dragons. With an agonised scream, the beast was engulfed in flame, its scales melting and its blood boiling. The beast writhed around in agony before crashing to the ground. Dead.

The other dragon stared at its fallen kin in horror, before glancing at Luxon warily.

"Drakis has no desire to die at your hand, wizard," the one-eyed dragon growled.

It turned, flapped its great wings, and fled into the sky.

CHAPTER 44.

Cliria cackled and clapped her hands in delight.

"A most impressive trick!" she giggled insanely. She ran a hand over the dead dragon's scales as she walked towards Luxon and the others. Her amused expression dropped as quickly as it had appeared, to be replaced with one of utter fury.

"Danon promised me dragons, and *you* have killed two of them!" she screamed hysterically.

Again, her expression changed.

The anger replaced yet again by the mirth of insanity.

"Never mind, never mind. More will come, and not just dragons – the entire Void will be my pets," she laughed, skipping through the splayed claws of the dead dragon.

"Not if I can help it, witch!" Ferran shouted. The Nightblade dashed forward; his tourmaline sword held high ready for the kill. He got within ten paces of Cliria but was halted by an invincible barrier. He tried to move but couldn't.

Sophia shot an arrow but it, too, froze midflight. Kaiden ran forward, his sword drawn. Before he could even raise the blade, he cried out as the pommel grew red hot, burning his hand. He dropped the sword just as the metal blade melted into a useless puddle at his feet.

Cliria wagged her finger like a parent scolding a small child.

"No, no, no. I will kill you three once I am done with Luxon."

With a flick of her wrist, the three were sent flying back to crash in a tangle of limbs. She smiled cruelly at Luxon.

"Let us see what you are truly made of."

Luxon stepped forward, yelling at the others to hide.

"You will pay for your crimes, Cliria," he said with more certainty then he felt.

An eerie silence descended upon them.

The tension grew to unbearable levels.

Each magic user stared at the other, both waiting for a time to strike.

Luxon glanced upwards to see the vortex widen further so that it now filled most of the sky above the city. He could make out dark objects falling through the breach. Cliria used the distraction to attack.

A wall of flame shot out from her hands and surged towards Luxon. He focused his attention back to the witch and the coming danger. Just in time, he whipped Dragasdol up and around, focusing his magic on casting a shield spell. The heat of the fire singed his cloak, but the brunt of the attack passed harmlessly by.

Cliria didn't wait for him to respond. She rained fireball after fireball at him, causing the magical barrier to shrink until it was just a few inches from his body. He gritted his teeth and focused on channelling all of his power through the staff. With a shout, he expanded the shield outwards to push the deadly flames back towards their caster.

Cliria batted the returned flames aside as though swatting a fly.

Luxon looked around, all the while maintaining his concentration on the shield. He smiled as he spotted the remnants of a shattered house.

With a flick of his wrist, the rubble floated into the air, and with a thrust of his arm, he sent the debris flying towards Cliria. The witch's eyes widened in surprise as the heavy stone and timbers came hurtling towards her. The flames ceased as her focus shifted to blocking. With expert skill, she cast her own shield which vaporised the incoming debris.

"Nice try, boy!" Cliria hissed. "But you are no match for the power of the N'gist."

She whirled Aljeron's staff above her head and muttered a dark incantation. Darkness seemed to engulf her; then she thrust the staff down into the ground. Black tendrils of energy spread out from the staff to envelop the dead dragon behind her. Luxon stepped back as the tendrils slithered and crawled towards him.

The bodies of ghouls and fallen warriors were devoured by the blackness.

Then they began to stir.

To Luxon's horror, the dead men began to twitch until they slowly began to rise. Their cold dead eyes focused on him. They let out an unearthly scream before shambling towards him. The rising dead men were bad enough, but then the dead dragon began to stir.

Luxon planted his feet and raised his staff. Memories of his lesson in the Void and the spell Danon had cast entered his mind. Sure enough, a wind began to blow. Fire sprang from Dragasdol to blow in the wind. The dead drew closer. He closed his eyes and concentrated; he pursed his lips and blew.

The wind turned into a howling gust, the fire joining it until a tornado of flame roared into life.

With one hand, Luxon pushed forward, sending the whirling flaming vortex into the undead.

The howling winds knocked them off of their feet, setting them ablaze and sending them flying in all directions. The now undead black dragon staggered onto its feet. With a roar, it reared back onto its hind legs, unleashing a fire of its own.

Once again Luxon cast a shield spell. The dragon fire knocked him backwards. Desperately, he tried to refocus, but Cliria launched another assault with her own magic. Luxon cried out as the shield almost buckled.

The stone beneath him cracked and splintered as he dug his heels in.

"Fear not Luxon!" a deep voice boomed.

Luxon looked to his right and sighed in relief as Umbaroth staggered back onto his feet. The silver dragon roared and lunged at the black dragon, his jaws once again clamping tightly over its throat. The dragon fire stopped, easing the pressure upon Luxon.

He dropped the shield and swung Dragasdol like a bat sending Cliria's magic back at her like a missile. The witch screamed as her own magic struck her at such speed that she couldn't block it. The fireball hit her solidly in the chest, setting her clothes ablaze and sending her flying backwards to crash into a heap.

Umbaroth meanwhile defeated the black dragon. With a sickening snap, the beast's neck broke. Umbaroth released his grip before destroying the carcass with his own fire.

Luxon pressed his attack. He ran at the downed witch and leapt into the air. As he went, he cast levitation to keep him off of the ground. He floated above her.

"It is over Cliria. You are beaten," he said coldly. He raised a hand, summoning the staff of Aljeron into it.

The staff flew into the air to land in his grip.

The witch glared at him. Her face was burnt, and her clothes were singed. She staggered to her feet.

"It is not over, fool," She spat. "Even if you destroy me, things have still gone to our plan. My beloved is back; his dark glory will consume the world. You think that by besting me, you have changed anything? There are many others like me, servants to his will."

Luxon floated to the ground to stand before her. He looked at the vortex above them. There was no other way. He swung the staff of Aljeron, smacking the witch back to the ground. Then he placed it on her head.

Cliria cried out in terror as he stood over her. Her face shifted and changed. Instead of the eyes once full of malice and hate were now wide and innocent.

"Where ... Where am I? The last thing I remember is walking through the Great Wood collecting mushrooms for grandmother and then ... nothing."

Luxon hesitated. Cliria had said that she had possessed the body of a girl.

"Alira?" he asked cautiously.

The blond girl nodded; her eyes full of fear.

"Do not fear. I will set you free," he said. His mind raced. Now was his chance to rid the world of the witch forever. He leaned down and whispered into the girl's ear.

"I know you are still in there hiding, Cliria. I will do to you what you did to me. You will seal the Void, witch. With no body to call your own, you will be trapped there for all time, and this girl will be free."

He stood back up and prepared himself for what he had to do.

Behind him, the girl's eyes darkened, her face contorting into that of the witch's once more. Reaching into her clothes, she pulled out a dagger. With a scream, she leapt to her feet and launched herself at him.

Before she could plunge the blade into Luxon's back, an arrow flashed past him and struck the girl in the hand. With a scream, she fell to the ground weeping.

Luxon spun around, sighing in relief as Sophia stepped out from the shadow of a fallen building.

"She's good at that," Ferran chuckled as he too emerged from his hiding place.

"Do what must be done," Kaiden said. He knelt down next to the girl. He stroked her hair tenderly. "Free her from the witch's foul taint."

Luxon took a deep breath and placed Aljeron's staff to the girl's forehead.

"I, the descendant of Aljeron, use this staff and the power of this foul witch to seal the Void and banish her blackened soul for all time."

The staff began to glow until it became blindingly bright.

The girl screamed as the witch was purged from her body.

More and more fell beasts were falling through the vortex, including more dragons, their roars echoing across the mountains.

Luxon raised the staff and aimed it at the breach.

"Seal it!" he shouted.

Light shot forth from the end of the staff to strike the vortex.

Thunder rumbled, and lightning flashed as the sky itself seemed to shake.

The vortex sputtered for a moment before it imploded with an intense flash. Luxon had to shield his eyes.

Slowly, he lowered his arm.

The sky was blue and calm once more.

The threat from the Void was ended.

Danon stood in the castle courtyard. Scattered around him like discarded toys were the charred bodies of the defenders. Rangers, soldiers, and knights had all tried to stop him. They had failed.

He looked to the blue sky in irritation; his plans for the Void had been thwarted, but the heir was in his grasp. With a flick of his wrist, he ripped the heavy wooden doors leading inside from their hinges. Panicked screams from the refugees cowering from within could be heard as he stalked inside.

Baron Lido charged at the monster coming for them but was swatted aside like a bug, slamming into the wall.

A group of women and children huddled together before him, their pitiful begs for mercy sounding sweet in Danon's ears.

Soon the whole world would be doing the same.

A young woman stood at the front of the cowering group.

Holding tightly to her hand was a small boy, a boy who watched Danon with no fear in his eyes.

Alderlade tugged on Elena's sleeve until she looked down at her charge. Terror gripped her as the lich stared at the boy. Somehow it seemed to know who he was.

"Lena, give me the shiny rock," the little boy said, his features set in a look of determination. Something in the lad's eyes caused her to reach into her pocket and pull out the strange stone. As she did so, the stone began to glow as it had done before. Soon it grew unbearably hot to the touch. Quickly, she handed it to Alderlade.

Danon glared at the stone.

"The key ..." He growled as he recognised it from ages long past. The last time his eyes had set upon it was when Zahnia had used it to retrieve the sword.

Danon stepped backwards as visions of pain and light flashed before his eyes.

Alderlade toddled forward, holding the now brightly glowing stone before him.

"Begone, bad man! Leave us alone!" the boy yelled.

Danon backed further away from the stone. Its light hurt his eyes, and for the first time in countless years, he felt fear. With a hiss, he spun away from the boy and the painful light.

"Go away!" Alderlade screamed. The stone shone brighter and brighter until it was blinding. With a final flash, the light faded, revealing that Danon had fled.

Elena hugged Alderlade tightly.

It was over.

The soldiers of Balnor moved into Eclin. Survivors of the siege emerged from their hiding places, stunned at the damage wrought upon their city.

Luxon and the others stood in the city centre. The wide square had been converted into a makeshift infirmary, with mages and healers hurrying about aiding the wounded. Umbaroth lay at one side of the square, his loud snoring echoing in the open space.

"Well, we did it. Danon is defeated, Cliria is banished, and the heir is safe and well. All in all, I'd say that was a good day's work," Sophia said cheerfully. Her face was covered in soot, and a livid red cut was on her cheek.

"And none of us died, which is always a bonus," Ferran added with a chuckle. Sophia smiled at him and wrapped an arm around his waist. "Also helps that Luxon seems to be invincible."

Luxon smiled at his friends.

"I wish. I'm just glad to be home."

"A lot of things will change now that there is a wizard back in the world," the Nightblade said. "The mages will no doubt elect you as their new leader."

Luxon looked away awkwardly.

"I don't know about that. I just want to go home and have a long rest."

"Back to Hannah, more like," Yepert chimed in.

The boy hadn't left Luxon's side since Cliria's defeat. He had vowed to never let his friend out of sight again.

"Where's Kaiden?" Luxon asked, flashing his friend a grin.

"He's not left Alira's side since the battle," Ferran replied. "With his order wiped out, he's got a lot of thinking to do."

They looked up as Davik approached them, a wide smile on his face. In his arms was a small boy.

"The Prince here wanted to meet the mighty wizard," he said jovially. Luxon shook the boy's hand; the prince chuckled in delight. The others bowed.

"It is an honour to meet you, my king," Luxon said, smiling at the boy. "I hear it was you who scared off Danon. I'd love to know how you managed that."

"I used this!" the boy said with a laugh. In his hands was a stone covered in runes. The shape of a sword glowed faintly on its surface.

"May I?" Luxon asked. The boy frowned a moment before handing over the stone. Luxon gasped. As soon as he touched it, he felt powerful magic coursing through it.

A vision flashed through his mind.

A golden sword casts back a cloud of darkness; images of a ruined tower nestled in the heart of a dark forest. Serpents writhe and fight; men in strange armour march over desolate battlefields and wage war. A huge lock with a square shaped keyhole; the stone belongs within it; on the other side of a mighty stone door lies the sword of the gods.

Luxon staggered backwards, dropping the stone.

"What is it?" Yepert asked, his tone full of worry. He took Luxon by the arm and held him steady.

Luxon looked at Davik.

"It's a key-" He muttered. He shook his head to clear it. "Keep that stone safe."

Davik raised an eyebrow. He leaned down and picked up the stone. Alderlade snatched it back to hold it tightly to his chest.

"Whatever you say- wizard," the old warrior replied uncertainly.

CHAPTER 45.

Sunguard

Cheering crowds lined the streets of the capital; ticker tape streamers filled the air and fireworks exploded noisily, casting dazzling light above the city.

Coming down the main avenue which led to the city's heart was a procession led by Archbishop Trentian. The old man held his head high as he walked, his long gold-threaded ceremonial robes glinting in the hot midday sun. A smile was on his face as he savoured the joy coming from Sunguard's citizens. The tyrant Rason was gone, and the true heir would sit upon the throne.

Behind him came a procession of a hundred other priests in similar garb, and behind them was a large horse-drawn carriage. Inside sat Elena, Davik and the soon-to-be-anointed King Alderlade the First. The little boy waved happily at the crowds.

Behind the carriage rode the Barons of Champia, Bison, Blackmoor and Robinta. Each man wore his finest clothes, and each had a highly polished sword on his hip. The young new Baron of Balnor rode alongside them, his face red with embarrassment.

Noticeable by their absence was the Baron of Retbit and the Baron of Champia, Ricard.

Luxon and the others were amongst the excited crowds.

He felt pride in having achieved what he had.

There would be a new king, one that would be guided by wise and noble men, and one that would give hope to the people.

"Retbit didn't yield," Ferran muttered darkly. "The fool will still press his claim."

"With the rest of the realm arrayed against him, Retbit will not last long," Kaiden said, placing a hand on the Nightblade's shoulder.

"He still has a large army, and rumours abound that fell things are afoot in his lands," Ferran replied.

Since his rout from Caldaria, the baron's forces had been mysteriously quiet. Even with Balnor weak as it was, the forces of Retbit had not crossed the Ridder River. Something was amiss.

Luxon's thoughts drifted to Accadus.

Now that he knew that it had been Danon whispering to him, he felt uneasy. The dark wizard had told him to spare his foe in Caldaria. Accadus had a part yet to play, he had said. Luxon kept his concerns to himself.

Davik lifted Alderlade up and placed him gently on the huge throne, before bowing deeply and taking his seat next to Elena in the front row.

The boy looked tiny; his little legs were unable to reach the marble floor.

Archbishop Trentian smiled at the grizzled warrior. In his hands shone the king's stone, which he placed at the throne's base. A priest stepped forward and carefully handed him a golden crown.

Gently, Trentian placed the too-big crown upon the wriggling boy's head. Alderlade cooed in wonder as the gold circlet touched his head.

"Alderlade, son of our beloved King Rendall, and his sole surviving heir, you are the rightful bearer of the Sundered Crown. Back in the days of the first kings, the crown symbolised the reunification of a divided people. Now it does so again."

The Archbishop then turned to address the packed cathedral.

"Here sits our new king. As he is so young, he will need a guide: a mentor to teach him how to rule, a noble to teach him wisdom and justice. Which of you will do this?"

He was met with silence. Sitting in the front row were Elena and Davik. Next to them were Luxon and his friends. All eyes went to Davik, who sputtered and shook his head.

"I cannot ..." he stuttered, his face going red.

Elena laughed.

"No greater teacher could a king wish for," she said gently.

The crowd began to chant his name until it grew into a roar of noise. Trentian laughed and banged his crook onto the floor to quiet the crowd. He looked at Davik with a smirk.

"It seems, Davik, that the people have chosen you to become regent until our king comes of age. Do you accept this great responsibility?"

Davik coughed. He was stunned. A wealth of emotions crossed his features as his mind raced. Eventually, his expression firmed.

"With great humility, I accept," he answered.

The crowd cheered.

Once again Trentian banged his crook on the marble floor.

"We have a regent. Now we must have a privy council. Who do you choose to rule alongside you until our king comes of age?"

Davik looked to the crowd.

"I anoint the barons who have proven their loyalty to the crown," he began, pointing to the gathered barons sitting in the second row. Each man stood and bowed, including the child Baron of Balnor. "And I also choose the one who saved us all so that we can be here today. I anoint the wizard, Luxon Edioz."

Luxon's eyes widened as he heard his name. Murmurs of discontent spread through the crowd.

The Archbishop stepped forward, annoyance on his face. He leaned close to Davik.

"Are you sure? He is a magic user. You know the law. No magic can be practised outside of Caldaria. It is only because of the dire situation in Eclin that he and his fellow magic users have not been arrested already!"

Luxon stood and took a deep breath.

"I have to decline,' he began slowly. 'Perhaps someday our new king will change the law that discriminates against my kind, but until that day I will respect the law," he said sombrely.

The rest of the ceremony passed without incident. Luxon and the others filed out of the cathedral; the fresh air was a welcome relief from the stuffy darkness of the old building.

"I cannot believe it!" Sophia growled. "After all you did ..."

Luxon smiled. "You cannot blame them. The scars of the Magic Wars run deep, and they do have a point – all that transpired was because of magic. Besides, I have other things I need to do."

Yepert looked at his friend in surprise.

"Like what? I thought we were going back to Caldaria?"

Luxon smiled at his friends.

"Cliria told me that my mother yet lives. I have to find her. I need to know that she is safe," he replied.

"Well you're not going anywhere without me," Yepert said stubbornly.

"I wouldn't have it any other way," Luxon laughed.

Luxon and Yepert said their goodbyes to their friends and made their way out of the capital. The sun shone brightly in the sky, and the birds chirped happily as they flitted to and fro.

They walked along the King's Road until they reached the top of a nearby hill. The view was breath taking. The tall spire of Sunguard stood proud and strong, and the turquoise waters of the flowing Ridder River glistened in the sunshine.

Sitting at the top of the hill was Umbaroth. The dragon had made itself scarce after the events in Eclin. Already, men had been drafted to hunt down the dragons that had escaped the Void.

Luxon smiled at his old friend. The long years he had experienced in the Void had made their bond strong.

"My friend," he greeted happily.

Umbaroth lowered his head so that it rested on the ground.

"I'm afraid that this is where we part ways, young wizard," the dragon said a hint of sadness in his deep rumbling voice.

Luxon's smile faded.

"Come with us," he said hopefully.

Umbaroth shook his massive head side to side.

"I cannot. For the first time in countless ages, my kind is back where it belongs. Many of my kin will be lost and confused. I must find them and keep them safe. I will find us a home, one where we can fly in the blue freely and without fear."

Luxon nodded in understanding. He placed a hand on the dragon's snout.

"I understand. May you be successful in your quest, old friend," he said, wiping his eyes as tears threatened to spill.

Umbaroth reared back so that he stood at his full height. He flapped his great wings and took the skies.

"If you ever need me, you know how to summon me!" he said as he flew off into the clear blue sky.

EPILOGUE

Accadus sat on his father's throne. At his feet lay the body of the man who had raised him. The blood oozing from his bloated corpse was still warm.

"It is done then?" a voice said from the shadows.

Accadus wiped the bloodstained dagger on his cloak before sheathing it into his belt.

"It is," he said coldly.

A figure stepped out of the darkness, a wicked grin splitting his face. His golden armour glinted in the candlelight. His face was hidden in shadow.

"Excellent. You will take his place as ruler of Retbit. Eclin was a setback but this ... this could work in our favour. What of your brother?"

Accadus snorted derisively. "His head is on a spike outside the city walls. He wanted to pledge loyalty to the child king. I did not."

"Good, good. We will bide our time. There are allies I shall seek out. When the time is right it will begin in earnest," the figure said darkly.

"What will begin?" Accadus asked.

The figure smiled.

"The true war for the Sundered Crown of course. The war that will see darkness reclaim the world. I will teach you, and you will be my apprentice, my most powerful weapon."

"Yes ... my master," Accadus said, bowing deeply.

The End

About the Author

Matthew Olney is the #1 Amazon best-selling author of *The Sundered Crown Saga, Unconquered: Blood of Kings,*
 among others. He lives in Worcester, England with his wife. Matthew loves history, fantasy, and all things sci-fi.

Learn more about Matthew at https://msolneyauthor.com/
Sign up to Matthew's mailing list

ONE LAST THING...

Thank you so much for reading. If you enjoyed this book, I'd be very grateful if you'd post a short review. Your support really does make a difference, and I read all the reviews personally so I can get your feedback and make my books even better.

Thanks again for your support!

Printed in Great Britain
by Amazon